Florence Marryat

Phyllida

A Life Drama

Florence Marryat

Phyllida
A Life Drama

ISBN/EAN: 9783337376925

Printed in Europe, USA, Canada, Australia, Japan

Cover: Foto ©Andreas Hilbeck / pixelio.de

More available books at **www.hansebooks.com**

BY

FLORENCE MARRYAT

(MRS FRANCIS LEAN),

AUTHOR OF 'LOVE'S CONFLICT,' 'MY SISTER THE ACTRESS,'
ETC. ETC. ETC.

A New Edition.

LONDON: F. V WHITE & CO.,
31 SOUTHAMPTON STREET, STRAND, W.C.

———

1883.

PHYLLIDA.

PROLOGUE.

THE reading of that letter seemed to exhaust Nelson Cole's stock of patience, for before he had finished it he jerked it from his hand, whence it fluttered to the ground.

'Crow away, my bantam!' he said to some imaginary listener, as he lit a cigar and elevated his legs until they formed a right angle with the mantelpiece. 'Crow away! You will have discovered your error long before you come to my age. Your theory is all very well *as* a theory, but it won't wash, my Saint Bernard, it won't wash.' But after a while spent in watching the rings of cloudy blue smoke, with which he was doing his best to fill the apartment, Nelson Cole seemed to determine that his friend's letter was too good to lie upon the floor, for he took the trouble to bring his legs down to their normal position in order that he might pick it up, and smooth out its creased pages on his knee. 'Poor dear Freshfield,' he thought, somewhat contemptuously as he did so, 'he is a deal too good for such a naughty world ! He sees no further beyond him than a week-old puppy. He ought to come to this country to get his eyes opened. He'd see a few marriages here and a few women that would make him view his impossible ideal in its proper light. How can a man live to eight - and - twenty and remain so green ? '

The letter, as it lay smoothed out on Nelson Cole's knee (or at least the part that had so much amused him), ran thus :—

'You ask me if I think of marrying again. No ; my dear Cole, that page of my life is, I believe, closed for ever. Not that I have lost the wish or the power to love, far from it—the difficulty is, that in discovering what I have missed, I seemed to have realised a paradise which is too great for attainment. Let me try and explain myself. You know that I married, partly to please my mother, partly to satisfy my conscience. My wife was pretty, amiable, well-bred, and fond of me. We never had a differing word in the course of our married life, and I am sure that she never disregarded a wish that I expressed. Added to all this, I had a tender affection for her, which I still retain for her memory. You will ask me then what more I could desire, and I cannot tell you, excepting this, that our union did not include the union of our souls, and our separation leaves mine still hungering to find its mate. I was fond of poor Alice, and I mourned her loss ; but, at the same time, I could have loved fifty other women as well as I loved her, and all at once, if the laws of my country had permitted it.' ('Hullo !' said Nelson Cole, 'here's a nice specimen of an English parson.

This is what they call a "muscular Christian," I suppose. Why, the fellow will be wanting to keep a harem next.')

'Now that is not the feeling one should have respecting one's wife. A man should as soon be inclined to be untrue to himself as to her, or to have another self as another wife. Once wedded, should be wedded for eternity, and death should come as a veil only, not as a divorce between man and woman. There should never be a second marriage, Cole ; there never *could* be, if the first proved the true union of soul to soul. I have made one mistake, you see, but I will never make another. My eyes have been opened, and the next awakening would be far more terrible than the first. Of course my mother will not admit my argument. She is a good mother to me, but she holds to the old-fashioned idea that parsons and doctors should be married men for the sake of their patients, as if one could preach truth all the better with a lie in one's right hand.

'No, Cole! I believe I shall die as I live, but I shall go through the world with my eyes open, and should I happily succeed in finding my soul's mate, whether she be clothed in rags or satin, seated on a dunghill or a throne, I will woo her till she is mine. But do not imagine that I believe in the possibility of such happiness—I only dream of it, as men dream of heaven.'

'Yes! and you may go on dreaming, my boy,' said Nelson Cole, as he twisted up the paper, and threw it this time upon the burning fire ; 'and you will die dreaming, take my word for it! Your "soul's mate," indeed! Show me the women with souls, and I'll soon find the men to mate with them. But I question with the followers of Mahomet, if

women have such things.   The Lotties and Dotties
and Totties of the present day go far to persuade
us they have not.   And your theory is a dangerous
one, Saint Bernard!   Going in search of your
" soul's mate " will lead you to wooing your neigh-
bour's wife perhaps—or striking up a paradisaical
wedding with your housemaid.   I am fond of this
boy with his Puritanical ideas and close shorn
monkish face, and wish I could go to England and
look after him a bit.   But it can't be just yet, and
I must content myself with a letter of sound practical advice.   The lad was always a dreamer, with
those blue eyes and white cheeks of his.   Ah! wait
till you come to forty, Bernard, then you'll know
how much a woman is worth striving for, or griev-
ing after.'

So thinking, our cynical friend reached down his
hat and overcoat, and prepared to leave the house.
He was a sojourner in the city of Chicago, in the
United States of America, at this time ; but only
for a brief period.   His profession, that of a civil
engineer, had led him out to the New World some
years before, and he had been reaping the golden
profits of an experienced hand and clever practical
brain ever since.   He had been employed in laying
down railroads in several of the States, and began
to feel himself quite a naturalised American, especially as he was well known, and sure of a welcome in most of their hospitable cities.   In Chicago
he felt himself peculiarly at home, having many old
friends settled there, and as he strolled towards the
principal theatre, he knew that he should be met
by a score of outstretched hands.   And from the
male portion of creation, Nelson Cole deserved the
cordiality extended to him.   He was a man of
about fifty—grey-haired, keen-eyed, clear-headed,

and critical—a bit of a philosopher, without an atom of romance in his composition, and wishing to be thought more hard and bitter than he naturally was. Essentially a man's man: fond of sport, politics, late hours and bachelors' parties, and eschewing—like the evil one—all assemblies where the female element predominated, or was the principal attraction.

What Nelson Cole really thought of women few of his own sex had never heard. He seldom mentioned them; apparently they engaged his thoughts as little as though they did not exist. Some men thought that he must have been cruelly disappointed or betrayed in his early days: others that he actually felt as little as he professed to do. But whatever their speculations, Nelson Cole remained a thorough good friend and boon companion to themselves. It was past eleven o'clock as he entered the theatre saloon, and the bar was crowded with noisy, chattering young men. The babble was so great, and the discussion so animated, that his entrance was at first altogether disregarded, and he had time to gather some notion of the subject of which they spoke.

'They say he has dismissed her,—it's a d—d shame!' cried one.

'I don't see that. I think she fully deserves it. The woman was intoxicated,' replied another.

'Intoxicated!' interrupted a third contemptuously, as though that word were far too weak. 'She was *drunk*—drunk as an owl;' and then the chorus swelled indiscriminately.

'But it's the first time, and it's deuced hard a girl should lose her bread for a single offence.'

'How do you know it's the first time?—not likely. A woman tries it on a good many times in private before she ventures to appear before the public in that condition.'

'Of whom do you speak?' asked Nelson Cole, and then the general attention was directed to him.

'Oh! here's Cole. How are you, Cole, old fellow? Glad to see you, my boy!' and so on, and so on. But amongst them all Nelson Cole addressed but one.

'Jack Neville!' he exclaimed, 'can I believe my eyes! Where do you hail from? I thought you were safe in San 'Frisco.'

The man he spoke to, a fine, handsome, sun-burned fellow of about thirty, coloured visibly even beneath the tan of a Californian sun.

'Oh, I left 'Frisco long ago, and have been lounging about the South for the last six months,' he replied hurriedly. 'I—I—got into a bit of a scrape down there, you know!'

'And serve you right, my boy, for herding with such a rascal as that Sandie Macpherson,' said Cole. 'I told you what he was from the beginning; and I only hope you've shaken yourself free of his clutches.'

'Be careful, Cole! some one may hear you,' interposed the younger man. 'Macpherson's friend, Pawley, was at the bar not two minutes ago!'

'Pawley may hear me or not,' replied Cole loudly. 'Nothing would give me greater pleasure than to have an opportunity of settling old scores with that detestable Scotch rascal.' But men, as a rule, dislike a disturbance in a public place, especially if it does not concern themselves, and the other loungers at the bar commenced to crowd about Cole, and reiterate the news that had occupied them on his arrival.

'Only fancy, Cole! poor little Stephanie Harcourt.'

'That pretty girl, with the blue eyes and golden hair.'

'Blue eyes, Marshall? What are you talking about? her eyes are as black as night.'

'Black eyes—rubbish! Why, the girl is as fair as she can be.'

'I tell you, her eyes are black, or nearly so; I've been close to them, and ought to know.'

'Well, well, never mind her eyes! interrupted Nelson Cole impatiently. What's the matter with the girl?'

'Why, she came in so drunk in the burlesque to-night that she couldn't stand, and Evans has dismissed her from the theatre.'

'That's nonsense! she could *stand* fast enough; only she had had a little too much, and forgot her part.'

'Broke down entirely in her singing, and you know she had *the* song of the evening.'

'Who *is* Stephanie Harcourt?' demanded Cole in an indifferent tone, addressing Jack Neville, who stood next him.

'I don't know,' answered Jack slowly, as he moved away.

'She's quite a beginner — only been on the boards a few months — and I think it's awfully hard lines on her to get her dismissal for a little mistake,' said another young man. Nelson Cole's hard voice fell like cold water on his enthusiasm.

'Drunkenness is never a little mistake with women : when they once begin, they go on, and Evans is quite right to check the first symptoms of it by a summary dismissal. He'll find plenty of girls to take Miss Harcourt's place. There are more than enough of them in the world, heaven knows!'

'You didn't expect to get any sympathy out of

Cole, I suppose?' laughed some of the men at the drinking-bar, as the person they spoke of elbowed his way from amongst them, and went to the private room of his old friend, the manager, where, after a little desultory conversation, he contrived to bring the subject round to Miss Stephanie Harcourt's offence.

'Sorry to hear you had a *fracas* on the boards to-night, Evans.'

'Yes, a disgraceful business! Little Harcourt perfectly intoxicated! I was rather afraid of it from the beginning. She's a strangely excitable girl.'

'Got connections in Chicago?'

'Don't know, I'm sure. I've heard some report of her being married, but I don't trouble myself about the affairs of my company outside the theatre. But I was obliged to make an example of her. I had no end of trouble last year with a woman named Harrison, who went on in the same way, so I gave Miss Harcourt her dismissal then and there.'

'Shall you miss her?'

'Not much. She's a sharp girl, but no particular talent, and I fancy she'll not find it easy to get employment on the boards again in *this* city.'

'Not when you've made a public example of her from your theatre, certainly,' replied Nelson Cole, with apparently the utmost indifference to Stephanie Harcourt's fate. Yet the girl's pathetic eyes and mouth, which he had noticed but cursorily in his visits to the Athenian Theatre, seemed to haunt him strangely for the remainder of the evening, and when he rose to return home, he passed out by the stage door and asked the porter if he knew Miss Harcourt's address.

'I can't say I do, sir; but I think that lady can tell us. Miss Vavasour,' he continued, addressing a tall, closely-veiled figure about to cross the threshold, 'can you tell this gentleman where Miss Harcourt lives?'

The veiled woman turned, and regarded Nelson Cole somewhat suspiciously.

'She lives with me,' she replied, with caution; do you wish to send her a message?'

'Are you her friend?' asked Nelson Cole, stepping out into the street beside her.

'I am, sir. Are you?'

'I should wish to be, Miss Vavasour! I feel for the misfortune that has overtaken her this evening, and if she requires assistance—it is a delicate thing that I would say, but perhaps you understand me—'

'It is a kind thing, sir,' replied the actress—they were walking slowly on together by this time—'and in her name I thank you for it. Her dismissal from the Athenian is a very serious matter, for she has no other means of support, but I hope she may get work somehow. You mustn't think this is a habit with her, sir—indeed—indeed it is the first time she has ever so transgressed. I have known her for eighteen months, and I can swear to it; but Mr Evans would not take my word.'

'And what was the occasion of this first transgression, Miss Vavasour? Do you know?'

'I am not sure if I should be justified in disclosing Stephanie's secrets, sir; but she has had great trouble. I can tell you so much, and an old friend met her out to-day and told her some good news and took her in and treated her to dinner somewhere, and I think it was the load off her mind and the excitement and the champagne altogether that did it.'

'Poor child! no wonder it had an effect upon her.   But what will she do now for a living?'

'I don't know, sir! You had better ask Stephanie herself. It is here that we live together. This is our door!'

'Thank you for the information. Of course I cannot intrude to-night, but to-morrow perhaps, if you would prepare Miss Harcourt for my appearance—'

But he had not had time to finish his sentence before the door of the house was thrown open, and Stephanie Harcourt appeared upon the threshold.

'Bella,' she cried to her friend hysterically, 'it is all over. I am dismissed without salary, and I can't even pay you my share of the week's rent! The sooner I go to the Tombs with that scoundrel the better!'

'Hush, hush, dear! there is a stranger present,' said Miss Vavasour compassionately.

But the girl was too excited to heed her caution.

'I might have known misfortune was at hand,' she went on passionately, 'for I met *him* to-day, you know who I mean—my evil genius. There has always been trouble for me following in the wake of Sandie Macpherson.'

At that name, heard for the second time that evening, Nelson Cole started; but he was too much a man of the world not to conceal his surprise.

'Stephanie! this gentleman wishes to be your friend, but this is not the time for you to speak to him. Come in now and let us go to bed, and to-morrow, when you are more composed, perhaps he will come and hear the story of your troubles,' said Miss Vavasour.

'I shall never be more composed,' replied the

girl incoherently. ' I have had so little good luck in my life. Why couldn't they have left me the little I possessed? But now I've lost everything, and I might just as well be in the Tombs with him as starving in the streets of Chicago. Oh, those horrid dreary Tombs! Why did I ever meet Jack?'

'Come in, come in,' whispered her friend in a soothing voice.

Nelson Cole tried to make his escape without further parley.

'I will call to-morrow afternoon,' he said, as he lifted his hat and turned away.

'Do you know Sandie Macpherson?' screamed Stephanie after him, and that name from her lips seemed somehow to send a chill through him.

What connection this poor little burlesque actress in Chicago could possibly have with the desperate and evil-disposed gold-digger of Sacramento Valley, whose villany had cast a secret shadow over his own life, he could not imagine ; but the fact of her having mentioned his name would have drawn him to her side again, without the inducement of wishing to befriend her poverty. He tried to persuade himself, in his free and easy manner, that the whole affair troubled him but little ; but the fact is that it troubled him very much, to the extent of preventing his going to sleep till the early morning, and not waking up until it was time to keep his appointment with Miss Harcourt. But when he reached her presence, it was a very different person who presented herself to him from the flushed and dishevelled Bacchante of the day before. It was a very pale and miserable-looking girl — half frightened and half ashamed — whom Miss Vavasour dragged rather than led into the room to be introduced to him. There was none of the brazen defiance of a woman used to vice in Stephanie Harcourt.

She looked rather like a child who had been detected in some fault and brought up for punishment.

She knew now what had befallen her the night before ; and it was so terrible to be presented to this grave, elderly man, who had seen her a prey to the most disgusting vice of which a woman can be guilty. But the worldly view that Nelson Cole took of the matter reassured her. If he had looked shocked, the girl would have shrunk from his scrutiny. Had he sympathised with her, she would have broken down,—but he treated it as a matter of every-day occurrence, as indeed it unfortunately was with the women he was most in the habit of seeing.

'Come, come, Miss Harcourt,' he said, as she held backward, 'this has been an unfortunate accident ; but accidents will happen, as we all know, in the best regulated families. You will not be surprised to hear that your face is well known to me, as it is to most of the inhabitants of Chicago, and perhaps your friend here, Miss Vavasour, has told you that if I can be of any assistance to you in this dilemma, I will. I am an old man, you see, and you need have no scruples in accepting my help. What can I do for you?'

'Can you get me other work?' demanded the girl shyly.

'Perhaps I can. At all events I will try. What do you wish to do? Do you intend to apply for another engagement in Chicago?'

'Oh no ; anything but that—anything but that,' cried Stephanie, with visible repugnance. 'I could not bear the shame of another public appearance here. If there were only work that I could do to be procured in the country—in the open peaceful country.'

'Do you love the country, then?'

'Oh! to find oneself there,' continued the girl excitedly. 'To wake up and find oneself amongst the primroses and violets, and the cool, cool grass, and the leafy trees and waving corn, and to know that one had done for ever with the noise and glare of the town, and the cruel bricks and mortar that seem to press upon one's heart, and keep all the joy and freshness of life from bubbling over.'

'Stephanie, do think what you are saying!' exclaimed Miss Vavasour. 'The gentleman asked you what work you would like best. You must excuse her wandering, sir,' she continued to Nelson Cole, 'for she is still weak and feverish, and I don't think she half knows what she is talking about.'

'Pray, let her talk as she will—I am interested in all she can tell me,' he replied; and, indeed, a colder man than himself must needs have felt some interest in the ultimate fate of the beautiful creature before him. For Stephanie Harcourt was beautiful, with more than the mere physical beauty of colour and shape. She was about eighteen years of age, with a graceful figure of middle height—a head of rippling golden hair—whether natural or artificial Nelson Cole was not skilled enough to determine, and pathetic eyes of some deep neutral tint, which looked just now like the eyes of a hunted animal. But her greatest charm lay in the far-off look of those eyes, as if her soul saw more than was presented to her earthly vision, and was filled with high and glowing thoughts.

As Nelson Cole gazed upon those upturned eyes, they reminded him of—he knew not what—and he turned away with a shudder.

'Have you ever lived in the country, Miss Harcourt?' he asked her presently.

'No! no! Never! I have been reared amongst the glare and the gas of cities. I can remember nothing but the smell of liquor and the sound of oaths, and the clash of the dice and the billiard balls, and the horrid, horrid bricks and mortar.'

'You must have had a strange experience?'

'Ah! you would say so if you knew all I have passed through before I came to Chicago—all the horrors that I saw in San Francisco. How I wish,' she went on passionately, 'that that place and everything connected with it, down to its very name, might be burned off the face of the earth!'

'You mustn't excite yourself like this,' said Nelson Cole. 'It is giving way to their feelings after that fashion that makes people forget themselves, as you did yesterday.'

'But that was an accident—indeed it was! How could I imagine a little wine would affect me so? And Jack said it would do me good. And we laughed and talked so much I did not notice how often he filled my glass, and I felt so well and happy until I walked out of the keen frosty air into the theatre, and then, somehow, all the lights seemed to close round me, and my head felt like a feather, and I seemed to be floating somewhere between the flies and the stage, until a crash came and I fell down. But it was all Jack's fault. He ought not to have given me so much champagne.'

'Is Jack your husband?'

'Who told you I had a husband?'

'You see I know it.'

'Ah! and so you may! Every one may know it now, if they choose, for it can't last long. Jack my husband! Oh no! he's only a friend; but we came across each other yesterday in the streets, and he gave me news of him that drove me mad.'

'Not mad with grief, I hope?'

'No! no! mad with joy! And what do you think the news was? That he's locked up for two years in the Tombs for forgery. Two years! Two long, blessed years. And I shall be free before he comes out, Bella, sha'n't I?' she cried, as she cast herself into the arms of her friend. 'Free from him and from all of them. Free to bury my secrets in the sea; free from that awful curse—'

'Hush, dear, don't talk so fast. Yes, yes, you shall be free, if there's any justice or truth in the laws of our country. But, meanwhile, you must live, you know, and this gentleman is kind enough to say that he will help you; and I do think if he would assist you to go to your friends for a little while, and try and forget all this misery before you turn your thoughts to work again, that it would be the kindest thing he could do.'

'Never fear,' said Nelson Cole, 'but that I will perform all that I have promised. Meanwhile, Miss Harcourt, your disclosures have interested me very much. May I ask the name of your husband?'

'Oh yes; it is no secret. He is a Brazilian, called Fernan Cortës.'

'And—pardon me, he is a rascal!'

'The greatest rascal that ever existed, sir.'

'My poor child, how came you to marry him?'

'I can't tell you that. I was frightened into it in a way that you would hardly understand. Only, thank heaven, I am now delivered from him.'

'But after his two years' incarceration are over, he will come out again and claim you.'

'I will have broken the chain by that time. I will have gone far away where he shall never find me.'

'And you met Cortés in San Francisco?'

'Yes, sir.'

'And that scoundrel Sandie Macpherson had some hand in your marrying him?'

The girl's cheek became as white as ashes.

'Who has told you that?'

'No one. I guessed it.'

'You have guessed wrong, sir. But I hate Macpherson. God forgive me. I hate him like my life.'

'You share the feeling with many others. He is a man universally detested.'

'But few know him as I do,' murmured the girl; 'all his cruelty, his artifice, his secret crimes. And my poor mother—can I ever forget her?'

'He injured your mother too?'

'Ah, sir, do not ask me to speak of it! Whom has he not injured? But when you hear me talk of the peace and quiet of the country, as if I were talking of heaven, remember that I can never disassociate the rattle and bustle and glare of the town from the thought of cruelty and crime.'

Nelson Cole left his seat and began to pace up and down the room.

'Did you live long in California?' he asked.

'Many years. All my life, until I came here.'

'Did you ever happen to meet there—a—a—anybody of the name of Summers?'

'A woman?' inquired Stephanie innocently.

'Yes; yes; well—a—a woman.'

'No; I never knew any woman there except my mother, till she died.'

'And you said yesterday that you had seen Sandie Macpherson in this town?'

'Oh yes, sir; I met him suddenly,' with a shudder; 'but he did not see me, and so I escaped him.'

'One would think from the way you mention him, that this man had a hold on you, Miss Harcourt.'

Stephanie glanced meaningly at her friend before she answered.

'No—not a hold—only—I am afraid of him.'

'And you would like to get far away from all the places where you are likely to meet him again?'

'Ah! so much—so much!'

'Well, I will put you in the way of doing so. There; no thanks. I have more money than I know what to do with myself—and if a few dollars can benefit you, you are welcome to them. But I suppose you ought to know my name. I am Nelson Cole the engineer, and you shall hear from me again in the course of the day.'

So saying, this eccentric man, without a single glance of admiration at the beautiful girl, who was sitting with her head bowed in her hands like a repentant Magdalen, seized his hat, and with a curt 'Good afternoon,' left the two women by themselves. And as he returned to his hotel, he was ready to laugh at himself for a fool for having been taken in by swollen eyelids and a downcast countenance.

'What is this girl to me,' he thought impatiently, as he traversed the streets, 'that I should offer to throw away my money upon her? A trumpery little burlesque actress who chooses to disgrace herself by drinking champagne with any Jack who invites her to celebrate with him her husband's arrest for forgery. And I must needs put my finger in the pie and offer to provide her with liquor for the next six months. I am a fool, and no mistake. And yet there is something in the child's voice and look that attracts me in spite of myself. I don't believe she can be all bad ; however, appearances are against her. Well, I've done the job now, and I can't draw back from it. I'll send her a bill for two hundred dollars to-morrow, and wash my hands of the whole affair.'

For the names of San Francisco and Sandie Macpherson rankled more in Nelson Cole's mind than all the troubles of Stephanie Harcourt. They had raised up the old bull-dog feeling in his breast, which for years he had attempted to quell by never mentioning the man whom he hated, nor thinking of him more than was absolutely necessary.

Yet here he was in the same town as himself, and Nelson Cole felt as if it were impossible for him to sleep until they had met, and had it out with one another.

But an excellent dinner had the power to soothe much of his resentment, and when it was concluded, he prepared, as usual, to finish up his evening at the theatre.

As he was putting the finishing touch to his attire before the mirror, some thought of Bernard Freshfield's last letter suddenly struck him, and he burst into a loud laugh.

'Oh, my saintly parson, with the impossible theory,' he exclaimed, 'you should see the end of a few of the marriages that are made in heaven before you attempt to foist your ideas of an eternal union on the world. The ignoramus ! why, his marriage with his Alice—innocent, inoffensive, and quickly brought to an end—*was* the true ideal had he only known it! Where will he ever find such another wife—to live with him peaceably for two years and leave him a free man at the end of them? He has had the luck of one in a thousand. Yet he continues to whine after the true soul union. Bosh! What would he say if he could see poor little Harcourt getting tipsy for joy, because her husband is locked up for two years, or knew of—of—a dozen other cases I could name where men have commenced their married lives with passionate congratulations, and ended them by cursing all mankind?

'My Saint Bernard decidedly wants his eyes opened for him, and they'll be opened some day by a woman of a different type from his beautified Alice.

'Well, well—it matters little. The only question is, whether it is possible to save a man from such suffering, or desirable to save him if it were possible? We must all live and learn. But the man who theoretically places woman on such a high pedestal as Freshfield does, is sure to find out his mistake. Woman was never meant for a pedestal. She is out of our reach there ; we want her in our arms. Consequently madam has to be pulled down and show her feet of clay. If we could only be content to worship them from a distance, or keep them under a glass-shade, how long they would last! But I mustn't forget my promise to the poor child, who tumbled so unmistakably from her little pedestal last night.'

So saying he enclosed a bill for two hundred dollars in an envelope, addressed to Miss Harcourt, and strolled off to the theatre, as if he had never done a kind action in his life. He searched eagerly there for Jack Neville, but he was nowhere to be seen.

'Jack Neville!' exclaimed an old Chicago man, who knew everything and everybody. 'You won't meet him here to-night, my boy. He's levanted to the South again; went off like a shot directly he heard a rumour that that old black-leg Macpherson was in the town.'

'And quite right of him too,' said another voice. 'Neville's burnt his fingers once in the company of Sandie Macpherson, and the less he's seen with him in the future the better.'

'Well, he needn't have been in such a blazing hurry with respect to Sandie this time,' interposed a third speaker, 'for the old man wasn't twenty-four hours in the town, and only passed through on his way from New York.'

'Is he gone again?' demanded Nelson Cole.

'That is so, sir. Sandie Macpherson is not the man to stay where he isn't sure of a welcome, and he is too well known to our force to be able to walk the streets of Chicago with any comfort by daylight. So he showed his sense by making tracks, sir, as soon as his business with us was concluded.'

'It is as well, perhaps, for him that he has,' replied Nelson Cole; and the subject was dropped amongst them. A few days after, a lurking desire to learn Stephanie Harcourt's plans, and to assure her that Chicago was delivered from the presence of her enemy, led him again to the actress's door, where he was met by Miss Vavasour alone.

'Oh, Mr Cole!' she exclaimed, 'I have been longing to see you, or to leave your address that I might deliver Stephanie's thanks to you for your goodness and generosity.'

' She received my letter, then ? '

' Indeed, she did. It conveyed new life to her.
She left Chicago the very next day ! '

' She has left already ! You surprise me. Where
has she gone ? '

' That I cannot tell you, for I do not know myself. I agreed with Stephanie, that since her desire
is to lose herself in a new name and a new existence,
that it was best no one should share the secret.
Oh ! she has suffered terribly, sir ; her young life
has been a chapter of horrors. You have done a
most benevolent action in aiding her to escape
from its consequences ! '

' I hope she may escape them, but I question if
it is possible. Anyway, she is safely out of the
city, and has friends, I suppose, to go to ? '

' Yes, sir ; she has connections, I believe, on the
mother's side, with whom she can find a refuge.
But I must not forget the packet she left for
you.'

She went to a drawer and produced thence a
tiny parcel tied up in paper, and directed to himself.
He opened it. It contained an ordinary wedding-
ring, and these words :—

' DEAR FRIEND,—I am too poor to give you
anything but my thanks. But keep this ! It was
my mother's wedding-ring. It is my best possession. It will remind you sometimes that I was
not ungrateful for your goodness. STEPHANIE.'

' Rubbish !' exclaimed Nelson Cole roughly ; ' what
did the girl mean by leaving me this ? What does
she suppose I can want with her mother's wedding-
ring ? '

' It was all she had, sir,' said Miss Vavasour

mildly ; 'and she was very grateful for your kindness to her.'

'Stuff and nonsense! You shouldn't have allowed it. Can't you send it back to her?'

'I do not know her address.'

'She will write to you.'

'I do not think so. I think she has gone away from us for ever.'

'Well, I suppose I must keep it ; but it was an absurd idea on the girl's part. What the d—l am I to do with somebody else's wedding-ring?'

He shoved it awkwardly in his waistcoat pocket as he spoke, and having wished Miss Vavasour good-day, turned into the street again. He would not have confessed the fact to himself, nor any other control for the world ; but he felt quite disappointed to find that Stephanie Harcourt had left Chicago without wishing him good-bye, or leaving any trace of her destination.

And when he reached home he transferred the little scrap of paper and the old wedding-ring carefully to a safe corner of his despatch box, where they could neither be discovered nor disturbed.

And then Nelson Cole went on his way through the busy hard-working world, and except for an occasional remembrance that made him smile rather than sigh, he forgot all about his adventure with the little actress in the city of Chicago.

———

CHAPTER I.

IT was a bright, beautiful afternoon in the height of summer—not a miserable, humbugging, make-shift for a summer, such as we have had for the last ten years, but a real, good, old-fashioned one, like those that Adam and Eve enjoyed in Paradise, before rain and cold joined league with the other curses of mankind to come out of their proper season. This had been and was still a glorious time, when all the fragrant essences of grass and herbs were drawn out by the hot sun, and perfumed the land long after he had sunk to rest, when the tangled blossoms rioted over the flower-beds in the profusion of their bearing, and the branches of the fruit trees and bushes, overweighted, hung to the ground, and the earth was warm and dry from early morn to dewy eve.

The noble acacias on the lawn of Blue Mount formed leafy bowers of themselves, and under the shade of one of them, in her ordinary dress, without fear of the exposure, sat Mrs Freshfield knitting. Mrs Freshfield was always knitting. No one ever encountered her sitting or standing on a week-day without a huge ball of worsted and two or four large wooden pins in her hands. What she manu-factured, or what became of the products of her labour, remained a mystery. The shelves of her mahogany wardrobe were piled with pounds of wool of various colours, which gradually became drawn into the general web and disappeared, to be re-placed by more; but where it went to in the form of stitches Mrs Freshfield seemed unable to account for. Her daughter Laura declared she made petti-coats for old sinners, who sold them as fast as they received them, so that each pensioner wore out about half-a-dozen in the course of twelve months.　But Mrs Freshfield was strictly pious, and in the habit of sternly repressing Laura's profane jests.　She had not been a young woman when she married her late husband, John Freshfield, the Sheffield merchant, who bought Blue Mount and its surroundings as a retreat for his old age.　Mrs Freshfield had been extremely pious even in those days, but her piety had not prevented her marrying the Sheffield merchant on account of his money.

Surely we have seen such things in the world before.　A golden bait is almost as irresistible to the elect as to the ungodly—only they call their temptation by a different name.　Mrs Freshfield thought that Mr Freshfield's riches would prove such a snare to him that he would require a help-meet like herself to counteract their evil influence. She married him to convert him (so she said), but she never succeeded in doing so, for he died as hardened an old sinner as he had lived, begging his physician with his last breath to keep his wife and her cant out of his room.　Thus deprived of the triumph of making a saint of her husband, Mrs Freshfield turned her attention to her children. There were two of them—Bernard and Laura, and although they were young people who dared to think for themselves in certain matters, they had certainly so far profited by their mother's training, that the young man was pure and refined and religious in his ideas to a degree extraordinary in this age of free thought and unbridled actions , and the girl, though light-hearted and full of fun, was as delicate and modest as any English girl could be.

Mrs Freshfield was an old woman.　She had

numbered nearly forty years when Bernard was born to her, and he was now past eight-and-twenty, and from the first she had always destined this unlooked-for blessing to the ministry of the church. Bernard had been brought up from an infant with the knowledge that he was to be a parson, and a parson he had conequently become. His father had left him ample means, and he had no need to work ; but it was his mother's wish, and he never dreamt of disputing it. Perhaps he sometimes regretted that he had yielded so easily ; he had his own thoughts and ideas about a parson's duty, and they clashed occasionally with the rules set down for him ; but, if so, he did not express his regrets openly, but laboured as faithfully as he could for the good of the inhabitants of Bluemere.

He did not live with his mother. On the occasion of his marriage he had taken a smaller but very pretty house about half-a-mile from the Mount, and he continued to occupy it and to keep a kennel of sporting dogs, which shocked Mrs Freshfield— and a couple of hunters, which horrified her still more. Indeed, the greatest calamities of her life were, that Bernard *would* wear a velveteen coat in the mornings and would *not* give up smoking. To be a smoking, hunting, shooting parson in a velveteen coat seemed, in poor Mrs Freshfield's narrow mind, very much like selling oneself to the devil ; but still Bernard was a good son to her, and she was a good mother to him, and so they managed to get on together, notwithstanding that on some points he would have his own way. A mother must not hope to exercise any influence but that of love over a son of eight-and-twenty, who possesses a couple of thousand a-year in his own right, and will come into all her property when she dies.

But Bernard had always been Mrs Freshfield's favourite child, and as she watched him coming across the lawn to her that afternoon, the old lady's eyes glistened and her hands trembled with the pleasure of seeing him again. For Laura was absent too, and she had the prospect of having the conversation with him all to herself, a pleasure she seldom enjoyed.

Bernard came up to his mother and greeted her affectionately. This young fellow, already a widower at eight-and-twenty, had a heart brimming over with love for all who loved him. He was not particularly good-looking—no one would have called him an Antinous or a Hercules, but he had a straight athletic figure—a kind, honest face, and blue eyes that were peculiarly tender and earnest in their expression. His widowhood had not sat very heavily upon his spirits, and he had never pretended it had done so ; but it had left a quiet subdued demeanour behind it, that was particularly noticeable when he was alone. Then he often sighed and heavily—not because his bereavement had bereaved him so much, but because it had bereaved him so little. He sighed for himself, because he seemed to have gained something where he had really lost, and it made him realise how little he had ever possessed. He was a strange young man, as these pages will show ; but he was honest to himself withal.

'Bernard, my dear,' said Mrs Freshfield, with some little show of excitement, 'we are to have guests to-morrow. The Muckheeps have been in London for a month, and are coming to spend a few weeks at Blue Mount before they return to Scotland.'

'Indeed, mother ! I hope you'll feed them up

well. They look as if they needed it—or at all events Miss Janet does.'

'Now, Bernard, my dear, I call that a very unkind speech on your part, and quite unbefitting your calling. It would lead one to think that you value your friends on account of their money or money's worth. If the Misses Muckheep—notwithstanding their good old blood—are not as wealthy as ourselves, it is their misfortune and not their fault.'

Mrs Freshfield delivered the phrase 'good old blood' with an unctuous smack, for, be it known, this very pious lady, who professed to despise the wealth of which she had a superfluity, cherished an overwhelming weakness for 'blood,' which was the only thing money could not buy for her, and would have given much to see her son contract a second alliance with some woman of 'family.'

But the Reverend Bernard did not seem to notice the maternal rebuke. His ear had been caught by another sentence.

'I wish, mother,' he said, as he took a seat beside her, 'that you would not speak of everything as either befitting or unbefitting my "*calling.*" The term is one that grates upon me. It insinuates that I had a spiritual call to undertake the work of a minister, and you know that I had no such thing. I became a parson because you urged me to the step, and wished to keep me by your side, and I entered the profession with far too little sense of its responsibilities.'

'Bernard, you don't mean to tell me that you regret it?' exclaimed Mrs Freshfield with horror.

'No, dear mother, I do not! Had I to choose over again, I might draw back from undertaking so much more than I feel myself able to perform ; but as the duty has been pressed upon me, I will discharge it as faithfully as I can.　Only don't try to make me out better than I am.　Let me work amongst my sick and suffering people in my own way, and comfort them with a friend's sympathy and advice, but don't set me up as an example of piety and virtue, because that you know I am not.'

'Bernard! I am sure that you are all that is best and most praiseworthy.　Mrs Pinner was saying, only the other day, that the life you lead is an example to any young man.'

'I am much obliged to Mrs Pinner for her opinion, but I should hardly think that her experience enhanced the value of her recommendation, and I don't think that a parson should be set up as a little oracle amongst his people.　It is the truth he preaches that should be worshipped—not himself. What! am I not a man like all the rest of them?'

'Oh, Bernard, my dear, don't say that,' murmured his mother deprecatingly.

'A man with all the tastes and feelings of a man,' he went on, 'and with no notion that I sin in indulging any taste that is not contrary to law.　If hunting and shooting and dancing and smoking are sinful, then they are sinful for everybody as well as for me, and we must all renounce them as evil habits.　But if they are innocent for my parishioners, then they are equally innocent for myself. And yet I know I shock you, my dear mother, and many other estimable people, by these worldly proclivities of mine, and you think I can neither go to heaven myself, nor teach my people the way there, unless I systematically look as if I were bound for the other place!'

'Oh, my dear Bernard, but then your sacred calling—'

'There you go again, mother! my "calling,"' said Bernard, as he rose to his feet and walked up and down the grass. 'I tell you if anybody "called" me to the ministry, it was yourself, and I am not going to make what may prove a harmless matter into a very evil one, by living a life false to myself and to my own notions of right, out of prejudice to the opinions of the world.'

'Well, well, my dear boy, pray sit down again and don't excite yourself in this needless manner. I don't know what I can have said to raise such a discussion. But the fact is, Bernard, the house is lonely to you since your great misfortune, and you don't care to stay at home as you ought to do. When are you going to dispel the shadow, my son, and brighten your home again? It seems quite unnatural, not to say wrong, to me, that a minister should remain unmarried.'

'Why so?'

But to this plain question Mrs Freshfield seemed puzzled to find an answer.

'I can tell you, mother. Because you think the vows a man makes to heaven are weaker than those he makes to a woman, and that though the latter may keep him in the straight and narrow path, he is not to be trusted to remain faithful to the former.'

'My dear Bernard, you really do say such things.'

'I only put your thoughts into words. It was with that idea that you threw me into the society of poor Alice, and persuaded me she was breaking her heart on my account, until I thought it was my duty to marry the girl, and tell the first lie that had ever passed my lips before God's altar.'

'Bernard, Bernard, it shocks me beyond measure to hear you speak in this manner, and of such a dear, good loving wife as she made you too.'

' I say nothing against her, poor girl ; God forbid
I should.   But as far as I was concerned, that marriage was a blasphemy and a sacrilege—a blasphemy
against love and a sacrilege of the highest human
sacrament that God designed for the regeneration
of mankind.'

' Well, I can't say I follow you, my dear.   She
was a sweet girl, and you made her an excellent
husband, and what more could anybody desire ?'

Bernard's quiet eyes were fixed upon the sky,
glowing with the first glories of sunset.

' I don't know if she felt the void,' he said, in a
low voice, ' but I wanted—completion.'

' Oh, dear ! oh, dear !' exclaimed Mrs Freshfield,
dropping stitches by the dozen in her perplexity.
' I don't understand all these new-fangled terms,
but I know what *I* want, Bernard, and that is to
see you happily settled again, and my little grand-
children toddling about my knees, before I am
called home to join your father.'

' Dear old mother,' replied the young man affectionately, as he laid his hand upon hers, ' it is a
very natural wish, and I hope it may be gratified.
But would not Laura do as well for the agent of
such happiness as myself ?'

' *Laura !*' ejaculated Mrs Freshfield emphatically.
' No—not at all.   In the first place, Laura's children
could never be the same to me as yours, Bernard.
They would not be Freshfields; and in the second,
a girl can't marry when she chooses, and a man can.'

' Oh, that is only a mother's partiality,' laughed
her son, ' and I am afraid the marriageable young
ladies of Bluemere would not be disposed to record
your assertion.'

' Nonsense, Bernard !   There are a dozen in
Bluemere alone who would jump at you.'

'Let me hear the roll-call, mother. Who knows but what I might take a fancy to one or two of them.

Mrs Freshfield bridled with importance. She really thought her son was beginning to look at the matter in a practical light.

'Well, my dear, there is Mrs Norman. She is not older than yourself, and her father's cousin is the Earl of Carisborough!'

'Mrs Norman! The pretty widow at Willow Cottage? No, no, mother, she paints!'

'Only on occasions, Bernard; and you could soon break her off that.'

'She won't do, I tell you. It is of no use.'

'Miss Warrender. You have often remarked how handsome she is.'

'The sorrowful lady with a secret in her life? Mrs Bernard Freshfield's former life must contain no secrets, mother. It must be open to inspection as the light of day.'

'You can have no such objection to make to Nellie Palmer.'

'Pretty little, timid, bashful Nellie. I am afraid she's too shy for me. Those girls who can never look you straight in the face are invariably flirts when your back is turned.'

'Annie Warren, then, who was our poor Alice's bosom friend, and nursed her like a sister in her last illness. Her chief pleasure lies in the parish work, Bernard, and I am sure she loves you already.'

'And for that very reason I would never make her my wife. Dear little charitable Bluemere would say at once that we had settled the matter over Alice's dying bed. No, mother, none of these women will do to fill the vacant place, and I have only been having a little pleasantry with you in even talking of them. I shall never marry again. I feel sure of it, because I see no chance of meeting the woman whom I could love.'

' Not if you continue to be so fastidious.' replied his mother, vexed at finding he had only been in jest. ' But I suppose we may depend upon seeing you at dinner to-morrow to welcome our guests. You know what a dear. good creature Miss Muck-heep is. and what a hearty interest she takes in everything that concerns your calling.'

' Yes, yes,' cried Bernard hastily, as he jumped to his feet. ' If you wish it, I will be here.

' Of course I wish it, and Bella too ; such a sweet. unaffected girl, without the least pride about her. although her father, the Laird of Muckheep. can trace his ancestors back to the time of the Picts and Scots.'

' Just so, when they were a party of untamed savages, and wore nothing but skins. if so much. I hope Miss Bella is a little more civilised than she was on the occasion of her last visit here. for I remember thinking her a terrible Goth.'

' My dear Bernard. her aunt writes me word that she is everything that is most charming, and imbued with the deepest religious feeling.'

' She will be an excellent companion for Laura. then, who is certainly not imbued with too much. I don't believe the monkey would ever come to church except for the pleasure of seeing me !'

' And you encourage her in it, Bernard ; deeply as I regret to say it. Laura would certainly be more attentive to her religious duties if you spoke with more severity against her neglect of them.'

' And make the duties as hateful in her eyes as I should become myself. Would you have me set up as an ogre or janitor to my only sister, instead of a loving friend ? No, mother, I cannot do it. Let Laura follow her own inclinations. An unwilling sacrifice can never be acceptable.'

'Well, my dear, I cannot help thinking you are far too lax in your ideas, and I wish you had a dear good partner to consult with you on all these knotty points.'

'Good-bye, mother, you shall see me at dinner to-morrow,' exclaimed Bernard, as he turned away and walked rapidly across the lawn, fearful lest another minute's conversation might renew the vexed question of a second wife.

CHAPTER II.

As he retraced his steps towards Briarwood (as his own house was called), followed by a couple of setters and a greyhound, his face was more thoughtful than usual. For notwithstanding Mrs Freshfield's doubts and his own modesty, this young man felt more deeply than he cared to acknowledge the responsibilities of the post he had undertaken. He earnestly desired to show a good example to the people under his charge, and to advise them profitably on the best means of regulating their ives ; but the difficulty with Bernard Freshfield was to make up his own mind as to which was the best example and the best way. He knew, of course, that a pure and charitable and useful life was obligatory on all who called themselves

Christians ; but it was in the smaller matters, in the petty laws laid down by custom, the rules observed because everybody else observes them, the thousand and one fretting obligations imposed upon men by disciplinarians, lest a ‘ brother should offend,’ that Bernard Freshfield hesitated to do more than tell his parishioners to judge for themselves.   He had seen certain parsons, in their endeavours to drive men like a flock of sheep to heaven, afraid to dance or sing, or join in merriment of any kind, and he knew how futile those endeavours had proved, to do more than make their fellow-creatures hypocrites.   He had watched these ministers, setting themselves up as gods amongst the people, and arrogating to themselves the power they deprecated in those of another faith, of refusing communion, or marriage, or burial to the persons whom they, in their infinite wisdom, deemed unworthy of such privileges.   And he had marked how their refusals had hardened the hearts they should have melted, and drawn down curses on their own heads instead of blessings.

He had seen parsons who had frowned openly with the world at the wife’s adultery, the maid-servant’s seduction, the apprentice’s theft ; pass over (also with the world) the master’s dishonest dealing, the gentleman’s fornication, the fast woman’s coquetry, and the mistress’s ill temper, because they were unrecognised sins, and they did not feel they had any right to meddle with them. Bernard Freshfield did not play the parson on this wise.   Where he saw what appeared to him to be wrong, he spoke openly, whether it was to poor little Jack with a dirty head, playing at pitch-and-toss with a stolen halfpenny on Sunday, instead of going to school ; or to the squire’s son, lounging about his father's park on the same day, with bloodshot eyes and aching head, cheerful reminiscences of his debauch of the night before ; and whatever fault Bernard found himself called upon to tackle, he always had a pleasant way of making the offender understand that if he had not committed the same sin himself, he most likely would have done so under similar circumstances, until the humbled heart felt that, given the resolution and the opportunity, it might rise to be as high as the parson himself. Consequently our hero was a universal favourite in Bluemere. The dogs naturally adored him, because he was their veterinary surgeon, as well as their friend, and the little children followed suit—for the love of babies and animals cannot be separated. The old men and women regarded him almost as a son ; the married couples made him their confidant and arbitrator in all their disputes ; the youths voted him the jolliest of companions, and, as for the girls, if one or two of them in that peaceful village of Bluemere had gone a step too far, and raised their hopes to a vested partnership in Briarwood House, and if their parson knew it, and felt a little flattered by their preference, what matter ? He was but a man, as he said himself, and a young man after all, and the blood of youth runs as hotly in the veins of a parson as in those of an officer in the dragoons. The absurdity is, to suppose that, by forcing a man into a particular profession, you can change his nature, and, with impunity, refuse him those licences which the world freely allows to another, and the consequence of which is, that the majority of our English parsons—let those deny the assertion who can disprove it—who have adopted the church, just as soldiers adopt the army, for a living, are only so many more proofs of the power the world's opinion has to turn a man, otherwise honourable, into a living lie.

Bernard's mind was occupied with some such thoughts, wondering what there existed in himself, different from other men, that he should have been elected to walk as a shining light amongst them, when his attention was arrested by the mention of his own name.

'Mr Freshfield,' called a voice as he passed by, ' I wish you would come in and speak to me for a few minutes. I tried so hard to catch you after service last Sunday, but you were too quick for me. It seems an age since you gave me a call.'

Bernard turned at once, and, with his usual courtesy, greeted a tall, angular, prim-looking old lady, who, with a shawl pinned round her head, was talking to him over a low hedge of French laurels. It was the same who had told his mother that the life he led was an example to all young men.

'Certainly, Mrs Pinner, I will come in if it will give you any pleasure. No, don't let my dogs through the gate. They will make havoc in your pretty little garden, and they are used to wait for me outside. Is there anything that I can do for you? he continued, as he followed her into a sitting-room on the ground floor.

'Oh! I have a thousand things to consult you about relating to the parish, Mr Freshfield, but, of course, this is not the time. It is past five o'clock, and you must be going home to your dinner.'

'Never mind my dinner if you require my services,' he replied good-naturedly.

'Now that is so like you, Mr Freshfield, never thinking of yourself—but no! I will not be so selfish —what I chiefly wanted to ask you was, if you could spare us any evening this week for just a muffin and a cup of tea, you know, and a little quiet conversation. It would be such a privilege—and I am particularly desirous to introduce you to my niece.'

Now, if there was one phase of parish life which poor Bernard particularly detested above another, it was the muffin and cup of tea Mrs Pinner alluded to, which generally took him away from his late dinner, and entirely deprived him of the post-prandial pipe. But it was one of the little mortifications to which he made it a rule to subject himself, holding the opinion that no man is fit to guide others who is not master of his own appetites, and that to give up our inclinations for the sake of our fellow-creatures is one of the highest phases of love. So he answered readily, if not cheerfully,—

'I will accept your hospitality with pleasure, Mrs Pinner—if you cannot transact business with me as well in the morning. But I was not aware you had a niece—'

'Well, she is not a niece, Mr Freshfield. I was wrong to call her so—she is a sort of cousin on the mother's side, and very distantly connected ; but she has been lately left an orphan, poor thing, so I asked her to stay with me for a few months, though I'm afraid she will be obliged to earn her own living when they are ended. But I think I can trace a providence in her coming to me. She has been very carelessly brought up, and it would be a blessed thing, wouldn't it, Mr Freshfield, if we could guide her feet into the right way before she left us again ?'

Bernard, who hated all cant, took no notice of Mrs Pinner's pious hope.

'Is your cousin young?'

'Yes. Quite a girl; but with the strangest ideas. She does not seem as if she could make enough of the country, and would idle all her time away if I allowed it.'

'Let her idle it away, Mrs Pinner. I daresay her heart is sore from her late losses. This beautiful country in this beautiful weather will speak surer peace to her than we could do in any amount of words.'

'But it seems so sinful to me, Mr Freshfield, to see a strong, hearty girl doing nothing day after day, when there is more parish work than there are hands to do it with.'

'Do you think so? I think Bluemere is admirably looked after. Sometimes I say *too* well looked after, particularly when I find that Miss Warren has countermanded half the orders that I have given for the relief of my parishioners.'

'Ah. Miss Warren; but see how she works, Mr Freshfield, and what a head she has got. I always call her your right hand. And then she is so devoted to your interests, and she is afraid the old people impose on your good nature and get more relief from you than they really require. I am sure Miss Warren is quite an example—I often say so, and would make a model clergyman's wife.'

'She'd better go to the next parish then,' remarked Bernard curtly. 'I know the new rector who has just been appointed there is a bachelor.'

'Oh, Mr Freshfield. you are always full of your fun; but you know that Bluemere would be quite lost without Miss Warren. And she was kind enough to offer to introduce Miss Moss to the Sunday school, but I am sorry to say she refused.'

'Is Miss Moss your cousin?'

'Yes. And it's such things I want you to talk to her about, Mr Freshfield, for her notions of religion quite shock me. Only think—she wouldn't go to church with me last Sunday, but sat all day in the garden reading some frivolous story. I was ashamed that my servant should see such a thing. And she doesn't seem to have any more knowledge of the Scriptures than a heathen.'

'And do you think no one can be religious without knowing the Scriptures, Mrs Pinner?'

'Well, of course, I know there are some who have been taught as it were of heaven itself; but Phyllida appears to be as ignorant as a baby.'

'Well, I must come and make the acquaintance of your fair barbarian; but please don't present me to her in the guise of a schoolmaster, or we shall make no way at all. Let me talk to Miss Moss after my own fashion, and I daresay we shall come to an understanding by-an-by.'

'I am sure you are only too good to take the trouble, Mr Freshfield. Shall we say Thursday for our little cup of tea? And I don't think I'll tell Phyllida that you're coming, for she seems to dislike the sight of strangers so, that, ten to one, she may run out of the house just to spite me.'

'You seem to have got a bargain on your hands,' said Bernard, laughing, as he rose to take his leave. 'I suppose, as I do not see her, that Miss Moss is not indoors at present.'

'No, she disappeared after our early dinner in her strange fashion, and I haven't set eyes on her since. I'm sure it's very good of you to promise to come to us, Mr Freshfield, and we shall look forward to it with pleasure. Quite alone, you know—a muffin and a cup of tea—next Thursday at seven—thank you so much.'

And with Mrs Pinner's murmured sentences pursuing him like buzzing flies, Bernard passed down the garden path, and, whistling to his dogs, took his way to Briarwood. He had intended to make two or three calls on the road ; but as he looked at his watch he was surprised to see how long Mrs Pinner's conversation had detained him, and determined to take a short cut home by the fields instead. His house of Briarwood was built upon a hill, and the land surrounding it was his own property. Bernard cleared a high fence, and making his way through some low brushwood which he was keeping as a pheasant preserve, entered a grove of larches which formed a foreground to his residence. He was pacing the narrow path with his eyes downcast and his thoughts far away, when he was startled by hearing a low cry of fear, followed by a hurried exclamation. Bernard looked up. His three dogs were leaping violently, and, as it would seem, with murderous intent, against the slight figure of a girl, dressed in black, who held something to her breast with one hand, whilst with the other she attempted to ward off the boisterous attacks of the excited animals. Bernard whistled to them, and then finding they did not instantly obey him, he sprang forward and belaboured them well with the stout stick he carried in his hand. But here the girl interposed to save her assailants from further punishment.

'Oh, don't beat them—don't beat them!' she cried. 'They didn't mean to hurt *me*, the beautiful creatures, only I was so afraid they would kill my little kitten.'

And she displayed to him a fluffy white and tabby creature with pale blue eyes, of a few weeks old, who was still spitting and scratching with all its puny might, and clinging to the sleeve of her dress.

'Go to heel!' exclaimed Bernard, in a voice of thunder to his conscience-stricken hounds, who slunk behind him, and then he took off his hat to the stranger, and trusted that her favourite was not hurt.

'Oh no, they didn't touch her ; I was only afraid they would. Poor things,' she said pityingly, 'how unhappy they look! Do pat them and speak kindly to them again.'

'I had better not,' replied Bernard. 'At all events until the temptation to transgress is out of their reach. They are apt to presume upon indulgence. You love animals I see,' he added with a smile ; for he loved them so well himself he felt affinity with all who shared his tastes.

'Very much — particularly dogs! they are so faithful and affectionate. I like them ever so much better than I do men and women.'

Bernard laughed.

'You think me foolish, perhaps, or wrong, as Mrs Pinner does—she says it is sinful to waste time and food on animals when there are so many poor people starving and in want of help.'

' If we neglected our fellow-creatures to lavish time and substance upon animals, I should feel inclined to agree with Mrs Pinner ; but it may not lie within the range of our duties to attend to poor people, and these dumb creatures are certainly confided to our care. It would be wicked to neglect them. But from what you say, I presume I have the pleasure of speaking to Mrs Pinner's niece.'

'Yes; I am Phyllida Moss. And do you, then, know my cousin Pinner?'

'Very well, indeed.'

'I am glad of that. Then perhaps she will not think it wrong of me to have spoken to you—cousin Pinner thinks everything wrong. She says she is going to bring the clergyman of the parish to talk to me about my doings.'

'Indeed! Have you been very naughty, then?'

'I can't say. I didn't go to church last Sunday —that is what bothered her.'

'Don't you like going to church?'

'Not much; it's all so prim and stiff, and the sermons make me sleepy. I like going out by myself on the hill-side and sitting on the grass and thinking better. I put my head right down in the grass and no one knows, who doesn't do that, what wonderful sights and sounds there are to be heard and seen there. The wee, wee flowers, no bigger than a pin's head, like little red and blue stars with golden eyes that grow down amongst the blades; and then the insects that talk to one another, and carry their food about and build their snug houses, for all the world as well as if they were giants. And I think you know that to lie and listen to all this and think about it, and how it came to pass, does one more good than sitting for two hours within four walls and hearing a lot of things you don't care about.'

'And so do I, a thousand times over.' said Bernard heartily. 'And you have never seen the parson of Bluemere yet, then, Miss Moss?'

'No, and I reckon I don't want to, either.'

'Why not?'

'Oh, because cousin Pinner thinks so much of him; it frightens me. You see I haven't been brought up amongst parsons myself. I am not good, it's no use denying it; and what's more, I don't feel as if I ever should be.'

'Why should you say that? I am sure your impulses are good, even from the few words we have exchanged with one another.'

'I don't *feel* good. My life's been all trouble and misfortune, and that makes one hard. But it's nonsense for me to talk like this to a stranger!'

'I wish you wouldn't look on me as a stranger. I know Mrs Pinner so well, that it is only natural I should know you also.'

'You won't tell the parson?' she said, with an arch glance.

As Bernard Freshfield met her eyes, he thought —and truly—that he had never seen so lovely a woman before.

She was dressed exceedingly plain in a suit of deep black, but her bronze-coloured hair was tucked up in profusion under her plain straw hat, beneath the brim of which gleamed at him large, soft, long eyes of the clearest brown, which reminded Bernard somehow of the eyes of his favourite setter Rose. Her nose was straight ; her chin pointed ; her mouth a perfect bow ; and her dark lashes lay on her cheek like a fringe of silk. It was a child-like face without being an innocent one—that is to say, it had an open confiding expression, and yet the languid eyes showed that the girl had passed through the experience of this world, and known its sorrow. When Bernard Freshfield came to know Phyllida Moss more intimately, he found she was a strange mixture of child and woman : of careless mirth and thoughtful despondency; but in the moment of their first introduction, he only thought her as she stood there conversing as freely with him as if they had been acquainted all their lives, with the little kitten clinging to her breast—simply charming.

And with each sentence she uttered, she charmed him more.

Her last words almost upset his gravity, but he managed to reply that he would not tell the parson.

' Well, then, I think long prayers and sighs and groans and texts, and all that sort of thing, you know, nonsense. I knew a man once,' with a shudder, 'oh, the very worst man I ever knew, and when it suited his purpose not to lie and gamble and cheat, he used to go to prayers instead, and pretend to be pious, and it worked with some folks, I suppose ; but it sickened me, and that's the truth, and I've never felt as though I could say a prayer since.'

' Mrs Pinner tells me you have lost your father and mother. Were they good parents to you ? '

' My mother was—an angel ! and she's one now, I know. Nothing could knock that out of me.'

' Doubtless she is. And you used to tell her all your troubles. I daresay ? '

The tears rushed to Phyllida's brown eyes.

' Ah, I used ! God bless her ! and she was never weary of listening, though she had enough of her own, poor soul ! '

' And it comforted you to go to her ? '

' Of course it did. Who can comfort one like a mother ? '

' But she wouldn't have cared for your confidence if it hadn't been true, if you had pretended to be in trouble when you weren't really so ? '

' Well—no—how should she ? '

' The church is like your mother, Miss Moss, and her children's prayers are their confidences.

Whilst you have nothing to tell her, I say keep away, and don't insult her by a pretence of requiring her consolations.

There was a pause between them for a moment, and then Phyllida inquired,—

'Are you the parson ?'

'I am ; but don't let that fact frighten you. You see I am not very formidable.'

'Oh no ; only perhaps I have said things I shouldn't.'

'Not at all. There is no good in a parson, unless you can speak your mind to him."

'And do you think my mind is very wrong ?'

'I think you have had some great trouble, and it has hardened you.'

'Oh, no, no,' commenced the girl vehemently, 'it has not hardened me! I love the flowers and the birds and trees more than I can tell you, and the little children and the animals, and I love to get out amongst them and try to fancy myself a child once more, and to begin life over again with them. That is what I want, sir, to begin life over again, to forget all that has gone before ; to wipe it out as if it had never been, and to feel a girl again with the birds and flowers, a girl as I used to do before my mother died,' she said in a low wailing voice.

Bernard felt very paternal ; he often did feel paternal when pretty girls bestowed their confidences on him.

'My poor child,' he replied, 'I understand you so well ; I can sympathise with every word you have said. I too have known trouble, Miss Moss, very heavy trouble, not only from domestic loss, but from doubts and fears upon religious matters, similar to if not identical with your own. Will you therefore try and look upon me not only as a friend, but as a fellow-searcher after truth, and help me with your confidences as I will help you, if possible, with my experience.'

'But I'm not fit to be your friend, Mr Freshfield—the friend of a parson. You don't know how careless I am. Mrs Pinner calls me a perfect heathen.'

'Child, you don't know of what you are talking. It is far more likely that the parson is not fit to be friends with you. But please speak of me by any name but that; I do not like it. I would rather the people of Bluemere thought of me only as their friend.'

'As a friend, then, sir, good evening. Kitty and I must be going homewards, or Mrs Pinner will have reason to think that we are lost.'

'Good-night, my child! Depend on it, it is not for nothing that we have been led to meet each other in this fantastic manner, and that your lips have been unsealed so freely to me. Good-night; it will not be long before we meet again.'

And as Bernard Freshfield turned to watch the graceful figure in black descending the hill, cuddling the mewing kitten to her breast, he felt a strange exhilaration, as if a new interest had suddenly sprung up in his uneventful life.

* * *

CHAPTER III.

THE following morning Mrs Freshfield was considerably startled by receiving a note from her son :—

'MY DEAR MOTHER,—Since you make a point

of my dining at Blue Mount to-day, you must let me bring my friend Anderson with me. He turned up expectedly at Briarwood last night, and I cannot leave him to spend the evening alone.—Yours affectionately,   BERNARD.'

Now, Charles Anderson was an old college chum of Bernard's, to whom he was deeply attached. The young men had gone rather different ways since starting in life, Anderson having become deeply imbued whilst at Oxford with High Church tendencies, which had subsequently led him to the communion of Rome. But Bernard and he had never severed a link of their early friendship in consequence, and it was one of Mrs Freshfield's grievances against her son, that he stoutly refused to relinquish any part of his intercourse with Anderson. The old lady was busy when the note arrived giving her housekeeper sets of sundry linen sheets and frilled pillow cases wherewith to furnish forth the bedchambers of the expected visitors ; but this piece of intelligence was too dreadful to be kept to herself, and she trotted off at once to communicate it to her daughter.

' Laura ! ' she exclaimed, with the most helpless, hopeless look upon her countenance as she came upon that young lady copying a profane love song, ' can you conceive it possible that Bernard proposes to bring Mr Anderson to dinner here this evening ? '

' Oh, I *am* glad,' replied Laura blithely ; ' Charlie Anderson is so entertaining, he'll help to take the Miss Muckheeps off our hands.'

' Laura, I am surprised to hear you speak in this manner of a person who has proved himself to be so utterly without principle. Have you forgotten

that Mr Anderson is a Roman Catholic—a Papist
—an Apostate?'

'One name is enough for him at a time, isn't it
mamma? But he is Bernard's friend, you know,
notwithstanding, and I cannot see what his tenets
have to do with his being an amusing companion.'

'Your poor brother is sadly mistaken in keeping
such a friend—it is unaccountable in one who pro-
fesses to hold the pure Protestant faith as it was
transmitted to us by the glorious Luther. And to
bring him to my table too, and to sit down with
Miss Janet Muckheep. It is an insult.'

'I am sure Bernard would much rather dine at
home, mamma ; you know how he hates a dinner
party. If you object to Mr Anderson's presence
here, why not write and tell Bernard so quietly,
and let him enjoy the evening with his friend at
Briarwood.'

'No, Laura, my conscience would not permit of
that. Who knows with what principles this poor
lost soul might not imbue your unhappy brother?
We must make the sacrifice, if it is only to keep
Bernard under our own eyes.'

'Well, mamma dear, let us make it then, and say
no more about it. Though I must say you do not
give dear Bernard credit for much steadfastness of
purpose or knowledge of his own mind.'

'My dear, I know human nature better than you
do, and I grieve to say that some of your brother's
doctrines are anything but orthodox. However,
we must make the best of this annoyance, and
trust it may be overruled for good.'

By which Mrs Freshfield meant that she trusted
her conversation and that of Miss Muckheep might
have some influence in causing the unhappy Mr
Anderson to see the error of his ways. She loved

to throw a stone at all Popery and Papists, and this Papist in particular,—having made of himself as it were a fearful example almost within their gates—but she had had no intention from the beginning of being deprived in consequence of the glory of seeing her son at the head of her table. So she resigned herself, though not without many Protestant groans, to the inevitable, only hoping that Miss Janet Muckheep might not discover the principles of her fellow guest. The expected visitors arrived in the course of the afternoon, and were received by Mrs Freshfield much after the same fashion as that in which Abraham entertained the two angels. Indeed, if her real mind with regard to Miss Janet Muckheep could have been laid bare, it would have been seen that Mrs Freshfield did regard her as very little lower than the angelic host. She was not a woman of strong mind or fixed principles, notwithstanding her stock of platitudes, and the old Scotchwoman's eternal cant and dragging in of holy names and holy subjects in everyday conversation was accepted by her as the very quintessence of godliness.

Miss Janet Muckheep was the sister of a man who was styled (or styled himself) the Laird o' Muckheep, or *The* Muckheep, and Miss Bella was his daughter and her niece. The laird had married early in life, and lost his wife within two years of the marriage, since which bereavement he had spent most of his time abroad. He had left his infant daughter at Barrick-gallagas Castle, as his feudal domains were grandly termed, under the charge of his maiden sister, and had only visited Scotland at intervals since. Miss Janet affirmed that the laird's feelings would not permit him to live on the spot where he had buried his wife;

but less partial judges were not surprised that he should find pleasanter habitations than the bleak tumble-down castle of Barrick-gallagas on its stony barren lands, and more cheerful society than that of Miss Janet and Miss Bella Muckheep. There, for five-and-twenty years, therefore, had they lived together, until the younger lady had developed into a full-grown woman, and the aunt had drilled her into what she considered a perfect model of lady-like deportment and religious training. But at five-and-twenty Miss Bella was still considered and treated by her aunt as though she were a child, and scarcely permitted to eat or drink, to walk, or talk, without an injunction or a caution from her duenna.

Miss Janet herself, now an old lady of sixty, was the picture of a strong, active, hard-featured Scotchwoman. She talked such broad Scotch that it was difficult at times to understand what she said, but she professed to scorn to use the southern tongue as though it would be a disgrace to her, and she forbade her niece to! do so either. She was unpleasantly candid and outspoken, never taking heed to any one's feelings, and her religious doctrine was as hard and uncompromising as her features. Yet with all Miss Janet's cant and pro-fessions of Christian humility, she had, like her friend Mrs Freshfield, one great weakness, and that was for the family blood. She could never say enough on the subject of the Muckheeps and the feudal homage paid to them in their native country as lords of the soil. To hear Miss Janet talk of Barrick-gallagas Castle and its surround-ings, one would have imagined that she and her niece lived there in pomp and luxury like two queens, surrounded by their vassals. And one would have been rather surprised, if led by chance to visit this remnant of an age of princes, to find the two queens supping on oatmeal porridge, and waited on by a red-haired serving-maid without shoes or stockings, whilst the wind whistled through the ruined walls of their castle, and the thistles grew up to the tumble-down front door.

But Miss Janet did not consider she was telling or acting a falsehood by thus upholding the glory of the Muckheeps, and Mrs Freshfield, listening to her grand accounts, felt her own blood quicken at the thoughts of how her Bernard's wealth entitled him to seek a match with this impoverished daughter of a long line of Scottish kings, and tried to hit upon the best plan of introducing the matrimonial alliance to his consideration. And to her intense satisfaction Miss Muckheep's own conversation seemed to land in the same direction.

'Deed!' exclaimed the old Scotchwoman, as she peered like a witch over her spectacles, 'it's weel you and I have met for a crack this simmer, Mrs Fraichfield, for the laird himsel' talks of retairning to Barrack-gallagas in the fa' of the yair, and ance he sets his fut on Scottish ground it's little they'll let him or me lose sight of the cairs-tle again.'

'Your brother is coming home, Miss Janet? You don't mean to say so? What a delightful meeting is in store for you! How you must be looking forward to his return!'

'Ay. I don't say but we regaird it with as much pleeasure as is ret for puir sinfu' creatures to look fairward to that which may never come to pairse. But it is noo five yairs sin' the laird has seen the lassie theer, and I'm thinkin' he con-see-ders it time he should come hame and give her a tocher and a laird for hersel' Bella—heid!'

Which last mysterious sentence was not as English ears might have interpreted a caution only, but a straightforward direction to Miss Bella to hold up her head—that young lady being in the habit of stooping. Indeed, to judge from Miss Janet's constant animadversions on her deportment, it would be difficult to say what portion of her niece's somewhat redundant frame she did not misuse in the using. Bella, a stout, full-faced, red-haired young woman with blue eyes, high cheek bones, and the colour of a peony, jerked up her head, as a horse does when touched on the curb, gave a kind of snort, and went on with her work composedly. She had been used to these admonitions since her infancy, and never dreamed of resenting them at five-and-twenty.

'Oh, indeed! yes,' replied Mrs Freshfield sympathisingly; 'and I wonder that Miss Bella has not found a husband for herself before now. I am sure it must be her own fault that she is still single, sweet girl!'

'Ech, woman!' returned Miss Janet, 'but that's noo the way the lairds o' Muckheep marry their dairghters. I've brought up the lassie in the fear o' the Laird, and free from a' cairnal procleevities, and she kens too weel what is due to hersel', as a dairghter of *the* Muckheep, to cairst sheep's eyes at any carl that her faither hasna' chosen for her. Bella—back!'

Bella drew in the offending member with a suddenness that threw all the rest of her body out of gear; but Miss Janet did not seem to notice the awkwardness of her appearance, although poor Laura choked with laughter, and was sternly frowned down by Mrs Freshfield.

'I am sure you need not remind me, dear Miss

Janet, of how admirably you have trained your interesting charge, and the excellent principles with
which you have imbued her. Any one could see
from merely looking at your dear Bella how sweetly
Christian humility blends with the knowledge of
her ancient lineage in being descended from those
grand old Scottish kings!'

'Ay, but we're a' that!' replied the old Scotchwoman with pride. 'My brither himsel' would ha'
sat upon the throne o' Scotland if the country had
had its reets. The Muckheeps came in a de-reect
line from the fairst James, and the bluid has been
untainted on their side till noo. But I'm no sayin'
we can expeect the same to laist for ever; and if
the lassie there can find a gude mon, and a God-fear-
ing ane, to cheerish her innocence and keep her from
cairnal procleevities in a proper fashion for ane wha
has Scottish royal bluid runnin' in her veins, why.
the laird and mysel' would give her our blessing
with that of heaven. Bella—shoulders!'

Laura was too much interested in the conversation this time to care whether Bella carried her
shoulders up to her ears or down to her heels. She
was a sharp girl, and soon perceived, notwithstanding the fencing with which they carried it on, that her
mother and Miss Muckheep had the same notion
in their minds—namely that her brother Bernard
would make a very good match for the young lady
in question, and she shuddered at the mere anticipation of such a sister-in-law.

'Ah! you must look out for a good *son*, dear Miss
Muckheep,' sighed Mrs Freshfield, and then he is
sure to make a good husband—such a son now as my
Bernard has been to me. You can scarcely credit
how good he is—the residents of Bluemere say they
never saw such another young man—with such

principles—and such charity—and such unselfishness. He is quite a father to his people, though so young. I trust he may some day marry again, for he must feel very lonely in that fine place, Briarwood, with no lady to look after it. Such furniture, Miss Janet, it seems a sin it should not be used, and his income, too, a clear two thousand a-year besides his stipend. What is a young man to do with so much money all by himself? But, as he was saying to me only yesterday, he cannot find the woman he could love in Bluemere. For my dear son is very particular, and he will marry no one who has not received a strictly religious training of the good old-fashioned sort, or who is not of undoubted birth and breeding. " Above all things, mother," he said, " she must have good blood, and be a confirmed Christian." '

Here Laura, who had been listening in silent amazement to this extraordinary combination of requirements in a wife, broke in with her usual vehemence.

' Why, mamma, we have always considered Bernard such a radical. I didn't think he cared a pin about blue blood. I have heard him say he would take a wife off a dunghill if he found a true wife there. And I am sure poor Alice was not very aristocratic. Her grandfather was a cotton-spinner.'

' My dear Laura,' interposed Mrs Freshfield, ' pray do not bring in the name of that dear saint in heaven. Whatever she may have been is no concern of ours now. And as to your dear brother's principles, they are strictly conservative in every way, and the Queen has no more loyal subject than himself.'

Miss Muckheep, whose mouth had been watering at the description of Briarwood, and the fortune that maintained it, took up the cue at loyalty.

'Ay, but it's a fine thing is loyalty, Mrs Fraichfield, and ye would say so if ye could see the respeects and the hoo-mage that is ay peed to the lairds o' Muckheep when they stan' on their ain heather. King James himsel' cou'dna have received mair dairference fra the vassals of his coort. And the same dairference wad be peed to a' his de-scendents in a dereect line. And though the bawbees air unco' guid things in themsels, and I wadna be sayin' that the laird wad refuse the han' of his dairghter to any mon wha had the siller to keep her as would be expectit, yet I ken weel that sae lang as he had no cairnal procleevities he wad geeve the prair-feirence to ane wha held con-sairvative views. Bella —chin!'

Bernard Freshfield and his friend Anderson walked over to Blue Mount some little time before dinner, and Laura, alarmed at the conspiracy which she had detected, took an early opportunity to draw her brother on one side and confide her suspicions to him.

'Bernard, dear,' she exclaimed, as she followed him into the hall, where he went to deposit his hat and stick, 'isn't Bella Muckheep horrid? *Do* say you think so.'

'She is not charming, my dear Laura, either in person or manner, at all events, on a first acquaint-ance. But what is the matter? Why do you look at me in that extraordinary way?'

'Because—I know you will not believe me—but I assure you 'tis the truth—mamma and Miss Janet want you to marry her. They have been giving broad hints to each other on the subject the whole afternoon.'

Bernard burst out laughing.

'And you are afraid your innocent brother will

be entrapped into matrimony against his will, like
the forlorn heroine of the last romance you indulged
in, and led like a victim to the hymeneal altar, eh ?'

But Laura did not laugh.   She blushed.

'Not quite that, Bernie, only—don't be angry
dear—you remember how mamma persuaded and
cajoled and coaxed you before about poor Alice,
until there seemed nothing for you to do but to give
in.   You are so good to mamma, Bernie, and so
mindful of her feelings, that you forget to consider
your own.'

Bernard drew his sister into the morning-room,
where they could talk with greater freedom, and
when he got her there he took her in his arms and
kissed her.

'Thanks, dearest Laura, for your thought and
care of me.   But don't be afraid, little sister.   Your
big blundering brother will not make a second
mistake.   My eyes have been opened, Laura.   I
see and know now what love is, and I will never
accept respect nor friendship nor liking instead of
it.   It must come to me like a revelation from
heaven,—full, free. and without reserve,—pouring
upon me because it has no power to contain itself,
and glorified by passion as the sun tips the clouds
with gold and azure.   No more half hearts nor
modified affections, Laura.   My next love must give
me all or nothing, and receive the same from me.'

'Oh, Bernie, I am so glad to hear you speak like
that.   It is just my own idea of what a love that
terminates in marriage should be.   But I dare not
say so before mamma, because she calls me bold
and unmaidenly to hold such opinions, and I would
rather be thought anything than that.   She says
that if I esteem the man I marry, it is all I ought
to do before I am his wife.'

' A false principle, Laura, and one that may lead to any amount of unhappiness. Love comes from God, and marriage was ordained by Him, and the man who separates the two, who marries for convenience' or conscience' sake, or because he considers it advisable, commits a blasphemy against the God of Love, and deserves all he may suffer in consequence. I would rather marry a bad woman who loved me than a good woman who did not. Love might reform the first, but mere goodness could never make me love the other. Don't mistake esteem for love, dear. They are not the same thing, and they never will be.'

'And you are quite, *quite* sure, then, that you could never come to love Bella Muckheep?'

'Quite, *quite* sure, little sister. I am afraid that I am too fond of beauty ever to be able to enjoy an ugly wife. I like to be surrounded by beautiful things—to let my eyes dwell on them—to drink in each detail of their perfections. You know how I value my beautiful china, my pictures and statuettes. They are a never-failing source of pleasure to me. My wife must be the same. She must be lovely and lovable, or I will die as I am. Miss Bella's fat cheeks and unmeaning features will never tempt your brother to alter his condition. So you may take me back to her presence with the most perfect safety!'

When they re-entered the drawing-room Miss Janet was holding forth to Mr Anderson on the perfections of her favourite minister.

' Ech, mon !' she said, 'but ye should set oonder the Rairverend Doctor Felinus, if ye would hae pure darctrine, and the most ecstimable example. Ay ! but to hair him cairse the sinner, and depeect the tairrors of hell prepared for the licht-minded

and ungardly, wud mak each hair on your heed
stan' on eend.   He is a rare fine preacher is the
Rairverend Doctor Felinus.   It would be wairth
your wheele to traivel to Barrick-gallagas, jest to
get a waird of exhoortation fra' the leeps of sae
gardly a mon.'

'But my friend Mr Anderson does not belong to
the same church as Dr Felinus, Miss Muckheep,'
interposed Bernard at this juncture, 'added to which
he has dozens of celebrated preachers of his own
faith to whom he could listen with greater benefit
to himself.'

'Ay, but I canna believe it,' replied Miss Janet
decisively.   'No young mon could do better than
to leesten to the exhoortations and the prayers of
sech a meenester as Dr Felinus, while he expoonds
the glorious darctrines of Calvin, the great refairmer
of the wairld.'

'Why did you not tell us of him before!' exclaimed Mrs Freshfield enthusiastically.   'I should
have been so charmed, dear Miss Muckheep, to
receive your estimable minister as a guest beneath
my humble roof, and to have benefited by some of
the precious sayings that would have dropped like
honey from his lips.'

'You, mother?' said Bernard, frowning.   'What
should *you* want with the teachings of a Calvinistic
minister?   Haven't we parsons enough in our own
country to serve your need?   I can understand
your wishing to receive Miss Muckheep's friend at
Blue Mount, *as* a friend, but not to place yourself
under his ministration as a disciple.   And you of
all people, who (as a rule) are so especially hard
upon any one who dares to think differently from
yourself in religious matters.'

Bernard accompanied this last remark with a

glance at Charles Anderson, which made Mrs Freshfield colour with vexation.

'My dear Bernard,' she replied testily, 'you are utterly mistaken. It is true that I cannot tolerate a wilful turning from the truth—an abandonment of the faith in which we have been reared.'

'Come, come! we have had enough of that,' interposed her son authoritatively.

'But it does not follow,' continued Mrs Freshfield, 'that I should not derive spiritual benefit from association with a saintly man like Dr Felinus, the doctrines of whose church are precisely the same as our own.'

'That shows all you know about it,' replied Bernard. 'Dr Felinus may be, and doubtless is, an excellent man, but we do not require his teachings in Bluemere.'

'Ech, sirr!' chimed in Miss Janet, 'but ye coudna speak with greater heat if the gude dochter were a bluidy Peepist, reedy to massacre ye with the sward if ye didna sweer at ance, to adhere for aye to his demooralising and darmnatory dawctrines.'

'Madam,' said Bernard, 'I must ask you to drop all theological discussion for this evening, as my friend here, Mr Anderson, is a member of the church you speak of.'

'A meember of what?' exclaimed Miss Muckheep.

'Of the Holy Roman Catholic Church,' repeated Anderson reverently.

'And therefore,' continued Bernard, 'you will see that as his faith differs as much from mine as mine does from that of Dr Felinus. If we wish to spend a pleasant evening together, it will be wise to put our religions in our pockets, and think only of our dinner.'

'Ay, but a Peepist!' ejaculated Miss Janet. 'a real bluidy Peepist; it is awfu' to think on, and I canna say it is whut I expected in this hoose to be asked to seet down at the table with a disciple o' the scairleet woman!'

'Indeed—indeed, dear Miss Janet, it is not *my* doing,' interposed Mrs Freshfield.

'Mother, you forget what is due to my father's name,' said Bernard sternly; but his expression quickly changed as he turned to Miss Janet. 'Come, madam, look well at my friend, and you will see he is not so formidable an antagonist after all. Turn this way. Anderson, and let us have a good view of your apostate features.'

'Ech, sirr! but I'm no sayin' that the young mon has not a gude face of his ain; mair's the peety it should fa' doon to warrship blocks of stone and idols. And is it true, sirr, that the meeneesters canna marry in your misguided chairch?'

'Quite true, madam,' replied Anderson, with a bow.

'Ay! but it's an awfu' thing to conteemplate, and I sincairly weesh that the Rair-verend Dr Felinus had been hair to pint oot to ye the air-rer of your ways.'

'And I am sincerely thankful he is not,' cried Bernard, laughing. 'or we should have been victimised to listen to a religious argument that would have spoiled our dinner. 'Come, Miss Muckheep.' he added, as the butler announced that the meal was ready, 'let us leave our spiritual duties alone for awhile, and attend to the wants of the inner man. I am sure you are ready for your dinner as well as myself, and when it is over we will join in a bumper to the healths of the Archbishop of Canterbury, the Pope of Rome, and Dr Felinus, and feel ever so much better Christians for the act.'

And Miss Muckheep, although dreadfully scandalised at hearing the name of her favourite minister linked with those of two such reprobates as a pope and an archbishop, possessed too many 'cairnal procleevities' of her own not to relish the idea of a good dinner, and trotted off on Bernard's arm without another word.

'Mother!' he said, over his shoulder on their way to the dining-room, 'I have received such a nice long letter from dear old Nelson Cole.'

'Indeed, Bernard!' and what is his news?'

'Well, he won't be home yet awhile, I am sorry to say, but as that is the consequence of his abilities being appreciated in the new world, his friends must not grumble at it. And he says that when he does return, his first visit shall be to Briarwood.'

As the party seated themselves at table, Charles Anderson found himself next to Laura.

'Why do you look so solemn?' she whispered to him, laughing.

'I was only thinking—that is, hoping, Miss Freshfield, that you do not share Miss Muckheep's sentiments with regard to my religion.'

'I do not share her sentiments on any subject; you may rest assured of that,' returned Laura. 'And, above all things,' she added with a bright look that reflected itself immediately on her companion's countenance, 'I admire freedom of thought, and the courage that puts it into action.'

CHAPTER IV

WHEN Bernard Freshfield went to his mother's house that evening, he had fully intended asking his sister Laura to accompany him to Mrs Pinner's 'tea and muffin' on the following Thursday, and make the acquaintance of Miss Phyllida Moss. But somehow—he hardly knew why—when he had any opportunity of introducing the subject, a sudden shyness seized him and he said nothing. He was vexed with himself afterwards, and determined he would write to Laura—yet he did not write. Why was it? The passion of love could not have made this staid young man its victim at one interview—a single sight of that mobile face, those starry, far-seeing eyes and that sensitive mouth could not have thus shaken his reason in her equilibrium? No ; but he instinctively felt the approach of some great change ; and when the love of women does come upon man with an overwhelming force that bears down all barriers of circumstance or policy or difficulty before it, he has an inkling of what will befall him from the very beginning. The affection which is grafted upon esteem and a knowledge of character may last longer, but it knows none of the bliss that is born of mutual instinctive passion. It is the offspring of the reason we have cultivated—not of the nature which, however we may lower it, came as a gift from God, and is a part of His own essence. When spirit is destined to meet spirit in this world, they look out of the human eyes and tell the truth at once. So although Bernard Freshfield had only spoken in a grave and somewhat catechising manner to a young girl who, without being shy or reserved, had scarcely smiled once in answering him, he had an undefinable feeling at the idea of meeting her again—a desire that made him excited at the prospect, combined with a reluctance that almost induced him not to go at all. But it was *almost*— not quite. Something—the nineteenth century will laugh at me for calling it his fate, yet why should it not have been his fate since things happen in this world whether we will or no, and no power nor prayer of ours seems able to prevent them— something at any rate, that was stronger than his own inclination, drew him to Mrs Pinner's on Thursday evening, although he thought that he would much rather have remained at home. And when he reached his destination and found that Miss Annie Warren, decked out in white muslin and pink ribbons, was one of the guests invited to meet him, he thought so still more. Miss Warren, as has been already intimated, was a parochial light in Bluemere, although some people were un- kind enough to say she had not found out her vocation until there was a good-looking young parson for her to work under. She was a dark, Jewish-looking woman, with a profusion of black hair which she wore in innumerable twists, plaits and curls, and was now considerably over thirty years of age ; nevertheless she cherished very strong hopes of stepping into the vacant shoes at the rectory. She had made herself necessary to Bernard's late wife by taking all her parish and domestic duties off her hands, until the weak- minded Alice had imagined she could not order a dinner without the assistance of her friend. So it came to pass that, when the poor girl fell into the decline of which she died, Miss Warren not only attended to the wants of the villagers, but con-

stituted herself Mrs Freshfield's head nurse. And
the husband, however much he disliked her, could
not but appear grateful for a kindness which professed to be disinterested.

But when Alice died, Bernard found himself
placed in rather an awkward position with regard
to Miss Warren.

She had obtained so firm a footing at Briarwood
that she almost seemed a fixture there ; and it was
not without calling in the aid of his mother that
he could persuade the young lady that her duties
as nurse and housekeeper were at an end.

But as for stopping her interference in the
parish, he found that to be almost an impossibility.
Miss Anna Warren was always so ready to defer
to his wishes and carry out his directions, that
he could find no actual fault with her, and the
only objection he really had to her acting as his
lieutenant. was, that she so identified his interests
with her own that the people of Bluemere began
to believe they were similar.

She had an obnoxious habit too of speaking of
'*our* dear Alice' and '*our* dear lost saint,' for
which Bernard could not rebuke her, and yet
which jarred upon him more with each repetition ;
so that he did not feel particularly pleased when
Miss Warren came skipping to open Mrs Pinner's
garden gate,— she had an infantine habit of
skipping 'as if she were bounding on cork
soles,' which made her look terribly young,—and
scolded him for being late, as if he were her own
property.

'You naughty, naughty man,' she cried playfully. 'Here have we been waiting for you for
the last twenty minutes. I don't know what
colour the tea can be by this time, but the poor

muffins are as dry as a bone. But you *sha'n't* be scolded,' she went on, as she passed her arm familiarly through his, and led him triumphantly up the garden path. 'I daresay you are tired, poor dear, with parish work, and want your tea as much as any of us. Tell me what you've been doing this afternoon. Have you visited the almshouse, and, by the way, did you go and see the man at Gray's who broke his leg falling from the hay-car t?'

Bernard tried to wriggle his arm out of hers, but without effect.

'No ; I haven't been to Gray's,' he answered somewhat curtly, 'nor to the almshouses either I was too much occupied with other things.'

'Your sermon for next Sunday, perhaps ?' suggested Miss Warren. 'Well, I think it is better for you to write it early in the week You know how tired you generally are by Saturday afternoon.'

'Excuse me,' was the young man's reply, as he stooped down to tie an imaginary shoe-string, and thus released himself from Miss Warren's hold. He was determined not to be led into the presence of Mrs Pinner and her cousin like a sheep to the slaughter.

'Here he is!' exclaimed Miss Warren, as she preceded him into the sitting-room ; 'and now, Mrs Pinner, you must be good enough to let him have his tea at once, and not say a word to him until he has finished it, because he is just "done up" with work and worry, and I don't know what *your* opinion may be, but I think it is awfully good of him to come here and see us at all.'

'Miss Warren gives me credit for a self-denial of which I am utterly incapable,' said Bernard, as he shook hands with Mrs Pinner and two or three other ladies, and looked anxiously round the room for a form which did not appear ; 'for, in the first place, Mrs Pinner. I am as fresh as a daisy, having been asleep half the afternoon under my big mulberry tree : and in the second, I could have no greater pleasure than in fulfilling my engagement with you.'

'Ah ! dear Mr Freshfield, everybody in Bluemere knows how good and self-denying you are ; there is no need to try and hide your light under a bushel, sighed his hostess.

'No, indeed, and he couldn't do it if he tried,' pertly interposed Miss Warren. Who should know that better than myself, who have seen him under the most painful circumstances. Ah ! that sad, sad autumn, two years ago, when our darling lay, day after day, beneath the mulberry tree, and we never knew, from hour to hour, which would be the last. No one could have watched your behaviour *then*, Mr Freshfield, and doubted if you were self-denying or not.'

'Well, let us talk of something more congenial than my domestic virtues.' replied the young man hastily, as he turned his back upon Miss Warren. At that moment he positively hated her and her reminiscences, and could have boxed her ears with the greatest pleasure, had it but been consistent with his profession as a parson.

'I hope Miss Moss is well,' he continued to Mrs Pinner, 'and that I shall have the pleasure of seeing her this evening ?'

'Yes, she is well enough, thank you. She was here a minute ago, but went upstairs as you entered the gate. Miss Warren, my dear, will you call Phyllida for me ?'

'Such an extraordinary girl,' whispered Miss

Annie familiarly, as she passed his chair, 'it is hardly to be credited that such a creature belongs to the same race as our sweet lost Alice. I hardly know what you'll make of her! She is not *our* style by any means.'

Bernard shook his head impatiently, as though a gad-fly had buzzed past his ear, as Miss Warren, with an arch smile, left the room.

'I suppose Miss Moss has told you of our meeting in the Briarwood copse on Monday?' he said, addressing Mrs Pinner.

'No, indeed! What an odd thing that she should conceal it. Oh, Mr Freshfield, she is a very strange girl! I am almost afraid you will blame me for asking her to Bluemere. And so you have already seen her? And what was she doing at Briarwood? Not trespassing, I sincerely hope?'

'Indeed, *no*,' replied Bernard earnestly, 'Miss Moss was only taking an ordinary walk, and I trust she will make use of my grounds whenever she feels disposed to do so. And Mrs Pinner,' he continued in a lower key, 'I don't think you should speak of your cousin in such terms before strangers. You will give them an unfavourable impression of Miss Moss. I see nothing extraordinary in her myself; we had a long talk together, and her ideas are much the same as other people's, except, perhaps, that she expresses them more openly. And probably they are due to her bringing up as much as to anything else. Where did you tell me she came from?'

'She came to me straight from St Domingo, Mr Freshfield, where some of her mother's friends reside, and I believe you may call it her home, though she has travelled a great deal about. My cousin, Agnes Summers, went out to the West

Indies, where she married her first husband, and this girl is her daughter by a second marriage. However. I never knew either Agnes or the men she married, so it's of little consequence to me either way, only I hope I haven't done wrong in letting Phyllida come to Bluemere.'

'I am *sure* you have not.   Take my word for it,' replied the parson fervently, and Mrs Pinner believed in him so fully that she began to think that, on the contrary. she had done a very clever thing.

'Here is Phyllida!' she exclaimed, a moment after, as Miss Moss entered the room with Annie Warren.   She was still dressed in deep black, and the lace round her throat was the only ornament that relieved her sombre attire.   The two young ladies in white muslin, and the widow in purple satin, who formed the other guests, exchanged furtive looks and smiles at the simplicity of the stranger's dress ; but Bernard saw only the humid eyes and the marvellous complexion, and the parted lips like rose leaves with the dew on them, as he rose and clasped the hand she extended to him.   After Phyllida's entrance and the few common-place inquiries that succeeded it, a blight seemed to fall upon our parson as regarded conversation, and the ladies had all the chatter to themselves.

The tea and muffins duly made their appearance, and Bernard was conscious of being assiduously waited on by Miss Warren and Miss Masters and Miss Lacy, whilst Mrs Pinner and Mrs Norman talked to him in soft, purring tones, and he answered their inquiries at haphazard, and was half alive to what was passing round him.   For Miss Moss was sitting at an open window at the opposite side of the room, with her face from him, and he kept watching the soft evening light as it shimmered on the rippling waves of her rust-coloured hair, and wondering to himself why each time she made a movement, as though she would turn and look at him, a shock ran through his veins as if they had been subjected to electricity. It was quite time our young parson was recalled to himself.

'Now, didn't I say he was regularly "done up"?' ejaculated the shrill voice of Miss Warren. 'Look at his tea and muffin, both as cold as stones. As if he could deceive *me*,' she continued, in a tone of triumph, 'who have watched his moods for weeks together. Have you forgotten the time when I had regularly to *coax* you to take your breakfast, Mr Freshfield, and if I left you to yourself for a minute you'd be off and leave it untasted on the table? Ah, those were sad times, weren't they? but mingled with much sweetness, and blessed to both of us, I hope.'

'I am sure they were times that neither you nor Mr Freshfield can ever forget, live as long as you may,' chimed in Mrs Pinner, 'for the whole village mourned with you and with him. Such a life, and such a death. Ah,—sweet saint.'

'Ah, indeed,' sighed Mrs Norman, and all the young ladies looked mournfully sympathetic.

'We often think of you, dear Mr Freshfield, in your lonely rooms, and pray for you. It was a terrible loss to incur so early in life; but depend upon it, it was not sent for nought. It will be overruled, and there are happy days in store for you still at dear Briarwood.'

'I hope so,' replied Bernard simply, and he meant to say no more, but catching a glance of *too* much sympathy from the black eyes of Miss

Warren, he went on hurriedly, ' I know, my good friends, that you all feel for me, and mean it for the best, but I think it is almost as well not to allude to such things, at all events in company like the present. The past *is* past, you know, and I am a great advocate for burying the past as much as lies in our power. I think it was intended we should do so. I think the Creator meant us to be as happy as we can, consistently with an honourable living ; and that when He sends us trouble, He does not wish us to nurse it longer than is necessary. And, added to this, I feel almost as if I should be exciting your sympathy on false pretences, if I did not tell you that. whatever I may have passed through, I am very happy now. I can never feel really lonely, you know, with my good mother and sister to keep me company, and I have no present intention nor desire to have any other society than theirs. and that of my friends of Bluemere. So let us talk of something more cheerful than my past troubles, which, I can assure you, Mrs Pinner, have nothing to do with the present deplorable condition of my tea and muffin. It is a real shame of me to have neglected them : but if the truth must be told. I dined too late to make a good hand at tea, and I came here for the pleasure of your society only. Will you forgive me, and let some of these young ladies seal my pardon with a little of their charming music ? '

By which it will be seen that the Reverend Bernard Freshfield had not been able to keep himself entirely free of using the small change which passes current in village society. But whilst he caused the hearts of Miss Lacy and Miss Masters to flutter with excitement at his request, as they looked out their most pathetic ballads for his edification, Bernard's thoughts were fixed only on the silent figure by the window, which had not once joined in the general conversation. Phyllida had looked up suddenly, it is true, when Bernard said that it was a duty to bury the past, and her wonderful eyes had met his, and told him intuitively that she too had a past to bury ; but the glance had lasted but a second, like a flash of lightning though—like the lightning, it revealed so much, and he longed to see the dark lashes raised again. The young ladies were warbling 'Two Wandering Stars' together by this time, whilst Miss Warren turned over the leaves of the music, —for it was Miss Warren's *rôle* to appear as the benefactor, help, and guide of everybody in the parish, and Mrs Pinner was enlightening Mrs Norman on the subject of Miss Moss's antecedents. So Bernard left his seat, as nervously as if he were a school-boy, and approached the window where the stranger sat alone.

'Not one word for me this evening ?' he inquired, in a low voice.

'Do you require any? I thought you were so fully occupied,' replied Phyllida ; 'and what should *I* say in a company like this ?'

'Probably something more interesting than any one else. Mrs Pinner tells me you are a great traveller.'

The girl coloured visibly.

'She invented the information then ! *I* never told her so. I *have* travelled of course—who has not in these days ?—but not half as much as some people.'

'But you came from the West Indies ?'

'Yes, my mother had many friends there. I

thought at one time I would make it my home for good! But circumstances caused me to alter my mind.'

'I am so glad of those circumstances.'

'Why?'

'Cannot you guess? If they had not happened, we might never have met.'

'That would have been no great loss to you, Mr Freshfield,' she answered quietly. 'I am not a good subject for conversion. You will only waste your time attempting it.'

He was about to answer her, when Miss Warren distracted his attention.

'Mr Freshfield, isn't it wrong of Miss Lacy's brother? He is a clergyman, you know, in London, and he actually allows his wife to go to the theatres.'

'Really, Miss Warren, I am no judge of another man's actions. If Mr Lacy considers the play a suitable amusement for his wife, he is perfectly justified in letting her attend it.'

'But think of the scenes enacted there—think of the dreadful characters of the poor lost actors and actresses! I remember when our beloved Alice—'

'Hush! please don't let us revert to that name,' interposed Bernard; 'I am not aware that I was ever narrow-minded enough to attempt to bias the opinion of any one in any matter that is not strictly forbidden. My sister Laura is very fond of the theatre, and I have never tried to dissuade her from attending it.'

'But you don't go yourself, Mr Freshfield?' said Mrs Pinner.

'Because there is no theatre in Bluemere,' he laughed, and then he added, 'that is quite another thing. I may refrain from doing so for expediency's sake, but it does not follow that I consider it wrong. On the contrary, I wish I could indulge my very natural inclination that way. And I dare-say many are of the same opinion. What do *you* say, Miss Moss? Are you not fond of the theatre?'

He had to repeat his question before she answered in a very low but decided voice,—

'*No!*'

'Perhaps you have seen too much of it, and are already *blasé?*'

She shook her head again.

'It is not that—but if *your* conscience approves of it, don't try and persuade them to like it in order to follow your opinion. It is not the theatre, Mr Freshfield, but the company and the excitement and the late hours. Oh, let them continue to love the pure air of the country and the innocence and freshness that is around them, and don't imbue them with a second-hand taste for what can never do them so much good as harm.'

She spoke rapidly, and almost in a whisper, but he could hear every word, and marked the glow which overspread her features, and bespoke the sincerity which actuated her speech.

'Thank you,' he said in answer; 'you have be-come my teacher.'

'No! no! I did not mean that; it would be the height of presumption—only you do not know, you cannot tell.'

'Do you sing?' he asked, to fill up the pause. 'Will you sing for us?'

'Oh yes; Phyllida can sing. She has a very pretty pipe of her own,' replied Mrs Pinner, who with the rest had been unable to catch the sub-stance of what had passed between her cousin and the parson. But Miss Moss seemed unwilling to show off her accomplishments.

' *Do* sing,' urged Bernard, ' for *me.*'

' Are you fond of music ? '

' Of *music?* Yes. But one seldom hears it.'

Phyllida went to the piano and struck the opening chords of Ascher's song, ' Alice, where art thou ? '

' You can't sing that ! ' cried Miss Annie Warren, in a nervous heat. Phyllida looked up to her for explanation.

' Why not ? '

' Because—it's the very name. Oh, Mrs Pinner, please make her sing something else ! '

' And why are we not to hear Ascher's song ? ' demanded Bernard, who knew the ballad, and the reason Miss Warren objected to it perfectly well.

' Oh, if *you* can bear it, let her go on,' replied Miss Warren huskily ; ' but as for myself, I must ask leave to quit the room,' and with that she disappeared.

' What am I to do ? ' asked Phyllida, bewildered.

' Go on,' said the parson, and so she went on, and sang her song through to the end. When she had finished, every one except Bernard looked as grave as a judge.

' Thank you so much,' was his comment. ' I never heard anybody sing so beautifully as you do, before.'

She had sung the song in a manner most unusually heard in private life. For though she made no effort, and indeed had taken but little trouble in the matter, her voice was so well trained that she could not use it ill, and the simple song of love and death appealed to the hearts of all present.

When it was concluded, Bernard took possession of the chair by the window that she had vacated, and looked more solemn than before.

' There, you cruel girl, see what you have done!'
exclaimed Miss Warren, as she re-entered the room ;
' you have made him downright miserable, and no
wonder.'

' But he asked for the song himself. And why
should he mind it more than any other?' rejoined
Phyllida, glancing somewhat ruefully at the parson's
downcast face.

' He told you to go on because he was too polite
to stop you ; but it has awakened the most sorrowful memories in his breast. His wife's name was
Alice ; the sweetest creature you ever saw, and my
dearest friend, and we watched by her dying bed
together, and I know what he suffered, dear, dear
creature ! and what an excellent husband he was
to her, and more like a brother than a friend to
me.'

Phyllida's lip curled.

' Perhaps you will be able to console him, then,'
she said shortly as she turned away.

' Oh, Mrs Pinner, did you ever hear of such heart-
lessness !' exclaimed Miss Warren, as she repeated
the circumstance during a whispered confidence in
the corner of the room.

' It is a sad insight, my dear ; but perhaps the
poor thing has never been happy enough to know
what trouble is, and will be mercifully chastened
before long. But tell Mary to bring in the tray,
my dear. A little refreshment may rouse our dear
minister from his sad recollections.'

The little refreshment, which consisted of stale
sponge cakes and bad sherry, did have the desired
effect of rousing Bernard, for, in his anxiety to
avoid taking any himself, he waited so assiduously
on his fair friends, and talked so incessantly to
them, that they did not notice the fact that he

neither ate nor drank; and Miss Moss followed his example, she neither ate sponge-cakes nor drank sherry.

'I am glad to see the signs of a little feeling in your cousin,' said Miss Warren, with her mouth full, to Mrs Pinner. 'She cannot take any refreshment. She is evidently thinking over the mischief she has done.'

'Ah! these things are all ordained for us, and doubtless it will be overruled,' replied Mrs Pinner, and she would have heaved a pious sigh, only a bit of the stale sponge-cake went the wrong way and made her cough instead.

When the ladies rose to get their cloaks and bonnets, and Bernard realised that his term of purgatory was over, he looked round for Miss Moss in vain. It was a lovely summer night, and the village was as light as though it were day, yet Mrs Pinner's guests, Miss Warren in particular, had quite depended on securing Mr Freshfield's services to escort them to their homes. But their hopes proved futile. Mr Freshfield shook hands with them all at the garden gate, but remained inside of it himself.

'What *can* he be stopping for?' said Miss Warren anxiously, as they were compelled to start without him.

'Perhaps he has some parish matter to speak of with Mrs Pinner?' suggested Mrs Norman.

'Nonsense,' was the sharp retort ; 'as if she had anything to do with the parish! Mr Freshfield consults *me* only in such matters,—indeed, he leaves them to me to settle without any consultation. I always did the work for him in dear Alice's lifetime, and I have never relinquished it since.'

'Won't it place you in rather an awkward position if Mr Freshfield marries again ? ' inquired the widow, who, like all the eligible ladies of Bluemere, aspired to the post of parson's wife, and was proportionally jealous of Miss Warren's interference.

' I don't think so,' was the fair Annie's reply, delivered with a certain secret satisfaction that aggravated her rivals.

' Laura Freshfield told me she hoped her brother would marry again, and soon, too,' remarked yellow-haired Miss Lacy, ' and have another fair wife into the bargain, for she hates dark women.'

' As if Mr Freshfield would choose a wife to suit his *sister's* fancy ! ' ejaculated Miss Warren, with an indignant toss of her head, which resulted in silence, and lasted until the ladies parted at their respective doors.

Meanwhile, the parson, standing in Mrs Pinner's garden, had asked that lady's permission to light a cigar, which she, from the door-step, with her head enveloped in a woollen wrap, had graciously accorded. It was a very obstinate cigar, however, and after at least a dozen *allumettes* had been struck on the heel of his boot, and gone out of themselves, whilst Bernard's eyes roved up and down the house and garden path, he spoke again,—

' I don't think I said good-night to Miss Moss, Mrs Pinner. I hope she will not think me neglectful ? '

' Oh no, indeed, Mr Freshfield, but I will go and look for her, and if she has not yet retired I will send her out to you.'

And the old lady, who was very glad to get out of the night air, beat a hasty retreat.

As she disappeared, a slight form came round the other side of the house, and a subdued voice said,—

'Were you asking for me, sir?'

Bernard turned to her with alacrity. Oh, if Miss Warren could only have seen it!

'I was, indeed. I should have been sorry to return home without wishing you good-bye.'

'And I was waiting here to speak to you also, that is, if I could manage it, without the presence of all those women.'

'All those women have gone home,' laughed Bernard, 'and you may speak with impunity.'

'But it is no laughing matter, sir. I guess I have wounded your feelings to-night, and stirred up old memories which you desired to forget. I am very sorry for it—that is all I can say, but I did it unintentionally. I know what trouble is myself, and I would have bitten out my tongue sooner than carelessly rake up yours.'

'But, my dear child,' replied Bernard. 'I don't know to what you allude. You have done nothing this evening but afford me exquisite pleasure by your beautiful voice and manner of singing.'

'You grew silent afterwards, and Miss Warren accused me of cruelty in singing a song with that name in it. She said it was the name of your dead wife, whose loss you mourn so much, and I am sorry for it, since it may make you dislike me.'

Bernard's reply was slow in coming, and he prefaced it by placing his hand over the one with which she leaned on the top of the garden gate.

'I cannot speak to you openly,' he said, 'and yet I wish you to understand me. Will you believe me, Miss Moss, when I say that Miss Warren is utterly mistaken in thinking that I did not enjoy your song. And yet it made me feel sad in the midst of pleasure. Why? Because I have never yet found my " Alice ! " She is still in Shadow Land for me, and my heart is always crying, " Where art thou ? " You may think it very strange for a widower to speak like this, but I feel I can trust you with my secret. I have been a husband, but I have never been married. My wife —the woman who is to be *one* with me in heart and soul—I have yet to meet. And perhaps I may never meet her. Perhaps I may end my life still crying, " Where art thou ? " And that is what made me sad—not your sweet song, and sweeter voice.'

' Poor girl,' sighed Phyllida, with a sort of gasping sob.

' To whom do you allude ? '

' To your dead wife.'

' No, don't say that. Don't run away with the idea that because I had a want unsatisfied, she must needs have been unhappy. I thank God I sincerely believe she led as peaceful and contented a life as is possible, and died without the faintest idea but that I had done the same. She was a good, dear girl, and I was fond of her, and grateful to her for all her forbearance with me, but I was not happy with her—that is all.'

' Well, and I repeat my words,' said Phyllida, ' " Poor girl ! " doubly poor in having failed to come up to the requirements of the lofty position to which you raised her.'

' The " lofty position " of a parson's wife,' laughed Bernard. ' It is evident you are not imbued with English ideas, Miss Moss, or you would not have made such a terrible mistake. We don't think much of parsons in England — and as for the parsons' wives, they are nowhere.'

' But isn't it a great thing to be the wife of a

real good man,' said the girl thoughtfully ; ' to be his companion and his friend, and to learn to be as good yourself as he is ? '

' It is a better thing to be his all on earth,' replied this material young man earnestly. ' I am afraid too many women accept men as husbands on the score of their supposed goodness, and find afterwards that a sense of duty alone supplies a very unexhilarating sort of wine with which to fill the cup of life. Parsons' wives, as well as the wives of other men, Miss Moss, must build their married happiness on love—on true and mutual love—or expect it to fail them in their most urgent need.'

' I should think that to be the wife of a good man was sufficient happiness for any woman on earth. Think what it is — I mean only fancy what it must be—to be tied to a bad man, a thief or a murderer ' (with a shudder), ' always swearing at you or cursing you — and then see what a heaven the other would look like.'

' But you are imagining an extreme case, Miss Moss, such an one as could never enter except into your imagination. How you tremble. Do you feel the night cold ? '

' No, no ! ' the girl replied with a shaking voice, that sounded ominously like tears.

' You are sad,' said Bernard kindly. ' You are in trouble. What is it ? '

But all the answer Phyllida gave was to throw her hands up to her face and give vent to a sudden burst of grief.

' Oh, how I wish I was dead ! ' she exclaimed as she dashed the tears from her eyes with an impatient gesture at her own weakness ; ' how I wish I was at rest with your Alice or the thousand other girls that have dropped to sleep in this peaceful village before care or misery came upon them.

'Don't say that,' cried Bernard, startled out of all propriety by her unexpected emotion. 'If you only knew what I feel, what it would be to me,' and then, recalling himself just in time, he added more calmly, 'Miss Moss—Phyllida, if I may call you so—never do such a thing again as to wish for death, however tempted you may be. It is foolish and wrong. Death is not oblivion, remember, and whatever ills we have to bear in this life, may be doubled in the world to come. I guess—I feel that you have suffered : be patient, look on me as your friend, and some day you may gather heart to come and tell me all, and I will give you absolution for it.'

'Oh no—not you—not *you !*' exclaimed the girl fearfully. 'I could not tell *you.*'

'Then I will be your friend without receiving your confidence. Any way, I must—I *will* be— your friend.'

The soft brown eyes went up to meet the glance of his, and sunk beneath it. Bernard pressed the hand he had again taken in his own.

'Phyllida,' he whispered ; and then he heaved a sigh and turned on his heel and walked slowly down the lane.

She stood for a minute where he had left her, gazing after him.

'Oh, what is this ?' she asked herself with a sort of fearful joy.

'Phyllida,' said the shrill voice of Mrs Pinner, 'have you said good-night to the minister ?'

'Yes, cousin. I have said good-night to him,' replied the girl as she returned to the house.

CHAPTER V.

IT is the teaching of the world that has made us lay down the axiom that to act upon impulse is a folly. How few of our impulses are wrong. What benevolent impulses, and sympathetic impulses, and generous impulses we relinquish upon second thoughts, for fear that we may be 'taken in,' or 'make fools of ourselves,' or 'not show a proper pride,' and the world—the heartless, lying, snobbish world—may jeer at an impulsive error. Ah, better to be taken in a thousand times than break one heart (and that one perhaps our own) from a dilatoriness that can never be amended. Yet so strong is the influence of our childhood's teaching, that we seldom act on impulse without entertaining a host of misgivings as to whether we have not done wrong.

Bernard Freshfield felt so as he walked home that night. He had only done the most natural thing for a young and impressionable man to do, when brought in contact with a young woman in trouble. He had tried to console her, and he had permitted his voice and his eyes to convey the sympathy he felt. If he had followed his impulses to their full extent, he would have kissed the sweet, tearful face that was uplifted to his in the moonlight, but at this point he had restrained himself. Yet he blamed his own weakness as he walked home to Briarwood, and condemned his conduct as unbecoming his profession, and wished he had not said ' Phyllida ' in that particularly soft and winning voice as he left her side, or that he was at liberty to act and feel like other men of his age and position.

He vexed himself on every point, in fact, until he reached his destination, and made grand resolutions to be more circumspect for the future. What should a minister of the gospel, he thought, have to do with falling in love at first sight? It was indecorous and unseemly! Besides, it couldn't *be* love, ablaze in this manner at a moment's notice, and for a woman he knew nothing of, and had never seen but once before. It must be some baser passion, born only of a beautiful face and lustrous languid eyes, and it was his duty to trample it under foot as a temptation of the devil.

He went to bed in this praiseworthy frame of mind, and he waked in the morning with but one idea in his head—how could he contrive to meet Phyllida Moss again? He wanted to bring her to Briarwood—to see her walk through his rooms and sit in his chairs, and leave the influence of her enchanted presence behind her when she left again. A happy thought struck him! The Miss Muckheeps' visit to Bluemere as his mother's guests, rendered it almost imperative on him to show them some attention at Briarwood. He would invite the whole party over to meet Mrs Pinner and her cousin, and one or two other friends. They would not have a formal dinner only, they should spend a day there—a whole, long, sunny, happy, heavenly day amongst the flower-gardens and shrubberies of Briarwood. As soon as Bernard had conceived this idea, there was no longer any rest for him until he had put it into execution. He sprung from his bed, and walked over to Blue Mount, delighting his mother by appearing at the breakfast-table in the most affable humour with her and everybody else.

'We have had such a glorious summer, and the

country is looking so beautiful, that it really is a
sin for anyone to remain in bed when he may be
abroad with nature,' he said, in excuse for his early
visit. 'My old gardener, Armstrong, has turned
Briarwood into a perfect paradise. I hope you are
going to bring your visitors over to see my flowers,
mother? Are you fond of a garden, Miss Muckheep?' he added to Miss Janet.

'Ay,' replied the old woman in one long drawn-
out syllable. 'I'm no denyin' that the flo-ors air
as bonnie as the reest o' the wairks o' the creation,
but to be ower fond of a gair-den or a doog, or a
beestie of any sairt, is a cair-nal procleevity fra
which I thank the Laird I ha' been presairved.
Bella—een!'

'Ah, well,' replied Bernard, laughing; 'perhaps
I should have said are you an admirer of nature
instead, Miss Janet? Any way, if you and your
niece will honour me by accompanying my mother
and sister to Briarwood some day, I think I can
show you as pretty a flower-garden, on a small
scale, as is to be found in the county.'

Mrs Freshfield became quite excited at this proof
of her son's evident desire to make himself agreeable
to her friends.

'I am sure you will enjoy it, dear Miss Janet,'
she interposed. 'My Bernard is an excellent host,
and Briarwood itself is worthy of a visit. I want
you to see the rooms and the furniture,' she continued, in a lower and more confidential key. '*Such*
a drawing-room, all ebonised chairs and tables,
with pale pink hangings, and the library, too, in
solid oak and morocco leather. No expense was
spared, I can assure you, in fitting it up, for I felt
I could not do too much for the wife of my beloved son, as I shall feel again, if the happy day

ever arrives for me to welcome a new mistress to Briarwood.

'Eh, weel, woman, it's na' seelks nor sai-tins as ye maun set your mind upon, but a clean hairt and a reet speerit, and then a' the reest maun follow in due coorse. Not that I wudna be sayin' that a guid tocher is an eestimable thing to set up the hoose with, and I trawst that Bella's carle will be fain to geeve her foorniture accairdin' to her station ; but we mauna think too much of oor sinful bodies and the cawn-forts of this wairld.'

'No, no ; of course not,' replied Mrs Freshfield, who was rather taken aback by this unexpected rebuke, 'still I am sure you will say you never saw anything more elegant than the decorations of Briarwood.'

Bernard, meanwhile, had drawn his sister aside.

'I want you to write two or three invitations for me, Laura. They will come better from mother than from myself.'

'Why, Bernard, are you going to have a party ?'

'Oh no; nothing particular. Only a few friends will make the visit more agreeable to the Muck-heeps, and it is a good opportunity for me to pay off some old debts in that way.'

'To whom shall I write, then ?'

'To the Ashleighs. Ask Captain and Mrs Ashleigh, and their son. I have dined there several times this year.'

'Very good ; and who else ?'

'The Langleys ; they are nice girls, and have two officers staying with them. And, let me see ! You may as well ask Mrs Pinner and her cousin, Miss Moss.'

'Has Mrs Pinner a cousin ?' asked Laura in

surprise. 'When did she come ? I never heard of her.'

'I thought the village crier—Miss Warren—would have been sure to tell you all about her. Miss Moss has been in Bluemere for some weeks, and I have met her at the Pinners'.'

'And is she nice, Bernie ?'

'Oh, she's well enough ; a little barbarian, fresh caught from St Domingo, but with more in her perhaps than the generality of her sex—(no offence meant, my dear, and I hope none " took ").'

'Never mind, I am used to your compliments. But is it necessary to ask this girl, Bernie ? You can't have everybody.'

'She may as well come,' replied her brother indifferently, 'Mrs Pinner will not care to walk backwards and forwards to Briarwood alone.'

'Very well. Any more ?'

'No ; the others will be men, and I will write to them myself.'

'Not Miss Warren ?'

'Certainly not Miss Warren, she is detestable !' replied Bernard, with unnecessary warmth.

'Oh dear !' laughed Laura with a mischievous look. She was well aware of Annie Warren's aspirations with regard to Briarwood and its master, and was not sorry to think that for once that individual would be unable to boast of her intimacy with the family of Freshfield.

Bernard remained at Blue Mount all the morning, and it was arranged that the festivities of Briarwood were to take place on the following Tuesday, and to consist of a collation on the lawn at five o'clock, and a supper in the house at half-past nine. Croquet, lawn-tennis, and archery were to be the amusements of the afternoon, and the parson was actually rash enough to propose a fiddler and a dance on the green, to give them an appetite for supper, but Miss Janet nipped his frolicsome propensities in the bud.

'If ye will ha' seckit cairnal pairstimes at yon hoose of Bree-arwud, never expectit to see me within its wairls, Mr Fraichfield. You mak me bloosh to hear ye coontenence sic ungawdly pleesures. Na, na ; Bella doesna' set fut in Bree-arwud till ye can tell me there will be na sic profane seeghts to meet her ee'. Bella—shoolders !'

'Oh, no, no ! dear Miss Janet, Bernard was only joking. Were you not, my son ?' exclaimed Mrs Freshfield, horrified at the turn things were taking in her visitor's mind. 'He would never *dream* of anything so frivolous as dancing. Would you, Bernard ? We have all agreed long ago that it is a vain and godless amusement, and quite unfitted for one of his sacred calling.'

'Well, I don't know about *dreaming* of it mother,' replied Bernard frankly. 'I am afraid I very often *do* dream of it, and wish it were more feasible ; but I can assure you and Miss Janet that there shall be no dancing at Briarwood if the idea is the least offensive in your eyes.'

'That's my good son !' replied Mrs Freshfield, and so the matter was happily settled, and Bernard returned home to consult his housekeeper about the preparations for the coming entertainment, and to pass, as best he might, the few hours of feverish suspense which must elapse before he received an answer from Mrs Pinner.

It came at last, and it was favourable. It would give Miss Moss and herself the greatest pleasure to accept the Reverend Mr Freshfield's kind invitation for Tuesday next.

What else did he expect the woman to say, considering that all days were disengaged days in Bluemere, and an invitation to Briarwood or Blue Mount was considered the very height of honourable dissipation. Of course everybody said that they would come, and only too glad to do so.

Yet the foolish, love-stricken young man felt the hot blood course wildly through his veins as he read Mrs Pinner's commonplace reply, and he raised the old woman's crabbed writing to his burning lips.

The weather behaved as it ought to do on that particular Tuesday, and the August sun was streaming like a flame of glory over hill and dale and foliage and flowers, as Bernard Freshfield stood in the portico of Briarwood to receive his guests, dressed in a brown velveteen coat with a noisette rose in his button-hole. His mother nearly had a fit as she descended from her carriage and beheld his costume ; but no one thought of wearing Pall Mall suits in Bluemere, and she trusted that Miss Janet might not be aware of the English etiquette concerning the clothes of parsons, who, though they have been strictly enjoined to take no thought as to what they shall put on, are as particular about the shape of their collars and the brims of their hats as if they were young ladies in their first season.

However unorthodox might Bernard's coat and trousers have been, and that worldly and carnal noisette rose blooming so saucily in his button-hole, there was no fault to be found with his frank, smiling face and hospitable greeting, and he looked the very picture of a fine young Englishman as he welcomed his friends to Briarwood.

'How handsome Bernie is looking to-day,'

whispered Laura to her mother. ' I have not seen him so bright and merry since Alice died.'

'Happier days are coming for him, thank heaven,' replied Mrs Freshfield, with a gush of premature gratitude, as she thought of the round-faced Bella, who, attired in a Stuart tartan and a hat of purely Scotch manufacture, looked very much as if she had come out of a Noah's ark.

A cricket tent had been erected on the lawn, which sloped down to the copse where Phyllida first met Bernard, and from which even Miss Janet was obliged to confess that the view was like a peep of Paradise. The smooth turf ran for some distance green, pliant, and close shorn as a piece of emerald velvet, and the beds of flowers bloomed all round it like a belt of beauty and of sweetness. Shrubberies enclosed the garden on either side, shutting off the stables, the kennels, and the kitchen department. To the back was a pine grove to shelter the house from the east wind ; beyond the copse in front were richly pastured meadows where Bernard's Alderneys grazed, and his colts took their summer pastime. Look on which side you chose, Briarwood presented the picture of a well-ordered and well·kept English homestead. There was but one thing wanting there—it was a Paradise without an Eve!

Mrs Freshfield whispered something of this kind to Miss Muckheep, as the ladies followed Mrs Garnett, the housekeeper, to the room which had been prepared for their temporary use.

' Not in here, Mrs Garnett,' she exclaimed, as the servant turned the handle of the principal bed-room door.

' Yes, madam, his reverence gave me orders it was to be so.' Mrs Garnett replied, as she ushered the party into a large bedroom, magnificently furnished in the French fashion with white and blue and gold.

'Dear me, how very peculiar,' remarked Mrs Freshfield. as soon as they were alone. 'This was poor. dear Alice's bedroom, Miss Janet, and my son has never occupied it since she was called away. I wonder what made him order it to be prepared for our use to-day! It is very flattering; don't you think so? I know it is not *everybody* whom Bernard would admit to *this* room, and it is a direct compliment to you and dear Miss Bella. How sweet she looks!'

'Mamma! mamma! who is that lovely girl?' exclaimed Laura, interrupting Mrs Freshfield's confidences, as the door reopened to admit another party of guests. 'Oh, there is Mrs Pinner! it must be her cousin, Miss Moss!'

Phyllida, in a dress of some clear black stuff, made full and high to her throat, and which yet revealed the creamy fairness of her arms and shoulders—with a large Rembrandt hat upon her head, with a drooping black feather. and not a single ornament to clash with the perfect beauty of her features—did look pre-eminently lovely, and startled even her own sex with a first view of her charms. But she stood beside Mrs Pinner, silent and unsmiling ; without a single glance that betokened knowledge of her own fairness; and Laura's *second* thought concerning her was, how sorrowful she looked for one so young.

'Is this your cousin. Mrs Pinner; please to introduce me,' she said quickly.

'Oh yes! certainly, Miss Freshfield, with pleasure. Her name is Phyllida Moss. It was so good of our dear minister to include her in his invitation. She actually didn't want to come, but I told her that would appear most ungrateful to Mr Freshfield and all of you.'

'I did not think there would be so many people,' interposed Phyllida, 'but it is quite a party.'

'I understand,' replied Laura, with a glance at the stranger's mourning ; 'and you have not been out much lately. But now you have come, Miss Moss, I hope you will enjoy yourself, and try and make friends with me. There are so few companionable young ladies in Bluemere.

She had been smitten at first sight with the girl's pensive beauty, and was eager to know more of her. But Phyllida did not respond in like measure. Rather she smiled at Miss Freshfield's sudden enthusiasm as from the heights of a superior wisdom.

'I should have thought there were too many,' she replied, alluding to the young ladies, as she shook the dust from the skirt of her black dress.

'You overlooked my adjective,' said Laura merrily. But if you have finished arranging yourself, let us get out of this room. I can't bear it. It is the one in which my sister-in-law died.'

Phyllida looked round at the white and blue and gold adornments with interest.

'And does not your brother use it now ?'

'No, never! He sleeps in a tiny room at the other side of the house.'

'How strange !'

'Do you think so ? I should say how natural ; what do we want with harbouring unpleasant memories ? There is enough trouble in the world without that.'

'But when we have loved a person, can the memories be unpleasant ?' demanded Phyllida.

Laura laughed.

'I am not to be drawn into a philosophical discussion to-day, Miss Moss. I have come here merely to enjoy myself; besides, I don't think my brother has ever cared for anybody in the way you mean. Let us go down and secure good seats for this famous collation.'

And the first view Bernard had of Phyllida that day was linked, arm in arm, with his laughing sister Laura. The sight warmed his heart as he hastened to greet the two girls—and Phyllida's cheeks flushed red as the heart of a damask rose when she perceived him. The collation was perfect; and as Bernard kept on heaping good things upon Miss Muckheep's plate, his mother secretly wondered how he had contrived to import aspic jelly and plover's eggs. and truffles, and perigord pie to Bluemere, and why he had considered it worth while to do her guests such honour as this, when his native hams and home-made cakes and strawberries and cream, had been considered sufficient provision for all former parties at Briarwood.

'Ech, mon!' exclaimed Miss Janet, as he piled her plate with lobster salad, 'I'll nobbut be sayin' but your jerlies and sallets, and troofled tairkies air a' guid in their way, but dinna forgit that they air but cairnal pleesures, an' that in a few shairt yairs, we shall a' be where seckit things air unknown.'

'Well, we have no actual proof of that, Miss Janet,' replied Bernard, laughing; 'but if it *is* the case, let us make the most of them whilst we are here.'

'Eh, young man, but your puir feet air no in the reet pairth, if ye can airgue in sic a manner. I wish ye cou'd hear my gude brither the Laird o' Muckheep discoorse on seckit things. Ay, but he's a gude mon, and a Gawd-fearing, and treeds a' sic cairnal pleesures under his feet.'

' Why does your brother stay so much from home, Miss Janet ?' inquired Laura ; ' why doesn't he live at Barrick-gallagas Castle with Bella and you ?'

' Ay, but my dear, is it for the likes o' you and me to question the goin's and comin's of a pee-ous and Gawd-faering man like the Laird o' Muck-heep ? If he doesna' see fit to bide at Barrick-gal-lagas, ye may be sure 'tis the Laird's wairk as keepit him elsewheer. For my brither sheds the licht o' the garspel round him wheerever he goes as a shinin' ray, and when it is needed at the cairstle he will be ca'd hame.'

' Where is the laird now ?' asked Bernard, wishing to be polite.

' I canna' say for cairtain, Mr Fraichfield, but he's ay at Noo Yairk, or Cailifornia or the Valley o' Saicremeento, or any other pairt wheer his blessed teachins air most needed by the larist and ungardly souls, wha' he was bairn to refairm.'

' What is the matter ?' said Laura to her neigh-bour, Phyllida Moss.

The girl had turned as white as marble, and the blue veins on her forehead stood out like cords.

' Nothing, nothing : only the day is rather warm, she answered.

Bernard glanced towards her anxiously.

' Take a glass of wine,' he said, pouring out some sherry. ' You require it, Miss Moss, you have turned quite pale.'

But she pushed the glass from her, and turned her head the other way.

' You will not get Phyllida to touch wine,' re-marked Mrs Pinner. She is quite a teetotaller and cannot bear the sight of it. Perhaps you had better take a turn in the garden, my dear,' she added, ' if the ladies will excuse your absence. I am afraid the walk up here in the heat has been too much for you.'

But Phyllida refused to leave the table, declaring she was all right again, and sat out to the end of the meal. whilst Bernard kept looking at her white face anxiously, and blaming his own stupidity in not having thought of sending a carriage to convey her and Mrs Pinner to Briarwood. As soon as the collation was over, the old people disposed themselves on garden chairs and benches, whilst the young ones repaired to the lawn-tennis ground. and soon a merry party were sending the balls flying everywhere but over the net. whilst shouts of laughter accompanied each fresh failure or success. Bernard did not care to play himself ; he was not by any means a croquet and worsted-work parson ; but his young curate Frank Robinson enjoyed himself to the utmost, and tried hard to persuade Miss Moss to take a racket ; but she shrunk visibly from the mere idea.

'Oh no !' she kept on saying, 'I could not run like that before everybody. Indeed, I couldn't. I should trip over my dress and fall, or do something dreadful ; besides, I don't want to try ; indeed, I don't !'

' Don't tease Miss Moss, Robinson,' interposed Bernard ; ' the heat is trying her, and she would rather remain quiet.'

Mr Robinson departed with a bow, and Phyllida looked gratefully at the parson.

' Would you like to rest indoors till it is cooler ?' continued Bernard. ' I want to show you my house before it grows dusk. Will you come ?'

He held out his hand with a smile as he spoke, and she accompanied him without a word. Some remembrance of the last time they had been alone together in the moonlight, leaning over Mrs Pinner's gate, was doubtless in the minds of both, but neither spoke of it. The hall and sitting-rooms of Briarwood felt deliciously cool after the unsheltered heat of the garden, and Phyllida's colour began to revive. It was a relief to her to lose the sound of the loud laughing and talking that was going on outside ; to be led by Bernard into one pretty shaded room after another, and to be invited to repose on the luxurious chairs and couches, seemed like the peace and quiet of heaven after the rattle of the world. She followed him first to the drawing-room, which was quaintly furnished in the Louis Quinze style, with sateen of a pale pink colour, decorated with little cupids and ribbons in blue, and had a grand piano standing in one corner, and mirrors framed in ebony and gold to match the chairs and tables. Bernard wanted Phyllida to try the piano, but she shrank from awakening the echoes in that empty house.

' Don't ask me,' she said, with evident repugnance. ' It would seem like sacrilege to sing to that piano. I guess it was her's, and I should fancy she was listening all the while, and reproaching me for daring to use her things.'

' It will be very unfortunate for me if every one holds your opinions,' said Bernard gravely, as he closed the piano lid. ' Is my house always to be a house of mourning, because my first venture turned out a failure ? '

But he did not ask her to sing again, and he led her quickly through the other apartments, until they reached the library, which was hung with purple velvet and furnished with old oak. Bernard's writing-table and chair stood on a Persian carpet at one end of the long room, and over the mantelpiece hung an oil painting of a girl, with a delicate face and soft braids of fair hair and a lapful of flowers. Phyllida guessed it was the portrait of the dead wife.

'I shall keep you a prisoner here,' said Bernard playfully, 'until you look yourself again. Come, take off your hat and lean back in that chair ; it is my own particular lounge when I am lazy, and I know you will find it comfortable. Do you hear that sound ? It is my dogs baying to get loose ; it is about the time when the groom takes them out for exercise. I love to sit here and listen to their voices. They are company for me when I am alone.'

He threw open the window as he spoke, and leaned his arms upon the sill.

'Ah, Mrs Benson!' he exclaimed, as he recognised a figure walking slowly through the grounds, 'what brings you here to-day ?'

'I came to see you, sir, but they told me you had company on the lawn, and so I was just taking my way home again.'

'But that was wrong of Mrs Garnett. She knows I am always at the service of my friends. Is anything the matter ?'

'Rachel's gone, sir,' replied the old woman, and as she advanced to the open window, Phyllida could see that the tears were coursing down her cheeks ; 'she went this morning at seven o'clock, and her last words were a prayer and a blessing for you.'

'My poor friend,' said Bernard, as he took the woman's withered hand in his, 'I feel for you deeply.

It must be very hard to bear, now it has come—
though we expected it so long.'

'I would be the last to complain, sir. It was
written she was to go, and I kept her longer than
I had any reason to hope. And, thanks to your
goodness, my poor Rachel was ready for her change
when it did come.'

'Say, rather, thanks to the goodness of God, Mrs
Benson,' corrected the parson gently.

'No, sir, I can't unsay my words. I know of
course that it was the goodness of God as enabled
you to do it—so 'twould be if you gave a crust to
a starving creature ; but *you'd* give it all the same,
and if it hadn't been for your patience and long-
suffering and prayers, my poor Rachel would have
left this world as careless as she lived in it. It's all
owing to you, sir, as I can believe and trust that
she's in glory now.'

'But you mustn't say such things, Mrs Benson ;
indeed you mustn't,' replied Bernard, visibly disturbed by the old woman's laudation. 'I did
nothing more for your daughter than any other
man would have done under the circumstances—
Mr Robinson, for instance, or Mr Blackett, of
Riversdale, or any other clergyman.'

'Why didn't Mr Robinson do it, then ?' demanded the mother shortly. 'You know it isn't
the visiting nor the reading nor the teaching I
speak of, sir. It's the Christian love you gave my
poor child—and the sympathy, and the prayers
you prayed for her at home. I know you did now,
so it's no use denying it—that broke down all the
pride in her poor heart. And the last words she
said to me was, "Am I going, mother ? Then
may God bless Mr Freshfield for ever and ever."
Them was my Rachel's last words, sir,' continued the

woman, wiping her eyes, 'and I'll never forget them nor you, till the grave closes over myself.'

Bernard Freshfield looked as stupid and conscious during this harangue as though he had been detected in a crime. His fair cheeks crimsoned like those of a woman's, and he did not once glance in the direction of his guest.

'Mrs Benson,' he said, quietly ignoring all that had passed, 'don't go home until you have had some refreshment. Go to Garnett's room and get a glass of wine or a cup of her good tea. You are not fit to undertake the walk back without—'

'No, sir, don't ask me. I couldn't touch bit nor sup, nor would I have come up to-day if I'd known you were engaged. But she looks beautiful, sir— so peaceful and happy—and you'll come and see her, won't you, before she's screwed down? I know she'd like to think you did.'

'I will come the first thing to-morrow morning, Mrs Benson.'

'God bless you, sir! you've been more like an angel than a human being to us. And you'll bury her, too, sir. Won't you?'

'Of course I will!'

'Ah! it's a shame for every one to come a troubling you as we do, when you've had so many troubles of your own to bear. There's never a burying in Bluemere, but every one on us thinks of the day when you laid your sweet lady under the ground. But you trampled down your own griefs for our sakes, and may the Lord, in His infinite mercy, send you the happiness as you deserve at last. That was Rachel's prayer, sir, and it is mine as well.'

'Amen,' said Bernard solemnly ; and he leaned out of the window and watched the old woman's figure till it was out of sight.

When he turned to Phyllida again, it was with half an apology that their *tête-à-tête* should have been interrupted by a matter of parochial interest.

'These poor people are absurdly enthusiastic,' he observed, 'and fond of making mountains out of mole hills.'

But as he looked at the girl leaning back in the purple velvet arm-chair, with her hair lying somewhat loosely on the cushion, and her large eyes fixed upon the sky, he saw that there were tears upon her cheek.

'Phyllida!—Miss Moss—what is this? Are you ill again? Let me fetch you some iced water.' But all the answer she gave him was to catch his hand impulsively between her own, whilst she exclaimed, 'How good you are. How very good you are!'

'Indeed, *indeed*, I am not. You must not think so. You distress me by the idea.'

'Why do you try to hide it?' cried Phyllida, 'to live such a life as you do; what can be better? To teach people how to be good; to turn their thoughts away from this wicked, heartless world, and give them the blessed hope that there will be another, where we can begin life over again, and forget all the misery we endured in this.'

'Can you doubt it? Have you ever doubted it?' he said tenderly.

'Thousands and thousands of times. I have always doubted it. I do so now. What have I seen or heard to make me believe? My experience is, that the wicked succeed and the good are miserable; that our prayers go out upon the empty air, and come back to us unanswered; that the young and happy die, and those who long for death live on for ever. And no one has ever tried to teach me otherwise.'

Bernard looked very grave, for some of the girl's arguments were unanswerable, and he knew that neither Church nor Bible held the key to them.

There is but one thing that reconciles the trials of this world with the belief in the next—the love, human and divine, that sanctifies and alleviates and shares the first, and will endure unto the second ; and Phyllida knew no such love.

'If I had been taught like your Alice,' she went on vehemently ; 'if I had had a friend and a guide like her, I might have been a different creature with a different mind ; and yet *she*, who had everything in this world, died and left it, whilst I live on. Oh, how could she—how *could* she die,' continued Phyllida, raising her wet eyes to the portrait, 'with so much goodness and happiness around her ? Had she no energy—no courage ? The very thought of what I had to leave behind me would have *made* me live ! '

'Do you consider, then, that Alice's lot was such a happy one ?' asked Bernard softly.

'How could it have been happier ? You, who love and pray for even the poor of your parish, who are no relations to you, would not have done less for the wife of your bosom.'

'I hope not,' he replied. 'Alice was too good and pure to need my teaching ; but my sympathy and counsel were always hers to claim.'

'And yet she *died*,' said Phyllida.

'God called her,' said Bernard, 'and when His call comes it must be obeyed. If love and care could have kept her here she would have remained ; but she was quite content to go—contented, obedient, and resigned.'

'I should not have been.'

The words left Phyllida's lips almost unintentionally, but Bernard heard them, and the deep flush of passion mounted to his face. He forgot everything—their slight acquaintance, his staid profession, his utter ignorance of her antecedents—and remembered only that he was a man.

'Phyllida,' he exclaimed, in a low trembling voice, 'is it possible you envy her? Speak to me; don't keep me in suspense. You must have guessed what I feel for you. From the moment we met I knew that I and my fate had come together. Say you will fill her place. No, no! what am I dreaming of? Say rather you will fill the place in my heart that has never yet been occupied—that has been waiting for your image, my darling and my wife.'

He pressed upon her as he spoke; he would have taken her in his arms then and there, but Phyllida sprang from her seat and kept him off with both her hands.

'No! no! What are you thinking of? You must be *mad!* *I* your wife—*I*—the wife of a man whose life is spent in doing good! Oh! you do not know me—your eyes are blinded—you will be terribly sorry for all this to-morrow.'

Bernard stopped short, and put his hands to his head as if bewildered.

'You are talking reasonably, I suppose,' he said. 'Let me try and answer your words. I do not know you! Not if you count by weeks or months, perhaps—but love needs no such knowledge. I read your heart instinctively the first hour we met, and years could not increase the sympathy nor interest I feel in you. I do not know your parentage, nor antecedents, nor your character,

perhaps—but I do not want to know them. All
I want is, to be one with you henceforward. You
have felt sorrow—I want to comfort you. You
need instruction—I want to teach you. You have
no clear hope of nor belief in a merciful Creator
and a blissful hereafter—I want to give them you.
I want to make you happy and hopeful and good,
by infusing my life in yours. and showing you that
love is the great regenerator of the world. In one
word, Phyllida. I love you ' I cannot tell why
—I do not know how. I know only that you
must be mine, or I will go through life unmated.
Come to me, darling. See how open my arms
are to receive you! Come, and find your rest and
refuge here !'

But she shrank still farther from him, reiterat-
ing,—

'I cannot—I cannot. Oh, how I wish I could !'

'Child ! do you love me ?'

'I do not know! I am so bewildered I cannot tell—only I would go to you with perfect
confidence as I am.'

'And I would hold you safe against the world
by the force of my passion! What is it that
comes between us, then ? Is there any obstacle
to our marriage?'

She shook her head decidedly.

'Does it exist in your imagination only ?'

'I am not worthy.'

Bernard sighed, but remained steadfast.

'I do not ask your confidence. Some day when
you are my wife you will give it me without asking. Only—granted that you are right—it makes
no difference to my love. You shall but have the
larger, fuller need of it to absolve you from your
sin. I repeat, I love you !'

'Oh, Mr Freshfield! It must not, cannot be! You have only seen me three times altogether!'

'Three times or three hundred times are all the same to me! The more I see of you perhaps, the more I shall esteem you, but esteem is not love. As love is a free gift from God to man, so is it free from man to woman. I do not want to bargain with you for an exchange for my love. It is yours without limit or restraint, because I cannot help giving it to you.'

'And neither can I help loving you. Heaven have mercy on me!' cried Phyllida, with a burst of tears.

But Freshfield would not let them flow. He took her hands from before her face and kissed her passionately.

'My love—my darling—my true wife! Say you will come to me!' he exclaimed, as he held her in his arms.

'I must not—I cannot! Oh, do not ask me!'

'You have confessed your love for me, and I will not let you take it back again. Only for the sake of Bluemere I will give you time. How soon may I tell the world that you are mine?'

'I am not! I will not let you say so! But I will give you my decision in a month. And before that time you will regret you ever asked for it.'

'In a month! A long, drawn-out, weary month! Think of the days and nights of suspense that I shall suffer! Oh, my love! make it less than a month.'

'I cannot! It is far too short a period. I must have time to consider and decide what is right for me to do.'

'You might think and consider for twice two

hundred months,' said Bernard, 'but at the end of that time, Phyllida, you would be mine. It is fate —do not try to battle with it, for it will be useless. God has given you to me, and you are mine; mine for time and for eternity.'

He held her from him for a few moments, gazing at her as though he were drinking in every detail of her beauty; then, almost roughly, he kissed her upon brow and lips and bosom, and put her away from him.

Phyllida stood where he had left her, too much overcome to speak or move, whilst Bernard took two or three hasty strides up and down the room.

When he returned to her side, he was the courteous, smiling host of an hour before.

'Shall we go back to the garden?' he said, drawing her arm through his own. 'I think you are rested now, and will enjoy the cool evening amongst my beautiful flowers.'

But before they passed out of the library he stopped once more and gazed in her face.

'My wife,' he said, with a look of ineffable tenderness, 'my true wife found at last! Thank God! thank God!'

CHAPTER VI.

IT was about five or six days after that eventful party at Briarwood that Miss Annie Warren met Phyllida, walking very slowly and steadily, with her eyes fixed on the ground, beside the broad lake or mere, from which the village took its name, and which was on the road to one of the outlying districts of the parish. Phyllida had chosen that path, because she thought it unlikely she should meet Mr Freshfield there. She knew nothing of the patch of common beyond, and his parishioners who lived upon it. She had been hiding from him ever since that passionate scene in the library in which he had claimed her as his, whether she would or not ; and he was too delicate to break voluntarily on her seclusion, although he had paid more than one visit to Mrs Pinner, in hopes of seeing her. His mother and sister also had called upon Phyllida, and Laura had been disappointed on that occasion by Miss Moss's absence ; but Mrs Pinner had no idea where she was gone, although she had but run to hide herself amongst the cabbages at the back of the house as soon as she heard the carriage wheels. She was shy, in fact, of meeting any of the family, until the mighty question Bernard had raised between them should be settled, and all day long she walked or sat about in the loneliest places she could find, asking herself, ' What *shall* I do ? What shall I do ? '

Miss Warren could not comprehend such shyness. Had she been placed in the position of Phyllida, all the parish would have been acquainted with the fact twelve hours after. She could only imagine, therefore, that this melancholy air was put on to curry favour with the parson ; perhaps even to induce him to employ her in the parish, which her presence on the road to Brick Common seemed to verify. Miss Annie was in a spiteful mood that day, she had been so ever since the party to which she had received no invitation, and Miss Moss seemed a fit subject to vent it upon.

' You here ? ' she exclaimed with well-acted surprise as she came up with Phyllida. She had seen and recognised her full three minutes before. 'I *am* surprised. What on earth can *you* be doing at Brick Common ?'

'What are you doing here yourself?' retorted Phyllida.

'Oh ! *I* am at my parish work, of course. *My* hands are full from morning till night ; thanks to the entire confidence reposed in me by our dear minister. He gives Mr Robinson his instructions daily, but he never thinks of interfering with anything I may do. He has known me and my method too long, you see. And as for giving me a rival to share my parochial duties, I believe he would as soon think of cutting off his right hand,' continued Miss Warren with a laugh that was intended to be the height of confidence. 'For he knows that I should resign my position at once, and he would lose my services altogether.'

'I should think you need have no fear of any one wishing to supplant you, Miss Warren. Attending to old men and women cannot be very pleasant work.'

' Not if you look at it in a *worldly* light, certainly not,' replied Miss Warren, severely ; 'but why should I talk to you on the subject ? The wisest words fall unheeded on the ears as yet unstopped by grace. And what sort of party did you have at Briarwood last Tuesday ? I was so busy, I had no time to come.'

' Were you asked ?' demanded Phyllida innocently. Miss Warren grew very red, but stood to her ground.

' It will be a strange day, indeed, when there are parties given at Briarwood, to which I am *not* asked,' she said ; ' but everybody in Bluemere is talking of the extraordinary manner in which the invitations for this one were sent out. All Mr Freshfield's *dearest* and *oldest* friends omitted, and *perfect strangers* of whom he knew nothing, asked instead. Whoever counselled him did very unwisely. It has created quite a scandal in Bluemere.'

'But perhaps it was Mr Freshfield's own wish, Miss Warren. The society of strangers makes a pleasant change sometimes, in a dull place like this.'

'You don't know Mr Freshfield, or you would not say so—he is not the man to neglect those who have been with him through all his trouble. I expect the invitations were left to his mother and sister, and that old lady Miss Muckheep has got a finger in the pie. Everybody says she is mad, and Laura Freshfield is not much better. She doesn't care with whom she associates ; she actually walked straight through the village the other day on the arm of a Roman Catholic.'

'How dreadful !' cried Phyllida, laughing.

'Ah ! you may laugh, Miss Moss, but we in Bluemere have been taught to think differently from yourself; and our minister is like a beacon set on a hill—he can do nothing that is not known and commented on far and wide. I can tell you that poor dear Alice hardly dared do anything, until she knew what Bluemere would think of it. I remember once her taking a feather out of her hat, because some one said that it looked too gay— a minister's wife cannot be too particular, nor a minister in the choice of his friends. But *some* people will push their way anywhere. What did you do at Briarwood?' continued Miss Annie, who was dying to hear all about it.

'Can't you ask somebody else, Miss Warren, since you know every one in Bluemere? *I* am a stranger here, remember! Besides, I was not well on that day, and did less than any one else.'

Something in the girl's look and tone warned Miss Warren she had said enough.

'Of course I can,' she replied, jerking the heavy basket on her arm. 'I can ask Mr Freshfield himself for that matter, as I am just going to meet him. Good bye, Miss Moss. I wouldn't keep on this road if I were you—for Farmer Green's bull is allowed to roam about these meadows at his will, and he is dangerous with strangers.'

'Thank you; but I am not afraid of bulls,' said Phyllida, as her companion left her to herself. But as soon as Miss Warren was out of sight, she *did* quicken her steps, though it was not from fear of Farmer Green's bull. 'I cannot meet *him*,' she thought to herself; 'he will renew that subject, and I shall not know what to tell him. That woman is right—with all her spite and jealousy, she speaks the truth. A minister is like a beacon set on a hill. He cannot lower himself without lowering his profession. Oh, I must not—I *must not* do as he asks me. It would be so sweet to feel myself safe and good with him, but I am unworthy of it, and if he knew me as I am, he would not press me to share his happy home. I *love him*,' she continued, grinding her pretty teeth together. 'I feel I love him for all his goodness to me and every one. He is like an angel from heaven to me, and so I must not marry him. Oh, I will not—I will not. I will run away, where he shall never find me again. I will go back to my old life—I will do anything except tell him the truth. But it is hard—hard. Why was I created to be different from other women? Why should I be unfit to be a pure and happy wife and mother? Why must *I*, who long so much to be good and innocent and free from blame, refuse the very means which would make me so ? I could love him a thousand times better than that pale-faced, stupid-looking girl who was his wife ; but she would have borne his contempt more quietly than I could. For I would *kill* him before I would see his love change to hatred or indifference. Oh, how I wish I had never met him. I wish I had the courage to throw myself to the bottom of that lake and forget everything that has ever happened to me.'

She leaned far over the water as these thoughts passed through her mind, and looked down into its placid depths. They were dark but clear as a mirror, and as Phyllida gazed at her own reflection another face appeared beside hers, smiling eagerly. It was that of Bernard Freshfield. She started as if she had been shot.

'Take care, my love !' he exclaimed anxiously ; ' these banks are very steep and slippery, and unless you can swim, I would not answer for your reappearance after a submersion in the Bluemere. Of what were you thinking, Phyllida, that my sudden apparition should make you start so violently ? '

The answer was very different from what he expected.

'I was thinking how much trouble it would save me, to be lying asleep for ever down there.'

'Haven't I already told you that is wrong ?' he answered gravely ; ' besides, it is cruel to me. How do you think *I* should feel now if your dear eyes and mouth were closed to me for ever ? Would you trample down my new-found happiness with the memories of another coffin and another grave ? '

'It is for *your* sake I would do it,' cried

Phyllida passionately, 'that you might forget you had ever seen or heard me. Oh, Mr Freshfield, you must never speak to me again as you did last Tuesday. It is quite impossible. It can never be. You lower yourself by the mere idea.'

'That is *my* business, is it not?' said Bernard Freshfield; 'and if I tell you that I feel lifted up to the very heights of heaven by the feeling you have excited in me, how can you gainsay my words? Phyllida,' he continued, coming closer to her, 'you have given me the grandest gift that one mortal can give to another—you have taught me how to love. Henceforward I am greater, nearer to God, for the love I bear you, and I cannot, will not, give it up.'

'Think of your mother—your sister,' she murmured. 'Think of the people of Bluemere, and what they will say to such a folly on your part.'

His lip slightly curled.

'How little you know me, child, to imagine that the opinions of the world would sway my resolve! How little you must comprehend the depth of the passion I have conceived for you—unsought, un-wished for, but overwhelming, if you think that ten thousand relations or friends could stand in the way of its accomplishment! I love you, as man loves woman only once; and I will hold you against the world. Don't wound me by saying you cannot understand it.'

The girl turned suddenly and threw herself into his arms.

'I *do* understand it! Bernard, I understand it far better than you think. If you *must* have me, then, if it be necessary to your happiness to call me yours, take me! Make me your slave, your servant, what you will! I will work for you in secret, and love you in secret, and be grateful to you for the least sign that tells me you are happy in my love. But don't make me your wife, for I am not worthy.'

The young man's arms, which had been clasped tightly round her supple form, fell from her like failing reeds.

'What!' he exclaimed, '*mine* and yet not my wife ? Phyllida, do you know what you are saying?'

'Oh, it would be far better so,' she went on wildly. 'You have told me several times that marriage should be of the heart, and not dependent upon formal ties. Take me then for your true wife—if you will! I *will* be true to you, Bernard, in thought and word and deed; and I will never, never ask for more than you may choose to give me. But don't marry me. I have seen what marriage means. A gradual but sure decay of feeling and respect and courtesy. I could not bear that from you. The contempt of a good man would be my ruin. You shall not pull yourself down for my sake. It were better, far better, that I were lying in the waters of the mere.'

He put his arms about her then, and drew her forcibly from the spot. He seemed to be afraid lest she should really cast herself headlong in the lake.

'Listen to me, dear,' he said tenderly. 'I have told you how I love you. Now, I tell you that I would rather see you dead than slay your purity with my own hand.'

'And you despise me for proposing it.'

'Not so. If you *could* be dearer to me than you have already grown, this noble sacrifice of self would make you so. I know what a woman must feel before she consents to give up all that makes life valuable to her for the sake of a man. I am glad you said it, because it proves how much you love me, but you must never say it again. My wife must be above suspicion.'

'And of me you know—nothing.'

'Oh, don't say that! Has not my love taught me what you are? Have I not read the purity of your feelings—the warmth of your heart—the earnest desires you entertain for goodness and virtue. It is in you, Phyllida, to become all that is most honourable and good, and with me (and the help of God) you shall attain it.'

'I almost think I could,' she answered, weeping.

'And I am sure of it! Tell me, now, may I not claim your promise to be my wife?'

'No, no! not yet! You know we settled that we were to take a month's consideration.'

'*You* did,' he answered, smiling. 'Well, then, sweetheart, I will not worry you; but there is but one answer that I will accept at the end of that time. And now I must leave you, for I was on my way to Brick Common. This has been a dreary week to me without your presence, but it is so many days nearer the moment when I shall claim you for my own. Good-bye, good-bye.'

He went away smiling till he was out of sight, but her mind was full of perplexity and fear. The old question came to the surface, and Phyllida went on her way, wringing her hands and crying, 'What *shall* I do?'

When she reached home the point seemed solved for her. Mrs Pinner, like many another charitable Christian, had benevolently invited Phyllida to

Bluemere, more for her own sake than that of the girl.

She had thought it would be so pleasant to have some one to run messages for her, and do needle-work, and generally undertake the housekeeping. And when Miss Moss failed to display any domestic proclivities whatever, and preferred roaming about the meadows with a volume of Shakespeare in her hand to washing and combing Mrs Pinner's pet poodle Tiny, or accompanying her to the Dorcas meeting, held once a week, under the supervision of Miss Warren, her cousin began to wish she had never asked her to Bluemere. But she had a sister, a Mrs Penfold, also a widow, who lived at a little town on the sea-coast, called Gatehead, where she made her livelihood by letting furnished lodgings. As soon, therefore, as Mrs Pinner found that Phyllida was likely to prove only an encumbrance to herself, she wrote the most laudatory accounts of her beauty and goodness to her sister Penfold, in hopes that lady would offer to take her off her hands ; and since a young dependent relation, who is willing to make herself generally useful, is quite as desirable an inmate of a sea-side lodging-house as of a cottage in the country, the bait took, and Mrs Penfold was just as eager to get Phyllida to Gatehead as Mrs Pinner had been to induce her to visit Bluemere.

And this intelligence Mrs Pinner made known to her over the tea-table, where she appeared that evening, white, heavy-eyed, and languid

' Why, bless my soul, Phyllida !' exclaimed her cousin, and with reason, ' how ill you look. You have been sitting out in that blazing sun again without anything on your head. You will have a sunstroke some day if you don't take more care of yourself.'

' I have been in the shade all the afternoon,' was Phyllida's quiet answer.

' I have just received a letter from my sister, Maria Penfold. Such a nice letter,' continued Mrs Pinner. ' Maria is an excellent creature, one of the salt of the earth, and Gatehead is the prettiest sea-side place you ever saw.'

' Cousin Penfold lets lodgings there, doesn't she ? ' inquired Phyllida, who saw no sin in letting lodgings. But Mrs Pinner had some particles of the old man still clinging to her, and one weakness which she shared with the carnal-minded was a false shame with respect to the occupation of her poorer relation.

Mr Pinner and Mr Penfold had been equal in point of station in this world, but one had succeeded in business and the other had failed ; hence Mr Pinner's widow was a lady in comfortable circumstances in Bluemere, and Mr Penfold's was a lodging-house keeper in Gatehead, and the lady of Bluemere was very much ashamed of the fact. It was some time before she could collect her thoughts to answer suitably to her cousin's straightforward question.

' Well, my dear,' she said at last, she certainly *does* in a measure, but you will agree with me that it is as well not to mention it.'

' But it isn't *wrong ?* ' quoth Phyllida.

' *Wrong !* I should hope not, indeed,' replied Mrs Pinner, with a jerk of her head. ' It would be a sad day when any one connected with me by blood did anything that was *wrong.* Still, to let lodgings is not an occupation to which any of my father's daughters ever thought to come down, and therefore I have never said anything about it to my friends in Bluemere.

'I see! You are ashamed of cousin Penfold,' said Phyllida boldly.

'Phyllida, you really do have the most extraordinary ideas! How *could* I be ashamed of my own sister,—born of the same good parents as myself, and walking side by side with me in the light of the truth to heaven? Have I not already told you what an excellent creature is Maria? And she does not exactly let lodgings either. Her house is too large for her, for she is childless like myself, and an old gentleman and lady occupy the first and second floors. They are highly respectable both of them, and have been living with Maria for years past, so you see it is not like being a common lodging-house keeper to share her very comfortable home with them.'

'I see that cousin Penfold must be a nice woman, or they wouldn't have stayed with her so long. I wonder if she would be good to me too, and find me some occupation in Gatehead. For I am tired of this idle life, cousin Pinner, and it is time I did something to support myself.'

This was the very opening Mrs Pinner required.

'How strange you should say so, Phyllida, for Maria is most anxious to make your acquaintance. I will read you what she writes, "Do you think Phyllida Moss could be persuaded to pay me a visit at Gatehead? I remember her mother as a girl, though you do not, and should be glad to know her daughter. The sea-side is charming just now. Our little season has just commenced, and Gatehead is as full as it can be. If our young cousin would like to spend a few weeks with me, tell her to come before the fine weather is over." There,' continued Mrs Pinner folding up her letter, you see what Maria says on the matter, and you can make your own choice.'

But she was hardly prepared for the energy with which Phyllida entered into the new scheme.

'I will go at once,' she said. 'I shall enjoy it above all things; and I am sure the sea will do me good. How far is Gatehead from here, cousin Pinner, and can I start to-morrow?'

'You seem to be in a tremendous hurry to go,' replied Mrs Pinner, who, though she wanted to get rid of her visitor, was not over-pleased at her alacrity to leave. 'Gatehead is half-a-day's journey from Bluemere, and I shall have to borrow a time-table from the rectory before I can tell you at what hours the trains leave Westertown.'

'Don't think me ungrateful,' said Phyllida, as she took the old lady's hand; 'I am afraid I have been a great bother to you since I came here, and you have been very patient with me. Only—I have had trouble (as you know) and it doesn't seem to lessen, and I think the sooner I set to work the sooner I shall learn to overcome it.'

'Don't say any more, my dear,' replied Mrs Pinner; 'I'm too old to be a good companion for you, and you don't seem to have taken to the young ladies of Bluemere — but you will have gayer scenes and perhaps gayer friends in Gate-head; for though my sister Maria has been trained in the ways of grace, I sometimes fear that her heart still inclines to carnal pleasures and company.'

Phyllida heaved a sigh of thanksgiving on the spot. But she had another petition to proffer.

'You won't send to the rectory for the time-table, will you, cousin Pinner?'

'Why not, my dear? Our dear minister is always

but too ready to share his good gifts with his people!'

'Yes; but I don't want Mr Freshfield to hear that I am going to Gatehead. I think, perhaps—at least, I feel almost sure—that (in his capacity as minister, you know) he might consider it his duty to urge me to remain in Bluemere and try and live down any troubles with parish work, and so forth.'

'But, my dear,' commenced Mrs Pinner, who was alarmed at this prospect of recantation, 'Mr Freshfield could hardly take the parish work out of Miss Warren's hands—she does everything in that way, you know—it would be a positive insult to her! And where am I to borrow a time-table except from him? We travel so little from Bluemere.'

'Perhaps Miss Warren may have one,' suggested Phyllida.

'She may. That is a happy idea on your part, for her brother lives in London, and is often here on a visit. Shall I send Mary over to ask her?'

'Yes, cousin Pinner; and say why you want it. Miss Warren will not try to prevent my leaving Bluemere—I am sure of that.'

And the upshot of this conversation was, that Phyllida Moss and her box were driven to Wester-town the very next day; and she had reached her destination of Gatehead before her lover was aware that she no longer breathed the same air as himself.

It was the evening after her departure that he came sauntering up Mrs Pinner's garden path, hoping to catch the ladies over their frugal tea. But Mrs Pinner sat alone at the raddish-crowned board.

'Is Miss Moss still roaming?' he asked pleasantly, as he entered the little room. 'What an

inquisitive young lady she is. I do not believe
that there is a nook or corner of Bluemere that
she has not explored. She is a thorough lover of
the country.'

'Have you not heard that my cousin has left me,
Mr Freshfield? She went to my sister's at Gatehead yesterday,' replied Mrs Pinner, on whom
Phyllida had laid no embargo as to concealing her
destination. For she believed that once out of
Bluemere, she should at least be allowed as much
time as she chose, in which to make up her mind
respecting Bernard Freshfield, for a parson (so she
imagined) must remain at his post of duty until
she saw fit to rejoin him. When Mrs Pinner
made her announcement to Bernard, his face grew
as pale as ashes. She said afterwards (when circumstances had thrown their light upon his behaviour) that she guessed the truth from merely
looking at him. But that was not the case. At
the moment she only thought that he was ill, or
vexed at letting a probable convert slip through his
fingers.

'Dear me, Mr Freshfield,' she exclaimed, 'you
look quite poorly. Do sit down and have a cup of
tea. Yes, Phyllida went off to my sister Penfold's
yesterday. It was rather a surprise to me, as you
may imagine, for I had invited her to stay with me
over the winter, but I am afraid our ways didn't
suit her. She's rather flighty, and I have been
brought up, as you know, in the strictest principles,
and used to refer all my doings to the Throne of
Grace, and it did not suit the girl. Two cannot
walk together, as we know, except they be agreed.
And the ways of the righteous are as a stumbling-
block to the ungodly.'

'No, no tea, thank you,' the parson said in rather

a strange voice, as he put back the cup she offered him. 'To Gatehead, did you say?'

'Yes, to my sister Maria. She lives in Shirland Villas, Gatehead, and was kind enough to invite the girl to stay with her. Directly Phyllida received the invitation, she jumped at it—ungratefully, I cannot but say—and insisted upon going off the very next day. I wished her to consult you upon the matter, Mr Freshfield, for, as I said, what greater privilege can we have than a minister's advice; but she is a wrong-headed creature, and she wouldn't hear of it. She said you'd keep her here, and set her about parish work. Such nonsense! But I've often thought that Phyllida is a little wanting. I hope my sister Penfold may make more of her than I did. And you won't take any tea then, Mr Freshfield?'

'No, thanks,' he stammered; and then rising suddenly, 'I must go on to Blue Mount. I have something of importance to tell my mother,' and before his hostess could remonstrate with him he was gone.

'So strange, my dear,' as she observed to Annie Warren somewhat later, 'to leave me all alone in that way, and when I was just in the humour to enjoy a little company! Not like a minister, I must say; but still, as he went to Blue Mount, I suppose I must not complain. He said he had something of importance to tell his mother. I wonder what it can be.'

If Mrs Pinner could have followed her minister to Blue Mount, she would have been still more astonished. He entered Mrs Freshfield's private sitting-room with troubled eyes and ruffled hair, looking more like a man walking in his sleep than an animate being, and flung himself upon the nearest seat.   The old lady was alone, occupied with her eternal knitting.

'Good heavens! Bernard,' she exclaimed, as she looked up at him over her spectacles, 'what is the matter?'

'Nothing,' he said, starting. 'Do I look as if there were.   It is this diabolical heat.'

'*Bernard!*' cried Mrs Freshfield.

'I beg your pardon, mother.   I mean it is the heat that has upset me.   I don't feel at all well to-day.   It's enough to make any man seedy, to tramp over a parish from morning till night, in such sun as this.'

'You should wear a "solar topee,"' remarked his mother practically

'I want change—that is the truth—and I intend to take it.   Robinson can do the work of Bluemere very well for a few weeks by himself.   You know, mother, that I have not left the parish since my wife died.'

'No, my dear, you have not ; and a most excellent opportunity presents itself at present.   Dear Miss Janet was lamenting only yesterday that Dr Felinus was not here to accompany her and that sweet Bella back to Scotland.   What would be more charming than for you to offer these two estimable ladies your escort?   You would get a thorough change in the bracing air of Scotland, and see something of the beauties of that delightful country.   Bernard, it is a most happy idea on your part : and if you are put to any extra expenses in the matter, of course I will defray them.'

'What ! to go journeying about the country with that old woman ?   No, by Jove ! I won't.'

'*Bernard,*' again exclaimed his mother, in a tone of horror, '*what* has come to you this evening ? '

'I don't know, I'm sure,' replied the young man, passing his hand wearily over his brow. 'I am out of temper, I suppose, or out of sorts. Anyway, I can't be the Miss Muckheeps' escort. I must be free and alone, and I must start at once.'

'You surely will not leave Bluemere whilst my friends remain with me, Bernard? Think how strange it will appear, and what every one will say about it!'

'What do I care for what people *say!*' he exclaimed impetuously. 'The Muckheeps are no friends of mine, and never will be. Don't worry me on the subject, mother, for I came to say good-bye to you, and I shall start to-morrow.'

'Oh, this is terribly sudden! What can be the reason of it?' cried Mrs Freshfield. 'It is not customary for a minister to desert his flock in this way at a moment's warning.'

'My flock will be well provided for, or I should not leave it. The shepherd wants most looking after at present.'

'And where are you going, Bernard?' demanded Mrs Freshfield in a solemn voice.

'I cannot tell you. I am not sure if I quite know myself; but you shall hear from me as soon as possible, and perhaps I may be able to tell you the reason of my determination.'

Mrs Freshfield only shook her head in sorrowful protest against such vicarious doings.

'Well, good-bye, mother,' said Bernard, rising. 'I don't want to go into the drawing-room, nor to see Laura, nor anybody. I am not fit for any company but my own to-night. Tell them of my determination, and let them put what interpretation upon it they choose. It is hard if a man, who works as much as I do, cannot take a few weeks' relaxation without publishing his reasons to the world. I *wish it*, and I should think that ought to be sufficient.'

And so saying, Bernard Freshfield turned on his heel, and with the same fretful, despondent look upon his face, left the room. Such is the power that the thwarting of his fleshly inclinations may produce, even upon a man proverbially even-tempered, pious, and self-sacrificing !

CHAPTER VII.

GATEHEAD was a little place between a village and a town, situated on the borders of the Thames, where it joins the Channel waters, and sufficiently near London to have the nastiest dregs of its population poured into it by excursion trains three times a-week all through what it termed 'the season.' There had been a time when Gatehead was strictly dull and proper—when it had possessed no railway station, nor theatre nor hotel even of the most unpretentious order. Then, its residents were composed of old maids and widows and superannuated officers, who met daily on its one promenade, and gabbled of the iniquity of the Board of Guardians in wishing to pave the town, or introduce public conveyances, or give their sanction to the erection of a railway station at Gatehead. But those days were past. The old ladies and gentlemen were sleeping quietly in the churchyard, and were not likely to have their ears shocked by the ribald songs of drunken excursionists, nor their eyes by the flaming placards, which set forth that burlesque had found its way even down to that select retreat. But Gatehead was hardly improved by the change occasioned by the march of intellect. In the olden days it had been at least respectable, if dull. Now it was dull and disreputable. More than two-thirds of the houses were let out in furnished apartments to clerks' and tradesmen's wives, whose superabundant offspring occupied the entire beach, and made the welkin ring with their discordant cries. The few residents that remained in Gatehead were in the habit of letting or shutting up their houses during the warm months of the year, and resigning the town to a lower class of inhabitants, returning only when the winter had commenced, and the place was empty, muddy, cold, and unutterably depressing. It will be understood, therefore, that Gatehead was at no time a very desirable place to live in.

Phyllida Moss came to it in the noisy, vulgar, money-making season. All day long the station kept on disgorging troops of mechanics and petty traders and their families, who swarmed about the place like flies, causing a lively trade in cockles, winkles, shrimps, tea and bread and butter—likewise, it may be supposed, of beer and stronger liquors. All the days they spent with crimsoned faces and perspiring bodies on the beach or pier. All the evenings they danced in drunken glee up and down the principal street, the women with the men's hats upon their tousled heads, and *vice versâ;* or drove about Gatehead, packed into open carriages, a dozen at a load, sitting on each other's laps, shouting filthy songs, and presenting altogether as disgusting and degrading a spectacle of human nature as could be seen anywhere. But the letters of lodgings made their harvest by the drunken crew, and were compelled to be grateful for their patronage. When Phyllida arrived at the station, and (not having apprised Mrs Penfold of her coming) found herself obliged to elbow her way alone through the boisterous crowd, her heart sunk, and she almost wished she had remained in Bluemere. Her soul was naturally formed to dislike noise and publicity, and she shuddered at the idea of carrying her trouble about with her amongst such a herd of ruffians. She had hoped to find quiet and solitude in Gatehead, but it did not seem probable, and her thoughts went back longingly to the shady road to Brick Common, where she had gazed in the silent mere and heard that sweet, soothing voice—the sweetest voice Heaven ever bestowed on man—remonstrating with her on her unhallowed wish. There were no cabs, to carry her box or herself, at Gatehead station that day—they were all taken up by the excursionists. so Phyllida hired a porter with a truck, and walking beside him to Shirland Villas, presented herself in a very humble fashion at Mrs Penfold's door. Her knock was answered by a placid-faced woman in a mourning dress, whom she felt sure at first sight was Mrs Penfold herself.

'Are you my cousin Penfold?' she asked eagerly. 'I am Phyllida Moss.'

The lady—for a lady she was in everything, but perhaps her occupation—dropt the prim look she wore for a stranger immediately, and dimpled over with smiles of greeting.

'Are you really? You don't mean to say so?'

she cried, as she kissed the girl on both cheeks. 'Come in, my dear, come in,' she continued, as she pushed Phyllida into a little parlour on the ground floor.

'Never mind the luggage, Sarah will see after that. And so you have come to stay with me at once. That *is* good of you, though of course I didn't expect to see you quite so soon, but your room shall be ready in half-an-hour. Sit down, dear, and rest yourself; I am sure you must be tired,—and now you will have a glass of wine, won't you?'

'No, no, cousin Penfold; I never drink wine. I would rather have a cup of tea.'

'And so you shall, dear; anything that I have it in my power to give you,' replied the hospitable Mrs Penfold; and then running to the head of the stairs, she called out 'Sarah! Sarah! Miss Moss has arrived. Come up at once and see after her box; and take the mattress off the bed in the little room, and put it to the kitchen fire; and air some clean sheets, and let us have a cup of tea as soon as ever you can get it ready; and give an eye to Captain Barclay's cutlets, lest they should burn; and don't forget to take an extra halfpenny worth of milk for Miss Annadale's coffee.'

And then she returned to the parlour, and re-commenced purring over Phyllida. 'It is such an unexpected pleasure to get you here, dear, for you seem such a favourite with Charlotte. I hardly hoped she would let you leave Bluemere.'

'But I am not very well,' stammered Phyllida, 'and I want change, and since you were so kind as to ask me, cousin Penfold, and cousin Pinner consented to my visiting you—'

'Say no more about it, my dear. I am only too

glad to see you, and I hope the change may do you good. Gatehead is not a fashionable place, but it is very healthy ; and though I don't pretend to be a lady like my sister Charlotte, I can give you as many comforts, I hope, as she can.'

' But why are you not a lady as much as herself ? ' asked Phyllida. ' I am sure you look more so, cousin Penfold, for she is so fond of gay caps and dresses.'

' Well, my dear Phyllida,' said her cousin, laughing, ' of course we come of the same parentage, and received the same training. But poor Mr Penfold was very unfortunate in business—in fact, it was his heavy losses broke his heart at last ; and he left me almost penniless. So I had but the choice of two things—to live on the charity of my relations, or to earn my own livelihood, and I chose the latter.'

' And quite right, too, cousin ! Who would live on charity who was not obliged ? '

' So, as I possessed a little furniture,' continued Mrs Penfold, ' I thought the best plan would be to let furnished apartments. And really it is far less trouble than you would think. My two lodgers have been with me now for more than three years. Captain Barclay, a retired officer of the Royal Navy, is the quietest old gentleman you ever saw, and most simple in his habits ; and though poor Miss Annadale is rather crotchety at times, Sarah and I have got used to her ways, and generally contrive to satisfy her. They pay me sufficient to keep my house comfortably and respectably, and that is all I need. So you see, my dear, I am not so much to be pitied, as perhaps my sister Charlotte would like to make out.'

' Cousin Pinner has vulgar stuck-up notions,'

said Phyllida unreservedly; ' and the people she lives amongst encourage her in them. They are all stuck-up in Bluemere, and they disliked me because I cannot pretend to be pious when I am not. Cousin Penfold, I know I shall like you much better than I did her. I feel you are not a humbug, and I think it was that feeling, and the knowledge that you are not ashamed to work, that made me decide so suddenly to come to you. I want to work myself; but I don't know how to set about it. Will you help me to get my own living as you do ? '

' We will talk about that hereafter, Phyllida,' said Mrs Penfold. ' You must stay with me for some weeks, and we shall have plenty of time for discussing ways and means. Here is Sarah with our tea. Now you must eat this nice fresh egg (I know it is fresh, because the captain and I keep a joint poultry yard in the back garden), and some buttered toast, and you will feel all the better for it. Bless me! you are very like your poor dear mother,' continued Mrs Penfold as Phyllida removed her hat ; ' she had just such clear brown eyes as yours, and the same profusion of hair. But what have you been doing to your hair, child ? It is quite yellow in places, and the ends look as if they had been burnt.'

Phyllida grew scarlet.

' I was foolish enough to dye it once,' she answered ; ' but it will soon be all right again.

' *To dye it !* ' reiterated Mrs Penfold; ' that was a silly thing (not but what half the girls do it now-a-days), only it's a shame to touch such hair as yours. It's a lovely colour in itself, and as soft as silk. No, no, leave the dyeing to the old women my dear, and the red-haired ones, and depend upon it you look much better as the Lord made you. And how long is it since you lost your mother?'

'Years ago,' replied Phyllida, with a deep sigh.

'Ah, poor dear! she was never very strong as a girl, I remember, though I heard little of her after she went to St Domingo. It's such a distance, you know, and foreign letters cost so much money. But she went out with her father, who was a West India merchant, and we heard the report afterwards of her marriage. And so she married twice—dear, dear, what an undertaking ; and Mr Moss was your papa. And have you lost him long, my dear?'

'No, very lately,' said Phyllida, with a glance at her black dress.

'Ah, yes ; of course, thoughtless of me to ask. And you have been left without any provision?'

'Utterly so, cousin Penfold. I had only just enough money to bring me to England, and keep me till I heard from cousin Pinner. I should have gone out as a servant if she had not asked me to Bluemere.'

'We must find something better for you than that,' replied Mrs Penfold, 'and till we do find it, it will be hard if your own mother's second cousin cannot give her orphan daughter food and shelter. So consider yourself at home, my dear, until you can better yourself by leaving Gatehead. Think that you are my child. I wish, indeed, Heaven had given me such a child. I should never have missed the bit and sup I earned for her,' and the good creature fell on Phyllida's neck and embraced her heartily. And it really seemed as if she meant what she said. As soon as Captain Barclay's cutlets and Miss Annadale's coffee were served, Mrs Penfold invited her cousin to a ramble through Gatehead.

'If you are not too tired, dear, you will like to see our little town, and Sarah will attend to the old lady, so I am free. This is my holiday time,' she said, as she and Phyllida emerged from Shirland Villas upon the esplanade, 'when I go to see my friends or take a walk with them, or enjoy an hour at the play. And it freshens me up for the next day's work.'

'You are not so strict as cousin Pinner, then?' observed Phyllida; 'she says the theatre is the devil's playhouse, where he goes to gloat upon his future victims.'

'Does Charlotte say that? I didn't think she could be so wicked. No, my dear, I hope I try to live up to what I believe to be right, but I should be ashamed to hold such sentiments as those. I see no harm in the theatre, and I am very fond of going there. In fact, when we have a good company in Gatehead, I go two and three times a-week Would you like to go to-night?' continued Miss Penfold, thinking to please her visitor. 'They play "East Lynne." It is a pretty piece; I am sure you will like it.'

'No, no,' replied Phyllida, shrinking backward.

'Why, what is this, you seem almost as shocked as Charlotte herself. Have I wounded your feelings by the proposal?'

'No, dear cousin Penfold, indeed you have not, only I do not care for the light and the heat and the noise. Sometimes I think I shall never enter a theatre again. Let us go down to the beach. May we? I long to put my hands into that cool green water, and feel the fresh salt breeze blow in my face. I shall love to lie for hours on the beach, if you will not call it wasting time as cousin Pinner did, and gaze up into the sky or over the waters and " make believe," as children say, that Phyllida Moss died years ago, and I am quite another girl, who has only heard of her sad life and pities her for having lived it.'

'My dearest Phyllida,' cried the warm-hearted Mrs Penfold, ' this is not the way in which a young creature like yourself should view life. It is very sad to lose our parents, dear ; but in the course of nature they die before ourselves, and it is morbid to consider all happiness over for us because they are gone.'

Oh, it is not that—it is not that!' replied Phyllida, saying more than she intended.

'Then I can guess what it is,' said Mrs Penfold, looking very wise, 'and it will be cured before long, my dear, never fear.'

But something in the girl's sorrow-laden eyes checked any further jesting on her cousin's part, and she turned the subject to some less personal matter. The two women remained out late that warm summer's night, lingering on the beach and pier till the harvest moon had risen, and every ripple on the incoming tide was tipped with phosphoric light.

'Is it not beautiful?' said Phyllida, as she leant entranced over the railings of the pier. 'I have watched the water all ablaze like this at St Domingo, until I felt that to drop to sleep beneath those warm living waves would be heaven compared to the life of cold anxiety and doubt which we pass here.'

'But what kind of doubt, my dear?' inquired Mrs Penfold. 'I hope you have not had your mind upset by some of these terrible false doctrines that are going about now-a-days?'

'Not exactly, cousin ; though sometimes when I have seen how a poor girl like myself can pass through this world of temptation without a soul to succour her, I have doubted if there *is* anybody to look after us, or to care if we go to heaven or the other place ; yet I did not mean religious doubt, but the difficulty of deciding what is best to be done in certain actions of our lives. Have you ever felt that difficulty, cousin ? '

'Oh yes, my dear, often ! I remember when Miss Annadale wanted to take my rooms I had the most harassing doubts on the subject, which kept me awake for several nights, because she seemed to have no friends nor references, and I thought to myself where on earth was the rent to come from if she played me false ? However, she's proved as good a lodger as ever a woman had, so you see I might have saved myself the trouble of doubting her at all.'

' But with regard to one's friends,' said Phyllida wistfully, ' do you think it necessary to tell them everything one has ever done during one's lifetime, whether it be right or wrong, so long as we are good and faithful friends to them ? '

'My dear girl, what a question ! *No*, most decidedly not ! The world would come to a pretty pass, indeed, if all our friends turned into father confessors. Why, I don't even approve of confessing sins to a priest, for we were all brought up on strictly evangelical principles, and I can't bring myself to fall in with what they call High Church doctrine. Still, there's some sense in telling your troubles to a minister if you fancy he can help you out of them ; but as for laying one's heart bare to a friend, you take my advice, dear, and never do such a thing. Confess your sins to God. He is the only person who can forgive them, and so He must be the proper person to hear them.'

'Do you *really* think so?' said Phyllida, with a strange light in her eyes.

'Of course I do! Why, child, if it is no offence, in what religion may your parents have reared you?'

'In *none,*' replied the girl, in a low tone.

'What a shame! I can't help saying it, and I should have thought Agnes might have remembered the teaching she had at home better than that comes to.'

'Oh, don't blame my mother, my poor unhappy mother!' cried Phyllida hastily. 'Cousin Penfold, you don't know what she suffered before she died. Her life was one continual misery to her. Is it a wonder that she grew to disbelieve in a God or an eternity, or anything except the cruelty and wickedness of man?'

'Poor, dear Agnes! Then I suppose your father didn't treat her well?'

'Don't ask me about it,' replied Phyllida, with a shudder: 'don't mention his name to me, because I cannot bear it. Cousin Penfold, the first memory I can recall is of my mother's suffering! She was my all whilst she lived—I cared for no creature upon earth but herself—and, seeing how unhappy she was permitted to be, is it wonderful that I too came to doubt whether there was any God sitting up in heaven, or any life when this shall be ended?'

'Oh, you mustn't think like that, my dear. Brighter times are coming for you now, I hope, and you must try and believe that the Almighty is over-ruling your actions for you, and will make everything right in the end. And my advice to you, Phyllida, is to bury your past as much as lies in

your power.   Try not to think of it or speak of it.
Let it die a natural death, as all griefs do in time,
and begin a new life from the present.'

'It is all past and done with,' said Phyllida mus-
ingly; 'it can never trouble me or any one again,
thank God, and I should be only too thankful to
let it rest.   And you really think I shall be wise to
do so, cousin Penfold?'

'I think it is your *duty* to do so,' replied the
elder lady.   'And now we had better go in, Phyllida, for it is eleven o'clock, and Captain Barclay
will never allow any one but me to mix his glass
of toddy.'

'Can't I take that trouble off your hands, cousin
Penfold,' asked the girl, laughing; 'you must let
me help you, if I can, and I am famous at mixing
all kinds of drinks.'

'I think I will dispense with your assistance in
this particular,' replied Mrs Penfold, laughing also,
'or we shall have the old captain taking to drink
for the sake of seeing you stirring the lemon and
whisky together.   You are too pretty for a hand-
maid, my dear child, even for such a dried-up and
salted old gentleman as Captain Barclay.'

Phyllida seemed to have dropped a load off her
mind after this walk with her cousin, for she
laughed and talked quite merrily until it was time
to go to bed.   But with solitude the old distressing
perplexities returned to worry her, and Mrs Penfold
heard her moaning through her restless sleep.   She
concluded, therefore, that the girl's body wanted a
little petting as well as her mind, and commenced
the cure by insisting upon treating her as an
invalid.   She made her lie in bed late, and occupy
the sofa when she came downstairs, and fed
her with strengthening broths and jellies, till

Phyllida was obliged to remonstrate against being killed with too much kindness. And on the evening of the third day, as she was dressing herself for a walk, and Mrs Penfold appeared in her bedroom with a look of mystery upon her countenance, Phyllida wondered what new remedy was going to be tried upon her.

'Cousin Penfold,' she exclaimed, 'I can*not* take any more soup or jelly to-day. I feel filled up to the very throat! And I see you are bent upon physicking me. I can read a new remedy written in your face.'

'Yes, my dear,' replied Mrs Penfold seriously, 'I really have a new medicine that I want you to take. I have been studying your case, Phyllida, and I believe I have hit on the proper cure, and I must insist on your trying it.'

'Anything to please you, cousin! What is it?— food or physic? I hope it is not very nasty?'

'It doesn't *look* nasty,' said Mrs Penfold; 'but I haven't tasted it myself. Any way I am sure it will do you good. Come down and see.'

'Haven't you got it with you?'

'No; I left it in the parlour.'

'All right! I will come,' said Phyllida, as she adjusted her hat. 'You are too good to me, cousin Penfold,' she added, as she wound her arm round the old lady's waist. 'I should be ungrateful, indeed, to refuse to try anything you see fit to recommend to me.'

'I recommend this strongly,' replied Mrs Penfold, as they reached the parlour door. 'Go in, my dear, and take it at once; you will find it by the side of the table.'

So saying she pushed Phyllida gently into the

parlour, where she saw standing by the mantel-piece—Bernard Freshfield. Her first impulse was to turn and fly ; but the door was closed behind her, and Mrs Penfold was descending the kitchen stairs.

'Oh, Mr Freshfield!' she murmured with crimson cheeks, 'is this *fair ?*'

'I will answer your question by another, my Phyllida,' said Bernard, crossing to her side ; 'was it fair of you to run away from me without one word of warning?'

'I thought it best—I did not think you would be so foolish as to follow me—and after that day on the Brick Common Road,' said Phyllida, flushing violently, ' after what I said to you then, I did not feel as if I could meet you again.'

'After what you said to me on the Brick Common Road,' he answered, looking full into her eyes, 'you had no longer any right to think for yourself at all. Why did you not give yourself to me that day ?—a freewill offering—and is this the way you make a present? To give it one day and take it away the next. But you are mine, Phyllida, and you shall not rob me a second time.'

'I thought it best,' she reiterated. 'I *know* it is best, that you should forget me, Bernard!'

'It is not best, it would be the very worst ; besides, it is impossible. Phyllida, I have prayed for years to God to send me my soul's partner! Am I to be so ungrateful, now He has heard my prayer, as to turn away and take no notice of it ?'

'But perhaps you are mistaken,' she faltered ; 'people appear so different from what they are— you might find out afterwards that I am not the person you had imagined me to be! You know that I am not a good, religious girl! How shall I make a proper parson's wife?'

'I do *not* know that you are not a good, religious girl,' he answered, making her sit down on the sofa by his side; 'but if it is the case, I shall marry my wife for myself, not for my parish, and I shall keep her for myself into the bargain. I am not on the look-out for a female curate without stipend. I want a companion, a friend, a second self! Such an one I have found in you, Phyllida; and only one part of the question remains to be solved in order to settle it satisfactorily, and for ever. And that is, *Do you love me?*'

'The month is not over yet, she said, temporising with her destiny

'I will not wait a month now for your decision. I cannot! Had you remained in Bluemere I would have been patient, but your sudden unexplained departure made me so miserable, that I came away at a moment's notice, and do not intend to return home again without my wife.'

'Oh, Bernard, that would be far too sudden,' she cried. 'Think what a solemn thing marriage is. Once done, it can never be undone, and there Phyllida pulled herself up suddenly and was silent.

'What is the matter, my darling?' inquired Bernard tenderly; 'did anything frighten you? I know all you would say, Phyllida, and agree with it heartily. No one thinks marriage a more solemn sacrament than I do—a true marriage that is—one hallowed by God and approved by man, as ours will be.'

The girl shivered slightly, and pressed closer to him. Freshfield interpreted the act as a sign of compliance, and joyfully returned the pressure.

'To prove to you the solemnity with which I regard marriage, Phyllida, I will repose in you a little confidence. I will treat you as if you were already the beloved partner of all my anxieties, and you shall tell me if I have done right. Amongst my parishioners I have a man and his wife, as handsome and apparently as happy a couple as you could see. The husband especially is devoted to his wife and her children, and can see no fault in them. Some months ago the woman was taken dangerously ill—in fact, our doctor gave no hopes of her, and she sent for me. I found the husband almost heartbroken in the lower room. He could not speak for sobbing. All he could do was to point to the upper chamber where his wife lay dying. I went upstairs and found her in a state of great excitement. She knew she was given over, and she wished to speak to me before she died. What was my horror on receiving her confession to learn that for years past she had been habitually unfaithful to her husband, and that she was not even sure which of her children belonged to him. However, the unhappy woman was apparently fast passing away, and my duty was to soothe her last pains, by pointing her to the one source of forgiveness for all sin. I left her, as I thought, for ever in this world. What was my astonishment the next day to hear that her disorder had taken a most unexpected turn in the night, and she was in a fair road to recovery. In a few weeks I heard that she was up and about her domestic work again, as bright and beautiful as before ; and her husband adoring her more than ever, for having been restored to him, as it were, from the very jaws of death. Now came my difficulty, Phyllida! I had received the wife's confidence under the seal of confession, and although I have no High Church proclivities, I am a man of honour, and I consider that such a disclosure made at such a moment should be held as sacred as though it had never been revealed. And yet when I saw the woman as careless and unsubdued as she had ever been, and thought of the unfortunate man she was, in all probability, continuing to deceive, I wondered where my duty lay, and whether I could conscientiously permit him to live on, duped and betrayed, when it was in my power to open his eyes.

'I cannot tell you how long this matter puzzled me; for how long I thought over it and adjusted its pros and cons, and prayed to be guided to act aright. And to what conclusion do you suppose that I arrived?'

'I cannot tell,' said the girl half sobbing; 'tell me yourself, Bernard, I want to know.'

'Don't tremble so, my darling—the story has a tolerable ending. How I argued the matter out was thus: To tell the man the truth (always supposing I could have reconciled it with my conscience) would have marred his life, and could not have amended hers. It would have broken up a happy home, the influence of which may be the means intended by God to lead her into the right way at last. It would have cast the man, blaspheming Heaven, perhaps, for his disappointment, upon the world, and turned his love for her offspring into jealousy and hate.

'I saw no end to the miseries my breach of confidence might entail on the couple and their

children; and I saw no especial duty to urge me
to it.

'The fact that the wife had outraged the sanctity of marriage only affected herself; it could not
undo that sanctity which the husband had faithfully observed. And so I left them to themselves
and the mercy of God, who can bring hidden
things to light if He so chooses without our inter-
vention. Was I right or wrong?'

'Oh you are right—always right and always
good,' said Phyllida clinging to him; and if I
thought—if I were really sure that you believe as
you say, that a marriage of love is a sacrament
ordained of Heaven that none of the lesser circumstances of life should be permitted to out-
weigh—'

'If you were really sure of that, love, what would
you do?' whispered Bernard.

'I would marry you to-morrow, and feel myself
—oh, so blest, to be your wife!'

'Done with you!' cried our unorthodox parson,
as he smothered her with kisses. 'You have passed
your word, Phyllida, and you shall not retract it.
We *will* be married to-morrow!'

CHAPTER VIII.

WHEN Phyllida had thus stepped over the bound-
ary that divided hesitation from consent, she found
there was no retraction for her. Bernard had made
Mrs Penfold acquainted with his errand before he

had seen Phyllida, and she was naturally all on his side.   That her young orphan cousin should hesitate for a moment to accept a man, young, good-looking, a clergyman, and with two thousand a-year, appeared incredible to her ; and when Bernard called her in to take part in the general council, she treated all Phyllida's objections as mere affectation.   The girl wished Bernard to consent to her remaining a month or two at Gatehead whilst he prepared the minds of his mother and sister and the parish generally for their marriage, and Freshfield wanted the ceremony to take place there and then, in fact he vowed he would not return to Bluemere without her.

'But it would be shocking—indelicate,' urged Phyllida, 'for you to marry without giving them any notice ; what would they say ?   A clergyman's wedding is generally such a thoroughly parochial affair.'

'And would you like it to be so, Phyllida ? Would you like to go to church in Bluemere with every old woman in the parish gazing at you and picking holes in your dress or your bonnet ?'

'Oh no ; you know I should not.   I shall shrink from the scrutiny of the old women more than anything.   I don't think I could go through with it, without you by my side.   Only I am nobody, you see ; but for your own sake, Bernard, and for Mrs Freshfield's, ought you not to endure the miseries of a public wedding ?'

The young man looked thoughtful.

'There is something in your argument, Phyllida, and it proceeds from a good and pure motive, as all your proposals do.   But I think I can overcome it without infringing my duty.   In the first place, nothing would persuade me to take part in an ordinary wedding feast again. I did it once. I swore before heaven to love and honour a woman whom I hardly loved, and was not all sure I could honour, and I sat through the public breakfast that succeeded it, feeling like a criminal escaped from justice. We won't have anything of that sort again, *This* will be a very different wedding, my love, from the other—it must be celebrated in a different way.'

'But oh, Bernard,' cried Phyllida, hiding her face against his shoulder, 'if *she* came so short of what you desired, what shall *I* do?'

'You will do as I tell you?' said the young man fondly. 'You will marry me in Gatehead in the course of the next few days, and let the astonishment and the cackle of Bluemere subside before we show our faces there again! Mrs Penfold, come and plead my cause with this obstinate girl! You are, I believe, her nearest relation in England— give your sanction to my plan, and make Phyllida hear reason.'

'Indeed, Mr Freshfield, I see no cause whatever why you should not have your own way. If you were a young boy, or a private gentleman, or one of those nasty soldiers that run about making love to every woman they meet, why, I might say it would be better to wait, and see whether you didn't change your mind. But Phyllida mustn't forget that you are her minister as well as her lover, and that she is in a measure bound to follow your precepts, and certainly not responsible for acting wrong whilst under your direction.'

'Capitally put, Mrs Penfold. You are a first-rate advocate. Do you hear that, Phyllida? I am not going to *ask* you any more—I am going to *order* you. And your cousin says you are bound to obey.'

'I see that between the two of you I am not likely to get my own way,' replied Phyllida, smiling.

'Of course not, when it is a bad way. Listen to me, dear; this is what I propose. Let us get a licence, and be married as privately as possible in the church here. Then I will take you to Switzerland or to Paris, or anywhere you most fancy, and thence I will write and let my people hear the truth. Remember, Phyllida, that, as Mrs Penfold says, I am not a boy, and responsible to no one for my actions; and I have often told my mother that if I married again it should be as private a proceeding as the conduct of any other sacrament. Will you consent to this, dearest? Will you come alone with me and Mrs Penfold some morning, and take the vows that will bind us together for life?'

'I will do anything you wish me to do,' replied Phyllida. 'Henceforward, I am yours only to command.'

'May my orders never be more than the fulfilment of your own wishes,' said Bernard, embracing her; and then he rose and went to his hotel to dinner, and left the two women in a flutter of excitement at the unexpected turn events had taken.

'I *knew* there was a gentleman in the case,' cried Mrs Penfold, as she half smothered Phyllida in her excess of congratulations. 'I could read the signs in your eyes, and guessed at once you had had a disappointment in love. But, bless you, my child, what made you give the poor fellow the trouble of following you all the way to Gatehead? Though I daresay it will turn out for the best in the end; for a private wedding, in my opinion, is far more agreeable than a public one, and no one can blame Mr Freshfield for wishing to keep it holy; but why you didn't accept such a charming, well-mannered young man on the spot I can't imagine. And with a couple of thousand a-year of his own, too, and more coming in at his mother's death. Phyllida, my dear, you must have been crazy!'

'I only asked for a month to decide in,' said the girl. 'I suppose I always knew I should accept him (in the end), but I never thought of his money, cousin Penfold, nor even of his appearance! He is so earnest and so right thinking that I—I feel he is far too good for me.'

'Ah, well, my dear, that's a very proper feeling for a wife to begin her married life with; but you'll find it wear off in time. I remember when Mr Penfold first proposed to me, I fancied I should never be able to look to his dinners and the getting up of his shirts as he had been used to have them, but I found it all came easy enough when I was once mistress of his house. And so will you—and you'll make a first-rate parson's wife, take my word for it. But fancy your being married from my poor little place in Gatehead, instead of Charlotte's fine cottage *ornée* in Bluemere. Won't she be mad when she hears of it?'

'She will, indeed,' cried Phyllida, with sudden glee. 'They'll be mad all round! For, do you know, cousin Penfold, they thought me so wicked in Bluemere, because I didn't go to church, that the other ladies looked at me as if I were a strange animal, and cousin Pinner invited the parson to come and convert me!'

'And he *has* converted you, my dear, there's no doubt of that!' exclaimed the elder lady; 'but, Phyllida, I hope it is not true that you don't like

going to church, because that will look very bad in
a parson's wife, and, I feel sure, will be a cause of
annoyance to Mr Freshfield.'

'Oh, cousin Penfold, do you think I would
annoy him?' asked the girl, with her soft eyes
full of tears. 'No, not for worlds; and of course
I shall go to church when he does, for the pleasure of looking at him.'

'I am not sure that that is a right motive for
attending divine worship, my dear,' commenced
Mrs Penfold primly; but Phyllida shut her mouth
with a kiss.

'Don't talk like that, please. You do look so
like cousin Pinner when you say such things. I
know it's all true and right, and that *I* am in the
wrong not to think just the same, only I don't,
you know, and so it reminds me of my own
wickedness and makes me unhappy. Let us talk
about my clothes instead. They will need a lot
of consultation, for do you know, cousin Penfold,
I have only about eight pounds left, and I know
that will buy very little. So I must just get a
nice dress to be married in, and let the rest go.'

'My dear, that is very awkward,' said Miss
Penfold, looking puzzled; 'I never thought of
it; but you cannot be married without some
new clothes—it is impossible.'

'That is nonsense, cousin. If I am to be
married at all, I must be married as I am, because I have no more money.'

'We must find ways and means, Phyllida. It
is not much I can give you, but still I have a
few pounds in the Savings Bank, and Charlotte
ought, I am sure, to contribute a liberal sum towards your trousseau.'

'Cousin Penfold, of what are you thinking?

Do you imagine I would be so mean as to touch a halfpenny of the little provision you have put by for yourself, and after you so generously received me in your house? No, indeed! I would starve first! Neither would I accept anything from cousin Pinner. She does not love me, and I would not lay myself under an obligation to her.'

'But, my child what are you to do? Some one must provide you with such things. Mr Freshfield was thoughtful enough to give me a hint on the subject himself, and tell me to make what use of his purse I chose ; but, perhaps you are too proud to owe it to him either.'

'I am too proud to owe it to any one,' replied the girl. 'If Bernard insists upon marrying me, as King Cophetua did the beggar maid, he must marry me in rags. I will buy a nice travelling dress and hat with my money, that I may not disgrace him outwardly, and for the rest I will wait till I have the right to accept his bounty.'

Mrs Penfold was unable to make Phyllida change her mind, so the simple wardrobe with which she travelled to Gatehead was repacked, to be ready to accompany her on her wedding tour.

Bernard Freshfield was a very fond and happy lover during those few days of waiting, and as Phyllida sat with him on the beach, or strolled along the glowworm-lighted cliffs, and listened to the outpourings of his pure and high-toned mind, she felt sometimes terribly afraid, and sometimes deliciously happy, to think that her life would be so soon inextricably mingled with his own.

Mrs Penfold trusted her to order the dress in

which she was to be married and leave Gatehead with her husband, but was horrified on its being sent home to find that it was made of some black material.

'My dear,' she exclaimed, 'you can never wear this!'

'Why not?' demanded Phyllida, with wide-open eyes.

'*Black*, my dear! *black* at a wedding. Why, it's the most unlucky thing in the world, and will bring death to all your hopes of happiness.'

Phyllida's face grew pallid as a lily, whilst her eyes blazed with a sudden premonition of ill.

'Take it away,' she cried hysterically; 'burn it, do anything you like with the horrid thing. I would sooner be married now in one of Sarah's print frocks.

But Bernard was close at hand to soothe and quiet her.

'Please, Mrs Penfold,' he said, 'don't put such silly ideas in my little girl's head. Do you know that if I have contempt for one thing above another, it is for superstition. How can a colour possibly affect our life's happiness? It depends solely on ourselves and the goodness of God! If Phyllida wishes to please me she will wear this dress at our marriage, if only to prove that she is above such foolish fancies.'

'You are quite, *quite* sure, Bernard, that there is nothing in it?' demanded Phyllida, still trembling.

'Quite, *quite* sure my darling,' he repeated, as he drew her to him; and Phyllida wore the sombre dress on the day of her wedding as he had desired her to do. But Mrs Penfold's fears were not to be so easily allayed.

'I wouldn't have had it happen for a five-pound

note,' she confided to Sarah in the kitchen ; 'however, he wishes it, and he's a clergyman, so of course one's mouth is stopped. But I shall never feel so comfortable about this marriage as I did, and—you mark my words, Sarah—misfortune will come upon them in one shape or another before many months have gone over their heads.'

However, they were married one morning as early as custom would permit, and walked straight from the church to the railway station, looking as happy as if they were driving off in a carriage and four, pursued by old slippers and showers of rice. Phyllida still voted for the country and quiet, *vice* the bustle and sights of town ; therefore her husband carried her off to Lynton, in Devonshire, where they could enjoy the beauties of nature and each other's society to their heart's content.

And Mrs Penfold, notwithstanding the handsome presents which Bernard gave her in return for her kindness to Phyllida, felt very lonely when the beautiful face that had brightened her home for ten short days was gone again, and almost wished the parson had never found his way to Gatehead. Meanwhile things were rather dull in Bluemere. Miss Janet Muckheep was quite as annoyed as Mrs Freshfield at the sudden disappearance of her son, and notwithstanding the absence of all ' cairnal procleevities ' in her composition, exhibited decided ill-temper at the derangement of her plans.

' Hoot, Mrs Fraichfield !' she ejaculated ; 'sin your meen-ister sonnie ha' sic ill manners as to bide awa' fra Breear-wud whiles we stay at Blue Mount, it's time that Bella and I gang oor ways to Barrick-gallagas.'

' But why should my son's absence shorten your stay, dear Miss Janet, when you know how honoured

I feel by your visit here ?   I do not know but what Bernard will soon return.   He is only gone to the seaside for a little change.   I think the dear boy may be suffering from suspense and anxiety on a certain subject,' said Mrs Freshfield, with a meaning glance at the inanimate Bella. 'and has left home to collect his thoughts a little.   He may have conceived hopes which he fears may not be realised.'

'Ay,' said Miss Janet, 'but it's no the way to ken a lassie's mind to rin awa' fra the varry seight of her.   And I steel say, we ha' better be movin' hamewards, Mrs Fraichfield.   Blue Mount is na the anely hoose wha the doors stan' open to receive the seester and dairghter of the Laird of Muckheep; nor your meenester son the anely carle wha'll be prood to mix his bluid wi' that of the kings o' Scotland.   And so we'll be leavin' you the morrow, an' sic Mr Fraichfield ha' a mind to the dairghter o' the Muckheeps, he maun find his ain way to Barrick-gallagas Cairstle.'

'So foolish of your brother.' moaned Mrs Freshfield in confidence to Laura, as the carriage which conveyed the Muckheeps to Westertown rolled down the avenue ; 'and such a chance to miss !   I am sure Miss Janet was inclined to look favourably on his suit, and that sweet girl has been trained to obey her aunt in all things.   If Bernard had but remained and paid Bella a little attention, they would have been engaged before they parted.'

'I am very glad he didn't,' replied Laura bluntly. 'Mamma, how *can* you wish for such a thing ?   To see Bernie married to that red-checked booby of a girl !   Why, her accent alone is enough to set one's teeth on edge.   I'm sure I hope my brother has better taste. I know if he married Bella Muckheep *I* would never set foot in Briarwood.'

'Laura, I am surprised at you, after all my teaching and exhortation and care! How can you speak of a dear, Christian girl in such terms, and one with the oldest blood in Scotland running in her veins? Do you know that the lairds o' Muckheep rank as princes of the soil in their native country?'

'Soiled princes,' laughed Laura, irreverently; 'well, mamma, if the oldest blood in Scotland was to be recognised by its colour, I might be able to judge of its purity by the purple bloom on Bella's cheeks. Her complexion after dinner was just like pickled cabbage. But I must be content to accept the truth on your authority. Any way, I don't want to see it mixed with ours. A troop of little Bellas at the rectory would be "quite too awfully awful."'

'If you are going to take refuge in slang, Laura,' replied Mrs Freshfield loftily, 'we will drop the subject. But I must say this is not the way in which I expected my children to receive my most honoured guests. My son leaves Bluemere without even bidding them farewell, and my daughter'— witheringly—'my daughter ridicules to my face the most virtuous and religious young lady I ever had the privilege of meeting!'

'Oh, I know nothing against her virtue or her religion,' laughed Laura, 'although for aught I saw of either of them she might as well have had none. To me, Bella Muckheep is simply a very stupid young woman, who has been rendered more so than was natural, by never having been allowed to exercise her own faculties. However, as you say, mamma, pray let us change the subject, for we shall never agree upon it. Isn't it strange that we have not heard again from Bernie. It is nearly a fortnight now since he went away. I wonder if he is still at that place—what was it?—Gatehead, from which he first wrote.'

'I don't know, my dear, I am sure. Your brother has not condescended to make me the confidante of his proceedings.'

'Bernie always hated letter-writing, mamma ; but I think we must hear from him again soon. Ah, there is the old postman coming up the avenue. Three to one that he brings the letter we want. I will go and meet him.'

And away flew Laura down the carriage drive, with bounding steps. like a girl let loose from school. Mrs Freshfield looked after her with pride, and yet she sighed. She really loved these bright, outspoken. honest children. which she had brought into the world, but her own training had been so conventional that she was unable to reconcile their mirth, and apparently light treatment of serious subjects, with any deeper feeling. The religion she had been brought up in was like Miss Janet's—a religion of darkness and devils and hell. She had but the poorest conception of the goodness and love of the Almighty, and believed that He sat in judgment over the world, for the simple purpose of trying how many unfortunate mortals He could catch tripping, and condemn to eternal pains. A religion of brightness and beauty, and a Father's watchful love, such as Bernard held, she shook her head at, as an over confidence not far removed from actual sin. And, as for Laura, she could not believe but that the unfortunate girl was utterly unregenerate, and would remain so until reclaimed by some fearful loss or bodily

suffering. Mrs Freshfield's was truly a religion
and nothing more — a certain course of action
strictly adhered to, for fear of eternal damnation.
But as for the faith that Bernard had in God—
the faith that if his human wisdom led him wrong,
he had a Father who could make allowance for
the defects in His own creation—of that his mother
knew nothing, and so she was a most unhappy
Christian, who went moaning through this world
in anticipation of the torments of the next.

Laura came bounding up the drive again, holding a letter above her head, in token that her hopes
had been realised.

'Here it is, mamma,' she cried, as she came up
to the old lady. 'I knew there would be a letter
from Bernie to-day. And the postmark is Lynton.
He has got down to Devon. I thought he would
soon tire of the seaside at this season. There must
be too many " Bobs and 'Arrys " there just now
to suit his taste.'

She thrust the letter into her mother's lap as she
spoke.

'Be quick and read it, mamma! I am dying
to hear what our boy is about.'

Mrs Freshfield broke open the envelope, and
commenced to peruse her son's epistle. She read
part of the first page, and then she turned to the
second and third in an aimless sort of way, and
leaving them, began again at the beginning, whilst
her face twitched, and she bit her lip and changed
all sorts of colours. Laura, who was watching her
earnestly, grew quite alarmed.

'Mamma! mamma! what is the matter?' she
asked quickly.

Mrs Freshfield's answer was to drop the letter
in her lap and begin to cry. The tears of the

young are of little consequence, they come and
go like a storm in summer; but it is a terrible thing
to see an old person cry. Laura dropped on her
knees by her mother's side.

'Darling!' she exclaimed affectionately, 'what
can affect you in this manner? Is Bernie ill or
unhappy, or in any difficulty? Oh, mother dear!
you can't think what I am suffering. Don't keep
me in suspense!'

'Read! read!' ejaculated Mrs Freshfield, pointing to the letter.

Laura seized it instantly.

'Am I to read it aloud, mamma?'

'Yes! I must learn to bear it. Read me what
your misguided brother says.'

And Laura began,—

'"QUEEN'S HOTEL, LYNTON.

'"MY DEAREST MOTHER,—I have something to
tell you that I fear may startle—though I trust
it may not grieve you. And let me premise what
a dear good mother you have ever been to me,
and how much I love and reverence you in return. Don't think that I ever lose sight of your
happiness in any action of my life; but then I
have such a strong belief that my happiness must
necessarily be yours also."

'Mother, dear what is there to make you cry
in this?' demanded Laura, stopping short in her
perusal of the letter. 'Bernie writes as he always
does to you, in the most loving and dutiful
strain, like the very best of sons, as he has ever
been.'

'Go on—read what he tells me,' replied Mrs
Freshfield, in a tone of despair.

'"You have often expressed a wish that I should

marry again, and I have felt myself great need of the comfort and rest that a happy marriage can alone afford a man in my position. What will you say when I tell you that I have taken a wife? Your first feeling will be, perhaps, a rather natural annoyance that I did not previously consult you, and that I should have married away from Bluemere—"

'*Married!*' cried Laura, dropping the letter again, 'really and actually *married!* Oh, my dear, *dear* Bernie, how I do hope he will be truly happy at last.'

'I am afraid there is little chance of that, Laura,' said her mother solemnly; 'an union entered into without the blessing of either parents or friends can never be a really happy one.'

'I think my brother believes that the blessing of God is all that is actually necessary,' replied her daughter, 'and he has that, I am sure. And why should he not have ours as well?'

'Will you be good enough to proceed with Bernard's letter?' said Mrs Freshfield, who having nothing to say in refutation of Laura's last remark, considered it advisable to return to the grievance in hand. 'I confess I should like to know *who* it is that has seduced your brother to forget his duty.'

'Oh, to be sure; who *can* it be?' exclaimed Laura curiously, 'let me see—where was I? Oh, here.'

'"That I should have married away from Bluemere, but I had my own reasons for acting as I have done. To consult you in the matter when you had formed such different projects concerning me, would have been simply to raise a discussion which might have produced ill feeling between us, and with regard to Bluemere, I had long determined that I would never again undergo the horrors of a formal wedding amongst my parishioners. Added to this, I made up my mind to marry Phyllida Moss—"

'Who?' cried Mrs Freshfield with horror.

'Mamma! mamma! don't look like that—you frighten me. Yes; it really is *Phyllida Moss*, the girl who came to Briarwood with Mrs Pinner. I heard she had left the village a few days before Bernard. It must have been a concerted plan between them, and—good gracious me, mamma, he has only known her about three weeks!'

'Get me my bonnet and shawl, and order round the pony chaise,' exclaimed Mrs Freshfield indignantly; 'this is some doing of that wicked woman Mrs Pinner, and I will go and tell her so to her face. She always had a sly catty look to me.'

'Pray, mamma, don't do any such thing. You are not in a fit state to discuss this matter with any stranger; besides, we don't know that Mrs Pinner is even aware of the event. I met her yesterday, and she said her cousin was staying with her sister. Listen to the rest of the letter, mamma. It may contain some consolation.'

'Phyllida Moss!' ejaculated Mrs Freshfield; 'a girl of whom we know nothing, who may be a heathen or a Mahomedan. Why, I heard your brother himself call her a barbarian.'

'Oh, that was intended as a compliment, mamma. I saw Bernie admired her the day we met at Briarwood. And she is very lovely—you will allow that—you said yourself you had never seen such a pair of eyes.'

'Beauty is vain, Laura, and a fine pair of eyes

will not give us admittance into heaven. My
poor, misguided son! Led away by one of the
daughters of Heth to take part in a disgraceful
elopement.'

'Hardly that, mamma. You must not forget
that Bernie was twenty-eight last birthday, and has
no occasion to elope with any one. But shall I
finish the letter?'

'Yes, yes, go on. I may as well hear the
miserable story to the end.'

'"Added to this, I made up my mind to marry
Phyllida Moss rather suddenly, and I could hardly
expect those who do not know her as I do to
enter into the feelings which caused my resolution.
I am not going to expose myself to your ridicule
by indulging in a lover's rhapsody upon the merits
of my young wife; but you have seen her face,
and it is but an index to her mind. Phyllida is
pure and innocent as a child, and entirely devoted
to me.

'"I look forward to a life of complete contentment in her society, and feel for the first time that
a dual existence can be truly one. I do not wish
to remain away longer than is necessary, and hope
to take my wife home to Briarwood next week.
Let me have a line to say that she will find a
mother and sister to welcome her to Blue Mount,
and I shall be entirely happy.—Ever, dearest
mother, your dutiful son,

"Bernard Freshfield."'

'You will send him that, mother, will you not?'
cried Laura eagerly, as she finished the letter.
'You will write to dear Bernie and tell him that
all *we* can do to increase the happiness of his
married life is his without the asking. And, for

my own part, I *feel* we shall like her,' continued the warm-hearted girl. 'I took such a fancy to her sweet, sad face that day at Briarwood ; and there was something in her, I can hardly tell what it was, but very different from other girls of her age—as if she had passed through some great experience that made her look down upon idle chatter and gossip and games. That is the right sort of wife for our Bernie, for he hates the ordinary type of young lady. Don't you think we shall love Phyllida, mamma ? We *must*, you know, for Bernie's sake.'

'We will *try* to do so, my dear, at all events,' replied Mrs Freshfield ; 'but whether she will prove worthy of our affection is an unanswerable question. If your brother chooses to marry a girl he has only known for a month, he must take the consequences. But I will never forgive Mrs Pinner for having kept us in ignorance of what was about to happen.'

And, notwithstanding all her daughter's efforts to prevent her, the old lady insisted upon being driven in state to Mrs Pinner's cottage as soon as ever the carriage returned from Westertown. She found that lady in a very gay and festive cap, streaming with lilac ribbons, and a shawl woven of many colours, like Joseph's coat, upon her shoulders, poring over a cheerful publication, en-titled 'The Opening of the Sixth Seal, or the Final State of the Wicked.' She came forward with alacrity to welcome her visitor, but Mrs Freshfield loftily waved aside her proffered hand.

'I see that you have put on your wedding finery to receive me, Mrs Pinner,' the lady of Blue Mount commenced with icy dignity ; 'but I should have considered it more *decent* and suitable to the occasion, if you had appeared in a garb of mourning.'

Poor Mrs Pinner, to whom this address was as intelligible as if it had been delivered in Arabic, could only gasp in answer, 'I really do not understand you, Mrs Freshfield.'

'*Not understand me!*' exclaimed her visitor. 'Oh, do not add duplicity to your concealment, Mrs Pinner. You must have known the preconcerted purpose for which your niece (or whatever she is) left Bluemere.'

'My niece—do you mean my cousin Phyllida Moss? She is staying with my sister Maria at Gatehead.'

'And do you mean to tell me that Phyllida Moss has not written to you, nor your sister Maria, nor my son, nor anybody?'

'Written to me! Why? On what subject? Mrs Freshfield. What can you mean? I have heard nothing from Gatehead for the last fortnight.'

'Then, if I am to believe you, Mrs Pinner, you have been as wilfully kept in ignorance as myself, and this misfortune must have been brought about through the machinations of your unprincipled sister at Gatehead.'

'Oh dear! oh dear! What has she done?' cried Mrs Pinner piteously.

'*Done!* She has just done this. She has married your cousin Phyllida Moss to *my son*, the rector of Bluemere.'

The 'Final State of the Wicked' went down to the ground with a crash.

'*What!*' ejaculated Mrs Pinner, in ear-piercing tones.

'You may well ask *what!*' replied Mrs Freshfield, sinking into a chair. 'I have just received a letter from my son, dated from Devonshire, where he is staying with your cousin, and they have been married for a fortnight.'

'Oh! that wicked, wicked girl!' cried Mrs Pinner, tumbling into another chair. 'I might have guessed what would come of her never going to church, or reading the Scriptures, and all her other heathen, godless ways. And my sister, too, to dare to consent to such a clandestine proceeding! I always said that Maria was most carnally minded, and needed the rod of divine love to bruise her hard heart before she could take her stand with the elect.'

'And yet you confided Miss Moss to the care of so worldly a person,' said Mrs Freshfield sharply.

'Dear Mrs Freshfield! What could I do? The girl was her own mistress, and insisted upon leaving me! The ways of grace did not suit her —she sighed for the leeks and garlic of Egypt, and her example was not edifying to the young creatures that come to my house. But little did I guess the purpose that was in her mind. Married to Mr Freshfield! the wife of our esteemed and reverend minister! He to whom we all look up as to an oracle, married to Phyllida Moss! Oh, it is quite incredible! Like some fearful dream.'

'If it appears so incredible to you, you may fancy what it does to me, Mrs Pinner! I shall not easily get over the shock I received this morning. My son is of course his own master, and should be able to decide for himself in such matters ; but I cannot but believe that in this instance his eyes have been blinded and his judgment led astray.'

'Led astray! I should indeed say so, and by that artful, designing girl too. What will the parish say? and poor dear Miss Warren, it will go near to break her heart. She positively dotes so upon the minister. And to think that *Phyllida Moss* is to be the mistress of Briarwood! It is too, too dreadful! It would serve her right if all Bluemere were to cut her. But you must absolve *me* from all complicity in this dreadful affair. I stood guarantee for neither her moral nor religious training. I told our dear minister plainly what a heathen she was, and that no words nor exhortations of mine made any impression upon her! Oh, she is the most ungodly creature, Mrs Freshfield; careless and irreverent to a degree! It is shocking to think of her having *presumed* to accept so exalted a position as that of your daughter-in-law and your son's wife.'

But Mrs Pinner had gone far enough in Mrs Freshfield's opinion, and at this juncture she pulled her up sharply. It had suddenly occurred to the rector's mother that it was slightly undignified for her to sit and listen to abuse of a girl who (whatever her faults might be) was indissolubly the wife of her son.

'There, there, Mrs Pinner, I think that is sufficient; you never said a word about this to me before, and I daresay your imagination is running away with you now. If you had no hand in planning this marriage, the least said about it the better; and if you take my advice, you will not repeat what you have said to me to your neighbours. My son is very determined, you know, and it may make things unpleasant in Bluemere, if it comes to his ears that his wife's character has been discussed in this familiar way amongst his parishioners. He intends to bring Mrs Bernard Freshfield home to Briarwood next week, and it behoves us all to receive her in a manner befitting our minister's choice. Whether it will prove a happy marriage for him is quite another thing, but I am sure he will be quick to resent the least affront offered to his wife.'

Mrs Pinner was sharp enough to take the cue.

'Of course, dear Mrs Freshfield, and I should never *dream* of mentioning what I said to any one but yourself, and especially when every girl in Bluemere has been setting her cap at the minister for the last two years. I am naturally very proud to think his choice should have fallen on my little cousin, who (notwithstanding a wayward disposition) has many excellent qualities, which will, doubtless, under dear Mr Freshfield's training, render her in time all that could be desired as a minister's wife.'

But Mrs Freshfield was not to be taken in by this sudden change of opinion. She gave Mrs Pinner some supplementary cautions, and then returned to Laura's presence, metaphorically wringing her hands.

'A nice thing your brother has done,' she commenced complainingly—it was a remarkable coincidence that, in these confidences between mother and daughter, whenever Bernard did wrong he was Laura's brother, and whenever he did right he was Mrs Freshfield's son. 'Mrs Pinner, who had that unhappy girl under her care whilst she was in Bluemere, says she is a perfect heathen— a godless, irreverent heathen — and everybody in the parish knows it.'

'I should like to wring Mrs Pinner's neck,' cried Laura. 'What business has she to speak of Bernard's wife in such terms? Why did you listen to her, mamma? I should have got up and left the room. Now that the marriage is a completed thing, we shall only cut our own throats by not making the best of it! I intend to call at every house in Bluemere and say it was the very thing we secretly longed for.'

'Just what I told Mrs Pinner, my dear, replied Mrs Freshfield, veering round like a weathercock. ' I took her severely to task for daring to mention anything but what was favourable of a lady whom my son has honoured by making his wife. But she is an impertinent old gossip, and I hope that Bernard will not encourage her visits to Briarwood.'

'I am afraid Bernie will be led entirely by Phyllida's wishes—at all events for the present,' laughed Laura ; 'our poor boy is very much in the chains,. mamma, and all that remains for us to do as good friends and Christians, is to lend our aid to rivet them as tightly on him as possible. Don't let us forget that it is *his* happiness that is at stake,' continued Laura, her bright eyes filled with tears of affection ; 'and make up our minds to see only what is good in Phyllida for Bernie's sake. And I'll tweak the ears of anybody whom I hear saying a word against her,' she concluded, with a sudden change of feeling.

Of course the parson's marriage was the one theme of discussion in Bluemere for many days after that. Never had more tea been drunk or muffins buttered, in the course of a single week, in the memory of the oldest inhabitant. The ladies, married and single, rushed from house to house, retailing the extraordinary occurrence over and over again, with such scraps of information as Mrs Pinner had gathered from her sister

Mrs Penfold. Lamentations ran high, and prognostications of evil were plentifully exchanged between the far-seeing ones. The young ladies were naturally in despair, and only the poor really rejoiced that the man they loved had struck out a new source of happiness for himself. Everybody in the village had been very anxious to see how Miss Annie Warren would bear the news, for her hopes with regard to Briarwood had been patent to the world. Many were the ambassadors, therefore, who were sent to her mother's house to ascertain, if possible, her feelings on the subject, and to gloat over, with true feminine charity, the disappointment which they trusted she would be unable to conceal.

But Miss Warren was too sharp for them, and not a soul caught a glimpse of her countenance until she had had time to place a mask upon it; but then the first thing she did was to walk over to Blue Mount with her congratulations, and deliver a panegyric on the bride.

'Such a pretty creature,' she said, in speaking of Phyllida. 'I am sure, Mrs Freshfield, that in your wildest dreams you never imagined a more beautiful daughter-in-law. She will be quite an ornament to Briarwood, and we shall all have to mind our personal appearance when she rules Bluemere. I used to say that everything Miss Moss—I mean Mrs Bernard Freshfield—put on, became her.'

'Yes, she has a lovely face, there is no doubt of that, Miss Warren,' replied Mrs Freshfield; 'and if she is not very conversant with parish duties at first, I shall look to you to give her a few lessons. You are quite my dear son's right hand (as you were poor Alice's), and I am sure he will be only too much obliged to you if you will make Phyllida as useful as yourself. He writes me she is a perfect child in innocence. Therefore we need not doubt she will prove as childlike in following her husband's wishes.'

Miss Annie Warren coughed, but that was all the answer she directly made to the old lady's remark.

'I shall be ready to help Mr Freshfield, as I have ever been,' she said, as she rose, basket on arm, to take her leave, 'whether it be with the parish or anything else. But I *fancy*, from what I have seen of her, that Mrs Bernard will do the parochial work her own way, and stick to it. Good-bye, Mrs Freshfield. We are decorating the church with white flowers for the minister next Sunday. He will receive the heartiest congratulations on his marriage from every one of his parishioners.'

And so Miss Annie Warren craftily concealed her feelings in her own breast. But they lay there unsubdued all the same, and only she knew what they were.

CHAPTER IX.

MRS FRESHFIELD having apparently condoned the irregularity of her son's second marriage, all Bluemere prepared itself to receive the bride and bridegroom with open arms. They would have rung the church bells, and decorated the village

with triumphal arches and floral welcomes, had
Bernard been weak enough to disclose the day
of his return. But he much feared the display
of some such manifestation, and kept the matter
a secret, even from his mother. So that she and
Laura were sitting in the drawing - room one
afternoon, waiting for the announcement of
dinner, and actually speculating on the proba-
bilities of Bernard's speedy advent, when they
looked up and saw him standing on the threshold, with Phyllida upon his arm. They had
driven over from Westertown in a hired vehicle,
and managed to reach Bluemere without a soul
being cognisant of the event. As they walked
up the carriage drive together, Bernard had said
to his wife,—

'Are you nervous, Phyllida? Does the idea of
meeting my mother make you afraid?' and she
had looked up in his face and answered,—

'Afraid! No; why should I be? If I was not
afraid of marrying you, I need hardly be so of
meeting your relations. Nothing can unmake me
your wife, can it, Bernard?'

'Nothing, my darling, thank God,' replied Freshfield. 'You are mine for ever and ever.'

So, as they stood upon the threshold together,
smiling, they looked more like people who feel
their presence brings a pleasant surprise than
offenders returning home to sue for pardon.

'Bernie!' cried Laura, in a tone of rapture, as
she jumped up and ran into her brother's arms.
'Oh! how delightful it is to see you again.
Mamma and I were just wondering when you
would return,' and then as freely, if not as
ardently, Laura embraced her new sister. 'Dear
Phyllida, we must be the very best and nearest of

friends, for I feel somewhat I shall love you very much.'

'Don't be too sure,' replied Phyllida, smiling. 'I have only one merit, and that is, I am Bernard's wife.'

'And that would be all-sufficient,' said Laura heartily. She forgot for the moment how powerless the fact had proved to make her love the girl who mouldered in the churchyard.

But Bernard, who had got over the first rather tearful greeting which Mrs Freshfield bestowed upon him, now took Phyllida's hand and led her up to his mother.

'This is *my wife*,' he said gravely. 'I will not ask my friends to love her until they do so for her own sake, but I want them to remember always that, in my eyes, *she is sacred*.'

Mrs Freshfield had not quite made up her mind whether she should receive the bride as if she were a duchess or a milk-maid, that is, if she should curtsey to the ground with mock humility, or express her welcome in the most familiar of nods. But Bernard's address contained so much of warning, that the weaker nature succumbed to his. She took her daughter-in-law's hand, and kissed her on the cheek as she said,—

'My dear, I do not anticipate having to love you for any reason, excepting that you are yourself.'

'You are all too kind to me,' faltered Phyllida, in return.

She was looking very lovely in some soft grey costume, that her enraptured husband had purchased for her, and when (the travellers having shaken the dust from their garments and removed the effects of a railway journey) the family sat down to the dinner-table, the ladies of Blue Mount were compelled to admit that a fairer guest than the second Mrs Bernard Freshfield had never graced their board. The old servants who had been in the family for any number of years could hardly take their eyes off her as they moved about the room; and Bernard's spirits rose to a most unclerical height as he observed the favourable impression she made.

As for Phyllida herself, except for an occasional glance of affection at her husband, she seemed perfectly unmoved by the silent homage paid her. She neither blushed nor giggled; no consciousness of her position as a bride made her hurried or nervous. She leant back in her chair as easy and unconstrained in her manners as if she had lived at Blue Mount all her life. Yet Laura could not help observing that the pathetic expression she had marked in Miss Moss's countenance had not deserted that of Mrs Bernard Freshfield, and that Phyllida still looked more like a lovely martyr than a happy bride. She admired her sister-in-law all the more for being so different from ordinary young ladies, but the look in her face haunted her and raised a host of conjectures which she dare not breathe to any one but herself. Almost as soon as dinner was over, Bernard asked for the carriage to take them to Briarwood, as he was afraid the long railway journey had fatigued his wife.

'And do you mean to say Mrs Garnett does not know of your arrival?' said Laura. 'Why, Bernie, she'll have a fit. She has sent over here every day for the last week to ask if we had heard when you were coming home.'

'I told her she might expect us any night,' replied her brother, 'so she is sure to be prepared with all we shall want, and I knew if I let her know the exact time, she would confide it to all Bluemere. I want Phyllida to have a day or two in which to become acquainted with her new home, before she is seized upon by all the cackling old women of the village.'

'You will have a very beautiful home, my dear,' said Mrs Freshfield solemnly to Phyllida, 'and I trust you will keep it so. There is, to my mind, no more fitting occupation for a young wife than the personal superintendence of her servants' daily work. The eye of a mistress is a better guide than any amount of experience.'

'I don't agree with you there, mother,' exclaimed Bernard, who was inducting himself into his overcoat; 'and I beg you won't upset all the ideas with which I have been imbuing Phyllida for the last fortnight. The fittest occupation for a young wife is making love to her husband, and that is all she is going to do for the next ten years.'

At this Laura laughed merrily, and Mrs Freshfield looked scandalised.

'But, my dear Bernard, surely you would not advise Phyllida to entirely neglect her household avocations?'

'No, I don't advise, I *order* her to neglect them. I am not going to have her turned into a housekeeper or head cook. What do I pay old Garnett fifty pounds a-year for, if it is not to take all such domestic worries off my wife's hands?'

'But, my dear son, you must think of others as well as yourselves. Your wife is placed in a very prominent position, and will assuredly be looked up to as an example by all the ladies in Bluemere.'

'Oh dear, I hope not!' cried Phyllida.

'But it is the case, my dear,' continued Mrs Freshfield, 'and no wishes can alter it. A clergyman's wife must live for the parish, and not for herself. Every mother in Bluemere should be able to point to you when she wishes to exemplify to her daughters what a virtuous and useful life culminates in.'

Phyllida looked timid, and moved closer to her husband. Bernard bit his lip, and as soon as he saw his opportunity rushed in with his usual impetuosity.

'Look here, mother dear! I know you mean it all for kindness, but please don't let us have any more of that. It is true that I have accepted the parish, worse luck; and am bound in many things—I may say in most things—to sacrifice my own natural inclinations in deference to my position. But my wife has bound herself only to me; and, once for all, to prevent any future misunderstandings on the subject, I do not intend to let her have anything to do with the parish or its affairs. I hate and detest the model parson's wife who considers it her duty to poke her nose into every cottage door as if it belonged to herself, and lay her commands upon its inmates as if they were under her rule. I will not have Phyllida do it. I married her for myself—to be the mistress of my house and servants, and my daily, hourly companion and friend, and I don't mean to give her up to any one, not even for a minute.'

'Well, Bernard, all I can say is, that I think you are sadly mistaken on this as on many other subjects,' remarked his mother quietly. She never attempted to argue with her son.

'I am sorry we differ, mother, but friends must

agree to differ sometimes. Another thing that Phyllida and I intend to dispense with is the abomination of wedding calls. Please let Bluemere know that there will be no particular day on which they can visit Briarwood, and find my wife dressed in a prismatic silk, sitting up to be looked at behind a silver basket piled with indigestible cake. We shall always be pleased to receive our friends, and when we are at home they will be sure to find us either in the garden, or the stables, or the kennels, or the piggeries, or employed in some other occupation equally congenial to our mutual tastes. So, good-night, mother dear, and good-night, Laura. Come over to dinner with us to-morrow, and see how we look sitting in state at our own table. Come, love, it is time we were off.'

And Bernard handed his wife into the carriage, and drove away with her. Mrs Freshfield returned to the drawing-room, dismally shaking her head.

'Laura! Laura! I am afraid this is all terribly irregular.'

'Not the marriage, I hope, mamma?'

'My dear, you know what I mean. I always considered your brother far too lax with poor Alice. He allowed Miss Warren to usurp all the parochial duties, and it will be worse still with Phyllida. He will ruin her with indulgence. To spend her days in the garden or the stables or the kennel—you heard what he said—I ask you candidly, *is* that the proper way for a clergyman's wife to amuse herself?'

'I should think the proper thing for her was to do exactly as her husband wishes. I don't understand a grown woman being ruined by indulgence, mamma. Depend on it, many more have been ruined by repression. And I don't think Phyllida could do parish work if she tried. She doesn't look that sort of person, does she?'

'No, not at all that sort of person—anything, in fact, but that sort of person,' reiterated Mrs Freshfield with fearfully mysterious meaning as she sighed profoundly.

Laura thought it best to change the subject. As the carriage drove into the gates of Briarwood, Bernard turned towards his wife and took her in his arms.

'We are nearly home,' he said. May it ever prove a true *home* to you, my own dear love, a true refuge and haven from every earthly ill and annoyance. If *I* can make it so, it shall.'

Phyllida buried her face in his.

'Oh, Bernard! you are too good and trusting. Suppose—supposing, after all, that I should prove a disappointment to you?'

'I do not think that is possible, but were it so, the remembrance of the happiness you have already given me would go far to soften it. But do not fear that I expect too much from you. We are neither of us faultless, and as I hope you will exercise forbearance towards me, so do I anticipate sometimes having to call mine into action for your sake. We shall have, like all other mortals, to contend against many disadvantages in one another. We may not hold the same opinions ; we may not like the same people ; occasionally our tempers will clash and cause us some uneasiness. But we love each other, and in all the rest I shall leave you free—free to exercise your own ideas and go your own way—perfectly satisfied if from that way you return to the shelter of my arms, and find an answer for every vexatious question of life in my never-failing love.'

This was the welcome she received to Briarwood, and as the carriage stopped beneath the portico, and Phyllida was handed into the luxurious hall, and saw the servants over whom she was thenceforth to reign as mistress, she seemed to realise, for the first time, what a stupendous change had taken place for her, since but a few weeks back she had been thrown on the protection of Mrs Pinner. Yet she turned from it all and threw herself into her husband's arms, and assured him a thousand times, —'It is *you—you* only that I want.'

She would have resigned her new possessions, in the first triumph of feeling them to be hers, for a simple luxury that her waiting-maids enjoyed with impunity and thought nothing of—'a conscience free from offence.'

The rector had not been within the walls of Briarwood twelve hours before every one in Bluemere knew he had returned ; but as no notification of the fact was made public, they were obliged to control their impatience to see the bride until she should appear in church on Sunday. Only Mrs Pinner was bold enough to invade the sanctity of their home without an invitation, and she had completely changed her tactics in speaking of Phyllida, and laid claim to double the amount of consideration she received before, in right of her cousinship to the parson's wife.

Knowing that Phyllida's ideas of religion, if honest, were rather peculiar, Bernard had purposely abstained from expressing the least wish that she should accompany him to church on Sunday, as it was his firm intention, unless he could bias her mind, to leave her actions free.

When he came down on that day, however, preparatory to starting for the morning service, he found her ready dressed and waiting for him in the portico.

'Are you coming with me, my darling?' he said, with pleased surprise.

'Of course I am,' she answered. 'Did you think I should remain at home?'

'I thought very little about it, love, excepting that I wish you to do exactly as you like; and you have told me you do not like going to church.'

'No more I used to—no more I do now, in fact—only I want to go with you.'

'And I am only too delighted to have you, my Phyllida. The church would look very empty to me without your dear face; but I want you to feel quite, quite free in this matter as in all others.'

'No; don't say that,' she whispered, gazing up into his face with sweet, troubled eyes—'don't let me feel free, Bernard, now that I belong to you. *Make* me good, whether I want it or not. You promised you would, and I will try—indeed, I will—if you will only *order* me to do everything that you think is best for me.'

'You dear child,' replied her husband, 'if we all regarded the Almighty with the same feelings with which you regard me, the evangelical Christians might shut up their hell at once.'

'Are you an evangelical Christian, Bernard?' demanded Phyllida.

'No, Phyllida.'

'Do you call yourself High Church, then?'

'I don't call myself anything.'

'But what are you?'

'Your husband, darling; that is quite enough for you; and now if you are coming to church with me we must have the carriage.'

'I can walk, Bernard.'

'I don't wish you to walk. I know many people think it very wicked to use their horses on Sunday, who think nothing of the wickedness of using their servants; but my notions on such subjects are peculiar. And one is that it will do our horses less harm to trot for a couple of miles than it will do my wife. So, go and sit down again until the carriage comes round.'

It would have indeed been a terrible disappointment to Bluemere if Mrs Bernard Freshfield had not appeared in church that morning, although her defalcation would have afforded them just cause for a little extra malice over their tea-cups. Every pew was crowded with eagerly expectant faces as Bernard led his young wife up the aisle and placed her in her seat, and the whispered comments that followed her appearance ran through the congregation like the buzzing of bees. Every woman's bonnet was thrust into the bonnet of her next neighbour, and they would have been struck dumb by the apparition in the parson's pew, except for the pleasure of saying that they were so. Those who had been so unlucky as to only catch sight of her back, asked each other in awestruck tones if it could possibly be Mrs Bernard Freshfield; but when, on changing her position, Phyllida let the whole church have a view of her profile, there could be no longer any doubt on the subject. But what had come to her? What wonderful transformation was this from the somewhat reserved young lady in a black merino dress, who had excited their comments as Mrs Pinner's cousin?

As the service commenced and Phyllida stood up with the rest, the responses went entirely out of their heads. They had expected naturally to see her bloom forth in wedding garments ; but the dress she wore : the golden brown velvet costume, with point-lace ruffles at her throat and wrists, and a couple of yellow roses nestling under her chin, and a broad-brimmed hat of some white, furry material that enframed her sunny hair like a snow-drift—it was the amazement of this style, unknown in Bluemere, that caused so much ir-reverence that morning. Where had she learned to dress in such a manner ? From whom had she acquired the taste ? Who had taught Phyllida Moss to carry her head like a princess, and wear her fashionable garments as though she had never been used to any other ?

They had expected to see her come back blush-ing, confused, and ready to sink under the unex-pected honour conferred upon her, and here she was, receiving the silent homage of their curiosity, as if she had been some earl's daughter who had condescended to marry Mr Freshfield ! It was incredible. Poor Mrs Pinner was assailed from so many quarters at once upon this point, and spoke so much louder than she intended to do in answering her assailants, that Mr Robinson had to cough her down in the middle of the service. But as soon as it was over she had her revenge.

' *Where did she learn to dress so ?* Really, Mrs Norman, one might think my cousin had never been in any society to hear you ask such a ques-tion ! Haven't I told you that her parents lived in St Domingo, and mixed in the highest circles there, which are chiefly composed of French

people, Phyllida tells me, and are of course up
to all the French fashions.'

'But she has such a *peculiar* dress on ! Do you
think it pretty ?' demanded Miss Lacy. 'My
mamma thinks a light-coloured silk would be so
much more appropriate for a bride.'

'Ah, your good mamma has lived in the country
all her life, my dear, and cannot be expected to
know the fashions. My cousin has come straight
from London, remember, so she can hardly be
mistaken.'

'Whether it is the fashion or not, it is a very
extraordinary dress for a minister's wife to appear
at church in,' remarked another young lady spite-
fully. 'I am sure Mr Freshfield must have been
hurt by the evident surprise it occasioned. And
his dear mamma too and Miss Laura, I didn't envy
them having to sit in the same pew with her !'

'You had better not talk at random, Miss
Masters ! I have seen my cousin naturally
(although it was Mr Freshfield's wish that *no one* in
the village but myself and his own relations should
intrude at Briarwood until his wife had appeared
in church), and Phyllida told me only yesterday
that her husband admired that dress so much that
he had ordered one exactly similar to be made for
his sister Laura. But perhaps you will not believe
that I am better informed than yourself, and perhaps my being cousin to Mrs Bernard Freshfield,
and cousin-in-law to the rector, does not warrant
my knowledge of their private affairs,' concluded
Mrs Pinner grandly.

Miss Masters tossed her head.

'I am sure I meant nothing of the sort. If Mr
Freshfield likes his wife to attend church in a
scarlet gown, or no gown at all, it is all the same

to me.   I only expressed the general opinion in
saying her costume was peculiar.   And as for her
hat, I never saw such a thing in my life.   Did
you, Miss Warren ?'

Miss Annie Warren, just issuing from the
church door, was not in the most amiable temper.
It had been a weekly custom of hers during the
lifetime of the late Mrs Freshfield to drive home in
the rector's carriage after the morning service, and
spend the rest of the day at Briarwood.

Alice had liked her society, and Bernard's
affection for his wife had been of too milk-and-
water a description to resent the presence of a
third party.   But he had no intention of allowing
his *têtes-à-tête* with Phyllida to be intruded upon
more than was absolutely necessary.   So that
though Miss Warren waited outside the vestry
door in the old fashion, and would have gladly
renewed her former footing at the rectory, all she
had received from the newly-married couple was a
shake of the hand, and Bernard had driven off,
looking the picture of happiness, leaving her, with
a very empty feeling at her heart, to find her way
back to her friends as best she could.   But Annie
Warren was made of different material from Miss
Lacy or Miss Masters, or any of the other misses
who populated Bluemere.   Her disappointment at
the rector's marriage had been bitter and severe ;
her hatred of the rector's new wife was bitterer
and severer still.   Hers was not a nature to forget
or forgive easily, and there was a trace of Indian
blood in her veins that imbued it with a still more
vindictive instinct ; she could *wait* for her revenge,
but it was not part of her plan to quarrel with Mrs
Pinner, or indeed with any one ; and it would have
been the height of impolicy in her to do anything

to widen the breach which was already yawning between the Freshfields .and herself. So she reproved Miss Masters' unkind speech in a thoroughly Christian-like and womanly way.

'I am surprised,' she said, 'to find that the admirable lessons we have just heard, and the prayers in which we have joined, have had no better effect than to make you discuss hats and dresses, Miss Masters. What can it signify what people wear? What they *do* is of the only real consequence, and we may be quite sure that Mrs Bernard Freshfield's conduct will have the approbation of our dear minister in all things ; may we not, Mrs Pinner?' she added, with a honied smile.

'Indeed we may, my dear,' replied Mrs Pinner, delighted to find so staunch an ally where she least expected it ; 'such a couple you never saw, they are perfectly devoted to each other, and Mr Freshfield seems as if he couldn't do too much for his wife. Have you been to Briarwood yet?'

'No ; I did not like to disturb them so soon after their return, though I *am* such an old friend,' rejoined Miss Annie, who had the greatest difficulty to prevent her eyes flashing the lightning with which they were laden.

'Come up with me this evening, will you? I am sure they will be delighted to see you ; and as for myself, of course, I am always welcome in my own cousin's house. It will be a nice walk for us, and if you will take a cup of tea with me first I shall be very pleased.

'Thank you, dear Mrs Pinner. I will be with you about six o'clock,' replied Miss Warren, who wanted to find out a great deal more about the bride's antecedents than she at present knew.

Meanwhile Bernard and Phyllida, unconscious of

the treat in store for them, having taken their luncheon, sat together on the lawn under the chestnut trees. There were only two services on Sunday in Bluemere, and the curate, Mr Robinson, conducted the afternoon one, therefore when his morning duties were over, Bernard had the rest of the day to himself. Phyllida was lying back in a low chair with her eyes fixed upon the sky ; and her husband had been watching her, and thinking how beautiful she was, for the last ten minutes.

'Phyllida,' he said suddenly, 'I shall have to give you a pew at the back of the pulpit !'

'Why, Bernard ? '

' Because you are too fascinating for a parson's wife, and I keep looking at you instead of my book, and I know I shouldn't. I must try and forget you, my darling, at all events whilst I am reading prayers ; and the only way to do that is to put you out of sight.'

' I would rather not see you either, Bernard. It made me miserable to see you dressed up in that night-gown thing this morning. I wish you could read the prayers in a pretty tweed coat—like the grey one you used to wear at Lynton—with a rose in your buttonhole.'

Bernard laughed.

' I wish I could, too, Phyllida, for I can assure you I dislike the " night-gown " quite as much as you do ! But though I believe my views are as broad as those of most men, I have not yet reached the pitch of appearing in the pulpit in a tweed suit. But how could my surplice affect you to the extent of making you *miserable ?* '

'Oh, it seemed to raise you so high above me. I looked up at your grave face, and I thought, 'What can I have in common with a minister of religion?" It made me feel I can never be good enough for you. Bernie, I like you so much better in a shooting-coat—don't you know! I guess you are nearer to me that way.'

'I guess I can't be nearer to you than I am, you little Yankee!'

Phyllida turned sharply.

'Why do you call me a Yankee?'

'Why, aren't you always telling me that you "*guess*" this and you "*guess*" that?'

'My father had been to America—I suppose that is the reason,' she said nervously.

'I daresay it is, for you have several other Americanisms which you must have picked up from some one with whom you have been familiar. But you are charming, nothwithstanding, Mrs Freshfield.'

She smiled at him, but still she sighed, and lay quiet for a few minutes more, gazing up into the sky.

'Bernard, why is it necessary for everybody to think the same?'

'What do you mean, Phyllida?'

'Why may not everybody try to get to heaven in his own way? Why must there be different religions and churches, and why must everybody who belongs to the same religion hold just the same opinions, and repeat the same prayers, and go to church at the same time? Why must it all be so formal and prim, and every man think just the same as every other man? Do you understand me? Why mayn't we do as we like, so long as we do what seems to us the very best?'

Bernard rose from his seat by her side, and began to pace hurriedly up and down the shaven turf.

'Have I said anything wrong? Are you angry?' demanded Phyllida timidly.

'Angry! No! How should I be, and with you? But your words have touched a tender chord in my breast, Phyllida, and renewed a question that is ever tormenting me. I have never dared to say as much to any other mortal, but I would have my wife familiar with every phase of my character.'

'Why may not man, in the matter which so nearly concerns his future, think for himself, instead of being compelled, on pain of eternal damnation, to adopt the opinions of those set over him, whether his intellect can approve them or not?'

'Why, indeed! This is the question that has haunted me ever since I became old enough to think for myself, and has infused a doubt in my mind that poisons a profession I might otherwise love to hold. I know what I believe myself. I have thought it out and argued it out, and proved it by testimony, which to my mind is incontrovertible—therefore I am happy and contented in my faith, and desire no other. But why, because *I* believe such and such things, must my neighbour necessarily believe them also? What my intellect approves with ease, *his* may utterly refuse to embrace; whereas another dogma, which I cannot grasp, may commend itself highly to his senses. This, then, is my difficulty—not what to believe myself, but what to teach others to believe. To attempt to cram a faith down a man's throat whether he will or not, is tantamount to forcing unpalatable food into his mouth. What good will it do him when swallowed? I have sat for hours, thinking it my duty, trying with all my might to make some old sinner believe the same truths as I do, and the result has generally been that I have left him more obstinately determined to go his own way than before. And how can we tell—this is the gist of the whole matter—whether *that* way, however wrong it may appear in our eyes, may not be the very means by which the man is fore-destined to be eventually saved ? For, mark you, Phyllida, sin is as absolutely a necessary component of the world's economy as virtue. If there were no sin, there could be no virtue. Who could exercise forgiveness without offence—generosity without debt—charity without malice—courage without temptation ? To call forth the corresponding grace there must be evil ; and surely, so long as we individually exercise the virtues within our power, we may safely leave the evil with Him who created it. You asked me this morning if I were an evangelical or a High Church Christian, and I answered you neither. For I don't want to belong to any sect at all, and my error has been to belong to any Church. If I could give up my profession to-morrow I would. My mother is the only person who keeps me in it. It would make her so unhappy if she thought I even contemplated such a step, and I owe my mother much, dear Phyllida. She has been a good mother to me.'

'And you cannot love her too much in return,' cried the girl warmly. 'Oh, my own dear, dear mother ! What would I not give to see *her* once again.'

Bernard came up close to his wife, and gazed into her tearful eyes.

'I suppose,' he said lovingly, 'the dear, good, charitable, Christian world, who take a delight in condemning every one to hell-fire who differs from

themselves, would call you a very godless sort of
little heathen; but I hold one such speech from
your lips as worth all their whining, canting platitudes about their duty or their religion.   My mother
has not been very cordial in her welcome of you,
my darling—I have seen that, and so have you—
but those sweet, unselfish words came straight
from your noble heart and have gone up like
incense before the Throne.   There was more true
Christian feeling in that one sentence than in half
the sermons in the world!'

'No, no,' cried Phyllida, visibly distressed.
'Don't say that—don't think it, Bernard.   I know
what my own heart is.   The worst you can think
of me is better than I am.'

'I will not speak of it if you desire me not, my
darling, but you must leave me to think of you as
I choose.   But I have told you now the difficulties
of my position, Phyllida.   As a layman I should be
the happiest fellow in creation, but the duties that
have been thrust upon me are burdensome.   I am
bound to preach much that I cannot accept, and
I dare not honestly proclaim what I believe myself, so my conscience is constantly warring with
my sense of obligation.   My friend Anderson has
tried very hard to convert me to his own opinions;
but to leave the church I am in for another would
not better my position.   I search each one in turn,
and I find the same fetters everywhere.   The priest-
hood—I use the term advisedly, and intend it to
embrace every description of minister—preach the
faith in which they have been ordained, and
will have it that man can be saved in no other.
This is what grates against my common sense and
my knowledge of the Almighty, and I want to
preach that man can *not* be saved by any laid down

plan, but only by God, and in God's own way, and that to further such an end God requires no church, nor prayers, nor opinions, nor ceremonies. He wants only our love.'

And as Bernard spoke thus, he too lifted his eyes to heaven in a silent prayer.

'You see the reason now, my darling wife,' he continued, 'why I will not lay the slightest restriction on you with regard to religious duties. I will have you do exactly as you feel inclined. The means which suit me may harden you; the set prayers that help another soul to heaven may drive you from it. Be free then, my sweetheart, and be happy and true, and when I love you most, think that it is but a spark, a flicker, an imperfect reflection of the flame of love which emanates from your Heavenly Father to yourself, and has done from the beginning of the world.'

Bernard had found out by this time that Phyllida's nature was variable and easily excited, but he was hardly prepared for the passionate burst of weeping with which she received his last words. She cried so violently and unrestrainedly that he was afraid the attention of the household would be directed to it, and it was with some difficulty that he soothed her emotion and restored her to her usual calmness before their unwelcome visitors, Mrs Pinner and Miss Warren, were announced.

CHAPTER X.

ONCE more settled at Briarwood, with Phyllida for his daily companion, and surrounded by his home interests, Bernard Freshfield's private life left him nothing to desire, and his wife experienced (what few women do) the privilege of being a good and clever man's friend, without being compelled to be his echo. He left her absolutely free, body and soul, and no prisoner set at large ever valued his liberty more. The season, though far advanced in September, was still mild enough for out-door enjoyment, and to ramble through the plantations, followed by the dogs; or to take the lessons on horseback which her husband had commenced to give her; or to sit under the trees for a whole forenoon, happy and lazy, without being questioned as to the propriety of her actions, was perfect bliss to Phyllida. What thoughts passed through her yet girlish brain as she sat, silent and impassive, beneath the chestnut trees, Bernard never asked and never wished to know. He considered the soul of a woman to be as much her own property as the soul of a man, and that no one had a right to peer into its secrets except Him from whom it is impossible to hide them.

Yet he studied his young wife's character anxiously, if not officiously. Even during the short time they had been married, he had been obliged to confess to himself that she was a puzzle to him—for her nature seemed made up of two parts, and they were utterly opposed to one another. In company she was always somewhat reserved and silent. Mrs Freshfield thought she was **stupid** and unused to society, and Laura trusted she was not of a cold or uncongenial disposition. Mrs Freshfield's disappointment at her son's marriage to a girl of whom, as she said, 'No one knew anything,' was too recent to admit of her showing more than politeness to the mistress of Briarwood; but Laura was nervously anxious, both for her brother's sake and her own, to make friends with her new sister. But the result was certainly unsatisfactory. The more the warm-hearted Laura poured her confidences into Phyllida's ear, and pressed for hers in return, the more did Bernard's wife seem to shrink within herself and become silent and abstracted. Her husband would have been as unhappy at this state of things as his sister, had he not known how differently Phyllida behaved when alone with him, and attributed it entirely to her shyness with strangers.

'Wait,' he used to say to Laura, 'till Phyllida has become as familiar with you as she is with me, and you will find that she is a perfect child in all her ways and manners.'

And he had reason to say so, for when they were alone together no gay unthinking child could pass more rapidly from one phase of feeling to another. Sometimes she would be hilariously gay, and chatter and laugh by the hour. The wildest, most enchanting creature that ever held fast the senses of man!

When she was in this mood (which occurred by far the seldomer of the two) Phyllida would sing snatches of sportive little songs, with an archness and *abandon* that held her husband breathless with surprise and pleasure; or she would dance before him as naturally as a child dances to its mother on the nursery floor; or she would seize the nearest thing at hand, a shawl, a table napkin, a coloured scarf, and twist it about her head and shoulders, and transform herself to some one else, and under that guise act a dual part, keeping up an imaginary conversation, which evolved such sparkles of wit that Bernard, remembering her usual quiet demeanour, would be fairly startled, and wish that all Bluemere could come and admire her versatility as much as he did. At such times she appeared a perfect woman of the world, a little hard perhaps, but with the most consummate ease, and a thorough knowledge that she was charming. But her general demeanour (and it was always strikingly so after one of these outbursts) was so subdued as to be almost melancholy. Bernard would detect her in the act of heaving a sigh sometimes that seemed to come from the very depths of her heart; and she would start and blush when accused of it, and turn it off with a merry declaration that it was all indigestion, and that if she continued to eat so much and do so little, she would soon be qualified to go round the country in a caravan as the 'Fat Lady.' And then she would jump up, declaring that in that case she must have some dancing dogs to accompany her, and let all the dogs loose, and make them dance with her upon the lawn and chase her through the shrubberies, whilst her husband watched her gambols with the purest pleasure. Only sometimes (much as he admired the languid far-away look in her lovely eyes) he wished that the dogs and flowers, and all the other innocent joys in which she revelled, had the power to chase it away, and leave her free to delight in them alone.

When, after the lapse of a few weeks, it became patent to Bluemere that Mrs Bernard Freshfield had no intention of taking any part in the parochial work, the whole community felt aggrieved, and her mother-in-law made it the fruitful theme of many a discussion with her daughter Laura.

'If Bernard does not wish it, mamma,' Laura would say, ' I cannot see how Phyllida can possibly undertake it. Surely her duty to her husband is her first duty; and you know he always said he would not have his wife pottering about the labourers' cottages with a basket full of flannel and tracts. The parishioners of Bluemere have no cause to complain ; they can have all their wants supplied and their troubles inquired into at Briarwood, and I believe they much prefer going up to Mrs Garnett to having ladies visit them.'

'Laura, it is useless of you to try and defend your sister-in-law's conduct. You speak as if she were a perfect child instead of a woman ! Do you mean to tell me that she married my son without the slightest thought of the responsibilities of the position she undertook ? A clergyman's wife to do nothing but ride on horseback, and drive about the country on the box-seat of her husband's curricle, and pay calls and receive them—why, it is perfectly iniquitous ! And she dresses in a manner to which, I am sure, she must have been quite unaccustomed. Every one at Sir George Wynter's the other night was staring at her white *moiré* and the costly lace with which it was trimmed—pearls round her throat too ! That foolish boy is spending all his substance on her, and for a person of whom one knows *absolutely nothing !* It is no wonder people stare at the exhibition of so much folly.'

'Say rather, mamma, they stare at so much beauty! Phyllida is the prettiest woman that has been seen in this part of the country in my remembrance, and I don't wonder poor Bernie is half off his head about her. I heard people saying at Sir George Wynter's that she was a perfect picture; and I think, mamma, that you ought to be very proud of your daughter-in-law.'

'Well, well,' replied Mrs Freshfield, but half-mollified, 'her beauty should not prevent her doing her duty, and I think Bernard is much to blame not to insist upon it. He lays everything on Miss Warren's shoulders in a manner that few young ladies would bear so quietly. That poor girl positively attends to everything, from the Dorcas society and the mothers' meetings to the school prizes and the harvest festival. It is most unfair that Bernard's wife should not share her labours, and I think she would be quite justified in resigning her post.'

'Oh come, mamma,' cried Laura, laughing, 'don't make a grievance out of that, for you know that Annie Warren undertook the parish work entirely of her own accord, and Bernie would like nothing better than to see his way to relieve her of it. He says she is the greatest plague he has, and makes more mischief in the village than he has time to undo. Miss Warren would probably consider herself very much injured if Phyllida were to enter one of the cottages without her leave.'

But in this surmise Laura Freshfield happened to be mistaken. Strange to say, Miss Warren was as anxious now that Phyllida should share the burden of her parochial work, as she had been before to prevent her doing so. Her hopes of becoming the mistress of Briarwood being unmistakably blighted, she did not see the advantage of toiling for the remainder of her life in the service of the parson. And it maddened her as she went her daily rounds with a heavy basket on her arm, and a thousand annoyances to beset her way, to think of the girl she had so looked down upon as Mrs Pinner's cousin taking her ease at Briarwood, clad in the costly robes her husband purchased for her, or visiting the best houses in the county, and being declared the *belle* where-ever she appeared. So she was very much bent on letting Bernard know, in a perfectly amicable manner, that if his wife did not intend to take her share of the parochial duties, he must find some one that would. Consequently, as he sat at breakfast one morning, with Phyllida in a cash-mere and satin quilted dressing-gown in a chair very near his own, Miss Warren, with the inevit-able basket on one arm and a large roll of brown paper under the other, walked into the room un-ceremoniously and opened fire with an exclamation of surprise.

'At breakfast, at half-past ten in the morning! What a shocking waste of time! Why, I hardly thought I should find you at home, Mr Freshfield! Isn't this the day that was fixed for distributing the garden seeds to the men at Brick Common?'

'I believe it is,' replied Bernard, crossing his legs and unfolding a newspaper. 'Robinson has gone over there, I suppose? I told him to see to it for me.'

'Dear me! I made sure you would distribute the seeds yourself. The cottagers will be very much disappointed, and I don't think Mr Robinson knows anything about the matter.'

'He must find out, then,' said Freshfield curtly;

and then wishing to make amends, he addressed his wife, 'Phyllida, are you not going to ask Miss Warren to take a cup of coffee?'

Phyllida blushed, and moved towards the tea equipage.

'I beg your pardon, Miss Warren. Which do you prefer, tea or coffee?'

'Thank you, I will take coffee,' replied the unwelcome visitor, depositing her load on the floor, and drawing a chair to the table, 'I have been so busy all the morning, I have hardly had time to think of breakfast. *My* work would never be done if I lay in bed after six o'clock. No one knows the cares of a parish, except those who undertake them, and I really have more on my hands than I can well accomplish. It will be impossible to go on in this way much longer without help.'

'Let me know what part of it you consider too onerous, and I will relieve you of it at once, Miss Warren,' exclaimed Bernard. 'I have the names of half-a-dozen ladies on my list who have asked me to give them some work to do in Bluemere, and are only waiting to pick up the crumbs your busy hands let fall.'

But this was not what Miss Warren was striving for. She wanted to see Phyllida (who, she believed, would hate such work) forced or shamed into doing it.

'Naturally, Mr Freshfield, all who call themselves Christians, or wish the world to think them so, must desire to labour in the vineyard. It should be a privilege, and with right-minded persons it is so. And therefore I have been waiting to learn what share of the duty your wife intends to take upon herself, before we dis-

cuss the propriety of letting others unsurp her
right of choice. Of course Mrs Bernard *does* intend to become a visitor amongst her husband's
people. It would be a noticeable fact if she did
not,' concluded Miss Annie, with a hard stare at
Phyllida, who began stammering,—

'I will—will—do anything that Bernard wishes
me to do—but—but—'

'*But,*' said Freshfield, wheeling round his chair,
so as to face Miss Warren, 'I do not wish my
wife to meddle in the parish affairs at all; more,
I do not intend that she shall do so. She has
not been used to such work, and she doesn't
like it, and I have plenty of assistance without
hers. If the ladies of Bluemere find it irksome,
Robinson will take it off their hands, and if it
becomes too much for him I will get a second
curate. So you see, Miss Warren, I have provided
against all contingencies, and intend Mrs Freshfield to stick to her own business, which is to
look after me.'

'Oh, of course if that is your decision, Mr Freshfield, there is no more to be said on the subject,'
replied Miss Warren tartly. 'It is very unusual,
and it will excite some discussion, but I daresay
Mrs Bernard will not mind that. But a rector's
wife is a very noticeable person, and the parish
expect more of her perhaps than of others. This
morning, for example, I quite thought I should
secure Mrs Bernard's co-operation in covering the
school-books. I have the paper with me, you
see, and was on my way to the schoolroom,
when I looked in here. Indeed, I half promised
the teachers that your wife would inspect the
premises to-day, and know they will be prepared
to see her. It seems so strange that she should

have returned home nearly a month, and not even been over the schoolrooms or almshouses yet.'

'Well, she is not going over them, certainly not as a duty; neither can she cover old school-books, Miss Warren. Indeed, she is bound not to leave home this morning, as we expect the Ashleighs to lunch. If, when Phyllida is better acquainted with Bluemere and its people, she likes to visit their cottages from a feeling of friendliness, I shall be the last person to wish to deprive my parishioners of what is such a pleasure to myself; but it is no duty of hers to do so, and I will not have her think it.'

'Well, I suppose I had better ask Miss Masters or Mrs Sedgewood to help me,' replied Miss Warren, with an air of martyrdom; for no one could be expected to put fresh covers on three hundred books in a morning with one pair of hands.'

'Please leave them altogether,' said Bernard, 'and I will see they are covered without laying myself under an obligation to any one.'

'Oh dear, no, Mr Freshfield! What I under-take I will do, even if I die under it. No one shall ever have it in their power to say that *I* shirked any part of the duty that falls to my share as a labourer in the Lord's vineyard.'

Bernard was afraid he might be tempted to say something rude, and thought it best to change the conversation.

'Give me another cup of tea, darling,' he said, addressing his wife; and then, just as she was handing it to him, he added, 'I have had such a nice letter this morning—I must read it to you by-and-by—from a very old friend of mine, now in America—Nelson Cole!'

Something must have startled Phyllida at that moment, or the evil eye of Annie Warren was fixed upon her, and made her hand unsteady; for down went the cup and saucer with a crash, deluging the table-cloth with hot tea, and when Bernard looked up at the unexpected clatter, he was horrified to see that his wife had sunk back in the nearest chair, and was staring at him with wide-open, frightened eyes. He sprang to her side in alarm.

' Phyllida, Phyllida, my darling! What is the matter? She is ill—she is fainting! Please open the window, Miss Warren, and give me a glass of water from the sideboard. Thank you. She will be better now. What can have been the cause of this sudden attack?'

'I don't think Mrs Bernard is *ill*,' remarked Miss Warren, with quiet malice. 'I was watching her face all the time, and I imagine it was something *you* said that upset her nerves.'

Phyllida turned her head and looked at the speaker. Their eyes met, and from that moment the two women knew that they were enemies.

' It is untrue,' she answered slowly, but her voice faltered as she spoke. 'I *am* ill—faint. I don't know what is the matter with me, but it is nothing that you said, Bernard.'

'I don't see how it *could* be,' he remarked ingenuously. ' I was only speaking of my friend's letter. Miss Warren's visions of parish work are much more likely to have upset you, Phyllida.'

' In which case, perhaps, I had, better take my leave?' said Miss Warren, 'though I can scarcely accept the blame you would like to impute to me, Mr Freshfield. Your wife's constitution must indeed be delicate if she cannot even bear the

N

mention of her duty. Our dear lost Alice, frail
as she was, had a soul which could at all times
take an interest in the wants of others. Dear
saint! Were she but on earth, she would be the
first to lighten me of my heavy burthen. But
those days are over. Shall I send Mrs Garnett in
to attend to Mrs Bernard?'

'No, thank you, Miss Warren. I can do all
that she requires for her. Good morning. If
Phyllida is quite recovered I shall ride over to
Brick Common this afternoon, and hear what the
men have to say about their plots of ground.'

As soon as they found themselves alone, Bernard poured out his whole wealth of tenderness
upon his wife, and implored her to confide
to him the cause of her sudden fright or illness.
But the girl was resolute in evading his questions.
It was the weather—the change of season—she
was over-tired—she had not slept well the night
before—it was everything or nothing. It was
anything, in fact, but the effect of what she had
heard or seen.

'And I am so sorry I interrupted you,' continued Phyllida in a low voice that still trembled,
'because you were going to tell me something
about—about—a friend of yours—in—in—America, and I want to hear all—all—you can tell
me of him, Bernard,' she said, with white lips.

' I will read you his letter, my darling, or
you shall read it for yourself—if you would
like it better. He is a dear old fellow, but
rather a rough diamond, not a lady's man by
any manner of means; but we have always been
the best of friends and companions, notwithstanding the difference in our ages; for I suppose
Cole must be fifty by this time. He was very

kind to me when I was a youngster, and though he has been in the United States for the last five years, we keep up a steady correspondence, though not a very constant one. And he writes so kindly, too. I believe he really cares for me.'

Phyllida came and seated herself on her husband's lap, and clasped her trembling arms round his neck.

'And is this friend of yours—this Mr Cole,' she asked, 'going to live all his life in Chicago?'

'In *Chicago*, dearest! What put that in your head?' said Bernard, with a look of surprise.

'Didn't you say he was out there?'

'No; I don't think I mentioned any place in particular, but he *has* been in Chicago several times notwithstanding. He has been employed on the railway there. He is a civil engineer. You will laugh when you read his letter, Phyllida. He "chaffs" me so for saying I shall never marry again. But that was six months ago, you know, before I met you, my darling! What *will* he say when he hears my resolution is broken? I shall never hear the last of it.'

'Don't tell him, Bernard. It can be of no consequence to him, and I should not like to be laughed at, if I were you.'

'Oh, I don't mind his fun, it is all good-natured. And I could not keep such an important piece of news from old Cole. How do you suppose I could write a letter without mentioning you, when I think of nothing else?'

'You will be telling him the colour of my hair and eyes, and all that nonsense,' said Phyllida wistfully, so that he may know exactly what I am like.'

'I might try, darling, but I should never succeed.

How do you suppose I could put such a dainty little witch on paper? The best part of you is what can never be described. But I shall certainly make an attempt to let my old friend know what a pretty young woman Mrs Bernard Freshfield is.'

'Perhaps,'—said his wife slowly, and as if she spoke with a great effort—'perhaps Mr Cole will be coming to England soon, and able to judge for himself.'

'No ; he won't, you conceited girl—worse luck. I wish he were ; but he says there is no chance of his return. The fact is, his services are too valuable, and they won't let him leave the States. I expect he will remain there now for the rest of his days.'

Phyllida heaved a sigh—was it of relief?—and rose demurely from her seat.

'I will go upstairs now,' she said, 'and keep quiet until the Ashleighs come,' and her husband saw no more of her that morning.

Her spirits appeared so depressed, however, after this conversation, and experienced so little relief from the bursts of gaiety in which she had hitherto indulged, that Bernard became quite anxious on her account, and began to have all sorts of fanciful ideas on the subject of the change. At one time he declared Bluemere could not agree with her. At another that she had not sufficient excitement, or that she had too much fatigue, and the entertaining of company at Briarwood exhausted her strength, until every old woman in the parish was laughing at the parson's 'fads' about his pretty wife. Phyllida herself was the last person to encourage his alarm. She smiled serenely whenever it became patent to her, and tried hard to force a hilarity she did not feel in order to allay it, but her efforts were too obvious to have the desired effect, and Bernard watched her every look and movement with the greatest concern. At last her mood changed, apparently as unreasonably as it had arisen, but whether causeless or not, sunshine burst forth again at Briarwood, and seemed destined to illuminate it for evermore. It was as if some heavy oppression had suddenly been lifted off Phyllida's mind, or some dark cloud cleared from her brain ; and she commenced to dance along the path of life like a child that had but just wakened to the reality and joy of existence.

Bernard could not account for the happy change, but he kept the day as a red letter one in the calendar of his memory. It was on an afternoon in October. one of those days we sometimes get at the close of the year, that are more precious than any in summer, when the whole land is made glorious by a sun whose rays enliven without scorching us, and the rich autumn foliage beautifies the country with one mass of colour. Bernard had some important parish work to look after, and Phyllida had set forth alone in her little pony chaise, which she had learnt to manage admirably, to pay a call upon the Ashleighs. She had become a favourite with most of the families round about Bluemere, and especially with the one in question. Captain Ashleigh. who was an old naval officer, could never sufficiently praise the beauty and amiability of the rector's wife, and Mrs Ashleigh thought her one of the sweetest girls of her acquaintance. So that Bernard was glad she should go and spend the morning with them, hoping their society might have the effect of raising her spirits. His own business kept him from home till late in the afternoon, and as he walked up the drive, on his return to Briarwood, he saw Phyllida waiting in the porch to receive him. But could this be the pale, listless girl he had parted from in the morning? Bernard looked at her in astonishment. Her cheeks were like a damask rose; smiles dimpled on her face and shone out from her eyes; her little feet danced with impatience whilst she waited his approach. Her husband quickened his steps in glad surprise.

'Why, my darling, what is this?' he exclaimed. 'Who has been working miracles in my absence? Have you met an old friend or made a new one? Or is Captain Ashleigh a necromancer, and has he been giving you a dose of the elixir of life?'

'Yes, yes, Bernie.' she cried, laughing, and clapping her hands, 'that is it. I found an old bottle amongst the captain's dusty books, and drank its contents before I knew what it was. And you see what it has done for me. I am quite well again now, and mean to live for ever.'

'Seriously, I hardly know you,' said Bernard, as he came up to her; 'my darling, you look lovelier than ever. I am so glad you enjoy riding and driving, and that it agrees with you. You are not the same girl I put into the pony chaise this morning.'

'No, dearest, I am not the same girl,' she exclaimed, as she pressed against her husband's side and clung to him. 'I feel as if all the world was changed for me, and I should never feel unhappy or depressed again. Oh, how wicked I have been to give way to such feelings, and when I had you —*you*, for all my own!'

'It was illness, my Phyllida, that made you so

melancholy. How could you help it?' said Bernard tenderly; 'but I cannot tell you how thankful I am for your recovery. What did the Ashleighs say, love? Did they not remark upon these sparkling eyes and glowing cheeks and happy smiles?'

'Bernard, dear, I never saw them. They had gone out for the day to Westertown.'

'Never saw them, child! What have you been doing, then, all this time?'

'Not much, I think; resting myself, and dreaming, and feeling—oh, so happy! When I arrived at the Ashleighs, Bernard, the old butler asked me to walk in; he thought "Master Edward," as he calls him, was about the grounds. So as I was rather tired, I went into the library, and there—'

'What did you do there, Phyllida?'

'Oh, nothing—nothing in particular, only read the captain's newspapers, and—'

'Ah, he is a rare old fellow for newspapers, I know, and takes them in from all parts of the world.'

'Yes, yes, Bernard,' interrupted his wife excitedly, 'and they are very interesting, and so I sat reading them, and—and—oh, I am so glad to be back again with you,' she cried disconnectedly, as she flung herself into his arms—'back again here in my dear, *dear* home, safe and well with you. For as I sat in that library, Bernard, a sudden fright seized me, and I thought, supposing—supposing—something were to happen to you whilst I was away, and I should never see you more—or die before we met again—and, as the thought struck me, I rushed out to my pony chaise and jumped in, and drove home as fast as ever I could. But you had not returned—and it has seemed hours—weeks—centuries, since I waited for you here! Oh, if anything *had* happened to prevent our meeting, it would have been too, *too* terrible—and just now!'

'My dearest girl,' said Bernard, 'you are still too much excited for health. Try and calm yourself, Phyllida. To think that you should love me like this is the purest pleasure I could experience; but you must not give way to idle fears. God is above us all, remember, and my life and yours are always safe in His hands.'

'Oh yes, Bernie, and I will never be so foolish again—never! I am all right now, indeed I am—and so—*so* happy, you cannot think.'

She gazed into his face with her sparkling eyes as she spoke, and he thought he had never seen her look so beautiful. There was perfect peace and contentment at Briarwood that day, and for many months afterwards, and Bernard never thought to inquire more closely into the reason of so unaccountable a change in the demeanour of his wife. That it *had* changed was all he cared for. Neither did it seem likely to distress him again. From the period of her visit to the Ashleighs' library, a calm happiness settled down upon the young mistress of the rectory, and she was an altered being. The feverish bursts of gaiety with which she used to startle her husband entirely disappeared; but they were succeeded by an equable cheerfulness that was far better suited to domestic life.

She now sought the society of Laura Freshfield as eagerly as once she had repulsed it, and responded with so much warmth to her overtures of affection, that the sisters-in-law became devoted friends. This happy result was followed by a participation in all Laura's pursuits, either in the parish or out of it, and before long it was no unusual occurrence for Bernard, on entering the house of a sick parishioner, to find his wife sitting by the bedside and beguiling the tedious hours with her reading or conversation.

The 'parson's bonnie lady' was soon as much loved in Bluemere as himself, and every day her husband's heart seemed to twine its tendrils faster and closer round her own.

Meanwhile, there was no more devoted wife in the country than Phyllida.

Her love for Bernard was so mixed with reverence and gratitude that she seemed never to be able to do enough to express it to him. She loved him more with the affection a dog bears to its master, than the wives of the present century think it dignified to display. There was none of the overweening pride of power in Phyllida's manner, although she could govern her husband by the lifting of her little finger. On the contrary, she was humble and low-minded in the extreme. She would watch his face to see if she could read his thoughts before he spoke them, and run to fetch and carry for him like a little dog, taking a delight in forestalling the servants, and even his own wishes.

Bernard would reprove her lovingly for such undignified behaviour, but she did not alter it. To wait on him, to obey his slightest word, and to accompany him wherever he would take her, seemed to fill up the measure of her existence.

Of course her conduct could not be unnoticed at Blue Mount, and even Mrs Freshfield was compelled to remark that although she 'was afraid poor Phyllida did not come of very good blood, there was no doubt she made Bernard happy, and that was, after all, the main thing.'

'But that is not all, mamma,' Laura would reply indignantly. 'Phyllida does almost as much good in the parish as Bernie himself. I don't mean to say she carries about a basket like that detestable Annie Warren ; and why should she, when she has plenty of people to carry it for her? But she takes care that no comfort for the sick shall ever be wanting from Briarwood, and she goes and sees them, and talks to them ; oh, in such a nice way, just as if they were her equals! The poor people about here perfectly adore Phyllida, mamma. They say she is a " real lady, without any pride in her ; " and call her the "*parson's bonnie wife*," and the "*parson's angel*," and all kinds of pretty names. And the scarlet fever is very bad over at Brick Common now, you know—the Tanners lost two of their little ones last week — and Miss Warren has left off visiting them, but Phyllida goes all the same, and she sat up a whole night with poor Mrs Tanner when she was in such distress. And Bernie, although he is very nervous about her, won't tell her not to go, because he says she is one of God's angels, and under His especial care. Isn't that nice ? '

Mrs Freshfield's answer was somewhat cautious.

'Well, of course, my dear, it is very good of your sister-in-law to try and comfort the poor creatures, and if your brother does not forbid her to do so, no one else has the right to interfere. Still, I think Phyllida might have some consideration for *you* and others of her friends, to whom she is very likely to bring home the infection.

Laura glanced at her mother somewhat contemptuously. Was this the fruit of the religion upon which Mrs Freshfield had moulded her life for the last sixty years,—to tremble at the proximity of a pestilence that, at the worst, according to her own creed, could only throw open the gates of that heaven which she believed she should walk straight into? The girl, with all her young life before her, had no such fear!

'You needn't be afraid for *me*, mamma,' she answered; 'but if you think there is any chance of *your* catching it, I will go to Briarwood and stay there until the danger of infection is past.'

But Mrs Freshfield, whatever her private opinion, could never have consented to let the public know that she was not ready for glory, and so Laura and Phyllida worked on together, heart and soul, and spared neither time nor trouble till the fever had abated, and the little ones were running about Brick Common again in their usual health.

CHAPTER XI.

MRS PINNER had a grievance—a daily and hourly grievance—and I regret to add that it was a worldly one, full of envy, malice, and all uncharitableness. Bernard and Phyllida had asked her sister, Mrs Penfold, to spend Christmas at Briarwood, and Mrs Penfold had accepted the invitation. Mrs Penfold had actually left Captain Barclay and

Miss Annadale to the tender mercies of Sarah, and such assistance as was considered necessary, and come to play at being a fine lady in Bluemere. To Mrs Pinner, who had never been invited to do more than dine at the rectory, the thought of her sister Maria living in the very bosom of Bernard Freshfield's family, and located in the best bedroom, with amber hangings, was gall and wormwood, and all the more so because she dared not confide her jealousy to any one but herself.

Her whole comfort consisted in reading the 'Seventh Vial,' and shaking her head over the delightful conviction, that when it was opened she should be able to hear from her throne of gold, even above the twanging of her harp-strings, the frizzling made by her sister Maria as she was tossed like a pancake from one infuriated demon to another in the nethermost hell.

'To think,' she said to herself, 'that Maria, who was ever one of the worldly-minded, leaning to all sorts of gaiety and carnal pleasures, should be living at Briarwood and driving all over the country in a carriage and pair, with that stuck-up Phyllida by her side; whilst, if they ask *me* to dinner, they don't even send the pony chaise to fetch me. The poor minister must indeed have been led astray from his duty by that girl before he would have dreamt of setting up my sister Maria over one of the elect. And to see the gown she wore to church last Sunday, too! Black silk at ten shillings the yard, if it cost a penny. The woman must be robbing her employers to be able to pay for such luxuries. I am greatly afraid her feet are already set upon the broad path. And the way in which Phyllida and she spoke of those disreputable lodgings at Gatehead before all the servants, perfectly shocked me ! What respect can they entertain for their minister after hearing such a confession ? I thought I should have swooned. I must ask Maria to spend a quiet evening with me, and talk to her about such things. After all the trouble I have taken to live amongst these people as my father's daughter, and one of the Lord's chosen should live, to have a sister who lets lodgings come and sit down at my very door, is *too* trying ! I must entreat her, if she has no respect for herself, at least to have some for me.'

Meanwhile Mrs Penfold (who was not yet aware of the feelings to which her advent had given birth in Mrs Pinner's breast) was enjoying herself, as she had not done for years past, beneath the hospitable roof of Briarwood.

Bernard Freshfield had not forgotten the kind part which his wife's cousin played at the time of their marriage, and there was no false shame in his manly nature to mar the pleasure with which he repaid it.

Had Mrs Penfold been a duchess she could not have been waited on and served more assiduously than she was at Briarwood ; and Bernard would have had her take up her residence there altogether and make it her home, had she not been too independent to accept his offer.

' Your husband is an angel, my dear,' she said to Phyllida, ' and you are the very luckiest girl I ever heard of ; but I couldn't be happy eating another person's bread whilst I have two hands of my own to earn it with. And what would the captain say if he heard I was going to desert him for good ? Why, it was with the greatest difficulty I could get his leave to come here at all. I was quite a fortnight coaxing it out of him. And poor

Miss Annadale cried when I left Gatehead, Phyllida—actually *cried*; but she is not quite right in the head, you know, my dear, so it is excusable on her part. And I should have been truly sorry to miss seeing you in your happiness. What a good, dear husband you have, child, and what an elegant home! You are indeed a fortunate creature. And the cloud you once spoke to me of at Gatehead, Phyllida—that depressing, uncomfortable feeling that I told you was so unnatural—it has all passed away now of course, my dear, and you are quite happy and contented,' concluded Mrs Penfold somewhat curiously.

Phyllida flushed deeply, and for a moment did not answer. Then she said slowly,—

'Yes, cousin Penfold, I am *very* happy, and *very* contented—sometimes I think I am too happy for it to last—and always that I am far happier than I deserve. And if the old depressing thoughts return at times to damp my pleasure, I put them away, and hope I am right in doing so. For they could only make my husband anxious about me; and you told me, didn't you, that it was my *duty* to bury all the past and begin a new and better life for the future?'

'I did indeed, my dear, and I meant it. You have many more luxuries and blessings than most people, and all you have to do is to let your heart overflow with thankfulness, and make dear Mr Freshfield as perfectly happy as you can. It would be a sin to rake up old memories that can do no good, and only infuse bitter into the cup which Heaven has been good enough to fill for you.'

'Yes, that is what I thought,' said Phyllida, with a sigh of relief.

'I am going to ask you if you will spare me for this evening,' continued Mrs Penfold. 'My sister Charlotte has written to ask me to take tea with her, and I don't like to refuse, as it is some time since we have been alone together, and she mustn't think I've grown proud because I'm visiting at Briarwood.'

'No; she shall not do that!' replied Phyllida, laughing; 'and so I will send you down in my little pony chaise, cousin Penfold, and you can order it to fetch you again at any time you like.'

So at six o'clock that evening the pony chaise deposited Mrs Penfold at the door of Mrs Pinner, who received her in a purple merino gown, with a pink ribbon at her throat, and artificial roses in her cap; yet looked, nevertheless, with righteous sorrow at the plain but rich dress worn by her sister, and which was one of the numerous presents showered upon her by her young relations.

'I am pleased to receive you in my humble abode, Maria,' commenced Mrs Pinner solemnly, 'for I almost feared that the attention you have been receiving at Briarwood would make you despise the hospitality of one who has little to offer you beside the divine food, which is provided for all those who earnestly hunger after it.'

'Well, I don't know why you should say that, Charlotte,' replied Mrs Penfold briskly, as she laid aside her outdoor garments. 'I have never refused an invitation of yours yet, that I am aware of; but it is not many that you have extended to me since I lived at Gatehead. I supposed you were ashamed of me because I let lodgings?'

'I cannot say that I consider letting lodgings a fit occupation for one of our father's daughters— the daughters of a minister of the gospel.'

'Yes, a Dissenting minister, elected by his own sect, who held his services in a barn,' replied Mrs Penfold ; ' but father was a shoemaker before he turned preacher.   I suppose you haven't forgotten *that*, sister Charlotte ? '

' I have not forgotten what is due to myself,' said Mrs Pinner, bridling ; 'and it surprises me, Maria, to hear you allude to poor father's misfortunes in that heartless manner !   It is the same thing with your own calling—you speak as openly of your lodgers and your lodgings as a duchess would mention her country seat.   I *do* wish you would have a little consideration for what *I* must suffer in the eyes of my friends by such a confession.'

' Well, I am sorry if I have hurt your feelings, Charlotte, but your friends can't be worth much if the fact of my poverty makes any difference to them.   Mr Freshfield and Phyllida are not ashamed of it, as you may plainly see.'

' Oh ! the poor minister,' said Mrs Pinner, tossing her head, ' is completely led by what his wife says ; and as for Phyllida, I daresay she has her own reasons for keeping on good terms with you. She has not forgotten, doubtless, that, but for your assistance, she would never have been married at all.'

' I don't know why you should say so, Charlotte.   *I* had no hand in the matter, except in accompanying them to the church.   The young people had made up their minds long before they saw me.'

' Mr Freshfield does not seem to be of your opinion, Maria.   He told me the other day he owed his wife to you.   And he tries to pay off the debt by making you handsome presents, if

I am not much mistaken,' said Mrs Pinner, with a spiteful glance at her sister's silk dress.

'Yes, indeed, he is most generous and kind to me,' returned Mrs Penfold, 'although I hope he does not consider that he owes me anything. He has given me four or five most handsome dresses (this is one of them, Charlotte ; just feel this silk —it must have cost a lot of money), and a fur-lined cloak for the winter, and one of the most complete writing-tables you ever saw—just the very thing I wanted, and fits into my recess as if it had been made for it. Indeed, he has been good enough to propose that I should take up my residence altogether at Briarwood and relieve Phyllida of the troubles of housekeeping ; but that is an offer I could not accept.'

'The minister seems to have a deep sense of the obligation you have put him under,' remarked Mrs Pinner sarcastically, 'and it is a very handsome return for just going to church with them. I suppose the marriage was all right and regular?'

'Why, bless my soul! Charlotte, what a question to put about our own cousin. Of course it was. I saw the licence myself ; and as I am one of Phyllida's nearest relations in England, I had a perfect right (the minister told me) to give her away.'

'Well, there was no one to object to it if you hadn't. I suppose the girl *has* relations in St Domingo, since her parents lived there, but she never received a letter while she stayed with me, which I thought rather peculiar. Has she ever mentioned any one to you, either on the father's or the mother's side? because you may remember Agnes Summers' people settled in the West Indies too.'

'No, she never has; and now you mention the circumstance, it *is* peculiar,' replied Mrs Penfold meditatively.

Now Mrs Pinner, notwithstanding she professed to know all about Phyllida to the Bluemere people, and plumed herself considerably on the fact of her being the rector's wife, was in reality excessively curious to find out something more about her cousin's antecedents, and it was chiefly with that object that she had asked Mrs Penfold to take tea with her. She knew that, however alienated her sister and she had been of late years, and however stiffly they had met each other at Briarwood, the familiarity of a close relationship is not easily dissolved, and that a cup of tea would probably soon loosen the string of Maria's tongue. And she was not mistaken. When the ladies were comfortably ensconced before the tea equipage, and the buttered toast had been sent up exactly to their satisfaction, the conversation became more sisterly and confidential.

'Of course,' observed Mrs Pinner, 'I was as pleased as yourself that our cousin should make so good a marriage. We have plenty of young ladies in Bluemere, — pious, well-trained, and domestic girls,—and it was a matter of great surprise when the minister passed them over in favour of Phyllida Moss. For though I cannot deny she fills the position well,—in point of looks and dress, and so forth,—yet Phyllida has not yet been "*called*," Maria, and if you have any remembrance of the teachings of our estimable parents, or knowledge of the ways of the elect, you must confess that what I say is true.'

'Phyllida doesn't *talk* much,' replied kind-hearted Mrs Penfold, 'but she *does* more than many ladies in her position would trouble themselves to do. She is constantly employed amongst the sick in the parish. And she is a most devoted wife, Charlotte, no one can deny that. Mr Freshfield perfectly adores her.'

'Is it a justifiable thing for a clergyman to *adore* a frail mortal creature, or to let his friends think he does so? Oh, I see a sad difference in Mr Freshfield since his marriage, Maria, though I would say so to no one but yourself. But he is always in a hurry to get home now, and scarcely ever has time for a chat or a cup of tea, as he used to have. And his marrying Phyllida was a sad blow at Blue Mount! I have that on the very best authority.'

Mrs Penfold was about to reply, when her attention was directed to a figure coming up the garden path. It was that of Annie Warren, eager and excited, from a certain circumstance that had just taken place at Westertown.

'I am afraid you are going to have a visitor, Charlotte,' she said, 'and that our conversation will be interrupted.'

Mrs Pinner glanced from the window.

'My dear, it is only Annie Warren, one of the best creatures in the world, and devoted to me. You can speak as freely as you choose before her; in fact, she is a bosom friend both at Briarwood and Blue Mount, and knows as much about Phyllida as we do.'

'I could not discuss such private matters before a stranger,' replied Mrs Penfold.

But Miss Warren's enthusiastic and gushing manner soon drove this resolution out of her head. She entered the room evidently brimful of news, or eager to extract some information from her hostess.

'You dear, *dear* thing,' she cried, falling upon Mrs Pinner's neck,—(Miss Warren had been rather given to displaying this exuberant affection for Mrs Pinner lately),—'I am so glad to find you have a friend to talk to; I was half afraid you were alone this evening. Your sister, is it? Oh, I *am* pleased to have an opportunity of making her acquaintance. I might have guessed she was your sister though, for she has just your own sweet smile! I hope you are going to make a long stay in Bluemere, Mrs Penfold? It will be such a treat for dear Mrs Pinner to have you here. She is always talking of you, and longing for your company. Aren't you, dear?' concluded Miss Warren affectionately.

'Come, come, you naughty girl,' replied her hostess, delighted at the small homage paid her, 'you must take off your hat and sit down and have a cup of tea with us. No, not one more kiss. You know it is all nonsense, and you don't mean it.'

'How *unkind!*' said Miss Annie, with a reproachful glance, 'when you know you are my very best friend. Do you think *I* would have run away and left you for the first person who asked me, as somebody else did?'

'Well, I don't know,' replied Mrs Pinner, with unintentional sarcasm. 'If the *minister* had been the person, I think you would.'

'*The minister!*' cried Miss Annie, with ineffable scorn. 'No, indeed, Mrs Pinner, the minister would never have had the power to tempt *me* away from any one. If ever I marry, my husband must be a man of sense and strength of character, and not a poor, weak creature like Mr Freshfield, who can be led by anybody.'

'Dear me,' said Mrs Penfold, 'you surprise me, Miss Warren. I have always considered Mr Freshfield to be a young man of so much determination and power.'

Miss Annie smiled.

'And yet you are staying at Briarwood, Mrs Penfold? How blind you must be! Can't you see how Mrs Bernard leads her husband by the nose? His poor dear mother is quite distressed about it. She nearly cried when she spoke of them yesterday afternoon. Oh, you mustn't mind my speaking so openly, but Mrs Pinner will tell you that I am quite like one of the family at Blue Mount, as I *used* to be'—with a deep sigh—'at the rectory, when my darling Alice was mistress there.'

'Yes, indeed!' echoed Mrs Pinner; 'and as you *ought* to be now, my dear, considering all the trouble you took on their behalf. Why, this dear girl was nurse and housekeeper, and everything, you may say, Maria, to the minister's first wife; and how he can ever forget it, passes my comprehension. But there will be a reward laid up for you, my dear, in the next world.'

'I know that, dear Mrs Pinner,' said Miss Annie modestly; 'but it comes a little hard sometimes, does it not? However, I have done my duty— that is my satisfaction; and if Mr Freshfield's eyes are blinded to it now, they may not be so always.'

'Don't you and Phyllida get on well together?' demanded Mrs Penfold bluntly.

'Oh, yes, my dear madam; and it is no question of getting on well—it is the sad incontestable fact that dear Mrs Bernard has not yet heard the voice of grace calling her into the fold, and the ways and words of her husband's former friends do not suit her. It was different with our sweet Alice. She was truly a child of heaven.'

'My cousin seems to take unusual interest in her husband's parish though. I heard Mr Freshfield reprove her to-day for going out in the rain to practise with the church choir.'

'Oh yes, her singing is charming, no doubt of that — almost too charming, one might say, for a private lady. Our organist, Mr Barnes, quite thought Mrs Bernard was a professional artist when he first heard her. He said there was a tone about a regularly - trained voice that was unmistakable. But (as I told him) that must be quite impossible.'

'*Quite* impossible,' repeated Mrs Penfold decisively.

'A professional artist!—our cousin,' ejaculated Mrs Pinner. 'Oh dear, what an awful report to get about the village! I hope you checked it at once, Miss Warren? It would be the death of poor Mrs Freshfield if it reached Blue Mount.'

'Of course I checked it, dear Mrs Pinner. I said how could it be, when Mrs Bernard came here straight from St Domingo. I am afraid the climate had an effect upon her health, Mrs Penfold —she is not very strong.'

'*Not strong!* You surprise me. I considered she had so vastly improved since her marriage. She looks blooming to me.'

'Ah, she has a nice colour sometimes ; yes, but these fainting fits are not a good sign.'

'I was not aware that Phyllida was given to that weakness. Does she faint often ?'

'I don't know, but she faints very easily. I was at Briarwood about two months ago, at breakfast time—I often run in on business matters, you know : *he* likes me to do so—and Mr Freshfield was in the midst of reading us one of his letters, when down she dropped in a swoon, or at least she *said* it was one.'

' Poor thing !' exclaimed Mrs Penfold concernedly ; ' you don't mean to say so ? '

' Yes,' continued Miss Annie, with her gaze fixed upon her two companions, ' it was just as he was reading a letter from an old friend of his, *Mr Nelson Cole.*'

But not the faintest token of recognition passed over either lady's face.

' It must have been the heat,' observed Mrs Pinner.

' I don't think so,' said Miss Warren ; ' I fancied it was something in the letter. Perhaps the name was familiar to her. Mrs Bernard always looks to me as if she had had trouble.'

' Ah, poor dear,' ejaculated Mrs Penfold, with an ominous shake of the head.

' What ! do you know anything about it, Maria ?' demanded Mrs Pinner curiously.

' I know Phyllida has had heavy trouble,' replied her sister, ' because she confided as much to me in Gatehead. She said her past weighed terribly upon her mind, and I told her it was her duty to forget it all as soon as possible. For what good does it do us to be always raking up old worries and fretting ourselves because we can't remedy them !'

' I don't think you were right, Maria. Perhaps it was the rod of grace designed to chasten her and keep her low ; we should be careful how we interfere with the designs of Providence. But doubtless you meant it for the best ?'

'Of course I did. I thought it a pity that a fine young girl like Phyllida should waste her life in lamenting things that could never be undone, especially when there was a good man like Mr Freshfield ready to help her to forget them.'

'And you have not heard the name of Nelson Cole before, then? He is not likely to be connected in any way with the past troubles of Mrs Bernard Freshfield?' said Miss Annie inquisitively.

'Not in any way that we know of, though of course he may have been a friend of her father's,' replied Mrs Pinner. 'We never knew Mr Moss, you must remember. Our only connection with Mrs Bernard comes through her mother, and as we never saw Phyllida till she came to Bluemere, she may have dozens of friends and connections of whom we know nothing.'

'It is strange you should have heard so little of her former life. She is not very communicative,' persisted Miss Warren; but at the same time she resolved to say nothing of the news she was burning to reveal. Since the two old ladies could not assist her, she was determined they should not spoil probable sport.

'And where have you been to-day?' inquired Mrs Pinner presently, as she glanced at her visitor's unusually festive attire.

'I have been spending the day at Westertown,' replied Miss Warren. 'My brother had business there, and as I wanted to do a little shopping I accompanied him. And we dined at the Crown Hotel, and they were so busy, you can't think.'

'Was it market day?' asked Mrs Penfold innocently.

'No; but there are several strangers staying

there, and all their luggage was piled up in the hall, and I—'

But here Miss Warren stopped short as though she could not trust herself to proceed any further. Presently she went on,—

'Is Mrs Bernard at home this evening, Mrs Penfold? Do you think I shall be intruding if I run in to Briarwood for half-an-hour?'

'I know she is at home,' replied Mrs Penfold, 'and I should not think, since you are so intimate with them, that you *could* intrude.'

'*I* should be surprised if it were possible, considering all you have done for the minister and his belongings,' interposed Mrs Pinner.

'Well, then, if you two dear creatures will excuse me, I will leave you again and run on there, because I wish especially to ask Mr Freshfield a question regarding the schools. Good-night, dear Mrs Pinner, and to you too, dear Mrs Penfold. I feel that I shall soon love you almost as dearly as I do your sister.'

The old ladies bid her good-night eagerly, not feeling sorry that they were to have a little further conversation in private together, and Miss Annie Warren went on her way to Briarwood with the sly, malicious expression of a cat tracking its prey. It was but a thread she had found in the chain of evidence her fancy had woven against Phyllida Freshfield, but a thread that might lead into a labyrinth of difficulties for the young couple at the rectory. On one of the trunks piled in the hall of the Crown Hotel at Westertown she had read the name of Nelson Cole.

———

CHAPTER XII.

MISS WARREN feared at first that she had had her walk for nothing. for the news that greeted her on arriving at Briarwood was that both Mr and Mrs Freshfield were out. The man-servant, who opened the door to her, and who disliked her as much as his master did, tried all he could to prevent her entering the house. He could not tell where either his master or mistress had gone, nor when they were likely to return ; it might be that night, it might be the next morning ; he was sure it would be useless her remaining in the hope of seeing them. But Miss Warren was persistent in her inquiries, and at last elicited the intelligence that Mrs Freshfield had been sent for in the middle of dinner to a young girl who was said to be dying, and that the parson had received a letter after her departure, which had compelled him to spend the night away from home.

So he had left Bluemere not half-an-hour before, and ordered the servants to sit up and await their mistress's return.

'A sick girl!' ejaculated Miss Warren ; 'that must be Sarah Jeffreys. No one else is sick at present in Bluemere. Dying! Pooh! nonsense. It's only one of her false alarms. She always thinks she's dying! Mrs Freshfield will see through the trick before she has been there half-an-hour. I shall sit down till she returns.'

Finding his remonstrances vain, the servant opened the door of the library. in which there was a large fire burning, and ushered Miss Warren to the room. She ensconced herself in Bernard's own arm-chair, and being left alone, fell to wondering

what business had called the parson away from
Bluemere. Could he have heard of the advent of
Nelson Cole and gone to Westertown to meet him,
and if so, would he bring him back to Briarwood ?
As Miss Annie speculated thus, and let her black
eyes range over each article in the room, they
lighted on a note which lay conspicuously upon the
writing-table. It was a half sheet of paper. hastily
screwed into the shape of a *billet-doux*, and
addressed to Phyllida in pencil—just such a note
in fact as a husband unexpectedly called from
home would leave behind him for the satisfaction
of his wife. Miss Warren had very few absurd
scruples with regard to the dishonour of prying into
the correspondence of another. She seized the
note with alacrity, and made herself mistress of its
contents.

'DEAREST PHYLLIDA,—I have just received a
letter from my dear old chum Nelson Cole, who is
actually in Westertown. He was suddenly dispatched to England on some important business
connected with his employers' firm, and says he
cannot go back without paying us a flying visit at
Briarwood. It is so good of the dear old fellow.
I am going to see him at the Crown Hotel at once,
and I shall not be back again until to-morrow
morning—perhaps not till the afternoon, if there is
anything to detain us there. But then I shall bring
him with me, and I am sure you will welcome him
for my sake.—Ever dearest, your loving husband.'

Miss Warren twisted the note round and round
in her fingers.

'I wonder if the servants know why he was called
away?' she thought. 'I don't think Edwards does,

because he did not seem quite sure if he had gone
to Westertown, or somewhere else.   Possibly they
are aware their master left a note for his wife in the
library, but then scraps of paper like this are easily
lost or mislaid.   It will be nothing very extraordinary if, when they come to search for it, they
find it is gone.   Yes ; I think I shall be quite safe
in destroying it.   *If* Mr Nelson Cole should prove
to have been a friend of Mrs Bernard's. as well as
of her husband, this note will give her time to prepare herself for meeting him.   She will be taken ill
before to-morrow, and have to go to bed, or to visit
the sea-side, or she will receive a sudden summons
somewhere, and leave Mr Freshfield to do the
honours of Briarwood alone.   *I* know their nasty,
shabby tricks ; and if ever a woman looks as if she
could be up to tricks, it's Mrs Bernard Freshfield !
So I will just drop this bit of paper in the fire, and
leave my lady to meet Mr Nelson Cole without any
warning of what is before her.'

She walked up to the fireplace as she thought
thus, and threw the note upon the burning coals.
In another instant it was reduced to ashes.   Then
Miss Warren rang the library bell, and walked
towards the door.

'You may show me out, Edwards,' she said,
as she met the servant.   'That girl Jeffreys has
evidentl y deceived poor Mrs Freshfield into imagining she is really ill !   It is nearly ten o'clock, and
I cannot wait any longer.'

'I said I was afraid it would be no use your
waiting, Miss,' replied Edwards. as he preceded
her along the warmed and lighted corridor, and
threw open the portals of Briarwood.   As he
closed them upon her, he muttered something not
entirely complimentary, to the effect that he wished

it were for the last time. Miss Annie Warren was thoroughly disliked in the rectory servants' hall. But when Phyllida returned nearly an hour afterwards, she received a very different sort of reception. It was not only because she was their master's wife that she was waited on so cheerfully by every dependant in his household. Her kind words and smiles repaid her servants for all the trouble they took for her; and Edwards opened the door almost as soon as she touched the bell, whilst Mrs Garnett appeared in the hall to inquire if she were cold or tired, and her own maid stood ready to divest her of her wraps, and exchange her walking shoes for easy slippers.

'No, I'm not tired at all, thank you, Mrs Garnett,' she said brightly, in answer to the housekeeper's inquiries, 'only very cold. There is a bitter frost to-night. But I am so glad I went. Poor Sarah is much worse. Dr Jenkyns does not think she will live till the morning ; and she was fretting so to see me. Where is Mr Freshfield ? In the library ?'

'My master is out, if you please, ma'am,' interposed Edwards ; 'he had a letter soon after you started, and was obliged to go to Westertown ; and he is afraid he won't be able to get back to·night.'

What a blank fell upon Phyllida's heart at the intelligence ! She had become so used to the cheering influence of that dear sunny face of Bernard's and to the tones of his voice, the prospect of passing twelve hours without him appeared terrible. Her sweet face fell to twice its usual length.

'Out !' she repeated. 'Gone over to Westertown, and at this time of night ! What can have taken him there ?'

' I don't know, I'm sure, ma'am,' replied Edwards respectfully. ' The master was in a great hurry, and hardly spoke to any of us. But I think he left a note or a bit of writing of some sort for you, ma'am—leastways I fancy he said so, but it may be a mistake of mine ; if not, I conclude, it must be in the library.'

' Oh, of course he would write,' cried Phyllida confidently, as she ran into the library, and searched on every table for a paper in her husband's hand ; but she could find none, for the good reason that, as we have seen, the note he left for her was resolved to nothing in the burning fire.

' I can't find it, Edwards,' she said, in a tone of disappointment.

' I'm afraid I must have been mistaken then, ma'am, for, as I said before, the master was in a terrible hurry, and spoke very rapid-like. But it's nothing bad as has taken him out, for he said he had had capital good news ; and he'd be home to-morrow for certain.'

' Ah, well, then, I must be content with that,' said his mistress with a half laugh ; but she felt a little uneasy nevertheless. It was so unlike Bernard to leave home without further explanation than he could afford to servants. Mrs Penfold's return was some sort of comfort to Phyllida, and they sat up late together, suggesting all sorts of reasons to each other for the parson's sudden disappearance, but were finally obliged to separate for the night without having come to any conclusion, excepting that they were equally anxious for the morrow to bring them the solution of the riddle.

Meanwhile, Bernard's capital horses had carried him quickly to Westertown, and he was enjoying himself thoroughly in the company of Nelson Cole, whom he found hearty and congenial as ever. He had had a double reason for setting off so speedily to welcome his old friend. Not only was he anxious to prove that his feelings were unchanged, but he felt rather shy at having to break to him the news that all his grand resolutions with regard to a second marriage were broken, and he was already in the possession of another wife. He thought he could stand the first looks of astonishment, and the cynical remarks that were sure to follow his announcement, better if he were alone with Nelson Cole than in the presence of Phyllida. So he had started off, determined to get it all over that evening, and bring his friend back to Briarwood the next day, fully prepared to greet and approve his choice.

The warm welcome he received as soon as he had placed his foot inside the 'Crown' was all that Bernard's heart could desire, and it was a long time before Nelson Cole could leave off shaking the hand of the 'boy with the monkish, close-shorn face, whom,' he had acknowledged to himself, 'he took so deep an interest in.'

'And is this really you, Freshfield?' he kept on exclaiming. 'Driven out seven miles on a winter's night in order that you may meet an old chum twelve hours earlier! I am glad of it. It is like yourself, my boy. It proves that your profession has not altered your nature, and that you still have a corner in your heart for the wicked ones of the earth, and a remembrance of the jolly old days at Oxford, when I used to give you youngsters suppers at my rooms, and help you to evade the vigilance of the dons in the morning. Ha! ha! ha!'

'When you used to be the very kindest and jolliest and most generous friend a young fellow ever possessed,' cried Bernard. 'No ; may I perish before I forget it—or you ! You can't think how delighted I was to receive your letter, Cole ! Your last spoke so definitely of your remaining in the States that it was the most joyful surprise. I think if it hadn't been for the servants, and that they would have thought it undignified in a parson, I should have jumped for joy. I know I ran off in such hurry and confusion, that I don't think they have the least idea where I have gone to.'

'That doesn't matter, my boy ! that's the best of a man being unshackled by any ties—he can come and go as he pleases without asking leave of anybody—in fact, he is *free.* And now you are come, you will stay, Bernard ? You must be my guest for to-night ; and to-morrow, if it so pleases you, I will run back with you to Bluemere and enliven your loneliness with a few days of my society.'

'I hope you will make it a good many days, my dear old friend,' said Bernard.

'I should like it above all things, but I fear it is impossible. A week must be the outside of my visit. I am due at Liverpool on the 10th of next month. But it is very good to see you, if only for a week, my son. And how well you are looking, boy. Not much like a disconsolate widower. eh ?'

'But I thought I told you I was *not* disconsolate !' replied Bernard sheepishly

'Ah yes, to be sure, you wrote me the most wonderful letter, all about the impossibility of your ever marrying again—wasn't that it ? on account of not being able to find a true soul union. But come, don't look so foolish about it. You're quite right, my boy, and the longer you stick to such principles the better. Looking out for a soul union may keep you from worse scrapes, and as you will never find it, the close of your life will see you just such another jolly, careless bachelor as I am.'

'But—but—perhaps what I told you I so earnestly desired, Cole, may not be so entirely out of my reach as you seem to imagine,' stammered the parson.

'Well look here, Bernard, we'll discuss that matter presently—it's too hard a nut to crack standing. Now, which are you for, dinner or supper?'

'Neither, thank you. I dined at seven this evening. In fact we—I had done dinner when your letter arrived.'

'Just so! well, I have dined myself, so we agree on that point. You smoke, I suppose?'

'Oh yes! That is a habit I cannot persuade myself to relinquish.'

'Why should you? Is it wrong? What can you manage over your pipe? I always take whisky and water.'

'And I will join you, Cole. I like nothing better.'

'All right, my boy.' So the order was given, and the two men sat down opposite each other with their pipes in their mouths, ripe to unbosom themselves of their dearest secrets. For what letting down her back hair is said to be to a woman, lighting his pipe is to a man, and crass ignorance alone supposes that the difficulty of keeping a secret is confined to one sex. But for a few moments they smoked on in silence, whilst Nelson

Cole was thinking into what a fine fellow young Freshfield had developed ; and Bernard considered in what words he should introduce the subject of his marriage, so as to excite the least amount of ridicule at the hands of his friend.

'And so you are living in fine style, I suppose. up at Briarwood?' remarked Nelson Cole presently ; 'that was a splendid pair of cobs you drove over just now.'

'Yes, they are considered good horses. I bought them of Lord Dinderslie, and I keep up a very fair establishment. I *ought* to, you know, with my income.'

'Two thousand a-year, isn't it, with another six or seven hundred from the living ? A very good income indeed for a single man, Bernard. How do you contrive to spend it all ?'

'Oh, it goes easily enough,' replied the other with a nervous laugh. 'I keep seven or eight servants in the house alone, and we have half-a-dozen horses in the stables, and my farm is more expense than profit to me.'

'What can you want with half-a-dozen horses? You can't exercise them all yourself, and eight servants too ! It's a mistake, Bernard, my boy. to keep people and animals eating their heads off. however large your income may be. You should see the establishment with which I travel in the States. One man—one horse ! It makes no difference to me if I am in New York or a village. I never exceed it, and it's enough for any one in the world.'

'Yes, I quite agree with you, Cole, if—if—that is, while a man is single. But otherwise one must keep up a certain establishment for the sake of one's position in the county, and—'

'Quite true,' interrupted Cole, 'only as you do not intend to marry again—'

'I know I wrote something of the kind to you—a long time ago, though, wasn't it?—but I have been trying to tell you several times since we met that—that—in fact—I *am* married again, and have been for the last six months.'

'*What!*' exclaimed Nelson Cole, pushing back his chair and staring in young Freshfield's blushing face; 'what is that you say? *Married again!* Found the soul union so speedily! Satisfied your heart's hungering after a true mate. O Jupiter! O Venus! Why can't you confine your machinations to us poor mortals who never boasted of our virtue, and not go turning the parsons upside down in this worldly fashion? Is it *possible*, Bernard? Married again? And where did you find her, my boy? In a palace or on a dunghill—clothed in satin or rags? Oh, ye gods and little fishes! you have upset all my calculations. I came here prepared to stare at a real live voluntarily elected monk, and I find nothing but an ordinary Benedict, henpecked, most probably, like the remainder of his species. *Married again!* I can't believe it! I must ring for some more whisky and water.'

'Go on laughing at me,' said Bernard. 'I quite expected it, and perhaps I deserve it; but all the same, Cole, I am very happy.'

'Of course you are happy, my boy. They always *are* happy for the first few months. Amaryllis retains every virginal charm that first attracted you to her, until some day she loses her temper or her figure, or bolts with your dearest friend. But *your* Amaryllis has servants and carriages and horses at her command, so perhaps she will behave herself, at all events till some one richer than you are spends a summer in Bluemere.'

'Don't talk like that—there's a dear fellow,' replied Bernard gravely, 'or at all events not of *my* wife. You don't know what she is, Cole, or you would not sneer at my faith in her. And I will not try to tell you: you will see her to-morrow. and be able to judge for yourself.'

'I'm no judge of women.' returned Cole curtly ; 'I have not seen enough of them to become so ; and I class them all in one lump as the natural enemies of man. They stick to him—true! as the horse-leech sticks to its victim until every drop of blood has been drawn from his lifespring. No, I am afraid you would not consider my opinion worth having, Freshfield. I don't deny the necessity of women in the world. I am only sorry when I see one of my friends in their clutches. They are creatures to be bent to our purposes — not queens to tyrannise over our fortunes.'

But all that Bernard Freshfield answered was,—

'You have not yet seen my Phyllida.'

'What did you say was her name ? '

'Her maiden name was Phyllida Moss. She is a cousin of one of our oldest residents in Bluemere.'

'You had known the lady a long time, then ? '

'No,' replied Bernard consciously ; 'a very short time, if you count by weeks.'

'How the deuce *should* I count ? ' said Cole ; 'I suppose she is handsome ? a pretty face will lead a man to perdition.'

'People tell me she is beautiful, but I hardly

seem to see it. I only know that she is mine, and that I love her.'

'An old story,' grumbled Cole, 'and one that thousands of fellows have told before. Only there is generally a sequel to it. There generally comes a day when they wish she belonged to anybody else. Ah, Bernard, my lad, I'm sorry to find you in the toils again; but so long as your wife doesn't forbid your smoking a pipe and drinking a glass of whisky and water with an old friend, you may manage to pull through life yet.'

'Phyllida is not that sort of woman,' said Bernard fervently; 'she leaves me as absolutely free as I wish to leave her; and I am sure, when you have seen her in her own house, that however little you may care for her sex, Cole, you will acknowledge she is all that a woman ought to be. I married her because I felt her to be so sweet and lovable. I longed for her daily companionship and sympathy, and I told her plainly that I did not wish her to take any part of the parish duty. Yet I put no restraint on her actions, and the result is, that her own sweet, womanly nature has led her to do more than many who assume such cares, from the mere sense of right. She is the angel of Bluemere. There is not a house that harbours sickness or trouble but what knows the comfort of Phyllida's presence. I have seen mothers swooning over their little one's death-beds in her arms; I have seen children die there. I have watched the looks of gratitude and eager expectation with which the sick have greeted her approach. I have heard the blessings that have been poured out upon her head, and I have thanked God, who, in giving her to me, has given her also to those suffering people, who require her perhaps more than I do. But what she is to me, Heaven and my own heart alone can tell! Laugh at me if you will, Cole, I only speak the truth.'

There was silence between the friends for some minutes after the young husband's speech was ended.

' I am not going to laugh, Bernard,' said Cole at length: ' I don't even feel inclined to do so. I daresay your wife is all that you believe her to be ; even if she were not, you are a lucky man to be able to believe it. But let us understand each other, old friend. I don't wish to say anything disrespectful of Mrs Freshfield. She may be an angel (and in that case you will allow that, in speaking of women, I do not touch her) ; but you are right in saying I don't care for the sex. I have had little reason to do so ; and much as I love you, I am not quite sure that I should have volunteered a visit to Briarwood had I known you had re-established a mistress there. I began life with much the same ardour as you have, my boy. I believed that every beautiful face I saw was the index of a nature as beautiful as itself, and I got into several awkward scrapes in consequence. But it took some years to break down my confidence. I went on and on, hoping against hope to find the ideal woman I sighed for, and when I did find her (as I believed), she turned out worse than the whole lot put together. Then my eyes were opened to see the sex as they really are, and I have been much happier since. I have left off expecting impossibilities, and am content to take woman for what she is, a weaker, more foolish, and rather less moral specimen of humanity than ourselves ; and that is not saying much for her.'

'Dear Cole,' replied Bernard affectionately, 'you must have been very hard hit to talk like this. I had no idea you had ever had anything to do with women. We always considered you such a regular Saint Kevin at college.'

'Which is as good as saying you didn't think I was a man! No, my boy, we can't do without women in this world—but we can avoid the error of believing them to be more than women. You are still young and—for your age—very fresh! When you have reached my time of life you will talk differently. I can only hope your awakening may not be as bitter as was mine. And now let us speak of something more congenial. I am anxious to take back an English hunter with me to the States. Can you recommend me to an honest dealer with a good stud?'

Bernard sighed. He would have liked to sit up half the night discussing Phyllida's virtues with his friend, but he saw that the subject bored, if it did not annoy him, and wisely dropped it. He could only hope that the sight of his wife's beautiful face, and the charm of her girlish manner, might have the effect of winning over Nelson Cole to his own way of thinking. But for that he must wait for the morrow. The next morning he drove his friend over to the stables of a well-known breeder, some ten miles distant from Westertown, so that it was far advanced in the afternoon, almost dusk, in fact, when he turned his horses' heads into the Briarwood drive. His heart was beating rapidly by that time, for it was the first occasion since his marriage that he had been absent from Phyllida for more than an hour or two, and he was impatient to look upon her again and to present her to his friend. As they came in

view of the house, which Nelson Cole admired
without stint, Freshfield could hear nothing that
was said to him for the eagerness with which his
eye roved over the lawn and garden paths, to catch
a sight of his wife's figure, and when he saw it
he became childish in his delight.　Cole was just
asking him, in what style of architecture Briarwood Hall was built, when Phyllida, clad in fur
and velvet, and followed by a rough St Bernard
mastiff and two or three smaller dogs, came quickly
round the house to meet them.

'Is it Elizabethan, or of a later period?' demanded Cole.

'There she is!　There is my wife!' exclaimed
Bernard in reply, as he threw the reins to his groom
and leaped to the ground.

There was no false shame about the parson.
Although the servants and Nelson Cole were
standing by, he took Phyllida in his arms and
kissed her fondly.

'How are you, my darling?　Did you think I
was never coming home again?　Of course you
found my note in the library?　And here is the
friend for whom I told you to prepare a hearty
welcome—my dear old chum, Nelson Cole.'

'New caught from the States, madam, at your
service!' said Cole himself, as he advanced to take
her hand.　But instead of offering it to him, she
fell against her husband heavily.

'Did you trip against a stone, dearest?　Are
you hurt?' he exclaimed, as he felt her weight.
But Phyllida was standing straight again in a
moment—straight, steady, and almost rigid.

'I—am—very—glad—to—see—you,' she articulated in measured tones, as she stretched out her
hand to Nelson Cole.

Bernard was disappointed. He had spoken so freely of her warmth and geniality of manner! Was this the best welcome she could extend to his oldest friend ?

'You know who this is, don't you, Phyllida ?' he interposed briskly. 'You have often heard me speak of Nelson Cole, who has been out in America for the last five years. It was such a delightful surprise to me to get his letter yesterday; but I told you all that in my note. You found my note, of course, darling ?'

Phyllida shook her head. Her lips seemed glued together; she could not speak.

'You didn't find my note? Silly child, where did you look for it ? I put it on the top of my blotting book. But let us come in to the fire. It is freezing hard again, and it strikes me we all want thawing. Come in, Cole, and welcome a thousand times to Briarwood !'

He drew his friend's arm through his own as he spoke, and led him along the lighted corridor and into the comfortable library, believing his wife to be by his side. But when they turned into the room he found she had escaped him. To his surprise, and somewhat to his mortification, his beautiful Phyllida, whom he was just going to show off with so much pride to his companion, had eluded his vigilance and slipped upstairs to the bedroom.

'Why, where's Mrs Freshfield ?' he demanded of Edwards, who had followed them in to turn up the lamps.

'I think my mistress has gone upstairs, sir, to remove her walking things,' replied the servant.

'How provoking,' said Bernard; 'I wanted to

introduce you to her, Cole; you couldn't see what she was like in that half light—you would have fraternised over this ruddy fire.'

'Never mind,' said the other cynically, as he warmed his hands. 'Mrs Freshfield has been good enough to leave us the fire. And I shall have the extra pleasure of seeing her *en grande toilette* at dinner. Women are never happy without their war-paint!'

'Phyllida need not have had any scruples on that score. She looks well in anything,' replied Bernard, in rather a vexed tone ; but Nelson Cole began to praise his house and furniture, and he was soon thinking of something else.

Meanwhile, Phyllida, with a face of the hue of marble, and limbs that felt turned to stone, had dragged her way up to her own room and locked the door against intruders. She must have time, she thought, to breathe, to consider, to plan. What was best to be done? Her first idea was (as Miss Annie Warren had anticipated) that she would run away ; that she could not wait there to encounter Nelson Cole again ; that it would be utterly impossible for her to go down to the dining-room and sit opposite to him at table under the full blaze of the lamps, with his keen searching eyes fixed upon her face.

As she half-sat, half-leaned upon her bed in the dusky twilight, with her hands clasping her head, and a strong shudder of fear and apprehension pervading her frame, a sickening scene, which she tried to shut out in vain, rose before her mental vision,—a scene of glare and gas—of crashing instruments and clamorous voices—a sensation of having done something wrong without being able to prevent it, and then of failing limbs and bitter insult, and a sudden dismissal into the dark frosty night—of disgrace, humiliation, and ruin?

Who was it that had undergone such things? Had any one told her the story of a poor girl thus tempted and fallen, in some remote age and clime, and which she had nearly forgotten until now?

Phyllida passed her hand wonderingly over her velvet and sable costume, and half smiled in a sickly, nervous manner to think she was so foolish as to imagine any one could believe it possible that such a girl had any connection with herself.

But then returned the agonising common-place thought, that *she must go down to dinner*, that there was no escape from that ordeal, and all the fearful struggle with self had to be fought over again.

How she wished she could run away till Mr Cole had left Briarwood, or lie in bed and pretend to be ill; but that was nonsense. She knew that she couldn't run away nor lie in bed—it was impossible; the deception would be too transparent not to be seen through at once; and if suspicion existed, it would make it stronger. There was only one thing to be done—she must stand to her ground and brave it out!

Yes; that was her only plan—she must brave it out. There was still a chance that Mr Cole might not recognise her. She must have changed very much since that time. Every one said her happiness had improved her looks; she was stouter and rosier than in the old days, and her hair was not the same colour. The effects of the golden dye had now completely disappeared, and she wore it in a different fashion. If she were only bold and confident, all would go well.

No one would dare to tell the wife of Bernard

Freshfield that he had seen her—*where?* but this idea overwhelmed Phyllida. Love for Bernard, pity for herself, and shame for the humiliating past swept like a tempest over her mind, and drove her beside herself.

'Oh! why did I ever do it?' she moaned; 'why did I consent to marry him? I tried so hard to make him see me as I am, but he was blind and deaf to everything but his love for me. Oh, that noble, generous love! Am I doomed to be more guilty than I have ever been before, in uprooting and blighting it for the second time? Bernard, Bernard! I wish I had died before we met! I wish I may die now, with the memory of your loving. trusting face upon my mind, rather than live to see it changed to scorn and loathing! Why—*why* could I not have found some way out of the difficulty, except by pulling him down to share my dishonour? Oh, husband, I never loved you so dearly as I do in this hour of dread that I may live to part with you!'

As she thought thus—moaning, weeping, and rocking herself to and fro upon the bed, Phyllida was startled by hearing Bernard's voice outside the door.

'Let me in, my darling! I want to speak to you.'

'Oh, Bernie! I shall be ready soon,' she cried, in stifled tones; 'I am very busy; cannot you wait till I go downstairs?'

'Be quick, then; it is nearly dinner-time. But what are you doing, child? Anne says she has been waiting to hear your bell for the last half-hour.'

'Making myself beautiful,' replied the girl, with an hysterical laugh; 'you know I am determined to make a conquest of Mr Cole.'

'I don't think you will find much difficulty, though he is such an old cynic. But don't keep us waiting, my darling; I am as hungry as a hunter.'

He laughed merrily as he turned into his dressing-room, and she leaped off the bed and lighted the candles on her toilet table. Her cheeks were white, her eyes were red and swollen; her whole face bore evident signs of strong emotion. 'This will never do,' she said with a sort of desperation to herself; 'this is not the way to brave it out. My craven looks would disgrace a whipped school-girl.' Then she plunged her face in cold water, and used sundry means to restore her features to their usual appearance, before she rang the bell for her maid.

'Put on my prettiest dress to-night, Anne,' she said, with affected gaiety, as the servant entered, 'for the master wants me to look my very best.'

'Will you wear the white cashmere, or the silk, ma'am?' demanded Anne.

'The cashmere, and the gold fillet through my hair. Twist it up as tight as you can, please. I don't like to feel it falling about my face. There. That will do! I am afraid I look rather pale this evening. The cold weather has set in so suddenly, I feel chilled—and poor Sarah Jeffrey's death this afternoon quite upset me. I know Mr Freshfield will stare at my eyes; the frost has made them red—but I can't help it. Thanks; that is quite sufficient, and the sooner I get down to the fire the better.'

Thus, talking rapidly in order to avoid her own thoughts, and anxious to rush at once into the thick of the battle, lest delay should bring hesitation or cowardice in its train, Phyllida gathered

her creamy skirts about her, and almost ran down
to the library, expecting without doubt to find her
husband there. But when she had entered the
room beyond retreat, she discovered its sole occu-
pant to be Nelson Cole, who, leaving his warm
corner by the fireside, advanced to meet his hostess.
His first impression of her was certainly a favourable one. He had done no more than catch the
outline of a graceful figure in the dusky afternoon ;
but here, beneath the lamplight, stood a woman
whom he decided at once to be a sufficient excuse
for any folly on the part of Bernard Freshfield.
Like some dainty creature stepped out of an old
picture she stood before him, and as his glance
travelled from the folds of her soft clinging dress
to the fair face set in its framework of chesnut
hair, and the starry eyes that beamed with a
half-anxious, half-frightened look, Nelson Cole
confessed to himself that he had seldom seen a
prettier woman. Yet, in the first blush of their
meeting, something in her features or expression
startled him ; some remembrance connected with
her returned again and again to puzzle his brain,
and his answers to her questions betrayed more
inattention than they should have done from a
gentleman visitor to so fair a hostess. Her manner too struck him with surprise. It was more
than timid or hesitating, it was positively nervous,
and except for her manner, his eyes might not
have been so constantly attracted to her features.

'Oh!' she exclaimed with a gasp as she caught
sight of him, 'I thought Bernard was here! I am
sure he came down long ago.'

'I have not seen him since he went to dress,
Mrs Freshfield,' replied Nelson Cole, as he scruti-
nised her closely ; 'but I daresay he will soon

make his appearance.   Will you not take this seat by the fire?'

'No, thank you, I prefer to sit here,' she said, sinking down on a chair in the background. 'Have you seen my cousin, Mrs Penfold? She is here, you know.   My cousin with whom I used to live—at least I lived more with Mrs Pinner than with Mrs Penfold; but they're both my cousins, you know, and they knew my mother when she was a child.'

Nelson Cole began to think Mrs Bernard Freshfield must be a little 'cracked.' 'What the deuce,' he thought to himself, 'does she suppose I care about Pinners or Penfolds. If this is Bernard's idea of a companion, Heaven help him !'

But Phyllida, unabashed by his want of reciprocity, went on rapidly, and in a jerky manner,—

'You have never been here before, have you ? No, of course not ; but we all think it very pretty —Bluemere, you know ; but then we live here, you see, and that makes a difference. But you don't live in England, do you ?'

'No ; and I don't wish to do so. I don't like it,' replied Cole, with his usual curtness.

'Oh, here is cousin Penfold !' cried Phyllida as the door opened to admit that lady and her husband, and Bernard too. 'Oh, Bernie ! where have you been ? I thought you would have been down ages ago ! It is very cold, isn't it ? Mr Cole says he doesn't like England—only fancy ! Cousin Penfold, can't you come nearer the fire ?'

Nelson Cole began to think his friend had married a great simpleton. But one fact did not escape his notice. (What *did* escape it ?) After her husband's entrance, and when he had ensconced himself in the chair next her own, Phyllida sunk into silence. Bernard occasionally addressed an observation to her, and Mrs Penfold made one or two common-place remarks ; but Phyllida neither spoke nor moved. She sat in the shadow, dumb and motionless ; only once or twice Cole thought he could detect her rapid breathing.

'Why is that ?' he pondered ; 'she is evidently not a chatterbox by nature. What made her run on in that absurd fashion when she found herself alone with me ?'

This speculation made him examine her more closely when they were seated next each other at the dinner-table, and he had the opportunity of doing so without being obtrusive. Yet his eyes wandered so constantly her way, with a thoughtful, meditative look in them, that Bernard observed the evident attraction Phyllida possessed for his friend, and began to rally him on it.

'When you've quite finished looking at my wife, Cole,' he said, laughingly, 'I want you to try this Madeira, which competent judges have pronounced to be of first quality.'

Phyllida reddened like a rose, and Nelson Cole became apologetic.

'I trust I have not been guilty of a rudeness,' he replied ; 'but Mrs Freshfield's face reminds me so powerfully of one I knew long ago, that it is difficult for me to refrain looking at her. The likeness is surprising. It quite puzzles me.'

'I did not think there were two faces like my wife's in the world,' exclaimed Bernard ; 'who was the lady, Cole, and where did you meet her?'

'Very far from here, and in a place of which Mrs Freshfield has probably only heard the name —the city of Chicago, in America! She was—'

But at this juncture Phyllida completely lost her presence of mind.

'It was not me,' she cried excitedly. 'How should it be? I don't know her; I never saw the place; I have never been out of England in my life.'

In her hurry and agonising fear, she completely forgot before whom she was speaking, and her agitated tones filled her hearers with surprise. Bernard looked across the table with open eyes, and Mrs Penfold commenced a mild remonstrance,—

'My dear Phyllida, what are you talking about? Never been out of England in your life, my dear, when you were brought up in the West Indies!'

'Oh yes, the West Indies, of course,' replied the girl with a scared look : 'but I meant I hadn't been in America. Why should I have been? What should take me there?'

'I should have thought from your accent you *were* an American,' remarked Mr Cole dryly.

'Her father was,' interposed Bernard, 'and I fancy she must have caught her accent from him. But Phyllida is not at all herself this evening. I am afraid you are not well, my darling. Have you been doing too much in my absence?'

'She has been at that girl Jeffrey's death-bed all the afternoon,' said Mrs Penfold, 'and I think it has tried her nerves. It's not good for a young person to be always seeing such sights, Mr Freshfield, and I do not think Phyllida is strong enough for it.'

'She is always considering others before herself,' replied Bernard, smiling at his wife. But Phyllida did not smile in return. She sat with her eyes downcast, flushed, palpitating and silent. And

Nelson Cole's gaze still continued, every now and then, to travel her way, and watch each change in the expression of her countenance. Bernard Freshfield took the greater part of the conversation on himself, and talked fluently on all subjects connected with his private and professional life. When the dessert was on the table, and they were comparatively speaking alone, Nelson Cole started the subject of drunkenness, and asked if that vice was prevalent in Bluemere.

'No, I am thankful to say it is not,' replied Bernard Freshfield, 'for, in my opinion, it is the most degrading that can attack mankind ; and I really don't know how I should cope with it. You can reason with men on their other follies, but a drunkard is neither open to reason nor amenable to kindness. It is the most obstinate and the most disheartening weakness one can be called upon to try and remedy. Thank heaven, my people are very little addicted to it !'

'We see an immense deal of it in the States,' said Cole ; 'in fact, a man who refuses to "liquor up " on the score of morality or prudence, is thought very meanly of, and the youngest lads are ashamed to refuse to drink ! Even women are not entirely free from the disgusting habit.'

'I suppose it must appear incredible to you, Mrs Freshfield,' he continued, addressing himself particularly to Phyllida, 'living in an atmosphere of purity and virtue, that a *woman* could even lower herself sufficiently as to become intoxicated ; but it is not an unfrequent occurrence. I saw once in Chicago—the very place I was speaking to you of—a beautiful girl, younger than yourself (and, may I say, almost as fair) in a state of helpless inebriation on the public stage, and—'

But at this juncture he was interrupted by Phyllida rising hastily from her chair.

'I am ill,' she gasped, with leaden-coloured lips. 'Bernard, I cannot stay here any longer. Let me go to my room,' and without another glance at her visitor she staggered to the door, followed by Mrs Penfold.

'See to her; call me if I am wanted,' said Bernard anxiously to the latter lady, as he held the door open for them to pass out; and then he returned to his seat at the table with a perturbed countenance, and pushed the wine across to his friend moodily.

'Is Mrs Freshfield often attacked like this?' demanded Nelson Cole, as he cracked a walnut.

'No, it is most unusual. I am quite alarmed lest she should be going to be ill; she is generally so well and active, and so full of conversation. She is the very light and life of my home,' said poor Bernard with a sigh.

'Strange that she should relapse so suddenly,' remarked Cole. 'I hope it is not my ugly presence that has brought the change?'

'My dear old chum, how can you speak so? We took her rather by surprise this afternoon; but Phyllida is as glad to see you as I am. I can answer for that.'

'Humph!' ejaculated Nelson Cole; and then after a pause he asked, '*Where* did you say you met her?'

'Where did I meet my wife? In Bluemere. She came on a visit to her cousin Mrs Pinner.'

'And where did she come from?'

'St Domingo, I believe. Her family were residents there before her birth.'

Nelson Cole started.

'St Domingo! I know the place as well as I do myself; bad cess to it ! and I ought to know her family.   How were they called ? '

' Moss.   Her mother was married for the second time to a Mr Moss.'

' What was her name before that ? '

' I do not know.'

' Are you acquainted with the father ? '

' No.'

' Nor any of the relations ? '

' How should I be, when I tell you they are all in St Domingo,' replied Bernard rather testily. ' I know none of them except her two cousins, and had I known only herself that would have been enough for me.'

' Naturally, my dear boy. Relations are only a nuisance ; but it is strange I never heard the name of Moss in St Domingo. I knew every one there.'

' Well, it's evident you didn't know *him,*' returned Bernard, 'and it's of little consequence either, as both her p arents are dead.'

' And Moss was an American, you say ? '

' I believe so.'

' I expect he was raised up San Francisco way.'

' How can you tell ? '

' By Mrs Freshfield's accent. It has the true Californian ring in it.   You can tell a man's State by the twang of his tongue in America.'

' Ah, *I* am not so learned,' said Freshfield, in a tone of annoyance.

' Of course not. It is strange how your wife reminds me of the face I mentioned, and the more I look at her, the greater resemblance I see between them.'

'I did not think there were two such lovely women in the world,' replied the husband proudly.

'You were right. No more did I. And Mrs Freshfield's eyes are very remarkable ones, you will observe, for colour and size and expression. You seldom meet brown eyes with so plaintive a look in them.'

'Like the eyes of a hunted deer ; we have often remarked it,' said Bernard.

'I should like to see her and my little Chicago friend side by side,' continued Nelson Cole ; 'they might run in a curricle together.'

'*I* shouldn't,' laughed the other ; 'one has been enough to upset my peace of mind. I don't know what would become of me between two of them.'

When the gentlemen returned to the library, Mrs Penfold met them with a request that Bernard would go upstairs and wish his wife good-night at once, as she had been very hysterical, and wished to take a composing draught. So the husband left the apartment, and Nelson Cole found himself *tête-à-tête* with the old lady.

'I trust Mrs Freshfield is not really ill,' he commenced politely.

'I hope not, sir, but I really do not know what is the matter with her. She appeared almost delirious to me just now from the rambling way in which she talked.'

'She will doubtless feel the cold very much this winter. I believe she came here straight from the West Indies.'

'Yes, I believe she did.'

'She has not visited America, then ? I should have thought from her accent she was fresh from the country.'

' I have never heard her mention it, but then you see, sir, we knew nothing of our cousin before she came to England last June, and she has never been very communicative since. I have heard my sister say that. from one or two words Phyllida dropped, she fancied she had travelled farther than she cared to tell ; but it was no business of ours, nor of any particular interest either. And I should think that a gentleman, newly come from the country like yourself, would be a better judge than either of us.'

' Yes. Were it not that Mrs Freshfield denies having been in the United States, I should certainly have said I had met her there. She has a striking face and figure, not easily forgotten. I never saw so close a resemblance between two people in my life.'

He went to bed, still puzzled and uncertain, turning over and over in his mind every reminiscence he retained of that time, yet unable to satisfy himself entirely on the subject. until, as he lay pondering over it all with himself, he suddenly jumped up and exclaimed aloud,—

' I have it ! I know what has caused this confusion in my mind. She has altered the colour of her hair. The golden wig has disappeared, *vice* a more clerical hue, and has set all my wits wool-gathering in consequence. But I am pretty certain now. and one more link in the chain will settle my last doubt.'

He went to his despatch box as he spoke, and drew thence from a secret drawer a small piece of folded paper.

' I will give Mrs Freshfield my little *souvenir* so look at,' he said. ' Her husband affirms that the is very sympathetic. The sad story of Stephanie Harcourt will be sure to appeal to her benevolent nature.'

He went back and lay down again on his bed, but he had no further sleep until the morning. At breakfast he was told that Mrs Freshfield had passed a very restless night, and was not well enough to come downstairs. He received the intelligence with perfect stolidity,—indeed he had quite expected it,—and would not have been surprised had he been told that her illness had turned out so dangerous she had been obliged to go away altogether. Women he believed to be endowed (in common with the lower animals) with any amount of instinctive cunning, in order to avoid danger. He smiled inwardly when he heard the news, and concluded that he had seen the last of Mrs Bernard Freshfield, at all events for this visit.

But he was mistaken. Phyllida was only trying to recruit her shaken nerves. She was shocked and horrified when she remembered how she had betrayed herself the evening before, and all her desire now was to remove the impression she must have made upon the mind of Nelson Cole. She promised herself, during those hours of solitude, that she would really be brave this time, and hear all her husband's friend might have to say to her without even changing countenance. She would listen to his story of the drunken actress at Chicago, and ask him what name she went by, and commiserate her sad fate, and say openly that she wished she could find her out and be her friend. She went downstairs at luncheon time full of these grand resolutions, and she trembled like an aspen leaf at the first sight of the man who held her destiny in his hands.

It was some little while before Nelson Cole could contrive to speak to her alone, but at last the opportunity occurred. Bernard was called out to baptise a new-born child, and particularly begged his wife not to leave the house during his absence.

' It is far too chilly, my love,' he said, ' and you will make yourself ill again. Stay by the fire with Cole and let him see that I have not overrated my wife's powers of conversation. I shall not be gone long.'

How little he dreamed what would happen during that temporary absence !

Phyllida stood where he had left her, before the fire, with one foot upon the fender. She was looking into the burning coals ; but as the hall-door slammed behind Bernard, she felt that her companion's eyes were fixed upon her, and in another moment his voice sounded in her ear.

' Mrs Freshfield, your husband tells me you have a superabundance of sympathy for those who suffer ! Will you read these few lines and tell me what you think of the writer ? '

He placed a paper in her hands as he spoke, and she unfolded it mechanically, and gazed at its contents.

' What is this ? ' she asked, in an awed tone.

' Cannot you see ? Are you short-sighted ? It is a wedding-ring. It was given me by the person who wrote the letter.'

She looked at the worn circle of gold long and earnestly, and large tears gathered in her eyes.

' Are you reading the letter, Mrs Freshfield ? Have you no curiosity to see what it says ? '

No. Apparently she had no curiosity. Nature was the only thing stirring in her breast just then, and it broke forth in a cry of pain as she raised her mother's wedding-ring to her lips.

Even as they touched it, she felt the grasp of Nelson Cole's hand upon her arm.

'*Stephanie Harcourt,*' he said, in a stern voice '*what are you doing here?*'

CHAPTER XIII.

PHYLLIDA gazed into the hard, determined face of Nelson Cole, and felt that she had nothing to expect from him. She had anticipated his accusation. In the solitude of her chamber she had imagined that just such a moment might arise when he would turn round and call her by her theatrical name, and she had thought she was fully prepared for the emergency. She had resolved to be so calm and brave, and to return his look with one of such complete astonishment as to disarm his suspicion, and leave him more puzzled than before. But when the time came, all her resolutions melted into thin air. It is difficult to keep a brave front before the truth. Even murderers, with their lives at stake, are forced by some inward power into confession. So, instead of staring her accuser out of countenance and haughtily demanding if he meant to insult her, Phyllida steadied herself with one hand against the library table, and with white lips faltered,—

'*You will not betray me?*'

Even Nelson Cole was staggered by this abrupt surrender. He had been certain of her identity before he placed the packet with her mother's wedding-ring in her hand; but he had expected to have somewhat of a fight with her, and to bring her to her knees only through threats of exposure to the world. And when she gazed up at him with tearful, pleading eyes, and made that tremulous prayer for pity, his task became a very hard one. He was a stern, cynical man, and he had a mean opinion of her sex; but he was not such a stoic as to be able to destroy all the hopes of such a very pretty woman without a pang. He took two or three steps backward in his surprise.

It *is* yourself, then!' he ejaculated; 'and you confess it? Upon my soul, I can hardly believe that it is true. Although I recognised you in the first hour we met, I can scarcely believe that any woman is capable of such an act of wickedness as this. Stephanie Harcourt, are you lost to all sense of decency, or are you mad?'

'Oh, Mr Cole,' she cried, trembling, 'don't speak to me like this. You were kind to me once before when I was in great trouble and distress, and I have never forgotten it. Don't turn altogether against me now.'

'*Kind to you before,*' he repeated, in a tone of contempt. '*What were* you before? answer me that. Am I to extend the same leniency that I showed to a second-rate actress, discharged for misconduct from the Chicago stage, to the woman I find living at Briarwood as the wife of my friend Bernard Freshfield? How did you come here? What devil sent you to Bluemere? And how dared you impose upon his credulity and trust in you ?'

'He *would* marry me,' she answered, weeping. 'I tried—oh, so hard!—to make him see what a bad thing it would be for him, and how much beneath him I was in every way; but he would not listen to anything I said. He declared his life's happiness was bound up in me, and so I gave myself into his hands to do as he thought best with.

'Don't talk rubbishy sentiment to me,' said Nelson Cole brusquely. 'This is a matter that is not to be mended with any humbug of that sort. You know that you are not his wife—that you cannot be—that you are the wife of that forger in the New York Tombs.'

'Oh no, no!' she cried passionately, clasping her hands together; 'indeed I am not. Cortës died in the Tombs three months ago. I read the news in the *New York Times;* and I know it is true. And it made me so happy—so very, very happy. I began a new life from that day.'

'Dead, is he?—and three months ago. But what difference does that make to you? You were married to Freshfield *six* months ago.'

'I know I was; but surely, sir, you do not suspect I was not free to marry him? I was divorced from Fernan Cortës before I left the States. I have the papers in my possession. I had no difficulty in getting free from a man who was locked up for two years for forgery.'

'Divorced!' said Cole contemptuously; 'pulled through by a Chicago attorney; and when Freshfield does not even believe in the legality of a divorce in his own country, why, in his eyes you are no more his wife now than you are mine.'

Her brown eyes dilated with horror.

'What!' she ejaculated. 'He does not believe in it?—he would consider it a farce, a fraud? Oh, Mr Cole, you cannot think I knew that? It is the first moment I have ever suspected such a thing. Do you think I would have dragged him down—*he*, who has been so noble, so generous, so loving, to me—to share such a lot as mine—had I not fully believed the past was done with for ever? Bernard not think me free?—still consider me chained to that dreadful man, and whilst his kisses were on my lips? Oh, my God! how I have been deceived!'

'*I* should rather say, how poor Freshfield has been deceived!' replied her companion. 'I am afraid to think what he will do when he hears that you have never been his wife.'

'Oh, don't say that!' exclaimed the girl in a voice of pain; 'don't think it. If you only knew all the love that has passed between us—the confidence we have exchanged—the delight we have had in each other's society—the thanks we have given to God for our happiness—you would not say we are not married. What *is* marriage but an union of hearts and souls—a mutual devotion—a tie that no misfortune nor trouble can unloose? And this is what Bernard and I feel for each other. Believe me, sir, we are true husband and wife. It would kill me to think we could ever be otherwise.'

'And do you suppose I can let matters go on in this way, then?' he asked roughly.

'What do you mean?'

'I mean that I came here to find that you have deceived my best friend; that you are still deceiving him; that he has not the slightest knowledge of your antecedents nor your condition, and that if I leave him in the same deplorable ignorance, I shall prove myself to be his worst enemy.'

'You will not *tell* him?' she screamed; 'you will not tell him of Cortës or my having been on the stage? Oh, Mr Cole, remember *he* is *dead*— he can never rise up to bear witness against me now; and I *am* Bernard's wife; indeed, *indeed* I am!'

'Stephanie Harcourt, if I acceded to your request, I should become *particeps criminis*, and I will not do it. Bernard Freshfield must learn the truth—if not from your lips, from mine.'

'Oh, I cannot, I *cannot* tell him,' she moaned; 'he has loved me so. You do not know how he has loved me.'

'I know that if he has the noble nature with which I credit him, that he will pretty soon *un*love you when he hears how he has been deceived. To think of your assurance in coming to a place like this, and taking your stand amongst respectable people, and finishing off by marrying a parson, beats me altogether. I have always known that your sex possess the daring insolence of the devil; that you will trample on proprieties, and carry your cheateries with a high hand, such as men would shrink from assuming; but I think your case is worse than any I have ever heard of.'

As he concluded he advanced suddenly, and grasped her again by the arm.

'In the name of evil!' he exclaimed, 'what made you leave America?'

She did not resent his rudeness. She only deprecated it by falling at his feet.

'Oh, sir,' she cried, weeping bitterly, 'you felt for me once before; show a little mercy to me

now. I came to England with the money you
sent me.'

' D—n my folly ! ' he interposed loudly.

' I came only desirous to find honest work, by
which to earn my living ; but my cousin Pinner
invited me to take a month's rest at Bluemere
first, and here it was I met him. Oh, sir, you
do not know, you cannot tell, the temptation it
was to me to let him love me. No starving creature with rich food in sight was ever more sorely
tempted to steal what was not his to take. But I
tried—indeed I did—to prevent his lowering himself by marrying me. I even asked him to take
me as I was instead—a lot like that, with such a
man as he is, would have been too good for me.
But you know his noble nature. He would do
nothing less than what was right in his own eyes,
and so he married me ; and I thought—I thought
—I hoped,' she went on sobbing, ' until you came,
that, by reason of his love and goodness, I might
live to become, some day, not all unworthy of
him. Oh, sir, you were my good angel once, and
took me away from all that was degrading me, and
gave me fresh hopes of life. Don't undo your work
now. Don't drag me again from the heaven you
helped me to attain, back to the misery from which
you lifted me.'

Nelson Cole was moved by her appeal. He felt
himself uncomfortably moist about the eyes, and
there was a husky sensation in his throat which
made it difficult for him to answer her. Yet his
mind never wavered from the idea that it had
formed of duty. He loved and respected Bernard
Freshfield more than he cared to acknowledge
even to himself, and he felt that he could not
leave him the dupe of a woman, whose antece-

dents rendered her quite unfit to fill the high position he had placed her in.

So, although he felt very much for Phyllida—more even than he had done for the trembling and shame-stricken girl whom he had visited and succoured in Chicago—he was firm in his resolution that Bernard Freshfield must learn the truth respecting her.

'You ask me an impossibility,' he replied. 'I am very sorry for the disgrace you have brought upon yourself; but you should have told Freshfield everything from the beginning. What right had you to conceal the events of your former life from him?'

'I know I should have done so. I have suffered for it greatly,' she sobbed, still kneeling at his feet; 'but I thought there was no chance of its ever being raked up again. I hoped it was buried and done with. I believed that that miserable episode need never be any more to me than a half-forgotten nightmare.'

'You thought, in fact, that neither I nor Miss Vavasour, nor any of your Chicago friends, would ever show their faces in the mother country! That was not very astute of you, Miss Harcourt. But supposing it had been the case, I think Mr Jack Neville can tell a few stories about a life even prior to the one you were leading when we met! I conclude you have not quite forgotten that scoundrel Sandie Macpherson, and the Sacramento Valley business, eh?'

She rose to her feet then, and confronted him with a face in which there was no visible feeling but that of indignant scorn.

'I have forgotten nothing—*nothing!*' she articulated; 'and above all that, every trouble I have encountered in this life—every sin I have committed —has been at the instigation or command of your sex. And you, too, are determined to hunt me down! I read it in your eye and the tones of your voice. Let it be so, then. I will make no further appeal to your pity or your generosity. Bernard Freshfield shall know the worst that you can tell him.'

'You will not break the news to him yourself, then? It will be the better for you, perhaps. You women have a thousand little wheedling ways, remember, by which you can induce a man to believe anything you choose, and to forgive everything, even against his calmer judgment! If you will tell the man you call your husband the truth with your own lips, you will probably be able to persuade him to marry you over again.'

'You have refused me your sympathy, Mr Cole; you might spare me your sarcasm! I am only a woman, you know, and cannot be expected to cope with it. And I would rather that you conveyed the intelligence you speak of to your friend. I don't think it—it—will make him happier, and there is no need that I should add more than my necessary share to his disappointment.'

As Phyllida pronounced, with some difficulty, the last word, she turned from him, and with drooping figure and bowed head left the room. Nelson Cole looked after her uneasily.

'D—n it all!' he thought. 'What *am* I to do? I'd give a thousand dollars not to have seen her at all; but having seen her, I cannot reconcile it to my conscience to leave that poor boy in ignorance of her identity! Why, I should be aiding and abetting one of the greatest deceptions I ever heard of. And a parson's wife, too! It beats everything that ever happened to me before. But *I* can't do the job. I must wait a few days and persuade the child to do the right thing herself— she will see on reflection that it *is* right, and will do it from love to him—and then they must slip away quietly somewhere, and be married over again to satisfy his scruples. Hang it all! she is a lovely creature, and I don't wonder at the boy going mad over her. And she's got some good in her too, poor little soul! and after all she is but a woman! Well, well, it's a most unfortunate business, and I wish I could guess how Bernard will take it. But at all risks it must be done.'

And so musing, Nelson Cole, half sorry for Bernard and half sorry for Phyllida, but quite believing that, however great a tempest his interference might provoke, the weather would settle down and be fair again after a while, walked round to the stables, and mounting a horse which Freshfield had ordered to be kept for his use, rode off, wondering how the poor little girl was bearing it all, and by what argument he could best induce her to tell her husband the entire truth. And the 'poor little girl' meanwhile, stunned by the calamity that had overtaken her, was walking up and down her own room, and resolving more determinately with every step, that she would die rather than tell it. The events of the last six months, during which she had gradually been learning to believe herself to be prosperous, respectable, and beloved, seemed to have slid past her like a dissolving view, and she was once more the disgraced and unprotected actress of Chicago, who had broken down in *the* song of the evening, and been ignominiously expelled. She shrank even from her own scrutiny, as in fancy she travelled back to that scene of humiliation, and felt as if all Bluemere had been witnesses of it, and she heard their voices reviling her for having dared to pollute their thresholds with her presence. She was no longer Mrs Freshfield of Briarwood—that dignity had been stripped from her like a stolen garment —she was Stephanie Harcourt, the burlesque actress, and the widow of a criminal who had died in the Chicago gaol. And she, who was all this and more, had pretended to be the wife of a good and pure and true-hearted man, who had believed in her and trusted her, and endowed her with all his worldly goods, and given her *his* mother and *his* sister to be hers also.

Tell Bernard! Go and look into Bernard's faithful eyes, and tell him she had never been his wife!—that she had seduced him into the commission of a crime that must be abhorrent to his feelings; listen to his reproaches; hear his exclamations of surprise and horror; see his looks of pain! No, no, she could not do it! she would die first; she would throw herself into the mere, as she had felt prophetically before all this misery came to pass that it would have been best to do.

And neither could she stay whilst Nelson Cole repeated the story of her disgrace—that would be almost worse than telling it herself, like standing in the next room with bated breath whilst some dreadful operation was being performed upon one's dearest friend, unable to help or comfort, because one had not the courage to look upon his inevitable pain. Phyllida told herself incoherently that she could neither use the knife nor see it used. She felt much the same as Charles the First must have felt when Lord Strafford went to his death, guilty to the last degree of the suffering about to be inflicted, but powerless to avert it, and too great a coward to see it put in execution.

Nelson Cole did not return to Briarwood till close upon the dinner hour. It was a raw, foggy afternoon, and riding in the dusk was not exhilarating exercise, yet he preferred it to the chance of encountering Phyllida without the presence of Freshfield, and being subjected, perhaps, to another series of piteous appeals for mercy. He had only time to run up to his bedchamber and change his spattered riding-suit before the second dinner-gong sounded, and he descended to the hall, where he met Bernard in evident perturbation.

'My dear Cole, I am so annoyed. Fancy, my wife has actually gone out, after all my cautions to her, and in this wretched fog. It is really too bad of my people. She is so good to them they think she is at their beck and call. I suppose some old woman sent up a request for her presence, and the dear child rushed off at once. But I must put a stop to it. I won't have her health sacrificed for the sake of the parish.'

Nelson Cole looked grave, but all he answered was,—

'It is, indeed, a foggy afternoon. I could hardly see an inch before me as I rode home, and more than once I thought I had lost my way.'

'Imagine Phyllida being exposed to it,' continued Bernard, in a voice of injury, as they entered the dining-room together. 'I do think, Mrs Penfold, you might have prevented your cousin leaving the house in such weather.'

'Indeed, Mr Freshfield, I am not to blame. I have been in my own room ever since luncheon, and have not even set eyes on Phyllida. I thought she was in the library with Mr Cole, where I believe you left her.'

'To be sure I did. What did she say to you about it, Cole? Have you no notion where she has gone?'

'Not the slightest, my dear fellow. Mrs Freshfield and I talked together for perhaps half-an-hour after you left us, and then she went up (I imagined) to her own room. It was not until I found she had no intention of returning, that I decided to take a ride. She did not honour me with any confidences as to her plans for the afternoon.'

'Well, it is useless saying any more about it,' replied Bernard, with evident annoyance. 'So let us think of our dinner. She is sure to be back before long.'

But the meal that followed was a very silent one. Bernard was fretting at his wife's absence. Nelson Cole, knowing what was in store for his friend, was naturally grave and thoughtful, and Mrs Penfold could hardly be very lively all by herself. So as soon as the dessert appeared, she rose from table and left the two gentlemen to entertain each other. Bernard sat silent for a few moments, then, striking his hand upon the table,—

'I will stop all my wife's visiting and nursing in the parish from this evening,' he said angrily 'I knew what it would be if she once began such work. Women can never do things by halves.

She will end by sacrificing me and her friends for her fancied obligations to the poor. She doesn't go into a single cottage after to-night. I don't care for this sort of thing, and I won't stand it.'

'Hullo, my boy!' exclaimed Cole, 'aren't you coming it rather strong? Mrs Freshfield may entertain a different opinion from yours. Women, as you justly say, seldom do things by halves, even to having their own way.'

'Phyllida is not like the rest of her sex,' replied Bernard; 'she is a child for docility and innocence.'

'Are you so sure of that, Freshfield? You always speak of your wife as if she had not an idea of her own ; as if she had never lived a life apart from yours ; as if, in fact, she were a nonentity. Now I don't think she is. On the contrary, I find that she has double the amount of experience of most females of her age.'

'Has she been confiding to you the history of her former life, then?' inquired Bernard jealously, knowing that no such confidence had ever been reposed in him.

'We have been speaking of it certainly, and I was surprised to find how far Mrs Freshfield has travelled and how much she has seen. I told her that she must tell the same story to you, and she promised me that she would.'

'It seems strange that my wife should tell you, a perfect stranger, of incidents that she has not considered it worth while to mention to myself. Are you sure she was not " chaffing " you? Phyllida is rather inclined to be mischievous when she finds a good subject to practise on.'

'No, I don't think it was "chaff," Bernard. I believe it was sober earnest. Neither does Mrs Freshfield regard me as a perfect stranger. We came to the conclusion this afternoon that we knew a good deal about each other—in fact, we are not quite sure that we have not met before.'

'Well, it's all high Dutch to me,' said Bernard pettishly, as he pushed back his chair from the table, and gazed thoughtfully into the fire. He did not relish the idea that his wife—who was so reticent with himself respecting everything in the past—should have been confidential with another man, and became more impatient than ever for Phyllida's return, that he might elucidate the seeming mystery. Nelson Cole, on the other hand, had made his remarks with the best intentions, hoping by them in some measure to prepare the husband's mind for the unhappy news that should greet him when he met his wife again. For he had little doubt in his own mind that Phyllida's absence was due, not to her active benevolence, so much as the perturbed state of her mind, and pictured to himself the unfortunate girl wandering about the plantations or shrubberies in that dense fog, vainly striving to reconcile herself to the inevitable, until he wished he had bitten out his tongue before he had said the words that had driven her from her home. They waited for two or three hours after dinner in vain expectation of her return, and then Bernard, having questioned all the servants, came into his friend's presence with a face the colour of chalk, and announced his intention of searching for his wife in the village.

'I am getting so alarmed, Cole,' he articulated, with chattering teeth, 'I hardly know what to do;

but to remain at home is impossible. Not a soul in the house saw Phyllida go out, which is very extraordinary, for the messages from the village always reach her through Mrs Garnett, the house-keeper. I have ordered my horse, therefore, and am going to ride over to my mother's. If she is not there or at Mrs Pinner's, I shall search for her in Bluemere, for I cannot allow her to remain out on such a night as this. Will you excuse my leaving you, old fellow ? You must know the state of anxiety I am in.'

'Can't I help you, Freshfield? Let me have another horse and ride over to Brick Common. It lies at some distance from Bluemere, does it not ?'

'Oh, she never could have been so mad as to go out to the Common on foot, Cole. It is a long way from this, and I doubt if she could walk it. Besides, it is dangerous ground down by the mere, and I would not allow you to traverse it without company. She must be at Blue Mount, though what has taken her there is beyond my comprehension.'

His horse came round as he spoke, and Cole watched him ride off through the fog with a heavy heart. A sudden fear lest the unhappy girl had attempted her own life in the mere had darted through him, and he felt that in such a case he should hold himself guilty of her death. He turned back into the house with a very grave face, and his spirits were not lightened by Mrs Penfold's melancholy forebodings.

'Do you think it possible anything can have happened to poor, dear Phyllida, Mr Cole ?' she whimpered. 'She has been so strange and unlike herself, both yesterday and to-day, that I quite fear the worst. I told you how she rambled last evening, and though I gave her a sleeping draught she talked all night of the most extraordinary things. And now to run away in this unaccountable manner, and without saying a word to anybody. It is really very unusual ; and if anything happens to her, poor, dear thing, in consequence, I am sure I shall never get over it.'

'What do you expect to happen to her,' returned Cole, in his gruff way, ' unless it is an attack of bronchitis or influenza? *That*, I should imagine to be a very likely result of such an act of imprudence on Mrs Freshfield's part, and the best thing you can do, Mrs Penfold, is to see that everything is prepared ready for your cousin to take a hot bath as soon as ever she returns home.'

'Oh, you are quite right, my dear sir ; thank you so much for the suggestion,' replied Mrs Penfold. 'I will go and see to it at once. Of course a hot bath, and just the least drop of brandy and water to take inwardly, that will be the very thing for dear Phyllida, to prevent the injurious effects of the fog.'

She left him to himself as she concluded, and Cole was thankful to be so left, for his anxiety was fast changing into apprehension. He did not employ himself, but sat there eagerly listening for the sound of the horse's hoofs which should bring Bernard back with news of her. They came at last, and as he entered the hall Cole went out to meet him.

'Well, my boy. and where is she ?'

'I can't find her,' replied Freshfield moodily, as he stalked into the library ; 'I have inquired at every house in Bluemere, but they have seen nothing of her. She *must* have gone to Brick Common. But it is too bad, too hard of her,' he continued, leaning his head in his hands; 'she knows how dear and precious she is to me, and might have guessed the alarm I should feel on her account. Besides, I asked her not to leave the house; you heard me, Cole? I asked her as plainly as I could speak not to venture out in this detestable fog.'

'I know you did, but I suppose Mrs Freshfield imagined it was her duty to go. Any way, my dear boy, it can't be helped now, and you must make the best of it. If your wife is at Brick Common, she will be safe enough till the morning, and you had better go to bed and forget this worry in sleep.'

'She *must* be at Brick Common,' repeated Bernard; 'there is no other place for her to be at; and she will be safe enough until the morning, as you say. And yet I don't think I can sleep, Cole, not being certain where she is, and I'd rather sit up in the library until I can start off to look for her again.'

'Then I shall sit up with you,' said Nelson Cole, and the household being dismissed to their beds, and the horses ordered for seven o'clock the following morning, the friends ensconced themselves in two arm-chairs opposite each other, and prepared to hold a vigil until dawn.

CHAPTER XIV

BERNARD FRESHFIELD was naturally very down-cast and disinclined to talk; but Nelson Cole told him so many stories of the vigorous life in the New World, that he became deeply interested, and the hours passed more quickly than either had anticipated.

'That is the sort of life that would suit me,' exclaimed Bernard, after Cole had been giving him an account of the gold digging in the Sacramento Valley, and described the lawless set of ruffians by which it was conducted. 'I should enjoy above all things the freedom and the freshness of such an existence, and I may add, of such a congregation. To do good to such a population would be a real triumph to the worker. The truths of the gospel, where they *did* take root, would fall with such tremendous power on the newly-turned surface of their minds. Such different work from grinding the same tune, day after day and year after year, to children so accustomed to the piping that they refuse to listen, and far less to dance. Cole, I should like to be a missionary in Sacramento Valley.'

'So you may think, Freshfield, but I fancy you would alter your mind when you had made a trial of it. The specimens *I* have met from Sacramento have not been promising subjects for conversion, I can tell you—murderers, gamblers, ruffians, thieves. There is no description of vice that does not take ready root in that congenial soil—a gold-digging encampment. I have reason to say so, believe me. Some day I may tell you why.'

Bernard was about to answer, when the wire of the house-bell grated as though the handle had been ineffectually pulled. It was now nearly six o'clock in the morning, and the sickly, dirty looking dawn, which succeeds a winter's night, was trying to struggle through the holes in the shutters.

'Hark! What was that?' said Cole, as they started simultaneously to their feet. A second passed and again the wire grated audibly, whilst the faintest of tinkles sounded from the bell.

'It is Phyllida,' cried Bernard, as he rushed into the hall, followed by his friend, and began hurriedly to undo the fastenings of the door. But when he threw it open there was no Phyllida upon the steps; only the figure of a little lad, not more than eight or ten years old, whose teeth chattered with the cold.

'Who are you, and what do you want?' exclaimed Freshfield, as he caught sight of him.

'If you please, sir, I've bring'd the letter, and the leddy said as how you'd give me a shillin' for bringin' of it, so I didn't wait longer than I was 'bliged to, cos the leddy says the sooner ye get it the better, so mother tell'd me to run over as soon as 'twas light.'

He fumbled in his dirty pocket as he spoke, and produced a crumpled envelope.

'Where *is* the lady?' exclaimed Bernard impatiently, as he seized the epistle. 'Where do you come from?'

'I don't know where she be now; she was a goin' off in the railway; but *I* come from Westertown.'

'*Westertown!*' cried Bernard, staggering backward.

'Come, Freshfield,' said Cole, 'go to the library and read your letter, whilst I settle with the lad. I suppose one can scarcely send him all the way back again without something to eat, so here's your shilling, my boy, and you can go down to the kitchen and sit there till the servants are about. It won't be long now before they're stirring.'

It took him a minute or two to usher the shivering little wretch to the kitchen premises, and when he reached the library again he unbarred and threw back the shutters in order to give his friend still further time to overcome whatever shock might be contained for him in that letter. But when, at last, he turned to look at Bernard, he was startled at his appearance. The young man was standing by the table, white, rigid and immovable, as if he had been turned to stone, with his eyes fixed upon the paper spread open before him.

'Why, Freshfield, old fellow, what's the matter now?' said Cole cheerfully.

'What does this mean?' demanded the other in a hollow tone.

'What does *what* mean?'

'This letter—her letter. Read what she says to me.'

Nelson Cole took up the paper, and read the following words:—

'BERNARD,—By the time this reaches you, your friend will have told you all he knows about me; and you will have learned how much you have been deceived. But oh, my darling, don't fret about it; I will never disgrace you more. I am going away where you will never hear of me. Only try to forget everything about me, excepting that I loved you very dearly, and had not strength to do what

I ought to have done. But indeed, *indeed*, I believed myself to be your wife.

'PHYLLIDA.'

'*What does it mean?*' again demanded Bernard Freshfield, as Cole came to the end of the letter.

'It means, my poor boy, that at last she speaks the truth.'

'The truth!—that paper! Take care what you are saying, Cole ; the truth that she disgraced me—that she only believed herself to be my wife. Why, I married her by special licence at Gatehead. She must be mad; you are all mad to imagine such a thing.'

'Bernard,' said Nelson Cole steadily, as he laid his hand on that of his friend, 'there is a great blow in store for you. Bear it like a man.'

'Who says I shall not ? Because I am a parson, do you suppose I am not a man—as good a man as yourself? But she says you know all about her. What can *you* know that she has not told to *me*—her husband ?'

'Unfortunately, a great deal. I wish it were not so. I knew her in Chicago, long before she came to England. I knew her there upon the stage, as a burlesque actress, and not as a very prudently behaved actress. The first time I met her, Bernard, was under very distressing circumstances ; she had just been dismissed from her employment for—for—in fact for intoxication.'

He glanced at the husband's face as he spoke. It looked as though carved in marble. Only the eyes glared like two balls of fire, and the dry lips muttered harshly the words, '*Go on.*'

'Why she came to England after that I do not know ; but she had no right to have married you, Bernard, without telling you the truth. She was a married woman, who had obtained a divorce from her husband, and six months ago he was alive in the New York gaol.'

'*It's a lie!*' cried the figure by the table; and Bernard Freshfield made a sudden lunge forward, as though he would have struck his friend. The next moment, however, he had fallen backward, striking his head against the steel fender, and lay on the hearth-rug, silent and immovable, with the blood oozing from a cut on the forehead.

Nelson Cole ran upstairs for a sponge and cold water, and having secured the door against possible intruders, knelt down beside the poor young husband, and administered to him as tenderly as if he himself had been a woman. So that in a few minutes Bernard Freshfield, ghastly pale and shivering, as though he had an ague, staggered to his feet again, and sank down in an arm-chair.

'There, dear boy, you are better now,' said Nelson Cole compassionately ; 'it's an ugly truth to swallow, Bernard, and no one knows it better than myself ; but you must learn to look it in the face, old fellow, and it will be none the easier for turning your head the other way.'

'It *cannot* be true!' murmured Freshfield.

'It *is* true, my son! Unhappily there is not a doubt upon the subject. A year ago Phyllida Moss was an actress on the Chicago stage, under the name of Stephanie Harcourt, and the wife of a notorious forger and criminal, called Fernan Cortës, then undergoing his sentence in the Tombs at New York. She tells me that she procured a divorce from Cortës before she left Chicago, and that he died in the Tombs three months ago ; but I am afraid that will not be much consolation to you. A divorce may be obtained in Chicago for the most trivial reason, and in the most irregular fashion. Couples divorce each other there for incompatibility of temper, or, as you see, on account of the husband being arrested, and the evidence of one party only is necessary to the decree. You must perceive, therefore, what an irregular proceeding it must be. When you met Stephanie Harcourt, she was, according to your own ideas on the subject, still the wife of Cortës, and without power to contract another alliance.'

'It *cannot* be true,' repeated Bernard, in a confused manner ; 'you must be mistaken. You are thinking of some one else.'

'Can't you believe the evidence of her own letter, Freshfield ? She only discovered that I had recognised her for certain yesterday afternoon, and her first act is to leave her home. Does not that prove to you that my statement must be correct ? '

'You frightened her, perhaps,' replied Bernard. 'She is not strong, and she saw no way of coping with your testimony. I cannot accept a statement that destroys my life, on the evidence of one witness alone.'

'Will you accept it on the evidence of two ? ' rejoined Cole. 'Jack Neville, who travelled with me from New York, is staying in London. Will you hear what he has to say on the subject ? '

'Who is Jack Neville ? ' asked Bernard in a low voice.

'He is a fellow who has been implicated in dozens of scrapes, and burned his fingers more than once ; but a sterling good fellow for all that, and one whose word you may trust to the uttermost.   I only knew Stephanie Harcourt in Chicago ; but he knew her in San Francisco, long before she went upon the stage.   Will you come up to town with me and interview Jack with respect to her ? '

'How are we to be sure that he will mean my—my— I would say. how can we be certain his description applies to Phyllida ?   Two women may singularly resemble each other.'

'True.   Take up her photograph, then, and show it to Jack yourself.   I see you have a very beautiful coloured portrait of her in the drawing-room, taken in white satin and pearls.   She is hardly likely to have worn white satin and pearls in Sacramento Valley.   I think if you show that to Neville, and he recognises it, notwithstanding its surroundings, to be the same woman he knew in 'Frisco, you may be satisfied also as to its identity with Stephanie Harcourt.'

Bernard did not reply, but moved unsteadily towards the door.

'Where are you going, dear boy ? ' asked Cole.

'To London—didn't you say so ?—to see this Jack Neville.'

'But you won't start without your breakfast surely ?   You can't do it, Bernard.   You will drop before you reach Westertown.   You don't know what a scarecrow you look.'

'Do you suppose I can eat or drink till I have satisfied my mind upon this subject ?   Oh. Cole, I am in hell—a raging, burning, intolerable hell ! For God's sake, let me do *something*, be it only to walk along the road to Westertown, or I shall destroy myself—or you ! '

'We will start as soon as it is possible to put the

horses into the carriage,' replied Cole soothingly.
'I am ready to go with you, Bernard, to the end
of the world, only you don't want all the servants
and that old woman, Mrs Penfold, to guess your
business before it is concluded, do you, old fellow?
You wouldn't like to think they were running
open-mouthed about the village retailing it to
each boor they met, and making it out worse
than it need be,—eh?'

The instinctive horror of men, and especially
Englishmen, to have their private affairs discussed
by a party of busybodies had the desired effect,
and Bernard Freshfield sank back in his chair
hopeless, but resigned to follow his friend's advice.

'Let me have brandy,' he articulated faintly,
'and leave me alone. Don't let any prying fool
come in here, Cole, for pity's sake! and make
all the necessary arrangements—there's a good
fellow; and tell—tell them what story you like—
only let us be off as soon as possible; for this
suspense is killing me.'

It was a difficult task which Bernard had
delegated to him; but Nelson Cole accomplished
it as diplomatically as was possible. He told
the servants that Mrs Freshfield had received
an urgent summons to the death-bed of a friend,
and that their master was starting at once to
join her. He saw that they were not taken in
by the deception, but it left them, at least, nothing
but conjecture to feed upon.

With Mrs Penfold he was compelled to be
more explicit. She would naturally have demanded to hear the names of people and places—
perhaps even have insisted on sharing the search
they were about to make for her cousin; therefore
he confided to her the fact that Phyllida's depar-

ture was wrapt in mystery, and that, for her sister's sake and her own, it would be prudent to adopt the fable he had invented for the benefit of the servants' hall.

But even as he advised her, he had little hope of her adhering to his counsel. The old lady's face twitched with curiosity and the delight of a mystery; and he felt that as soon as their backs were turned, her tongue would itch until she had confided it to some one else.

Yet, after all, he thought to himself, what did it matter? There was no doubt in his own mind as to the identity of Phyllida Moss ; and all the world of Bluemere must know her story before long. It was for Bernard alone that his heart bled. The women might fight it out between themselves ; he thought only of his ' monkish-faced boy,' and how best to shield him from the scandal and trouble that had come down upon him.

As soon as the hour arrived, he got him as quickly into the carriage as he could, and drove him with his own hands to Westertown ; thence to London, and to the rooms in the Strand temporarily occupied by Mr Jack Neville, was, comparatively speaking, easy work. For many broken hearts and blasted hopes go travelling about the world, and pursuing their usual avocations, as though nothing were the matter with them, to render the presence of one silent and abstracted man in a railway carriage any matter for curiosity to the rest of the passengers.

They found Mr Jack at home, doing the *dolce far niente* after a night of debauch — careless, handsome, and *insouciant*, as if he were still in San Francisco — and lying on two chairs, with a pipe in his mouth.

'Wake up, Jack, my boy!' was Cole's first salutation to him. 'My friend here, Bernard Freshfield, and I have come up to town on an unpleasant business, and we want your assistance.'

'What is it?' cried Jack, suddenly becoming animated; 'disagreeable, eh? sorry to hear it. Is it a robbery, or a forgery, or an arrest? Any way, I'm at your service.'

'I knew that before you said it, old chap. It's something worse than all three put together, Jack. It's a woman!'

Jack whistled, but made no further remark, except asking them if they had lunched, or if they wouldn't sit down.

'Well, we can talk as well sitting as standing,' replied Cole, taking a chair; 'but my friend, here, is rather anxious to see this business con-cluded, and so, to tell the truth, am I. And now, Freshfield, I think you'd better open fire by pro-ducing that photograph. I wish Jack to take it from your hands rather than mine.'

Bernard, with a face that had assumed a stern rather than a sad expression, now that he was under the scrutiny of a stranger, produced a parcel which he was carrying, and which, being untied, revealed an exquisitely painted photograph of the woman he had called his wife. He placed it in silence before Neville.

'Tell us who that is, Jack?' said Nelson Cole.

Jack looked at the portrait a moment then clapped his hand upon his thigh.

'By George! it's herself!' he exclaimed. 'How did you get this? Where was it taken? I wish I had a cool thou. laid on the chances of my picking out her face from that of any other woman in the world. She was always a little stunner;

and, by Jove! how handsome she's grown, and what a swell she looks! Rather different from her appearance after that last night in Chicago— eh, Cole?'

'Don't talk rubbish,' cried the other, impatiently. 'I asked you to tell me whose portrait it is.'

'Get out!' returned Jack; 'you know as well as I do. It's little Nessie Macpherson, of Sacramento Valley.'

'That—that isn't the name you mentioned,' said Bernard hurriedly, to Nelson Cole.

'No, it isn't; but it will lead to it. Tell us where you met Nessie, Jack, and where she went to, and all you may know about her; not for *my* satisfaction, you understand, but for that of my friend.'

'Oh, certainly, with the greatest pleasure!' replied Jack, pushing the portrait away from him. 'Only look here!—she hasn't got into a scrape, has she? You're not going to ask me to peach upon a woman?'

'Don't be afraid of that. She *has* got into a scrape (or rather she's got my friend into one); but it's nothing in which the truth can hurt her. So fire away, Jack, and be quick about it.'

The three men drew their chairs together, Bernard sitting between the others, like the ghost of Banquo at the feast of Macbeth.

'I met Nessie first in San Francisco,' commenced Neville. 'I tried my luck at the gold diggings there, and her father, Macpherson, who is one of the greatest rascals living'—('*The very greatest*, d—n him!' interposed Cole)—'kept a sort of public-house there, which was, in point of fact, a gambling hell, and Nessie used to serve at the bar. I think I noticed her more because she was so young—only sixteen—to place in such a position, than because she was so pretty. And Sandie Macpherson ill-treated her into the bargain. There wasn't a digger in the Valley that didn't feel for the child.'

Freshfield groaned, but he said nothing.

'Go on ; cut it short,' was the practical remark of Cole.

'I got into a scrape up there after a while—one of my numerous awkward jobs, you know, Cole—and had to run down South till the breeze had blown over. There was a nasty fellow there at the time, called Fernan Cortës, whom none of us liked, and he was implicated in the affair ; in fact, *I* had had to bear the brunt of his knavery. Naturally, the first thing I did on my return was to look up my friend to have it out with him, but I found he had mizzled from Sacramento Valley, and taken Nessie Macpherson with him. The father declared she was an obstinate hussy, and *would* marry Cortës ; but I heard a very different story from the diggers. They told me there had been a fight up at Macpherson's one day with a stranger, who declared he had been cheated at the tables, and that Sandie had held him down whilst Cortës knived him, and Nessie had been witness to the affair, and threatened to expose it. So then her father forced her to marry this Cortës—they can do anything they choose with a rough disorderly band like that—and packed her off with him, lest she should turn witness against them. I'm not sure if that's the real truth of the matter. I only tell it you a it was told to me.'

'But where did you meet Nessie next, Jack ? That's the most important thing.'

'Why, in Chicago, where she was acting on the stage under the name of Stephanie Harcourt.'

'You hear that, old fellow,' said Cole to Bernard; 'am I right or wrong?'

'Let Mr Neville go on, Cole. I have no hope left.'

'I had just come from New York then, having made the Valley a bit too hot to hold me again, and Fernan Cortés was arrested for forgery whilst I was there, and condemned to two years' imprisonment in the Tombs. I inquired after his wife in the city, but I couldn't hear anything of her, so I was all the more surprised to recognise her pretty face on the Chicago stage. Of course I found out her address—I wish to goodness now that I hadn't—and went off to carry her the news of her husband's arrest. I never saw a poor girl so delighted in my life; it was as if she had been condemned to death, and I had been the bearer of a free pardon. She went right off her head, and was like a mad creature. Then I was fool enough to give her a dinner at one of the swell restaurants there, and ply her with champagne —without any idea, of course, except that of keeping up her spirits, but it proved too much for her, and she was dismissed from the theatre that evening. I daresay Cole has told you that part of the story, Mr Freshfield, and I need not recapitulate. Nessie left Chicago, and I have heard nothing of her since, until you placed her portrait in my hand. And what the dickens is she doing now?'

'Worse than she ever did in all her life before, Neville. We owe you some explanation after giving you all this trouble, and I know you may be trusted with my friend's secret. I knew this girl

under the name of Stephanie Harcourt at Chicago.
I felt interested in her, as I suppose most men
would do if only on account of her beauty, and
when Evans dismissed her from the theatre, I
visited her, and sent her sufficient money to enable her to leave the city. What was my astonishment, on going to see my friend Freshfield
the other day at Bluemere—a clergyman, and a
man of property and standing in the county—
you won't credit me, Jack, but it's sacred truth
I'm telling you — what was my amazement at
finding that girl established at Briarwood *as his
wife.*'

'Heaven and earth!' cried Neville, starting
from his seat. What! Nessie Macpherson, the
daughter of old Sandie, a parson's wife! It's
impossible.'

'It *is* possible, my boy, and if I had died in
America, she would have probably gone on to the
end without detection. But I recognised her at
once, and when she found it was the case, she cut
and run.'

'Best thing she could do,' remarked Jack sen-
tentiously; 'she's a nice little thing, but as for
sticking up to be any man's *wife*, and a parson's
above all men—O Lord—'

'*Don't*,' ejaculated Bernard in a voice of pain ;
and then he added in a very gentle but manly
manner, 'Mr Neville, I daresay I must appear to
you in the light only of a very easily taken in
fool ; but you must remember that this—this lady
came to Bluemere under a feigned name, to stay
with respectable people, and I had no means of
ascertaining her antecedents. I — I — loved her
and believed in her. Tell me all therefore that it
is necessary I should know ; but don't say more,

at least till I am gone, for I am scarcely strong enough yet to bear it.'

There was such bitter unmistakable suffering imprinted on his features that the best part of Jack Neville's nature was aroused. He held out his hand to Bernard, with a firm friendly grasp,—

'I was thoughtless,' he said, 'and I beg your pardon. That you have been easily deceived by her, Mr Freshfield, is no blot upon your character, it rather redounds to your credit. I wouldn't give you twopence for the man whom a pretty woman can't take in. But I think now I have told you all that I can about the girl whose portrait this is, and who is without doubt the same that I knew under the names of Nessie Macpherson and Stephanie Harcourt. And what shall you do now about it?'

'She has left me. I do not believe her to be my wife. There is nothing left for me to do except to bear it as best I may,' said Bernard, in a broken voice.

'Shall you return to Bluemere?' demanded Nelson Cole.

'Certainly; because I have suffered a terrible shock is no reason that my people should suffer also. My duty lies in Bluemere. I had better return at once. And I carry one consolation with me, my conscience is at rest; I have not wronged her.'

'I had better return with you, Bernard,' said Cole anxiously.

'As you will, dear old chum; but it is not necessary—in fact, I would rather go alone. I must learn to fight with this grief that has come so suddenly upon me, and which is far worse than death. After a while, perhaps, if I hear nothing, I will ask you to make some inquiries for me.

She must not want, you know; but for the present
I feel stunned and unable to think. Let me go
home at once, Cole; I am like a wounded animal,
that wants to get out of the light and die alone.'

'All right, Bernard,' replied Cole, 'you shall do
exactly as you think best. After a few days you
shall be better able to decide for yourself. For
the present, I will remain with Neville. To-
morrow or next day, if you wish it, I will rejoin
you at Briarwood, for I shouldn't like to leave
England again, dear boy, without another shake
of the hand from you. And keep up your pluck,
old fellow. Remember there are as good fish in
the sea as any that came out of it.'

Bernard shook his head with a sad smile; but
he bade them farewell gratefully, and walked
downstairs again, as miserable a man as existed in
all England.

His friends talked very differently of Miss Stephanie Harcourt as soon as his back was turned.

'Fine fellow that,' commenced Jack Neville. 'I
like his cut. He's straight as a rule. I can read
it in his eye.'

'You'd say so if you knew him,' replied Cole.
'His only fault is being a parson. That man would
as soon shoot his own mother as do a mean or
dishonourable action. But how he can have been
so green as to be taken in by that little jade beats
me altogether.'

'Nessie's awfully pretty,' remonstrated his companion, 'and when she's well dressed, she looks a
thorough lady. Not that I often saw her in San
'Frisco.'

'Jack, my boy, I never knew, till I heard you
tell the fact to Freshfield, that you had been such
a long time in Sacramento. You must have known

that old devil Sandie Macpherson for several years.
Did you ever see or hear of a person named
Summers, who was connected with him there?'

'Summers! Summers!' said Jack reflectively.
'Let me see.   Do you mean a man?'

'No—a woman!'

'Young?'

'No,' replied Nelson Cole, as curtly as before;
'middle-aged.'

'Why do you want to know?'

'What's that to you, my son?'

'True.   However, I don't remember the name.
I knew a lot of women there, but I can't recall any
one of the name of Summers.'

Nelson Cole smoked in silence for a few minutes,
as though he were making up his mind to some
mighty effort—then he said suddenly,—

'Jack, had Macpherson (curse him) any one
living with him whilst you were there?'

'He had his wife,' replied Neville innocently.
But he was startled by the tornado of passion his
words roused in his companion.

' *Wife* '' he exclaimed vehemently, dashing his
pipe upon the ground; 'he had no wife.   He lied
if he said so.   The woman who lived with him
was only another of his victims, and rather a more
wronged and helpless victim than the rest.   Macpherson stole her—the cowardly scoundrel—as he
stole the money of men, and their reputations, and
their lives.'

'My dear Cole, don't put yourself into such a
white heat on the matter.   What was the woman
to you?   Did you know her?'

Cole paused to wipe the beads of perspiration
from his forehead before he answered,—

'Yes, I did know her—years and years ago, and

I knew her husband too, poor devil—and what he suffered when she left him, and I have sworn that, whenever Sandie Macpherson and I meet face to face, I will avenge his wrongs. She was a good and true wife to him, Jack (to my friend, you understand), until she met that devil Macpherson, and he led her astray—the arch-fiend alone knows by what means—for he is one of the ugliest dogs that was ever created.'

'You may well say that, Cole. He can never have been handsome at any time, with his freckled face and red hair, and what he used to look like in a digger's costume, with a beard to his waist, you may just imagine. He always went by the name of Sandie the Devil amongst the diggers, and well he deserved it. But this woman you speak of. Can it have been Mrs Moss?'

'*Moss* — Moss ; that is a coincidence, Jack. Stephanie Harcourt went by the name of Phyllida Moss when she came to England! It was under that name she married poor Freshfield.'

'Was it? Well, I conclude she took the idea from her mother.'

'Was Mrs Moss the mother of Stephanie?' asked Cole, with visible agitation.

'I have been always told so. But she is dead, as perhaps you know. She died when Nessie was fourteen or fifteen—about a year before this iniquitous marriage was brought about with that brute Cortës.'

'She is dead, is she?' said Cole slowly. 'Well, if she was the woman I mean, I am glad to hear it. Dead! escaped from his clutches—gone to a more merciful gaoler. Thank Heaven for her release! Poor Agnes.'

'That was her name, I know,' interposed

Neville. 'I have heard Macpherson call her by
the name of Agnes over and over again.'

'And what was she like, Jack?' said Cole
eagerly ; describe her to me as well as you can.
Let me be sure that it is my—my—poor friend's
wife that lies at rest at last.'

'She was a tall, slight woman—if you are
speaking of Mrs Moss—with dark eyes and hair—'

'Yes, yes ; go on, my lad, go on!' cried the
other hastily.

'A great quantity of hair that fell down to her
waist, and small hands and feet, and a French
accent, and—'

'It was she, without doubt ; it was poor Agnes
whom you knew. But why did she call herself
Moss instead of Macpherson?'

'That I cannot tell you. I thought perhaps it
was because Macpherson himself was in such evil
odour in California, and so often in scrapes, that
she preferred—like some American women—to
keep her maiden name; and it is quite certain
that Nessie was never styled Macpherson till after
her mother's death. You see Mrs Moss was a
sort of protection to the girl ; but when she was
removed, Sandie had her entirely in his power,
and a nice use he made of it.'

'Did he ill-treat her?'

'Shamefully. The whole Valley was up in
arms about it. For my part, I was not surprised
to hear she had run off with Cortés ; I should
not have been surprised to hear anything of the
girl, she suffered so much from his violence.'

'Poor child! Well, it will only add another
knot to the lash I have in store for that gentleman.
It is quite in accordance with the character I have
heard of him that he should ill-treat his own child.

I confess, Neville, that when I met you after that business in Chicago, and found that I had been assisting the daughter of my greatest enemy, I was sorry for it, and the knowledge of whose child she is made me sterner perhaps with her the other day than I need have been; but now that you tell she is only another of his victims, I will try and forget she is his flesh and blood.'

'But, my dear fellow, I don't know that she is. The general belief in Sacramento was that Nessie was *not* Macpherson's daughter.'

'What do you mean, Neville?' cried Nelson Cole, starting to his feet; 'not *his* daughter! Then whose daughter could she be? Was not this Mrs Moss her mother?'

'Oh yes; there is no doubt of that; but I imagined—I may be wrong, you know, but this was the general idea—that Mrs Moss had been married twice, and that Nessie was her child by the first marriage. Any way, she was several weeks old, I believe, when Macpherson brought the woman he called his wife to Sacramento; and I have been told, by those who knew him then, that he constantly disclaimed all relationship with Nessie. Now that you tell me that Mrs Moss was seduced from her husband by Sandie, the thing is clear enough—Nessie must be the daughter of the man she "deserted."'

'God in heaven!' cried Cole. 'Why did this never strike me before?'

'I wonder it didn't strike Mrs Moss's husband,' said Jack.

'Because, my dear boy, he had left his wife six months before in New York, whilst he went down South on business. And during his absence that reptile Macpherson used some of his diabolical arts by which to convince Agnes Summers that her husband was untrue to her, and she succumbed (as too many women do)—not to her passion, but to her desire of retaliation. And so her husband lost her; and so he has gone through the world since, waiting, but longing, for his revenge. And you really think that this girl is the child of—of—my friend?'

'I think it is very probable; I am sure the mother thought so, though she brought up Nessie to look upon Macpherson as her father; but perhaps that was to avoid trouble after her death, for she was a long time dying.'

'Poor Agnes!' murmured Cole thoughtfully, as he remembered the worn wedding-ring and the curious fashion in which it had reached him.

'Cole, did you say you were only waiting to meet Sandie Macpherson face to face?'

'It's true, my boy. I've tracked him from one State to another, but always missed him by a flash of lightning. He knows we have a heavy account to settle with each other, and slips through my fingers like an eel. But the day will come, Jack; sooner or later it must come.'

'Perhaps it *has* come, Cole, for Sandie the Devil is in England. I saw his ugly face—clean shorn, but still his own—only last night.'

'Where? where?' cried Cole, roused into sudden activity.

'He was pushing through a crowd when I caught sight of him, and I didn't attract his notice, as you may suppose. That man is my evil genius, and misfortune has always followed in his wake for me. So I didn't stop to shake his dirty hand. But he is in London, safe and sure.'

'Neville, I can't return on the 10th. This

matter must be settled before I leave England. The sleepers start by the *King of the Icebergs,* and I shall telegraph to Farquharson at once that business detains me here for an indefinite period.'

'Will it be wise, Cole, to let your friend's private affairs interfere with your relations with Farquharson ? '

'My connection with the firm, my annual income, and every prospect I have in life, may go smash before I will give up this opportunity of settling old scores with that scoundrel! Neville, you don't know—it is impossible to tell you— the bad blood that is between us!'

'I know one thing,' replied the younger man, laughing, 'that you are determined to have a slap at the old hypocrite, and I wish you all success. If I could help you to smash him I should be but too glad.'

'They don't allow Lynch law in this country,' said Cole ; 'but they'll have to stand it for once in a way if Sandie Macpherson and I cross each other's path, and they may give me six months afterwards if they will, but I'll have my revenge on him. It would be cheap at any cost.'

And then having made some appointment with his friend for the evening, Nelson Cole took his way slowly downstairs, with a mouth that looked as determined as a bull-dog's, and an eye that gleamed with the softness of a woman's. The one was for Sandy Macpherson, the other for Phyllida Moss.

'Poor child!' he thought, 'poor ill-used child! At any rate she is *hers*, and from this time forward I will stand her friend.'

CHAPTER XV

How Bernard Freshfield reached home that day, he said afterwards that he never knew. It is supposed that he travelled by cabs and trains in the same way that happy mortals (if there are any) perform their journeys ; but it was all done mechanically, and he was conscious but of one thought the while, that he was alive, and he wished that he could die. He was a good man ; but it was too soon for him to become reconciled to such an awful disappointment—the worst that had ever befallen him. He could not realise that it was true—that would have been impossible—but he kept on repeating mentally the intelligence that had been conveyed to him by Jack Neville and Nelson Cole, and wondering in a dull, stupefied way if they could be mistaken, and resolving that he would tax his wife with it, face to face, and then, waking up with a start, to remember that she was *not* his wife, and that she was gone.

Briarwood without Phyllida! It was incredible —it would never look like the same place again— but then that was a trifle compared to the rest ; *the world* would never look the same to him again, it was puerile fretting about Briarwood. As he walked home from Westertown (for he felt that when he *could* use action it was the only preservative against his going mad), he could not help comparing his feelings with those he experienced on losing his first wife. He had been very lonely then ; the house had seemed like an empty mausoleum to him, and he had never entered the hall for months afterwards, and encountered the stairs without recalling how he had watched the bearers carry Alice's coffin from her bedroom to the library, and had removed the lid to take one more look at her pale waxen face before it was hid away from him for ever. He had not loved her as he *could* love, but she had endeared herself to him, and no man can lose the woman who has been part of his life, without the loss being succeeded by a terrible sense of loneliness. But with the loneliness, however hard to bear, come rest, soli-- tude, and silence—three strong friends to help us to cope with sorrow. In his present position, Bernard could have no such assistance, and he felt as if the first he should never know again, and the other two he could not bear. *If* she had only died, he kept on saying to himself—meaning Phyllida, of course—died with her hand in his, true and loving to the last, like his poor, for- gotten Alice, he could have struggled with mis- fortune. But to think of her living still, though lost to him—the wife perhaps of some other man (since their union was proved to have been illegal), the thought was madness, he could not, dare not, think.

There were his people waiting for his return ; his work amongst them to be punctually per- formed. As he strode on through the gathering darkness (for it was late in the afternoon) he told himself there was but one way in which to meet the storm that had overtaken him, and that was by work—hard, constant, faithful work—and he would try no other remedy. He had been careless, perhaps. The charm of this woman's society and ways and manners had kept him too much by her side, and caused him to neglect his humbler friends. He had provoked the Almighty to send forth His thunders and lightnings upon him. In

the freshness of his grief Bernard Freshfield forgot
the heart and essence of the religion to which
he had ever clung ; he overlooked the ' All-loving,'
who had been to him as an actual fatherly presence, and called Him the Almighty instead.
How much some women will have to answer for
hereafter—the *charming* women especially, who
hold the power of drawing men after them and
detaining them there.   A woman has but too
often come between a good man and his God
before Bernard Freshfield's time.   But his nature
was too noble to succumb utterly to such weakness.   As he entered the grounds of Briarwood
it struck him, for the first time, that he should
have to give some explanation of the disappearance of Phyllida to his friends and servants.
He had been too much absorbed in his own
grief to think of it, and even now it troubled
him but little compared with all the rest.   After
all, what was the shame, compared with the loss ?
Only he must spare her name as much as he
possibly could.   He let himself into the house,
and walked into the library.   The lamps were
burning brightly. the fire had been well tended ;
it was evident that his servants had expected
him home again.   He rung the bell for Mrs
Garnett twice.   That was his accustomed signal
that he required her services, and he felt in his
present state of mind that he could better encounter a woman than a man.   The old housekeeper appeared, prim and spotless as usual, and
without a sign of disturbance on her countenance.

'I am glad to see you home, sir ; I was beginning to feel uneasy.   The days do close in so
soon now.   I suppose you will take your dinner
at seven as usual ? '

'Yes — no — ' replied Bernard incoherently. 'Dinner, oh yes, of course I will. I mustn't forget Mrs Penfold. By the way, that's what I wanted, Mrs Garnett. Please ask Mrs Penfold to come and speak to me here.'

'But if you please, sir, she's gone!'

'*Gone!* Where to?'

'I understood she had gone to stay with Mrs Pinner, sir; at least she packed up her box, and left word for the stable boy to take it over there on a barrer. Mrs Penfold was very curious like and upset in her mind all the morning, sir. She kept on saying that she'd better go, and that you wouldn't like to see her here when you returned, and I thought, perhaps, there had been a sort of misunderstanding between you. But it wasn't my place to say anything, sir, so I just let her go.'

'She must do as she thinks best,' replied Bernard indifferently, 'though there is no reason why she should not have remained at Briarwood. Any news from the village, Mrs Garnett?' he added, with a sigh.

'Well, yes, sir. As I was just saying to Edwards, they've been coming and going all day like a hive of bees. But it was the mistress they was after, and it was no use my telling them she wouldn't be home to-night. Old William Bennett has the rheumatics very bad, and wanted some of that famous liniment; but you see, sir, I hadn't the mistress's keys to get it. Then Mrs Sutton was taken ill, and sent up for her. As if she could be at all the labours in the village, as I told 'em. This evening, not half-an-hour ago, up comes John Wright to ask if she could step down to his little Katie, who had scalded her foot with upsetting the tea-kettle, and she kept on screaming out for Mrs Freshfield. I sent them down a roll of cotton wool, and said that would do the child more good than the mistress, even if she had been at home. They think they can't do anything without her now, sir. It's here, there, and everywhere, they want her, just for all the world as if she was their slave.'

'Poor creatures! poor creatures!' groaned Bernard, as he thought how his loss would reflect on so many. His manner alarmed the housekeeper.

'I hope there's nothing wrong, sir?' she said respectfully. 'Me and Edwards have been quite in a quandary all day, what with the mistress going away so suddenly, and you too.'

She was an old servant, who had served his family faithfully for many years, and he tried to tell her of his trouble, but broke down utterly in the attempt.

'There *is* something wrong,' he gasped, 'but don't speak to me of it yet, for I cannot bear it. Only do this for me, Garnett. You and Edwards have been more than servants to me ; be my friends in this predicament, and try to hold your tongues. I—I—don't quite think she will return,—not just yet, I mean,—but you shall know all about it by-and-by. And don't worry me with dinner. Only leave me alone and undisturbed, and make the best of it you can downstairs.'

The old woman curtsied to him and instantly withdrew. She had suspected the worst from the drift of Mrs Penfold's lamentations, and the alacrity with which that lady had removed herself and her belongings from Briarwood.

But the uneducated, however well-intentioned, can never leave a mystery to *be* a mystery. They must supplement it with speculations of their own. Edwards and Garnett had already decided that as no one knew *why* Mrs Bernard Freshfield had left her home, it was quite evident she did not go alone, and visions of mustachioed rakes, with gold-braided uniforms, and swords clanking by their sides, had been floating through their minds all day. It was not the slightest obstacle to their imagination that no officers had been seen in Bluemere or its vicinity since their master's marriage.

'I always did *hate* them milling-tary,' Mrs Garnett had ejaculated, as they discussed the subject together. 'I might have been married to a soldier myself; but I thank the Lord I wasn't ; for I've heard since as they're the ficklest and poorest and most trumperious lot. Poor Garnett always maintained so.'

And after her interview with Bernard in the library, she was still more certain that a 'nasty soldier' must be at the bottom of his undisguised misery, though she and Edwards were both too faithful to his interests to do more than whisper their suspicions in each other's ear. In the servants' hall they declared—and, let us hope, were forgiven for the pious lie—that the master had been with the mistress all day ; but as she was nursing her own aunt, by the father's side, and the complaint was not infectious, he had given his leave for her to stay away as long as she was required.

'And I'm afraid it will be some time before we see the mistress back again,' added Mrs Garnett (not content with having told a lie and done with it) ; 'for *I* know what her poor, dear aunt lies ill of, and it's a disease as will never rest until it's carried her off. And how I'm to satisfy all these poor people as come hollering after the mistress, whilst she's away, the Lord only knows. But if any of you jades go to disturb the master in the libbery or elsewhere,' cried Mrs Garnett, with a sudden change of manner, 'you'll lose your places. He's got more than enough to think of and manage, poor, dear gentleman, with the whole parish visiting thrown on his hands. So you mind what I say, and keep down here in your proper places, or it will be the worse for you.'

Meanwhile Bernard remained in the library, in silent torture, with his face buried in his hands, trying to disentangle the confused thoughts that tripped each other up as they rushed helter-skelter through his brain ; to reduce the chaos into order —to remember exactly *what* had happened to him, and to decide what influence it would exert upon his future. He had one especially hard task before him—to tell the truth to his mother. He felt he must tell it ; that it was due to her and to Laura that they should hear of the disgrace that had fallen on the family, through his means, from his own lips. He did not know how much or how little of the news had already circulated through Bluemere. Mrs Penfold's sudden departure seemed as though she was aware of it ; it would never do for it to reach Blue Mount by a stranger's hand. He pulled out pen and paper at once, and wrote hurriedly ; but his letter was addressed not to Mrs Freshfield—but to Laura.

'MY DEAREST SISTER,—A terrible blow has fallen upon me, which you must not hear from any one but myself. Phyllida has left me. She was never my wife. She was a married woman when she came to England, and Cole (who knew her in America) recognised her directly they met. Break this news to my poor mother as gently as you can, and talk about it as little as possible. And whatever you do, don't come to Briarwood, for I cannot speak on this subject nor see any one, at all events for the present.—Ever your affectionate brother,   BERNARD.'

He sealed his letter and despatched it by a groom, and then he went up to the chamber which Phyllida had occupied, and locked himself in, and spent the night amidst the relics of his lost love, with which it was strewn. She had taken nothing away with her apparently, except the plain serge dress she wore. All the costly fabrics he had taken such delight in purchasing for her—the delicate silks and satins ; the sable trimmed and velvet mantles ; the lace and jewellery, that had excited the indignation of her mother-in-law — were all there. She had left them behind her, seemingly with the utmost indifference, and gone forth into the fog and the darkness, unprovided and alone. Even her purse, containing the money with which he supplied her for the parish needs—('Judas's bag,' as the poor child had laughingly called it)—lay on the toilet table, and Bernard took it up mechanically and counted the contents. A five-pound note, two sovereigns, and seven shillings in silver. What had Phyllida taken with her? he thought in a dazed manner ; by what means did she intend to provide for herself in the future? But even such speculations did not cause any feelings of tenderness or compassion towards her. His whole heart was hardened by the blow it had received ; he would not remember that she had been the wife of his bosom ; he thought of her only as the woman who had deceived him and brought him to shame, who had been deceiving all her life (so his curdled nature was ready to believe), and who would go on deceiving till she died. He was rough even with the poor things she had left behind her, and kicked such as lay in his way to one side with his foot—a very different mode of procedure to the tenderness with which he had handled the reminiscences of the dead girl whom he had never loved with one tithe of the passion which was even then raging in his breast. Violent emotions must have their violent counter-parts. The deceived lover who can bless and pardon, has ceased to regret the infidelity he so readily condones, and a woman need never desire a better compliment from an old admirer than when he refuses to meet her altogether. She may rely that he feels himself too weak to bear her presence, or too strong ; too full of regret for the past, or too angry with the present. When lovers become friends, the passion of love has expended itself. Had Phyllida entered Bernard's presence at that moment, he might have killed her.

Meanwhile, it is impossible to describe the consternation with which his news was received at Blue Mount. Had he written to say that Phyllida had dropped down dead, it could not have surprised and shocked poor Laura more. She had grown so fond of her sister-in-law, they had become so confidential and friendly together, and read so much of each other's hearts and minds, that the revelation was as ghastly as though she had been told that her mother, whom she honoured above all women, had led a life of iniquity and sin.

Phyllida already married, and not to Bernard! Living at Briarwood, and making every one so happy there, and showing such a bright, sweet example to all who went to her for comfort or advice, and yet *not* Bernard's wife—the wife of some other man! Oh, it was incredible!—*it could not be!* Bernie's mind must have been led astray by some diabolical arts; his friend Nelson Cole must be mistaken,—or mad—or—or—anything, sooner than she could credit that Phyllida was not as good and pure as she seemed.

The dear, brave girl read her painful letter and kept the secret, hugging it to her breast as the Spartan boy concealed the fox that preyed upon his vitals—taking it out in the night, and perusing the horrible sentences it contained again and again, but still remaining steadfast to her first idea—that the thing was impossible.

She did not heed Bernard's injunction that he would not be disturbed either by her mother or herself, but slipped out of the house as soon as breakfast was over the following morning, and made her way to Briarwood without breathing a word of her intention to Mrs Freshfield. She opened the hall-door (doors are generally kept upon the latch in country places), and without ceremony entered the library. There sat her brother at his writing-table, pale, hollow-eyed, and stern, but still occupied just as usual with his parish papers. His greeting to Laura was not a genial one,—

'I thought I desired you not to come here?' he said gravely.

'I know you did, dear, dear Bernie; but how do you suppose I could obey such an order? I received your note—I need not tell you that; but I have not said a word about it to mamma.'

'Why not?'

'Because I don't believe what you wrote to me; because I think you must be labouring under some terrible delusion, and I want to see if it cannot be cleared away again.'

'It is not a delusion; it can never be cleared away. You might have taken my word for it,' replied her brother.

'No, Bernie, I cannot. I must hear everything about it, from beginning to end. I want to know what Mr Cole said, and why he said it, and what it was that frightened dear Phyllida away? Oh! Bernie, I love her so dearly—she is like my own sister to me. I cannot give her up at a moment's notice, and on the condemnation of a man who is a perfect stranger to me.'

'Oh, Laura, you might have spared me this ordeal,' groaned Bernard, with his face buried in his hands. 'I tell you there is no mistake— it is but too true—and the fact that directly she was taxed with her crime, she fled from my protection, is sufficient proof that she knew it to be true.'

'Who taxed her with it?'

'Nelson Cole. He knew her in America under the name of Harcourt.'

'Bernie, I hate this Nelson Cole. What does he mean by coming as a welcomed guest into such a happy family as ours, and spreading misery and dissension amongst us in this way?'

'You don't know what you are talking of, Laura. You cannot understand such a matter. No *man*, who is worthy of the name, could see his friend the dupe of an artful *intriguante*, without opening his eyes to his disgrace.'

'Bernard, how *dare* you speak of Phyllida by such a name?' replied his sister boldly; if *you* can forget in so short a time all she has been to you, *I* cannot. An *intriguante!* I would as soon believe myself to be one.'

'Oh, Laurie, Laurie, you don't know how much harder you are making all this for me to bear. Yesterday, I would have said the same as yourself—to-day, I cannot. But don't think that I would not blot out the conviction (if I could) with my heart's blood. God knows, I would die ten thousand deaths to restore Phyllida to the place she once held in my estimation!'

'And so would I, darling; so would I,' cried the warm-hearted Laura; 'and do you think it possible that a *bad* woman would have been able to gain such power over us as that? Do you imagine that a deceitful, lying adventuress (such as Mr Nelson Cole would wish us to believe dear Phyllida to be) could change all at once to the sweet, loving, sympathising soul who made herself the good angel of Bluemere? Why, brother, the people simply worship her. And you have let your fine American friend drive her away.'

'She went of her own accord,' sighed poor Bernard; besides, no sophistry nor arguments can alter facts, and the fact remains—she was a married woman.'

'To whom was she married?'

'Oh, what does it matter? To some low ruffian in the States; or rather she was divorced from him (but you know how I regard divorce), when she was cruel enough to go through the farce of wedding me.'

'Is her husband dead since then?'

'Yes.   He died some months ago.'

'Then you can marry her over again,' cried Laura confidently.

'Laura, of what are you thinking? Marry a woman who laid herself out to deceive me? Who lived here for six months with a secret that was eating out her very heart, and never disclosed it to her husband; who sat at my table and smiled in my face—'

'Yes, and who brought sunshine into your heart despite the canker in her own; who could make the poor happy whilst she suffered herself; who could watch by the bedside of the sick whilst she wanted comfort and consolation most of all. My poor, brave Phyllida! my dear, sweet sister. If everybody else turns against her, I will search the world until I have found her, and thanked her for all the love she showed to us.'

But Bernard turned away from Laura with offended dignity. How hard it is to knock his pride out of the very best of Englishmen. It is an integral part of himself. The poor man shows it is as openly as the rich, and both are rather proud of being proud than otherwise. Bernard Freshfield's heart was burning to relieve itself by tears; the mention of Phyllida's virtues touched him to the very quick; but he would not give way to the weakness of allowing any part of her to be good. *She had deceived him,* that was quite sufficient.

'I should be sorry that my mother should hear you speak in such a manner, Laura,' he said gravely. 'Whatever my—my—I mean whatever Phyllida was in Bluemere she can never be again, and she would never have been had her antecedents been honestly revealed to us. Cole knew her as a burlesque actress on the American stage, and—and—not always as quietly conducted as she should have been even there.'

'How *mean* of him to tell, even if he *did* know,' replied the girl, with flashing eyes. 'But I don't believe it, and I won't; and even if she *were* an actress, does that make her good deeds the less to be admired? It makes them a thousand times more valuable. It is not often a woman gives up all the excitement and gaiety of professional life to be the Lady Bountiful of an out-of-the-way village, and dispense liniments and bandages to the poor. You have made Phyllida rise instead of sink in my estimation by that announcement, Bernard, *I* can tell you.'

But the rock had not yet been smitten by the rod that should make the waters flow.

'It would be well if we all possessed so staunch a little advocate as yourself in our troubles, Laura,' he answered, with a sickly smile; 'but I must really ask you now to leave me. I have a lot of business on hand, and I am not in very good form for working.'

'Bernard, where is Phyllida?'

'I cannot tell you. Why will you continue to mention a name which you must know is agony for me to hear?'

'But you don't expect me to drop it for ever, brother, surely? A person can't come in and go out of our lives again in this fashion without leaving some trace behind. When are you going after her?'

'*Never!*' he said resolutely.

'I don't believe it.'

'You must believe what you choose, Laura.

It is impossible for you to read my heart. I can only tell you what is written there. And one thing is, that Phyllida Moss and I will never meet in this world again.'

'Then I don't envy your chances of meeting her in the next,' said his sister defiantly ; 'an unforgiving spirit will be, I should imagine, about the last to enter heaven.'

'Laura, will you be good enough to leave me to myself? You are increasing my torture to a degree of which I could not have believed you capable.'

'What am I to say to mother, then ? '

'Tell her the truth.'

'Yes ; when I know what *is* the truth.'

'I have already told you ; I have nothing more to say.'

'It will be a grand opportunity for mamma, certainly,' continued Laura, hoping by sarcasm to rouse her brother into action, 'for she is going to hold a regular levee of saints next week, and they will be as happy tearing poor Phyllida's character to shreds as your kennel over a defunct sheep. Miss Janet's brother, the Laird o' Muck-heep, is once more standing on his native heather, and she has volunteered a visit for all three of them to Blue Mount. It will be a sort of universal jubilee. I believe mamma entertains flattering hopes that the pious laird may take a fancy to transplant me to Barrick-gallagas Castle; and now that Phyllida is out of the way for good and all, Miss Bella may yet have a chance of reigning at Briarwood—the news will just reach them in time. I expect we shall have meetings called for praise and thanksgiving every day.'

'Laura, Laura you are going too far,' said poor

Bernard, writhing under the lashes she gave him.

' I shall never have gone far enough until I have found Phyllida again,' was the girl's parting shot, as she ran hurriedly from the room, lest she should break down under the crushing disappointment she felt.

She was to tell her mother then—there was no help for it—and she would have to undergo the purgatory of hearing the name which had become so dear to her vilified and abused in every possible way. How Miss Janet would hold forth on ' cairnal procleevities ; ' how Bella would blink her sandy eyelashes, and pull down the corners of her coarsely-moulded mouth, and profess to be too much shocked to take part in the conversation. How the hateful laird (for Laura hated the laird before she had seen him) would thank God he was not as other men are, and her infatuated mother would chime in and agree with everything they said, and think them the most pious people she had ever met.

Well, what must be, must be ; but though she was a brave young woman, Laura Freshfield felt that she would dearly like to have some one to help her in breaking the news to her mother ; some one to stand between herself and the inevitable storm ; some one to make the best of things, not only at Blue Mount but at Briarwood. And feeling thus, her thoughts seem to go naturally (as it were) to Charles Anderson, Bernard's greatest friend, and a man to whom he would listen, perhaps, sooner than to any other, because he had strong religious feelings, and had given up his best prospects in life for the sake of his faith. Mr Anderson was resident in London ; but our young lady was quite equal to despatching a telegram to his address ; and the same afternoon he appeared at Blue Mount.   Laura contrived to receive him alone (indeed Mrs Freshfield always shirked the young Catholic's presence, from dread of social contamination), and in a few minutes she had put him in possession of the terrible story.

'Go over to Briarwood and tell Bernie what to do,' she said. in conclusion ; 'he will take your advice, Charlie, when he would listen to that of no other.   He thinks so highly of your discretion and powers of judgment.'

'He flatters me, Laura,' replied Anderson, 'and you have set me a very difficult task, yet I will do my best for your sake and Bernard's ; but what *can* I say to him ?'

'Charlie, wasn't their marriage sacred ?'

'Of course, my dear Laura, all marriages are sacred : but in this case you see—'

'Oh, I am not speaking of its legality,' she interrupted hastily ; 'I know, of course, that the marriage ceremony would have to be performed over again ; but I am speaking of their hearts.   They truly loved each other.   Bernie used to say theirs was a perfect union ; that they were in reality *one*. How can anything that occurred *before* that marriage destroy its sacred unity ?'

'It is a hard question to answer, Laura ; you must give me time to think over it.'

'I cannot do that.   You must either go over to Briarwood at once. or break this dreadful intelligence to mamma ; for I tremble at every ring at the bell lest it should bring some visitor openmouthed to inform her of it.   But *do* go to Bernie first.   He would hardly speak to me this morning ; but to you he may confide something that will soften the blow to mamm.'

'I can refuse you nothing, Laura,' replied Mr Anderson, as he prepared to start for Briarwood.

CHAPTER XVI.

HE reached Briarwood at dusk, and found his friend Bernard still in the library, professing to read and write, but in reality doing nothing but stare into vacancy. He had not moved from his seat all day, nor taken any nourishment. The fire was nearly out; the lamps were unlighted; the desolation of the apartment bespoke the corresponding feeling in the owner's heart.'

'This is kind of you, Charlie,' he said languidly, as Anderson took his hand, but he never rose from his seat to welcome him; 'how did you hear the news? I can see you *have* heard it from your face; surely it is not in possession of the newspapers yet?'

'No, no, Bernard, no such thing; don't talk nonsense. I came down to Bluemere on receipt of a telegraphic message from your good little sister, who has an idea that the presence of an old and very true friend may prove some comfort to you in this trouble.'

'Nothing can comfort me, Charlie, and no one. It is a wound past cure. The sooner I bleed to death the better.'

'Yes,' said Anderson reflectively, 'and meanwhile what is to become of your profession and your parish and your people?'

'I need have no fear for them,' replied Bernard. 'They could not fall into worse hands than mine. I have been altogether wrong from beginning to end. I see it more plainly now than I have ever done.'

'Indeed! this is news to me. I imagined that you and Bluemere were on excellent terms with one another, and that everything in the parish was working smoothly and well. How long is it since you found out it is altogether wrong?'

'Since she left me!' burst out Bernard passionately; 'since she took all the sunshine and hope of life away with her, and made me the most miserable man upon earth. It is she who has done it all, Anderson; I swear it. We were—we were so happy together, and now there is nothing before me but a wretched blank. I feel as if I were going to the devil, and it won't be her fault if I *don't* go there!'

'Bernard, you shock me,' said Anderson, 'and make me feel more strongly than ever how wise is our Church in prohibiting the marriage of her priests. A woman—one single woman turns out to be something different from what you expected her to be, and everything in consequence—your vows, your profession, your people, and your prayers—are to look after themselves, or worse. I couldn't have believed it of you.'

'I know what you would tell me,' replied Bernard wildly, 'that God is left, and whatever happens, He is always ours, and I know it—*I know it!* but oh, Charlie, old boy, He is behind a cloud. I cannot see Him or hear Him, or feel His hand; and I am going mad. I know I am. I am going out of my senses with grief and longing and fear.'

And throwing his head suddenly down upon his

outstretched arms, Bernard Freshfield gave way to one of those storms of emotion which men sometimes indulge in, and cried as violently as if he had been a child. His friend did not attempt to check him; on the contrary, he left his seat and walked round the room, professing to examine the pictures and ornaments, until Bernard should have had time to recover himself. But, by-and-by, whilst the parson was still catching his breath in the convulsive manner that succeeds passionate weeping, he felt a kind, warm hand laid on his, which, without looking up, he grasped between both of his own.

'Charlie, dear old fellow,' he sobbed, 'you have always been like a brother to me, but this is an ill you cannot cure.'

'I don't profess even to *try* to do so, dear Bernard,' said Anderson; 'but perhaps it may be ameliorated. When you feel strong enough for the task, I want you to tell me all the rights and wrongs of it.'

'There *are* no rights—it is all wrongs,' groaned the unfortunate husband, 'and it has humiliated me as nothing else on earth could have done. Fancy, Charlie, *me*, with my grand ideas of the sanctity of marriage, the greatest human sacrament in existence—the institution of God for the regeneration of mankind by a dual existence— taken in, duped, dishonoured by the woman whom I had made part of my very life. But I see it all now; my eyes are open. I worshipped her instead of the God who made her, and I am justly punished for my sin. But oh, if the Lord had but adopted some other means by which to empty the vials of His wrath upon me!'

'Bernard, did your wife—'

'Don't call her by that name. She is *not* my wife.'

'If I understood your sister rightly, she believed herself to be your wife, and you believed her to be so, therefore I think she has every claim to the name. However, I will call her Mrs Freshfield. You will at least not refuse to grant her the courtesy which is accorded to those women who assume her position, knowing it to be such.'

Bernard groaned, but answered nothing.

'When Mrs Freshfield left Briarwood, she surely gave an explanation of her actions to some one.'

'She left a note behind her for me.'

'May I ask what was in it, Bernard ?'

The parson unlocked a drawer in his writing-table, and taking thence a half sheet of paper, threw it across to his friend.

'You can read it if you like. There it is.'

Anderson took the note in his hands and examined it closely ; when he had finished the perusal, he simply raised his eyes and fixed them on those of his companion.

'Well ?' said Bernard, in a tone of voice as though he defied him to find any excuse for Phyllida in that.

'Well,' echoed Anderson, have you read this letter, Bernard ?'

'Of course I have read it.'

'More than once ? When you have been calm enough to decipher its meaning ?' persisted his friend.

'I don't know what you're driving at, Charlie. The words are plain enough—no one can misunderstand them.'

'I should have thought so, too, but it appears I am mistaken. May I read it to you ?'

'If you will, but I don't see the use of it.'

Anderson, not heeding the grumbling remonstrance, commenced to read,—

'"Bernard, by the time this reaches you, your friend will have told you all he knows about me ; and you will have learned how much you have been deceived."'

'There, you see what she says herself,' interrupted Freshfield. 'She acknowledges I was grossly deceived.'

'How could she do otherwise, poor girl?' replied Anderson; 'the question is, how far she was deceived herself. Her words tell how deeply she felt for you.'

'"But oh, my darling, don't fret about it. I will never disgrace you more. I am going away where you will never hear of me. Only try to forget everything about me, *excepting*"—read Anderson, slowly and emphatically—"*excepting* that I *loved you very dearly*, and had not *strength* to do what I *ought* to have done. But indeed—*indeed*, I believed myself to be your wife."'

'Does she say that?' asked Freshfield quickly, as Anderson came to a full stop.

'Does she say that! Of course she does. I thought you told me just now that you had read the letter.'

'So I did, when I first received it, but it was such an awful blow to me, my head was all in a whirl; and then I had to go with Cole to London and see a fellow called Neville, who had known her in the lowest possible position, and oh, Charlie,' continued Bernard, breaking down again, 'if you had heard what they had to tell me, you would never talk of there being any hope again.'

'Bernard, old fellow, confide the very worst to

me. You know I am to be trusted, and I cannot advise you unless I hear it. What are the most serious charges these gentlemen bring against Mrs Freshfield ?'

' That she is the daughter of some low ruffian who kept a gambling saloon in Sacramento Valley.'

' Well, that is unfortunate : but it is not her fault, and it has certainly left no traces on her behaviour. What next ?'

' She was married at sixteen to a man who turned out to be a criminal, Anderson, a forger, and got two years' imprisonment in a New York gaol ; and, meanwhile, Phyllida, who was on the stage—fancy the stage for *my wife*, Charlie !' (he interpolated with a shudder)—'got an irregular divorce from the brute, and came to England and married me,—*I*, who do not believe in any kind of divorce : and had I known her antecedents, would have avoided her even as a friend.'

' I thought you considered yourself a broad-minded man,' said Anderson ; ' however, let that pass. Did Mrs Freshfield consider her divorce to be complete. from a moral as well as a legal point of view ?'

' I suppose she did, from what she says here.'

' And married you, believing herself a free woman ?'

' Perhaps so ; but that didn't make her free.'

' Can you call to mind, Freshfield, whether in your courting days you ever questioned her as to her past ? It seems strange you should have married a woman who was an absolute stranger to you.'

' I am not sure if I did. I know she refused to marry me several times, and made me so mad, that I was determined to have her at all risks.'

'Rather a worldly sort of proceeding that for a parson,—eh, Bernard? and one that lays the onus of such a marriage more upon your shoulders than hers. Don't you think so?'

'Oh, I don't deny I was to blame, Charlie. I am only cursing my own folly in being so easily taken in.'

'I deny that you were "taken in." It appears to me you entered into the contract with your eyes wide open to the truth that they were not so; in fact, it suited your convenience to be hoodwinked.'

'I was infatuated with her,' sighed Freshfield. 'No woman has ever held me in such thrall as she did—'

'As she *does*, you mean. Now look here, Bernard, it seems to me the case stands thus—you meet a very pretty girl of whom you know nothing, and fall desperately in love and marry her nilly-willy. She (believing herself to be free) takes you at your word, and you probably said that you couldn't live without her. Didn't you, now?'

'Oh, I daresay I did. She made fool enough of me for anything.'

'She has certain unfortunate antecedents (I won't call them disgraceful, for they were not her fault. How could she help being married to a forger or thrown on the stage for a subsistence), and naturally, I suppose, she argues that if there is no need to disclose them, it will be the happier for both that you should remain in ignorance. It is not strict honour, you know, according to the code of rules men set down for one another—but you mustn't judge a woman's morals as you would those of our sex. They

are not reared under the same method. Besides,
I conclude she was in love, and everything may
go to the winds for a woman when she's once
thoroughly in love.'

'Charlie, what are you driving at?' demanded
Bernard, with open eyes.

'Nothing, my dear boy, unless you will answer
me this question. Do you still love Phyllida
Moss?'

A look of the deepest agony passed over the
parson's face, such a look as we may suppose
on the features of a man wrestling with God for
pardon for some mortal sin.

'*Love her!*' he ejaculated. 'God knows I love
her with every fibre of my wretched heart. Oh,
Anderson, that is the worst of it! I feel that I
shall never cease to love her to my dying day.'

'No, Bernard, that is the best and not the worst
of it. If these are your feelings, the sooner you
are re-united to that woman the better.'

Hope flashed into Freshfield's haggard face, as
the sun suddenly breaks out from behind a murky
cloud. His misery had been that re-union with
Phyllida seemed impossible, and when a friend
suggested to him what he had not dared to
whisper to himself, it seemed as if the idea would
suffocate him. He pulled at his round collar as
though he were choking, and rising from his seat
threw open the library window. It was already
dark as night, but the air was full of sound and
the baying of the dogs—those dogs she had so
dearly loved—was borne distinctly from the ad-
jacent kennel. Bernard leaned out of the open
casement for a moment to recover himself, then
he said, in a strangely altered voice, there was
so much fearful joy in it,—

'But how—*how* could that be, Anderson? If all my wishes tended to forgive her—'

'What the d—l have you got to forgive?' exclaimed Anderson suddenly. 'She is the victim of an error, or twenty errors if you like, into nineteen of which you led her, and all you have to do is to follow that girl—*your wife*, mind you—the woman whom you *made* your wife by love, and confidence, and union, more surely than any bands of law can do it—and satisfy the demands of your country and your conscience by marrying her over again. If you do not, Bernard—if you cast her off now, after having nurtured her in your bosom, to wander where she will—I shall look on you as no better than a seducer!'

And in his excitement Anderson walked up and down the room like a caged lion.

'But my profession — my people,' stammered Bernard. 'Can I bring her here again to reign in Bluemere, where every labourer's child will have heard her history?'

'Don't bring her here, then; you are an independent man. Take her anywhere that seems best to you. You have not married your people, but you *have* married her, and your first duty is towards her. What do you suppose it will benefit you to appear before the Almighty with five thousand converts shining like jewels in your crown, whilst the one soul you have sworn to protect and cherish is damned for everlasting, through the cowardice which would prevent your bearing the shame of your mutual error before the world?'

'Damned! my Phyllida! Oh, God forbid!' cried Bernard, with the tears running down his cheeks. 'May He condemn me to the very nethermost hell

if I neglect any means by which to save her soul.
But, Charlie, I took the vows of ordination as well
as those of marriage.   Can I keep both?'

'I see no obstacle to it, old friend.   It may not
be advisable to continue your work here. but there
is work waiting for you all over the world, wherever there are fellow-creatures to be taught and
souls to be saved.'

'Charlie, you have given me fresh life!' cried the
parson, seizing his friend's hand ; 'this is what I
longed to do. but feared lest the desire alone was a
temptation of the devil.   But you have cleared the
mists from my brain.   I can see God once more,
not as the stern Judge, condemning my folly, but
the loving Father who pities it. and holds out His
hand once more for me to grasp, as I grasp yours.'

'Keep fast hold of it, Bernard, and you cannot
go wrong.   And now, if you will take my advice,
you will send me back to Blue Mount to break the
intelligence to your mother.'

'Will it be necessary to tell her ?   Laura thought
not.'

'Laura, in her love for you, thinks only of what
will save you pain.   I am sure it is necessary, Bernard, for two reasons.   One is because concealment
must lead to deception, and deception is wrong ; the
other, that in order to thoroughly clear your wife's
character, everybody must know of the second marriage.   You cannot keep this matter an entire secret.
Little things will leak out here and there ; and unless you are perfectly open, the next thing you will
hear is, that you were never married at all.   Let
me tell Mrs Freshfield that, as you have discovered
that your wife was a divorced woman at the time
of your marriage, you consider it necessary to have
the ceremony performed over again, and she has

left Bluemere until it can be accomplished. This will be the truth (if not all the truth), and will be putting, I think, as good a construction upon the matter as we can.'

'Charlie, you are a true, good friend!' exclaimed Bernard. 'Your visit has raised me from the very depths of human misery to the hope of renewed happiness. My Phyllida! my darling! Is it possible that she may be mine again—mine by the laws of man, and with the smile of God upon our union? Oh, Charlie, it is too much—I cannot realise it!'

'Don't try to do anything but *act*, old fellow. You've been realising too much already, it strikes me; you look ten years older in a couple of days. A change of work will be the best thing for you.'

'What shall I do first, Charlie? It is you who must advise me.'

'Go up to town to your friend Cole. Tell him of your intentions. and get him to help you in your search. I fancy he is more used to that sort of work than you are.'

'True, true; and he is the best of fellows, though he *did* deal me such a terrible blow. I will start for London by the seven o'clock train; and you— what will *you* do, old chum ?'

'I shall return to Blue Mount, and try to smooth matters over for the old lady.'

'Give her my love, Charlie, and explain why I felt myself unable to carry the news myself.'

'I will explain everything; never fear.'

'You are the very best of fellows,' said Bernard earnestly. 'What can I ever do to repay you?'

'Some day I may put your gratitude to the test,' replied Anderson, laughing, as he bid his friend farewell.

CHAPTER XVII.

MRS PENFOLD was not staying with Mrs Pinner, although the housekeeper was quite correct in saying she had gone there. But in the afternoon of the day succeeding Phyllida's mysterious flight, and whilst Bernard was still in town, she had received a note by post, a faint scrawl in pencil, half washed out by tears, in which her cousin had told her partly the truth,—had said, at least, that she had disgraced Mr Freshfield beyond all remedy, and should never return to Briarwood again. And then Mrs Penfold had felt that the rectory was no longer the place for her, and that it would be more delicate to go at once before the parson came home. So she had packed up her small belongings and thrown herself on the hospitality of her sister. Perhaps, if Mrs Pinner had sympathised with her anxiety about Phyllida, or shown the least compassion for the unfortunate girl, cast upon the world for the second time, friendless and alone, Mrs Penfold might have prolonged her stay in Bluemere until she had ascertained what position the Freshfields intended to take up with regard to her cousin's behaviour. But Mrs Pinner's condemnation was so entirely without limit, that Mrs Penfold made up her mind to return to Gatehead the very next day.

'Be good enough, Maria,' Mrs Pinner had said, when her sister tried to make some excuse for the absent girl on account of her defective training, 'be good enough never to mention that disgraceful creature's name in my hearing again. We cannot touch pitch without being defiled, and I feel as if it would be a long time before my house and surroundings recovered the contamination they must have contracted from her presence here.'

But Mrs Penfold had a mother's heart. It was quite a mistake on the part of nature not to have given her children, for she would have loved them tenderly, and her thoughts and prayers, poor old soul, were with her erring little cousin night and day.

'Indeed, Charlotte,' she replied, 'I think you are too hard on her. Of course I cannot entirely understand her reasons for leaving Briarwood from the very incoherent note she sent me, but I can see that she thinks it her duty to go, and that she is very, very miserable in going; and a woman who does her duty, although it makes her wretched, cannot be altogether bad.'

'Stuff and nonsense!' said Mrs Pinner. 'You always were a simpleton, Maria, but I hardly thought you could be so silly at your age. Do you suppose it's likely she's gone *alone?* Did you ever hear of a married woman running away by herself? You must be a born fool to believe it.'

'Good gracious me! Charlotte, what do you mean? Who do you suppose she would take with her? Besides, I am *certain* she went alone. There were only Mr Freshfield and Mr Cole and the servants in the rectory at the time, and I can answer for it they all stayed behind.'

Mrs Pinner gazed at her sister with the supremest contempt.

'Well, if this comes of letting lodgings,' she began, when the other interrupted her,—

'Do you mean to insinuate,' she said indignantly, 'that Phyllida has disgraced us all by running away with *a man?* Oh, Charlotte, you ought to be ashamed of yourself. And when you know how devoted she was to Mr Freshfield, how can you say so wicked and cruel a thing?'

'Hoity, toity!' cried Mrs Pinner; 'here's a flare up about nothing. What do you suppose all the village are saying about it? Annie Warren tells me there is hardly a cottage where they have not heard the whole story, and put their own construction on it. Run away alone, indeed; a likely story. No one else will believe it if *you* do—not if she came back to-morrow with that smooth hypocritical face of hers and swore she'd only been on a round of parochial visits.'

'But who could she run away with?' gasped Mrs Penfold, staggering under the unexpected assertion.

'Who, indeed? As if my lady hadn't cunning enough to keep all her affairs secret. You know how close she was from the beginning. Don't ask who *is* it, but who may it *not* be. Any one, I should say, who would take her. Mr Anderson, perhaps, for want of a better. Those Papists will do anything if they're not found out, and Mr Anderson is one of the slyest looking men I ever saw.'

'Charlotte!' exclaimed Mrs Penfold, looking her sister full in the face, 'you are the very wickedest woman I ever saw.'

'*What!*' screamed Mrs Pinner.

'I repeat it, the wickedest woman I ever saw. You go to church twice every Sunday and read your Bible, and say your prayers, and you are always talking of religious things and using sacred names; but you haven't got as much charity in you as a grain of mustard seed. You made the worst instead of the best of poor Phyllida from the very beginning, and only left off abusing her when she became Mr Freshfield's wife, and there was everything to gain by keeping friends with her. And now that she is under a cloud again, poor little soul, though you know no more of the facts of the case than I do, you suspect her of the grossest iniquity without any better foundation than what your unworthy suspicions supply you with. But, in my opinion, you are much more to blame than she is (since you have enjoyed so many more privileges), and, instead of reviling her, you had better go upstairs and go down on your knees and pray to Heaven to change your hard heart, and make you more charitable to your fellow-creatures.'

During this harangue Mrs Pinner's face had gradually assumed the appearance of an infuriated turkey cock. Her wattles (if I may be allowed to use such an expression for a lady's double chin) had turned purple, her forehead was crimson, and every poppy in her cap shook as though under the breath of a tornado.

'Maria Penfold,' she ejaculated, as soon as she could speak, 'leave my house!'

'You need not take the trouble of turning me out, Charlotte. I wouldn't stay here if you paved my room with gold. No, and I wouldn't change places with you (although you do look down on me for letting lodgings), not if you were a duchess in your own right.'

'Leave my house!' repeated Mrs Pinner. 'I will listen to no more insults at your hands.'

'And you never will,' was Mrs Penfold's parting shot, 'for unless your hard heart is softened, and you begin to practise the religion which at present you only talk about, I shall take good care not to see you again,' and with that she sent out for the only vehicle to be hired in Bluemere, and was landed safely by the train in Gatehead the same evening.

But she had the consolation of receiving an unfeignedly hearty welcome on her return. Miss Annadale, who scarcely ever stirred out of her own apartments, came half way downstairs to greet her landlady, and Captain Barclay insisted on her sharing his roast chicken and mushrooms, and drinking a glass of Madeira with him in his snug little parlour, instead of sitting down to a solitary meal.

'First-rate wine that, Mrs Penfold,' said the old sailor, as he handed her a bumper of the rich coloured Madeira; 'drink it down. It will do you good, I promise you. That Madeira made four voyages round the Cape in my own ship, Mrs Penfold, so I ought to know its quality, if no one else does.'

And under the influence of the Madeira, and Captain Barclay's kindness, the poor woman unbosomed her griefs to him, and confided her fears with regard to her young cousin.

'Think of that poor young creature, captain, wandering about the world alone—and so pretty, too. What will become of her? I assure you I haven't slept a wink since it happened, for wondering what I can do to find her again. For whether she's right or wrong, she's too young to be left to herself, and I must have her back at Gatehead, as sure as my name is Maria Penfold.'

'Mrs Penfold,' exclaimed the old sailor, extending his brown hand across the table for her acceptance, 'you're a good woman, madam!—a good woman, never mind who the other may be. Let that pretty girl with the big brown eyes go about the world alone, without a friend or protector? By gad! no. Why, I'd protect her myself, if there was no one else to do it. But I don't see how you are to get at her, my dear, unless you advertise in the papers.'

'Why, of course, captain, that is the very thing,' cried Mrs Penfold, jumping up from her chair; 'and I'll have the advertisement written out and sent to the post-office this very evening. I suppose I'd better insert it in the *Telegraph* and *Standard.*'

'And the *Times*, my dear, the *Times*,' added the captain, who was used to becoming rather affectionate in his speech after dinner.

'And the *Times*, of course,' replied Mrs Penfold. 'What a help you are to me, captain. Whatever should I do without you?'

'And when you have dispatched your advertisement, you will come back again, won't you?' said Captain Barclay.

'Well, captain, if you *really* require me,' replied Mrs Penfold bashfully.

'*Really* require you, madam. I really require you every hour of the day. You don't know what my life has been during your visit to Bluemere—torture, Mrs Penfold, torture! Sarah has been very attentive—I have no complaint to make of Sarah; but she is not, and she cannot be, yourself; that is her misfortune, Mrs Penfold, and not her fault. I have missed you every day and everywhere. My bed has not felt the same, and my parlour has not looked the same, and this chicken, for instance—although Sarah has done her best with it, I am sure, her very best—yet this chicken is *not* browned in the way *you* would have browned it; eh, Mrs Penfold?'

'Well, you see, captain, it is impossible to put grey heads on green shoulders; however, I am home once more to attend to all your little comforts, and not likely to leave you again in a hurry.'

'Not if I know it, madam, not if I know it,' replied Captain Barclay, with a facetious wink at his landlady.

'Well, really, captain, I don't see how you are to prevent it; not if my mind were bent upon going, for instance.'

'There are ways and means, Mrs Penfold, ways and means,' said the captain, with another wink.

Meanwhile, we must return to Blue Mount. Charles Anderson only waited until Bernard was well out of the way to break the intelligence of her son's disappointment to Mrs Freshfield, and do what he could to comfort her, the poor old lady's grief and shame were but too genuine. A divorced woman was, in her eyes, quite as ineligible a subject for the marriage contract as a wife would be, and Anderson did not attempt to refute any of her arguments on this part of the matter. Only he kept on repeating the fact that Phyllida's first husband was now dead, and therefore, according to the laws of God and man, there could be no possible obstacle to her re-union with Bernard. But to his astonishment he found that Mrs Freshfield did not take this view of the subject at all, and was strongly opposed to the idea of her son having anything more to do with the woman who, in her opinion, had betrayed him. This mother, who had reared her child in the strictest principles of her own religion; who had dedicated him from his birth (as it were) to the Lord and His service, and who (Anderson would have supposed) could have but one desire in her heart at this crisis, namely, that Bernard should act up to his profession, and do what was right, commenced arguing against the advisability of a second marriage on the most worldly grounds.

'But it would be perfect madness,' she said, when Anderson confided to her the motive that had taken her son to town. 'Surely, Mr Anderson, you never gave Bernard such advice as that? By the Lord's mercy he has been delivered from the bonds of a strange woman, though, if he had only waited to consult his poor mother on the subject, he never would have married a person of whom one knew *positively nothing;* however, he was headstrong, and had his own way, and now that his evil has been turned into good, I consider it would be flying in the face of Providence to re-forge the chains that have been struck off him.'

'Do you mean to say then, Mrs Freshfield, that you would advise Bernard *not* to marry his wife again?'

'Certainly, I would, Mr Anderson. She is *not* his wife. You have said so yourself. She is only a most disreputable person—a disgrace to her sex—a—'

'Oh, pardon me, I never said so much as that, because I do not think it; but, even if it were the case, I am not sure but what it would still be Bernard's duty to try and reform her by the only means in his power.'

'Well, I consider your ideas of duty are far-fetched, Mr Anderson, and I am surprised to hear a member of *your* Church upholding the sanctity of marriage with a *divorce.* I am no friend to Popery—'

'No, indeed, you need not tell me that, Mrs Freshfield.'

'But I do at least agree with it in one particular, and that is, that had this woman's divorce from her first husband been ever so regular, it should not have permitted her to contract an alliance with my poor misguided son.'

'And I am not likely to gainsay you, Mrs Freshfield. I say nothing of the past, except that it is as sad as sad can be, and I feel deeply for my dear old friend ; but I think that his duty now lies straight before him, and that is to make the woman to whom he is already united by ties of the tenderest affection his wife by law.'

'Well, I am surprised to hear you say so,' replied the mother coldly. 'I was aware, of course, that poor Bernard was very much infatuated with her when he believed her to be a good and pure woman (though why he should have squandered a small fortune in decking her out in pearls and satin far above her station in life I never could understand), but I should have *thought* and *hoped* that, his eyes once opened to her iniquity and deceit, a *son of mine* would have turned from her with the loathing and disgust which she deserves.'

'Oh no, Mrs Freshfield ; don't wrong your own nature by saying so,' pleaded Anderson. 'What ! turn from those we love when they most need our counsel and assistance ?—look the other way when our dear ones, however erring, lift their tearful eyes to ours ?—shut the door upon the repentant sinner who is longing to receive her pardon from our lips ? That is not the way a merciful God deals with *our* trespasses—blessed be His holy Name!' said Anderson reverently, 'or we should indeed be the most forlorn and miserable of creatures. What should you say, madam, if your heavenly Judge dealt with *your* sins as you would have Bernard deal with hers ?'

Now, although Mrs Freshfield called herself a miserable sinner every Sunday, and perhaps two or three times in the week to boot, she did not in the least believe that she was so, and Charles Anderson's straightforward question considerably ruffled her dignity. That a man, and a young man, and above all other things a Catholic young man, should presume to talk to her in such a manner greatly offended her ; and she showed the offence in her answer,—

'If you intend to compare me with the person we were speaking of, Mr Anderson, we had better drop the subject ; for I cannot see that the two cases tally in the slightest degree. I do not need *you* to remind me that there is forgiveness in heaven for *all* who sin on earth, but I do not see how it is to be attained by setting this depraved young woman again in the position which she has polluted and disgraced, and when Bernard *might* have secured one of the most estimable and pious young ladies for his helpmeet—a girl with the oldest blood of Scotland in her veins, and descended from a line of kings—one who would have conducted herself in all things as the wife of a minister should do, and been an honour and blessing to the whole family.'

'Yes, it is unfortunate, doubtless, that he could not see with your eyes ; but these are matters, Mrs Freshfield, in which men will and ought to judge for themselves. An union entered into from any feelings, however pure—except those of entire and disinterested love—cannot be a real union. I have seen men marry, apparently from the best of motives —for conscience' sake—or for the good of others, but however unselfishly entered into, unless it is from love alone, marriage is no longer a sacrament, but sinks to the level of a legal contract.'

'And would you call my poor son's marriage with this dreadful girl a sacrament, Mr Anderson?'

'I do indeed, Mrs Freshfield, and would continue to do so even if he did not marry her over again. His heart is knit up in hers, as hers is no less in his, and *that* constitutes a true marriage.'

'I don't believe it!' interposed the old lady, trembling with excitement. 'My poor son's eyes were dazzled by her beauty till he could not distinguish right from wrong, and I consider that any one who persuades him to take that woman back again, is his worst enemy, and not his friend.'

'And you would wish Bernard never to see her again then, nor to inquire after her fate?'

'Decidedly I would. He has taken a wife from among the daughters of Heth as the rebellious son of Rebecca did, and you see what has come of it. He ought to thank Providence, who has helped him to escape so great a danger, and not fly in its face by courting it a second time.'

'And you would consider him free to marry again, if he felt inclined to do so?' continued the young man.

'Of course he is free! What claim can she bring against him? Oh, if Bernard would only see it in the same light, and put some dear good girl in the vacant place!'

'You think the divorce he has obtained from his present wife is more legal then, than the one *she* got from her former husband?'

'Oh, there is no question of divorce,' replied the old lady, tossing her head in a nervous manner; 'she never was his wife; and I would rather discuss the painful subject no longer, Mr Anderson.'

'Very good, madam. I have done Bernard's bidding, and therefore may take my leave of you. But I am glad I do not share your sentiments on the question of right and wrong; neither do I think they would receive endorsement from above.'

And Anderson quitted Blue Mount, leaving Mrs Freshfield with the very uncomfortable sensation of having been brought to task, and considerably worsted in the encounter. Laura was not present at this interview. Had she been it would not have proceeded with so little interruption, for this young lady coincided with the opinions of Mr Anderson on all subjects in a remarkable degree. But she received the full benefit of it afterwards.

'Such an extraordinary manner in which to be addressed by a young man of *his* age—not so old as my own son by a couple of years—and a Papist into the bargain!' exclaimed Mrs Freshfield, as she retailed the circumstances to Laura. 'I wonder what the world will come to next? but Mr Anderson may rest assured of one thing, that I know my duty, and I will do it. I should have liked dear Miss Janet to have been present at our conversation this morning. I know she will entirely coincide with the view *I* take of this disgraceful affair.'

'Oh, mamma dear,' cried Laura, 'don't say anything to that old woman about it. What business is it of hers? And of course if *she* hears it, Bella and the laird will hear it also, and we shall be obliged to listen to all their comments on the matter. It is not delicate, mamma; it is purely a family misfortune—which we should keep entirely to ourselves for Bernie's sake, if not for our own. And do oblige me by putting off the visit of these

Muckheeps, at all events for the present. They asked themselves, so it could easily be managed without giving them offence.'

Mrs Freshfield regarded her daughter solemnly.

'And you would seriously ask me, Laura,' she said, 'in this the most unfortunate crisis of my life —when the Hand of Chastening is so visibly upon us—to deprive myself of the counsel and advice of my very best and most valued friends?'

'Oh, mamma, they are not your best friends, believe me. Miss Janet is only a canting old hypocrite, and you have never seen the laird at all. If he is anything like his sister though, I hope he will cut his visit short.'

'*Cut his visit short!*' reiterated Mrs Freshfield, with much the same look that might have been expected of her had her daughter uttered a blasphemy; 'is that the way, I ask you, Laura, to speak of a man who has spent his life in doing good to his fellow-creatures, who has expatriated himself for their sakes, and relinquished the society dearest to him, in order that he might bring souls grovelling on their knees for pardon.'

'Well, mamma, if he has done all this, it is very good of him, but we have only Miss Janet's word for it, you know. And in any case, we don't want him to grovel after souls here—unless you have any particular work for him in that way yourself,' said Laura brightly.

But Mrs Freshfield was in no humour to respond to brightness—however innocent.

'I shall *not* put off my friends' visit,' she said sternly; 'neither shall I conceal from them the misfortune which has fallen upon us. They will advise me, I am sure, to do what is best in the matter for my unhappy son, whom *your* friend

Mr Anderson appears bent upon leading to his ruin.'

'I don't know why you should emphasise Mr Anderson particularly as *my* friend, mamma,' returned Laura, with a suspiciously bright colour; 'but I am not ashamed of him if he is, and I do not believe that he wiil give Bernie any advice but what is good and proper.'

'Wait and see,' was Mrs Freshfield's oracular reply, for she had a strong suspicion that if she told Miss Laura what she meant by 'ruin,' that the wordy warfare just ended with Charles Anderson would have to be fought all over again, so she wisely held her tongue. The arrival of the Muckheeps the day after was a grand event in her life, for, naturally, poor Phyllida's history had to be retailed from the beginning to the end,—from the first time they met her with Mrs Pinner at Briarwood, to the last time she had sat in that very chair dear Miss Janet was then occupying ('just as if she had been an honest woman,' as Mrs Freshfield indignantly added), and the two ladies wept and wailed and groaned and condemned together over the reputation which they considered dead, just (as Laura had prophesied) like two dogs tearing a carcase to pieces, and determined not to leave a shred without the mark of their teeth upon it. But the Laird o' Muckheep —before whom Miss Janet (and, consequently, Mrs Freshfield) mutely bowed, as though he had been one of the kings from whom he boasted his descent—took little or no part in the discussion.

He was a very different man from what Laura had expected to see him. She had pictured the laird in fancy to be very like his sister,—in fact, an old woman in 'breeks,' but, on the contrary, he

did not resemble her in the slightest degree. He
was a large-boned, muscular man, very plain, with
red hair, a dirty complexion, small ferrety eyes,
and a bottle nose. He was, moreover, very silent,
and allowed Miss Janet to do all the talking,
although he never deprecated the fulsome praise
she lavished on him, but allowed himself to be
worshipped with the most perfect *nonchalance*,
taking it apparently as much his right as some
ugly old Chinese god set up in a joss house
might do, and with about the same amount of
interest in his worshippers. Laura, whose eyes
were everywhere at the same moment, noticed
that whenever Miss Janet lauded her brother's
goodness and self-denial, the laird would wink and
blink, and become restless and uneasy, changing
the subject as soon as he could, and sometimes
in the most abrupt manner ; but as he never denied
the praise she gave him, the girl attributed his
manner to his modesty.

'Ainly to think, Mrs Fraich - field,' the old
Scotchwoman would cry, 'that this gude mon has
ex-peetri-ated himsel' fra his ain land far mair
than twenty yair in order to been-efit his peerish-
ing fellow-creatures.'

'Noo, noo, Janet,' the laird, who spoke as broad
Scotch as his sister, replied, 'it's mickle I have
dune. Let us tairn the soobject.'

'*Mickle!*' screamed Miss Janet, 'd'ye ca' it a
mickle thing, mon, to abide awa' fra your ain for
the space o' twenty yair, an' to pair-se a' that
wheele in preaching and praying and striving for
the puir sawls that wouldna' strive for themsels.
Why, it's joost the Laird's wairk that ye've gee-ven
up your varry life for, and it's a greet re-waird
will be laid up for ye in heaven.'

'Noo, noo, Janet, not me whoole life. Ye forgit that I vee-sited the cairstle ten yairs agoo,' said the laird, with a modest declaimer of so much merit.

'Brither, I maun hae me ain way, and Mrs Fraich-field here will uphoold me. It's a gran' wairk, and a blessed ane that you've geeven yair time to, an' we should a' be prood to claim ye as a freend or a relation. Bella—bar-ck!'

'Yes, indeed, dear Miss Muckheep,' chimed in Mrs Freshfield approvingly. 'We should indeed be proud, and we are (at least I can speak for myself) to welcome the laird back to England. Twenty years! it is indeed a long time, though none too long to devote to so noble a cause. And were your efforts much blessed out there, dear sir ? Did you bring many poor lost souls back into the fold ?'

'Yes, yes ; I had pratty gude soocess, madam althoo' a mon shouldna speak of what he has dune.'

'Hoot, brither,' interposed Miss Janet, 'but if ye air a bairning and a shining leeght, ye mauna pet yourself oonder the beed, bit upon a carn-dle-steek, that sae ye may geeve leeght to the whoole hoose. Dinna ye haud wi' we, Mrs Fraich-field ?'

'Indeed, indeed, I do, although your estimable brother's modesty renders his worth all the greater. Ah, we have been in great need of a missionary to do the good work here, I can assure you. What effect might not the laird's influence have had upon that poor misguided soul at the rectory ?'

'Do ye speak o' your sonnie the meenister, Mrs Fraich-field, or o' the hizzy he pet oop theer as his wife ?'

Laura who had been silently boiling over this conversation, here burst in with a remonstrance,—

'Please to remember, Miss Janet, that the lady you speak of is about to become my brother's wife by law.'

'No, no, Laura, I trust not—not if *I* can help it,' interposed her mother.

'You will not be able to help it, mamma ; and I think the less the subject is discussed with strangers the better.'

'Hoot, what is the lassie speering at ?' demanded Miss Janet. 'Ye dinna shoo muckle re-speect for your mither to interroopt her after sic a fashion, Mees Fraich-field.'

'I desire to show respect for my brother and his wife, madam, which is hardly to be attained by discussing their private affairs.'

'Laura, how can you speak so to Miss Janet, who, you must know, is in my entire confidence on this unhappy subject? We have just been consulting together on the best course for me to pursue in the matter, and I have made up my mind to follow your poor brother to London to-morrow.'

'Bernard will be exceedingly annoyed if you do so, mamma. He is quite old enough to manage his own business, and you will gain nothing by putting your finger in the pie.'

'Petting your feenger in the poy ? I dinna oonderstan' your dairghter's mode of speaking, Mrs Fraich-field. I never raired oor Bella after sic a fashion ; it wou'dna become a leddy o' Muckheep at a''

'No, indeed,' replied her hostess fretfully ; 'nor any lady in the world, I should imagine. Laura's *fast* mode of speaking shocks me as much as it

can do yourself. But to return to my poor, erring
son. What a consolation it would be to me if you
and the dear laird (who has had so much experience in winning back lost souls to the right way)
would accompany me on my sad errand to-
morrow. It seems almost too much to ask from
you, but I shall need both support and guidance
on the journey.'

'If you are resolved to go, mamma,' said Laura,
'for heaven's sake go alone!'

'Young leddy,' exclaimed Miss Janet, 'ye dinna
ken the reet way to speak to sech as air abune
yairsel'. Your gude mither is awa' to Loon-don
to try and breeng your puir brither back to a
sense of his re-sponsibeelities; and if I can be
of ainy cairm-fort or cainsolation to her on the
jair-ney, she maun depeend upon my coompany.'

'Ah, you are indeed too good to me,' sighed
Mrs Freshfield. 'What should I do without your
kind sympathy and counsel? If I can gain an
interview with my poor Bernard before his artful
friend Mr Anderson—a Jesuit in disguise, I verily
believe, Miss Janet—persuades him to sacrifice
himself afresh, and can bring him back with us
to Blue Mount, all may yet be well. The dear
laird's advice would be invaluable to him at this
critical period. He could so ably point out to
my poor boy the way to induce that young person
to abandon her depraved and godless life without
going to the length of marrying her over again.
An asylum is the place for her—some nice, respectable asylum where she will be plainly shown
the depths of her wickedness and sin.'

Here Laura rose hastily, and gathering her
work together, left the room.

'My poor child does not like this subject,'

continued Mrs Freshfield, with a compassionate
shake of her head. ' I have trained her carefully,
dear Miss Janet, and with many prayers, but her
heart, I regret to say, remains hard and stubborn
to this day. I believe that she even goes so far
as to *regret* her brother's merciful escape from the
thralls of the bond-woman.'

' Ay!' ejaculated Miss Janet. ' Ye should jeest
pet me brither upon her in prayer; her hairt
wou'dna' lang remain haird nor stooborn after
that. Mony and mony a hairt has he subdooed
and melted by his fair-vour, till it coudna' weep
eno.' Ay!—but he's a peen-acle of the temple
before wheech naething can stan' upreet.'

' And do you think I might really ask him to
accompany us to town to-morrow ? It would be an
immense favour ; but oh, so gratefully appreciated.
I cannot believe that Bernard will be able to resist
his eloquence ; however, he may be inclined to walk
in the downward path.

' Oh, the laird will go with us, dinna fear, Mrs
Fraich-field. He maun aye be wheer the gude wairk
is goin' on ; and if wairds o' his can tairn the
puir sinner fra' the eer-or of his ways, he will be
tairned, ye may reest assured o' that.'

' Indeed, indeed, I do. I feel as if an *angel*
were going with us to point out the right thing
to do, and the right word to say at the right time,'
cried Mrs Freshfield enthusiastically, as she clasped
the freckled and hairy hand of the Laird o' Muckheep between her own.

He turned aside with a conscious air and a few
muttered words of acquiescence ; but his hostess
was gazing at him through rose-coloured spectacles,
and attributed his confusion entirely to the humility
of his pious soul. And the next day, therefore, to

Laura's intense annoyance, her mother set out for London, supported on either side by a Muckheep' like sympathising friends upholding the chief mourner at a funeral.

'How angry Bernie will be by their interference,' she thought. 'It would have been bad enough if mamma had elected to go to him alone; but accompanied by that pair of canting old hypocrites, she will drive him nearly crazy, and when he has so much to trouble him, poor darling.'

She was full of such thoughts when a servant brought her word that Mr Anderson was in the drawing-room. She flew to meet him, in a manner most undignified for a young lady of two-and-twenty, and with a bloom upon her cheeks that looked suspiciously as though she were uncommonly glad to see him. Perhaps Charles Anderson guessed the truth; for as Laura ran up to greet him, he grasped her outstretched hands and kissed her straight upon the lips. She drew backward with a face of crimson.

'Oh, Charlie, you shouldn't have done that. You never did it before.'

'Perhaps not; but there must be a beginning to all things, you know, Laura.'

'Not to bad things, though.'

'Was that a bad thing then, Laura? Tell me.'

'Well, it can't be quite right, can it?'

'Why not?'

'Oh, I don't know, but it isn't the usual mode of greeting between friends, Charlie.'

'But we are not friends.'

'Aren't we?' she asked, with professed innocence. 'I thought we were the very best.'

'So we are; but something more, I hope, Laura. I love you dearly, and I am sure you know it.'

'I have hoped it, Charlie.'

'That's a brave woman to tell the truth at once. Then it's all right between us?'

'Between *us*—oh yes! but, Charlie, have you ever thought of mamma?'

Charlie laughed.

'Rather too often for my peace of mind, Laura. She doesn't like me; I am aware of that.'

'I don't think she has any personal objection to *you*, dear; but it's the religion. Mamma is frightfully bigoted, you know. I really believe that she imagines there is not the slightest chance of your going to heaven.'

'And what do *you* think, my Laura?'

'Oh, Charlie, I think you are everything that is best. I only wish I had the same assurance of salvation as yourself. To give up one's family and friends, as you have done, and all one's prospects in life for the sake of your faith, what more could any man do to prove his sincerity? It is a grander sacrifice than even the martyrs made of old. They gave up this life to gain a better; but you have given up all the comforts of the world, and chosen to walk through it without luxury or love, in order that you may remain true to yourself; and I have honoured you for it, dear Charlie, above all other men, ever since Bernard told me the story.'

'Don't make too much of it, Laura. If you could guess the consolations I have received in exchange, you would not think it such a sacrifice. And now, if I am to have your love into the bargain, I shall be more than happy, only you mustn't forget that I am a poor man. My father has cut me out of his will, and will not even hear my name mentioned in his presence. I have only the work of my two hands to offer my wife as a support.'

'That is not of the slightest consequence,' said Laura, indifferently, ' for I have money of my own, as well as Bernie. What *I* am thinking of is the prejudice of your father and my mother. Charlie, isn't it extraordinary that people who profess to love God with their whole hearts, and desire His glory above all other things, should quarrel with *any* form by which their fellow creatures strive to serve Him too?'

'It is almost incredible, Laura, yet we know it is true. But I cannot call such people Christians, even though they are my own flesh and blood. They are pious dogs in the manger: quite satisfied with their own position, and ready to snarl at any one who attempts to dispute it. I suppose it really did the ox more good to nibble at a few straws than it did the dog to lie on them ; but since he had no stomach for straw himself, he was too blind and selfish to see that the ox needed it. If my friends and relations have no eyes for the beauty of the Catholic Church, and no ears for the sublimity of her doctrine, I pity them, and I pray for them ; but I do not blame them, for the mind must be spiritually opened to view it as I do, only I cannot understand why they must needs quarrel because they cannot agree with me.'

'Do you pity me, Charlie?' whispered Laura, sidling up to him.

'A little, because you are going to fall into my clutches. Do you pity yourself?'

She shook her head.

'I am quite happy as I am. I do not know what I may become as the years roll on, but at present it seems to me as if life could never be

fuller of interest for me than it is. I have had
Bernie ever since I could remember, and now I
have got you, and I cannot tell which is the best
of you ; he as a Protestant or you as a Catholic.
And I hardly know which of you I love the best
either,' she added more shyly, 'nor, if I had to
give up one, which I should choose. So you
must let me be the link between you, Charlie, that
when you look at me you may both remember
that, as I bind you together by the names of wife
and sister, so the great Christian Churches should
be bound together in brotherly love by the one
Holy Name which alone can save us all.'

Anderson drew Laura closer to his side, and
repeated the operation with which he had greeted
her entrance, and this time she made no objection,
although the tears were shining in her bright eyes.

'Oh, Charlie, I am so happy!'

'So am I, dearest ; and you will really marry
me then, spite of all your mother may say ?'

'Mamma will come round after a time. She is
generally open to persuasion from Bernie or me.
You know how strongly set she was at first against
poor Phyllida ?'

'That reminds me, darling, that I came down
here this morning with news of Bernard. Let us
find Mrs Freshfield and tell her at once.'

Laura's face fell.

'Oh, I had quite forgotten. You put everything out of my head, Charlie ; mamma, I am
sorry to say, has just started for London to see
my brother. I begged and entreated her not to
go, for I am sure her visit will annoy him, but
she would not listen to anything I said ; and what
is more, she has taken those two Muckheeps with
her—the old laird and his sister—and you know

how Bernard dislikes Miss Janet. I am sure something very disagreeable will happen when they meet.'

Anderson became as grave as herself.

'I am exceedingly sorry to hear this, Laura, and I think, under the circumstances, it was the most ill-advised course your mother could take; and this morning, too, of all days.'

'Why not this morning, Charlie?' asked Laura in alarm. 'What has happened to make this day worse than others?'

'Nothing but what will make *you* glad, Laura, but, at the same time, will render Mrs Freshfield's visit rather *malàpropos*. Bernard has found his wife again.'

'Oh! Charlie, why didn't you tell me that before?' cried Laura, bursting into tears of pleasure and excitement. 'Phyllida home again! Phyllida with Bernard! My dear, dear sister found! Oh, I am so grateful, so happy! How can I repay you for bringing me such joyful news?'

'Kiss me again,' suggested the practical Charlie.

'I *will*,' exclaimed Laura determinedly, as she put both her arms round her lover's neck, and lifted her burning face to his. 'I would give you a hundred kisses, Charlie, if you wished it, for making me so happy!'

'All right, Laura ; go on.'

'No, no ; we mustn't be foolish. But tell me all about it. Where did he find her? Where are they now? How soon can they be married again?'

'Gently, Laura, you are going too fast. Bernard has received intelligence of his wife—he hoped to meet her again to-day—and as poor Phyllida seems to be in a miserable state of doubt and uncertainty as to whether she ought to return to her husband, he thought the presence of his dear little sister would be of great service to both of them.'

'Did he send you for me? Does he wish me to go to London? Dear, dear Bernie,' said warm-hearted Laura.

'Yes; indeed that is just what he wants, and sent me to obtain your mother's permission to escort you to his side. He thinks that if his arguments have no effect on Phyllida, your per-suasions are certain to prevail.'

'Of course—of course, I will do my very best, and if she will not return to him, I can at least remain with her. But, Charlie, mamma and those horrid Muckheeps will be there. Ought I to go up at the same time?'

'If you are not afraid to trust yourself with me, Laura, I think that fact is an extra reason for your making no delay in joining your brother. It is very probable, I am sorry to say, that they may burst in upon him just as he has been re-united to his wife, and I am afraid to think what may pass between them, or how serious a breach their visit may cause. Your presence will be an immense protection to your sister-in-law, and, I am sure, a comfort to Bernard.'

'Then I will get ready to go with you at once, Charlie. There is only Bella Muckheep in the house, and as she never does anything but knit stockings, she will not miss me for a few hours. I shall tell her I am suddenly summoned to join my brother. Ring the bell, and order the pony chaise as soon as it can be got ready, and I will be with you again before it comes round.'

And with a smile and a nod, Laura Freshfield

flew off to her own room, leaving Charles Anderson in a very contented and self-satisfied frame
of mind.

CHAPTER XVIII.

BERNARD FRESHFIELD had started for London
about a week before this, and made his way at
once to the hotel where he knew that Nelson Cole
had taken up his quarters. He found his friend
at home and alone, looking rather more haggard
than he had done at Briarwood, as though he
had been somewhat anxious and thoughtful since
they parted, and sitting at a table covered with
papers.

'Bernard, my boy!' he exclaimed, as our parson made his appearance, 'I am glad you have
come up to town again. I was just about to write
and ask you to do so. I have heard of some
business since I saw you last that will detain
me in England, so I expect to be stationary here
for the next few weeks; and I want you to spend
them with me. It will be ever so much better
for you than moping at Briarwood by yourself.'

'Thank you, Cole,' replied Bernard, somewhat
shyly, and there he stopped. Nelson Cole was
surprised at his manner and appearance. He
had expected to see him the very picture of de-
jection, but he looked rather cheerful than otherwise, although his eyes were heavy and his cheeks
pale. Yet there was an air about him as of one
who had passed through the suffering and found
peace on the other side.

'You are bearing this trouble better than I expected, Bernard,' said Nelson Cole, almost jealously.

'Am I? You don't know what I have gone through since we parted. But I confess I feel happier now than I hoped to do. I had my dear friend Charles Anderson talking to me for a couple of hours this afternoon, and he made me see things in a different light.'

'Ah, he is the pious Papist, is he not?'

'Yes, he is a Papist; and very proud of being so; and he is pious, like most of his faith. It is an exception to the rule when a Papist is not pious.'

'And he talked to you about heaven, I suppose, and the reward laid up for martyrs who sacrifice themselves to their opinions, until you fell in love with suffering, and are going to add a hair shirt to the loss of your supposed wife?'

'Cole, my dear fellow, why do you speak to me in this way?' exclaimed Bernard. 'I came up to London to tell you of the resolution I have, after much thought, arrived at; but if you are going to treat my confidence with sarcasm, you will frighten it away.'

'What resolution can you possibly have arrived at but one?' grumbled Cole; 'the girl never was married to you according to your own ideas. She has led you into spending some six months in what you would consider to be mortal sin; and all that remains for you is to do penance, and practise mortifications until you have purged yourself of even the memory of her unholy presence. I know you parsons. Everybody may go to the d—l so long as you save your own souls.'

'But — *was* it sin, Cole?' asked Freshfield wistfully.

'Was *what* sin?' said the other.

'My living with Phyllida. She believed herself free: I believed her to be so, and I cannot think that an Almighty Father will punish an unintentional error. If we sinned, it was not with our eyes open. No; it is the concealment she used towards me that hurts me so terribly. If I can see her soul purged of that, I shall be content.'

'And so you have come up to London, I suppose, to find her out, and bring her down on her knees for confession? Her husband is to be turned into her missionary, and treat her to a medley of passion and penitence, till the poor child will be totally unable to distinguish right from wrong. No, no, it must not be. I knew the girl in America, and I won't have her trifled with. You've renounced her — I don't question your right to do so, perhaps she is everything that is bad; but let the renunciations be final. There are plenty of parsons in the world beside yourself; and there is no need for you to go running after Phyllida Moss, and doubling her misery for the purpose of converting her.'

Bernard stared at his old friend in amazement. He hardly knew him. Nelson Cole, who had always appeared so hardheaded, cynical and ''cute,' was now working himself up into something very much like a passion, and on behalf of a girl whose condition he had been the very one to bring about.

'I don't understand you,' replied Bernard; 'in the first place, you are bringing accusations against me without any cause; in the second, you condemn me unheard. Was it *I*, Cole, who turned my poor girl out of doors, or pronounced her unfit to hold the position she did at Briarwood? Why, the blow has nearly killed me, and after a day and night of torture, I came here to tell you that I have made up my mind, at all hazards, to find her again, and persuade her to become my wife.'

Nelson Cole pushed the hair off his forehead, and looked up into his friend's face critically.

'Is that *so ?*' he asked incredulously; and have you well considered what taking Phyllida back again means in your profession and your family?'

'I have considered nothing but my own good and hers—we love each other, Cole—we belong to each other—we stand alone and apart—two in one, inseparable — indivisible — not, mark you, because the law made us so, but because our hearts were joined before our hands. I have been very angry and very shocked. I don't deny it. Your revelations seemed at first to have made a gulf between us that nothing could again bridge over; but I am calmer now. I can regard things in a truer light; and I see that my life and hers will be spoiled if they do not come together again. You laughed at me once for writing and talking of my soul's mate. But it was true. I found her in Phyllida, and in spite of everything she is mine, and she must remain so.'

'You intend to marry her again?'

'I intend, please God, to marry her again.'

Nelson Cole leapt from his chair and seized Bernard's hand.

'God bless you, my boy! God bless you!' he exclaimed. 'You have lifted a weight off my mind.'

'How could I imagine,' returned Bernard, 'that you would receive my news like this—you who were so hard upon her—Cole?'

'No, not hard, not *hard*. Was I? Poor child! poor child!' replied the other man. 'But if so, I am thankful you have the strength to remedy the harm I did her. Ah, Bernard, she loves you. I could envy you, my boy, for being so much loved, but I will not, for you deserve it. Only guard and protect her from herself for the future, and I will believe that for you at least there is a heaven and a reward laid up in it.'

Then perceiving the look of utter astonishment with which his friend still regarded him, and suddenly remembering that he was talking in a very different strain from what he usually employed, Nelson Cole drifted into a sort of apology for his words.

'I daresay I seem to be talking a great deal of nonsense to you; but the fact is, Bernard, I found out the other day, from a conversation I had with Jack Neville, that Phyllida is the daughter of an old friend of mine.'

'What! Do you mean the wife of the man Macpherson, whom Neville mentioned to us?'

Nelson Cole winced.

'Yes—his—his—wife. You are right. I find that I knew her, ages ago, and it has made me feel a great interest in the daughter. And you really mean to take her back? You are not afraid of any more facts cropping up to nip your new-born resolution in the bud?'

'I could be afraid but of one thing, Cole, and that would be any uncertainty respecting her husband's death. You are *sure* that he is dead?'

'I *am* sure. I have made inquiries since I saw

you last. The rascal was too well known to be able to pretend to die. He died in the Tombs, cheating justice to the last, as he had ever done.'

'Then I breathe freely, Cole, and Phyllida will be my own again.'

'But she may have done worse than that, remember,' said Cole, wishing to test the sincerity of Bernard's resolution. 'She was on the stage for a twelvemonth, and I won't be responsible for anything that happened to her during that period. Suppose she had half a score of lovers,—eh ? '

Bernard bit his lip, but answered calmly,—

'I have determined that all bygones shall be bygones. If Phyllida consents to be my wife, we will begin afresh from the moment of our marriage. She will never find me calling her to account for what took place before I knew her.'

'Few men are so generous as that,' said Cole, with a touch of his old sarcasm.

'Cole,' replied Bernard earnestly, 'don't you think that we men are rather hard, as a rule, upon our women. We allow ourselves every licence, but we call on them to be immaculate. They must not only be modest and single-minded, but they must live as though they were perfectly passionless and without feeling of any sort. Since I have entered the Church, men have naturally been more shy of bestowing their worldly confidences on me, but when I was a wild young fellow at Oxford, and up to any kind of spree myself, I used to hear and see what married men did when away from their wives, and even then, careless as I was, it shocked me. I used to think how surprised those men would be if, when they went home, their wives (having become aware of their behaviour) refused to receive them ; and yet what would *they* have said if the same infidelities had been practised in their absence. They would have called their women by every foul name they could think of, and declare them unfit to be the wives of honest men. And the law would have upheld them. But there is another law than that of man, Cole, and I am trying hard to look at this matter according to the law of God.'

'Well, I believe, for your satisfaction, that Phyllida was always as good as gold in that respect; but she got tipsy one night—there is no doubt of that. You heard Jack Neville confirm my statement.'

Bernard was gazing before him with dreamy eyes.

'Because she heard that the brute to whom she was tied was locked up, and she would be free from his persecution for two years,' he answered. 'Poor child! How she *must* have suffered to create such a reaction!'

'Oh! that's the way you take it. But isn't there just a chance of her relapsing?'

'Do you think so?' cried Bernard, with sudden energy, springing to his feet. Oh no, no—not whilst my arms are round her to save her! My poor darling!—my poor betrayed and outcast Phyllida! If any such terrible harm should follow that one fall to degradation, it will be laid at *his* door, not hers—at the door of *him* with whom she was forced into an unholy marriage; and I will fight *for* her and *with* her until we have stamped out the last foul memento of that horrible sacrifice. Oh no, Cole, don't think it. She cannot—she *shall* not fall again, with my love standing between her and temptation!'

Nelson Cole seized both his hands and held them as if they were in a vice.

'My boy!' he exclaimed,—'my noble-hearted boy! The woman who mates with you should be an angel.'

'She *shall* be one,' said Bernard, 'if the prayers of a lifetime can make her so. Don't tell me any more of her past; let us think only of her future. She is more to me a great deal than the love of my heart; she is a soul that God has put into my hands to save.'

And Bernard looked like a saint as he pronounced the words.

His friend wrung his hands again and sat down; then they both laid their enthusiasm aside for a while and became practical.

'I was only testing the stuff you were made of,' said Cole, 'and you have come nobly out of the trial; and now to business, Bernard. Do you know where that poor girl is?'

'Indeed, I do not. I am here to ask you to help me to trace her.'

'I have been thinking about her a great deal since we parted, and I imagine that old lady, Mrs Penfold, will be better able to find her than ourselves. Didn't you tell me she was very kind to Phyllida at the time of your marriage?'

'Very kind, indeed. We were married from her house in Gatehead.'

'Don't you think it is probable that Phyllida might again seek shelter with her cousin at Gatehead?'

'Perhaps so; but Mrs Penfold is still at Bluemere. She is staying with her sister, Mrs Pinner.'

'Write to her, then, and ask her to go home, and be ready to receive Phyllida there. Then we will advertise as if from her cousin, begging the girl to return to her protection. I think we shall catch her that way. Of course we could put the matter into the hands of detectives ; but the less publicity about these domestic affairs the better.'

Bernard taking his friend's advice, wrote to Mrs Penfold to Bluemere ; but as she had [already left Mrs Pinner's the letter was forwarded to Gatehead, and reached there the very morning that the following lines appeared in the *Standard*, in answer to Mrs Penfold's advertisement :—

' *Phyllida to Gatehead.—I cannot accept your offer. By-and-by, when I am independent, I may see you again, but not now. Many, many thanks, and may God bless you.*'

Mrs Penfold cut out the advertisement, and enclosed it in a letter (which might have been a chapter out of the Lamentations of Jeremiah) to Bernard, who immediately carried it to Nelson Cole.'

'*Independent*, indeed!' exclaimed the latter. ' How is such a child to make herself independent in a howling wilderness like *London*, unless it be by returning to the stage, and she will find a difficulty in doing that. She is sure to look in the *Standard* again for another appeal, Bernard. We will insert one that is certain to bring an answer.'

'But how will that enable us to ascertain her address ?' asked Bernard anxiously. ' Each day that we are separated now seems like a purgatory to me.'

'Patience, my son, patience. All things come to him who knows how to wait. This is the sort of thing I should advise you to insert in the paper :—

'" *Gatehead to Phyllida.—Mr F. has consulted me about putting the case in the hands of the police. Do you wish him to find out your address or not ?*"'

'And what do you expect her to reply to this?' asked Bernard ruefully. She will only say "No." I feel that the shock of discovery has driven her from me for ever.'

'Bernard, my boy, you're a very good "cuss," but I calculate you've not been "raised" in the States. This message will be in Phyllida's hands to-morrow at latest, and she will be in a regular fix about the police. Nothing frightens a woman like the law.'

'But what's the good of frightening her, poor darling ?'

'I'm coming to that, my son. The first effect of her fright will be to make her rush to the *Standard* office with an answer to the advertisement. She will write to beg Mrs Penfold to prevent her from seeing *you*.'

'Well—'

'Well, I guess I shall have my eye on that office all the day, and when she appears to insert her advertisement, I shall drop down upon her— sharp.'

'Oh, Cole ! to-morrow—actually *to-morrow !* Is it possible that to-morrow I shall hold her in my arms again ?'

'*Possible* ; but only possible. Suppose she refuses to accompany me home ?'

'Surely she will not refuse when she hears how we long to have her back again.'

'Don't know. Women are fickle cattle to shoe behind. But if she accompanies me here, she may refuse to see *you*.'

'Oh no, no. She loves me, Cole, believe me. She must yearn for me as much as I do for her.'

'Good ; but then there is another risk of failure —so don't be too sanguine. She may not go to the office herself, but send a messenger.'

'And in that case, what *shall* we do?' asked Bernard mournfully.

'In that case, my chum, we must try the effect of another advertisement. But let us see what to-morrow will bring first.'

The two men passed that evening together with a certain degree of cheerfulness, but Bernard was not too much absorbed in his own troubles to observe that Nelson Cole looked forward to the morrow with almost as much anxiety as himself. It was with difficulty when the morning arrived that he could let him start on his quest alone—he was so sure that if he stood on the opposite side of the way, or up the next street, or under a doorway—that Phyllida would not perceive him until it was too late to make her escape. But Nelson Cole would not hear of his accompanying him, and made him promise into the bargain to keep to his own rooms in the hotel, until he was invited to enter those of his friend. And so the unfortunate parson, left behind in that state of mind when it is quite impossible to fix the attention upon anything, threw books and papers consecutively to one side, and ended by casting himself, face downwards, upon the bed, whilst he worked up his brain to a pitch of madness by reviewing all the happiest scenes he had passed through with Phyllida, and trying to realise what would become of him if they never occurred again.

Meanwhile Nelson Cole took up his station opposite the office of the *Standard* paper, and watched carefully all who went in or came out. He felt more certain of success than he had confided to Bernard, for several reasons of his own. In the first place, he argued that when women are very anxious about a thing, they always like to do it themselves—they will not believe that any one else can do it so well; and secondly, Phyllida was a stranger in London, and not aware perhaps of how easily an advertisement can be sent, with a few stamps, through the post; and thirdly, she was not likely to be in a position to command the services of any one to do the errand for her. So he kept up a steady tramp on the opposite pavement, with his keen eye watching the approaches from every quarter. About two o'clock she came, dressed in her serge costume, pale as a sheet, and with dark circles under her eyes, but still Phyllida, and looking so lovely that every man's head turned to gaze after her as she passed. She came on fearlessly, though evidently labouring under the deepest depression. But she had no idea that any one in that vast crowd would single her out for notice, and when Nelson Cole, crossing the road, placed his hand upon her arm and said the word 'Nessie,' he frightened her so that she screamed. That name reminded her of all that was most terrible in her young life, and she turned about, half-expecting to see the face of Sandie Macpherson scowling at her, or the ghost of Fernan Cortës at her elbow. And when she recognised Nelson Cole, she seemed hardly less alarmed.

'Oh, Mr Cole, why are you here? Why do you call me by that name?'

'I came here solely to find you, child, and I

called you " Nessie " because I knew your mother, and I used to call her so.'

'You knew my mother, and yet you told *him* of me. Oh, I do not believe it! You are making some pretence in order to do me further harm. Let me go, Mr Cole ; pray, let me go. I never wish to see or speak to you again.'

'Phyllida,' said Nelson Cole earnestly, 'will you believe me when I tell you, that I wish now I had been dead before I confessed that you were recognised. But it is too late now for regret. Let me try therefore to make you some amends. You have said that I was kind to you once—'

'Oh yes, you were indeed,' she interrupted him gratefully ; 'what should I have done if you had not come to my rescue at that miserable time in Chicago ? Why, I never could have left the city. I could not have come to England—I should not have seen *him.* Ah !—' and here Phyllida put her hand against her side as though to still a sudden pain.

'My poor child, you think after all, perhaps, that *that* did not turn out such a kindness. Well, well, never mind it now. I thought I saw my duty plain before me, but you were a little goose not to take my advice and tell Bernard yourself. But, Nessie—'

'Not Nessie, Mr Cole, *pray* not Nessie.'

'Phyllida then, if you prefer it ; come back with me to my hotel, Phyllida, and let us talk matters over quietly.'

'There is nothing to talk over, sir, and there is nothing to be done. I have disgraced him without remedy, and the sooner he and his friends forget my existence the better.'

'But I am of a different opinion. I have been

talking with Jack Neville since I was at Briarwood.
Do you know, by the way, that your old friend
Jack is in town.

Phyllida slightly shuddered.

'No, Mr Cole, I had not heard it before ; but I
would rather not see him.   He will remind me of
the past.'

'I had no intention of proposing it, only I found
out from what he told me that I had been acquainted with your mother, Mrs Moss (as she
called herself), and you are very like her, Phyllida
—very like.   I know now what it is in your face
that attracted me from the first.'

But to Phyllida it was evidently a matter of
complete indifference whether Mr Cole was attracted by her or not.   She moved uneasily from
his side, trying to elude him.

'Will you let me pass into the office, Mr Cole ?
I have business here.'

'What is your business ?   To insert an advertisement in the *Standard ?*'   Don't throw away
your money, Phyllida ; you must have little
enough, because I tell you it will be useless.'

She looked at him in astonishment.

'How can you know what my advertisement is
about ?'

'I don't know the words of it, but I am sure of
the substance.   It is to entreat your cousin, Mrs
Penfold, not to let Bernard Freshfield put the
detectives on your track, and I can help you in
that matter better than twenty Mrs Penfolds.'

'How can you do so ?' she asked faintly.

'Because Bernard will not act without consulting me, in fact the business will be put into my
hands to work as I choose.   Now, Phyllida, I
will make a compact with you.   Come home with

me and let us talk quietly over the matter, and I promise Bernard shall not have your address until you give it him yourself.   Is it a bargain ? '

' Yes, I will go with you,' she said ; for she was dying to hear all·about her husband, and how he had borne the revelations which had been made to him.

She stood quietly enough by Cole's side until he had hailed a cab and placed her in it ; but as soon as they were driving towards his hotel, she startled him by hiding her face upon his arm and bursting into a flood of tears.

' Oh, Mr Cole,' she sobbed, ' I don't bear you any enmity—indeed I don't—for I know it was your duty to tell him, and it was to my shame that he should have been kept in ignorance so long.   But my heart is breaking, indeed, indeed it is!'

' Hush, Phyllida ! Hush, my child,' he found himself saying, in the most paternal manner, as he smoothed the long tresses which had fallen from under her hat.

' I did not dream I was doing him an injury,' she went on, weeping ; ' how should I ?   I didn't know that *anybody* considered a divorce illegal. And, Mr Cole, I was never really married to that other man ; for I ran away from him the very same day that my father forced me into it, and hid in a digger's hut until Cortës had left the valley.   So I believed I was quite—*quite* free—to do as I chose.'

' Yes, yes ; I understand it all now,' replied Cole soothingly ; ' and so will he, some day.   I will take care that he does.   But you must try and compose yourself, Phyllida, for here we are, close to my hotel, and you would not like the waiters to see you in this condition.'

She drew herself up then, and dried her tears, and pulled her veil over her face, and walked up to his private sitting-room with a dignity of which he had hardly thought her capable; and Jack Neville's assertion that 'Nessie always looked like a lady' came back to his mind as he watched her.

'And now,' he commenced, when they had seated themselves, 'tell me first what you intend to do.'

'I am going back to the stage, Mr Cole. I find my style of acting is all the rage in London just now, and I have already had a very favourable interview with one of the managers.'

'Yes, I suppose you will get an engagement, Stephanie, if it is only for your beauty. But of course, then, you have relinquished all idea of returning to Bernard Freshfield?'

She gave a sudden cry, and put up her hand to her face.

'Oh, Mr Cole, don't! You know that he would not take me back.'

'I am not so sure of it. He is very much attached to you, and I believe he would be ready to condone everything if you wished to return.'

'Oh, I couldn't!—I couldn't! He may think so now in the first agony of parting; but he would say differently when we had settled down into a quiet life again. Think what I have done to him —he who is so good, so pure, so pious, so fond of his mother and sister, so anxious to do honour to his profession. I went amongst them all as his wife; I took all the privileges of a wife, and the respect and esteem. And what has it ended in? That he doesn't believe me to have been free till Cortès died, and that for six months I betrayed him (by my cowardice in not telling the truth) into the commission of a sin for which he must look on me with abhorrence, I—I—who would have died for him!' she continued, with a fresh burst of grief.

'Listen to me, my dear,' replied Cole; 'all that you say is very true, and had you *not* believed yourself to be free, and deceived him into thinking you so, I daresay this would have been an awkward matter to mend. But I have talked with poor Bernard on the subject, and however grieved he may be (and he has been terribly cut up about it), he absolves you from blame in the matter.'

'He *absolves* me!' she repeated with surprise. 'Does that mean he thinks I was right?'

'Not quite that, Phyllida. He regrets deeply that you were not more open with him, but he does not consider the injury has been so great as to prevent your living together again. Bernard wants you to return to him.'

A gleam of joy shot over her countenance, but it was immediately succeeded by her former gloom.

'He is wrong,' she answered, 'even to wish it. Nothing can unmake me. I was never fit to become one of his family; and on looking back, I think I was mad ever to think of it.'

'But if your husband desires you to return, it becomes your duty to do so.'

'He is not my husband,' replied Phyllida.

'My dear, I think that question is open to doubt. If your divorce was a legal one, he is at any rate your husband by law.'

'*My husband by law!*' she echoed; 'oh, Mr Cole, you don't know Bernard if you can speak of him like that; you don't know what Bernard can make a woman feel a husband to be, if you can name the name in the same breath as *law*.　Do you imagine I could endure to know myself to be his wife *by law*, and miss all the holiness and sanctity which made the title sound like a blessing to me every time he uttered it?　Do you think I could accept what the law would give me, and know that the esteem and love which he showered on me (but which I had no right to take from him) were dead and gone for ever?'

'Perhaps not; but supposing they are not dead?'

'I should bring him to shame all the same.　I should cause him to be pitied by his neighbours and avoided by his relations.　Fancy a parson with a wife whose antecedents must not be inquired into.　Oh, Mr Cole, do not let him find me out; persuade him to leave me alone.　He shall never be troubled again by so much as the mention of my name, for I will not let people know that we have ever met.'

'I don't think Bernard will consent to that,' replied Cole gravely.　He was beginning to fear that the task he had taken on himself would prove a less easy one than he had imagined.

'But he must—he must!' cried Phyllida wildly.　'I will not meet him; I will not speak to him. I have been a curse upon his life, and if my heart breaks under the ordeal, I will separate myself from him for ever; and were I to see him come into this room this very moment, I would—Ah!—'

But at this juncture Phyllida turned, and seeing Bernard himself standing on the threshold, gave a shriek of joy and flew into his arms.

'Hang you, Bernard!' cried Nelson Cole, with affected anger, 'I thought I desired you to remain in your own rooms until I requested the pleasure of your company here.'

But he might have talked for ever before the lovers would have heard a word of what he said.

'Forgive me, love, forgive me!' Phyllida was crying, as, having slid from Bernard's arms, she fell at his feet, and twisted herself like a snake about his knees; 'I did not know what I was doing; I never thought that I was injuring you; I saw only one thing, and that was my love, which would have led me to die for you if my death could have done you any good. Oh, say you forgive me — you who first taught me that there is forgiveness for the worst of sinners—say that you do not believe that I wilfully deceived you—that you will not curse me for having blighted all your hopes in life?'

'I will say nothing, my Phyllida,' returned Bernard, as he attempted to raise her from the ground, 'until you come to my heart—to your rightful resting-place—and tell me what you wish from there.'

'Oh, Bernard, I am not worthy.'

'If you are not worthy, no woman is. It is your home, dearest, by the rights of our mutual love, and until you come home, I will not speak to you.'

Then she suffered him to lift her drooping form, and clasp it in his arms, and their lips met, as if there had been no stain between them, and she had been the daughter of a duke instead of a disreputable gold digger, who kept a gaming-table in the Valley of Sacramento.

'You know all—*all*,' she whispered.

'All, dearest, except one thing which I wait to learn from your own lips. There has been an irregularity in our marriage, Phyllida. Will you marry me over again?'

' *Over again ?* ' she repeated, startled at the idea of so much happiness.

' Yes, over again. You are free now, by the universal Law of Death—and as a free woman, I offer you my hand. Will you accept it, Phyllida ? '

' Oh, Mr Cole,' she exclaimed, turning to their mutual friend, ' tell Bernard this must not be. Tell him of what we were talking before he came in.'

' Well, my dear, I don't know of what you *were* talking, unless it was of your determination never to see nor speak to him again. And if you are going to keep your other resolutions as well as you did *that* one, why, I don't think you require any interference on my part.'

She reddened and was silent.

' Phyllida,' said Bernard, ' we don't want Nelson Cole nor any one else to settle our affairs for us. You are my wife, darling—I can never regard you in any other light ; and if you won't come back to me, I shall have to walk through life alone, for I certainly should never think myself justified in marrying any one else.'

' There, now, you see,' interposed Cole, ' if you don't marry him, Phyllida, you'll have another set of sins upon your head, and by your own account you can't afford that.'

' But your mother and Laura ? ' said Phyllida timidly to Bernard.

' Laura is only too anxious to see us re-united, darling,—and as for my mother,—well, she *is* my mother, and not my wife.'

' But the Bluemere people ? ' continued the girl with a shudder.

' I shall not take you back to Bluemere, or at all events not for some time. We will have a holiday first, and enjoy some travelling together.'

'Come over the duck pond with me,' said Cole ; 'there's lots of sight-seeing for you in the States.'

'Done with you !' exclaimed Bernard heartily. 'If Phyllida agrees, so do I. And now, my love, when is this marriage to be ?'

'When you like, dear Bernard.'

'I should *like* to-day, but as I suppose it's too late, I like to-morrow. I have a brother parson close at hand to whom I will explain matters, and he will do it as privately for us as possible. You will come with us, Cole ?'

'Oh, yes,' returned Cole gruffly ; 'as I was the cause of the split, I should like to see the knot tied again, and give the bride away. And don't you think it would be kind to telegraph the intelligence to Mrs Penfold and ask her and the old captain she writes about to join us at luncheon afterwards.'

'Oh, yes ; let us have cousin Penfold, by all means,' said Bernard. 'I owe the old lady another sealskin cloak for the rapidity with which she advertised for my darling.'

'And now, Phyllida,' said Nelson Cole, 'I had better see you home, and Bernard can let you know the time and place for to-morrow's meeting by this evening's post.'

'Oh, can't she stay the evening and dine with us ?' asked Bernard in a tone of injury.

'No ; she is tired out with all this excitement ; she will be much better at home.'

'Let me go with her, then,' replied the other eagerly.

'You will do no such thing ; I shall take her myself,' was the curt rejoinder ; and Nelson Cole began to hurry Phyllida from the room.

'She flung herself once more into her husband's

arms, and then turning to Cole, she caught his hand, and timidly raised it to her lips.

'How can I ever thank you,' she murmured, 'for bringing me home again ?'

'Won't you give him a better one than that, Phyllida ?—he deserves it,' said Bernard laughing.

The girl raised her head and kissed Cole upon the forehead ; and as he felt the touch of her lips, the blood mounted to his face as if he had been a boy.

'Fancy a kiss from Agnes's child making me feel like that !' he grumbled to himself in a cynical manner, as he hurried after her down to the cab which was waiting to convey them to her home. He was ready to laugh at himself for his weakness, and yet the remembrance of Phyllida's kiss was with him through his dreams.

The next morning was as bright as the season could contrive to make it, and the three people who went to church so early. and returned to the hotel in time to greet Mrs Penfold and Captain Barclay on their arrival from Gatehead, could not have looked brighter had it been a morning in the leafy June.

'Not in black this time, my dear,' whispered Mrs Penfold approvingly, when the two gentlemen had taken possession of the nice bluff old captain, and she had a moment alone with Phyllida.

'Oh no, cousin Penfold,' replied the girl smiling, as she contemplated her soft grey velvet dress. Dear Bernie telegraphed yesterday for Mrs Garnett to send up some of my things. He said we wouldn't have any mistake *this* time. Oh! he is so good to me, and after all that I have done. I feel so happy, cousin—just as if it was too much to bear, and I must die.'

'Oh no, my dear, you mustn't say that,' replied

Mrs Penfold, who took everything she heard *a pied de la lettre.* 'Mr Freshfield was good enough to write and tell me all about you, and though I don't say you ought not to have told us of your former marriage, yet it's all over now, thank heaven! and certainly no one has a better right to Mr Freshfield than yourself. Ah, all marriages have their twofold aspects, and you have found out the truth already. Well, well,' and Mrs Penfold sighed in a mysterious manner, which seemed to say, 'do ask me a little more about it.'

Phyllida took the hint.

'What is it, dear cousin? *Your* marriage was happy enough, I know, for you have often told me so.'

'Yes, my dear, so long as it lasted,' replied Mrs Penfold, still mysteriously.

'You would like it to come over again?' said Phyllida sympathisingly, and with a happy glance at her Bernard.

'I should indeed, my dear; but what would people say? I shall be fifty-two next birthday, remember.'

'Dear cousin, what *do* you mean?'

'Why, my dear I thought you would have guessed it, from his interest in you and so forth. Captain Barclay, a thorough gentleman, Royal Navy, you know, Phyllida—none of your merchant services, my dear; but then, as I tell him, "Captain, what *would* the world say?"'

A light broke in on Phyllida.

'Is it true? Oh, I *am* glad! Never mind *the world*, cousin Penfold. Think of yourselves, and what your *hearts* say; that is the only thing worth a moment's consideration. Take a lesson from my Bernard. You see how little he cares for the world; and he is so good—so perfect. And a true marriage is such a holy thing. Oh, I think you will be very happy with the dear old captain, and I am sure that he is nice.'

'Ah, he *is* that, my dear—essentially nice, and has become so used to my ways that he cannot eat his dinner unless I cook it, nor sleep at night unless I make his bed. So I hope I shall make him comfortable in his last days; and our little incomes put together will enable us to keep the house entirely for ourselves. I shall not dare tell my sister Charlotte until it is all over; but I felt I should like to hear you say, Phyllida, that you consider the plan a good one.'

'I consider it the very best plan in all the world,' cried Phyllida heartily; but as she spoke the door was flung open, and before the waiter could announce the coming visitors, she found herself clasped in Laura's arms.

'Phyllida, my dear, *dear* sister! My darling Phyllida, have you really come home again?' exclaimed Laura in an outburst of affection and kisses, as she strained her sister-in-law to her heart.

'Yes, yes. I am home for ever now,' returned Phyllida; 'we have just come back from church. We have been married again this morning;' and the two girls cried together for joy.

'But please to explain your presence here,' said Bernard, when the excitement had somewhat subsided. 'We are delighted, Laura, to welcome you and dear old Anderson to our wedding breakfast, but I confess I should like to understand why you two giddy young creatures are running about London together, and what brought you up from Bluemere on this particular day?'

'Why, where are mamma and the Muckheeps?'

exclaimed Laura suddenly, looking round for them.

'We have not seen them. Did you expect to meet them here?' replied her brother.

'They started for London an hour before we did, that is what made Charlie bring me up to you, Bernard, because we feared—we were not quite sure, that is to say, how you would like the intrusion of strangers at such a time. Where *can* they be? I am astonished they have not yet arrived. They must have mistaken the hotel.'

At the idea of her mother-in-law's appearance, Phyllida turned pale and crept to her husband's side. Bernard put his arm firmly round her.

'Never mind,' he said cheerfully, 'we are not going to wait luncheon for them, I can answer for that, for I ate no breakfast this morning, and am as hungry as a hunter. So, my dear friends, will you take your places—(ah! Charlie, how good it is to see *your* face here, my boy)—and join my heart in its thanksgiving for the very happiest meal I've ever sat down to.'

The waiters, who had been busy spreading the table whilst this conversation was carried on, now announced that all was ready, and the party sat down to luncheon. How merry they were; and yet not so merry perhaps as cheerful, for though Laura blushed and giggled a good deal, remembering the scene that had taken place at Blue Mount that morning, and Mrs Penfold simpered in a matronly way under the attentions of Captain Barclay, Phyllida's sweet face turned paler and paler as the moments went on, and each one brought nearer to her the dreaded advent of Mrs Freshfield; and Bernard also, although he felt brave as a lion in defence of his young wife, wished heartily that the anticipation of the interview had not spoiled their luncheon. At last, however, as the meal had nearly drawn to a conclusion, it came. A querulous voice was heard approaching by the vast staircases of the hotel that led to their apartments, and Laura and Bernard simultaneously exclaimed, 'My mother!' The waiter in attendance heard them, and threw open the door, and Mrs Freshfield appeared first upon the threshold, transfixed at the scene that met her view.

'What is this?' she exclaimed angrily, as her eyes rapidly took in the presence of Laura and Mr Anderson and the rest of the wedding guests.

'*This*, mother,' replied Bernard, as holding his wife's hand firmly in his own, he rose to his feet to confront her, 'is my wedding breakfast ; Phyllida and I have been married again this morning.'

'*Married again !*' gasped Mrs. Freshfield ; 'and when I have travelled all this distance at *my* age to try and save you from being once more shackled with the chains of ungodliness ; when I and my dear saintly friends, the Laird o' Muckheep and his blessed sister, have hastened here at the call of duty to try and snatch you as a brand from the burning, to find you once more in the power of Satan, is indeed too hard.'

'Hadn't you better have some luncheon, now you are here ?' replied her son practically.

'Hoot, Mrs. Fraich-field,' exclaimed the voice of Miss Janet, somewhere from the background, 'didna I tell ye it was rai-sh to leave Bluemere without the wreet·een dirrirc-tions in your han' o' the hoose wheer yon misguided young mon had heeden himsel' If ye had taken my advice, ye wouldna ha' dree-ven my brither an' mysel'

round Loon-don for mair than twa hoors whiles
ye tried to re-cairl the neem o' the street, an' ye
wood ha' been in time, maybe, ta raiss-cue heem
fra' the weels o' the evil one.'

'Mother,' said Bernard, if you and your friends
like to take your places amongst us *as* friends, we
shall be glad to see you ; but if you have journeyed
to town for the express purpose of insulting me
and my wife, the sooner you go back to Bluemere
the better.'

'Oh, sir,' exclaimed Mrs. Freshfield, turning to
some one who stood behind her, ' can *you* not say
a word in season to my unhappy son ? '

'Ay,' replied the voice of the Laird o' Muckheep, ' when I can *see* him, madam, mebbe I shull
be tauld the reet thing to say to tooch his hairt ;
but at this moment, Mrs Fraich-field, its naething
I *can* see but the toop o' your ane boonet.'

'I beg you ten thousand pardons,' said Mrs
Freshfield, as she made way for the laird to
appear upon the threshold ; ' in my terrible grief
and disappointment I could think of nothing but
myself.'

But at the sound of the laird's voice, Phyllida
had risen suddenly to her feet and clung to her
husband, almost convulsively.

'What is it, my darling ? What do you fear ? '
Bernard was saying tenderly, when his mother's
saintly friend came to the front.

'See, see ! ' shrieked Phyllida, as she pointed to
him ; ' I knew it was he. I recognised him from
his voice. There stands *my father !* '

She did not hide her face, but she pressed it
close against her husband's breast, whilst her eyes
glowed like living coals, and every feature was
expressive of the keenest horror.

' *Your father !* ' repeated Bernard. But by this time a fearful oath had rung through the room—such an oath as comes from the lips of a man, but seldom in his lifetime—such an oath as the condemned felon in the dock might level at the one who had been the cause of his standing there, and it had issued from the lips of Nelson Cole.

'Sandie Macpherson, by all that's holy !' he exclaimed, as he started to his feet.

The Laird o' Muckheep turned livid—the sweat started to his forehead, and his limbs shook under him. Miss Janet was the first to come to the rescue.

'Hoot, mon,' she cried, 'ye dinna ken wha ye speak to—Sandie Macpherson, indeed. It's my brither, the Laird o' Muckheep, wha stan's befoor ye ; a mon wha has spended his life in bringing back lairst sools to the ane foold. What wood ye ha' in callin' the laird by sic a neem as that ? '

'The Laird of Muckheep ?' cried Phyllida ; ' it is not true. His name is Macpherson, and he is the greatest enemy I ever had. There stands the man, and let him look me in the eyes and deny it if he dare, who forced me to marry his colleague Fernan Cortës, for fear I should betray the murder I saw them commit between them.'

At the word ' *murder*,' which sends a thrill through every breast, the luncheon party rose to their feet simultaneously, and shrank in horror from the man who stood in their midst.

' Ye boold-faced hizzy,' interposed Miss Janet, ' to ca' the Laird o' Muckheep out o' his ain respeected name.'

'I don't know what his own name may be,' continued Phyllida, 'for he has had a dozen names to my knowledge, but he knows that what I say is true. He knows that I saw him hold Norris the Englishman down by the arms, while Cortës stabbed him in the back with his bowie-knife, and that when I threatened to expose his villany, he locked me up in a room until he brought a man to marry me to Cortës, and that he had to hold me himself whilst the vile ceremony was performed. Answer me, Macpherson ! ' cried the girl, with eyes of fire; ' is it not the truth that I am telling now ? '

' Phyllida, he is too much of a cur to do you justice,' exclaimed Nelson Cole ; ' it is a man alone who ought to deal with him, and it is a man who will bring him to his knees. Do you know *me*, Sandie Macpherson ?' he said in a voice of thunder, as he strode up to the quondam gold-digger of Sacramento Valley, and glared in his face. ' Do you know *me—Nelson Cole ?* Answer that.'

Macpherson glanced round the room once or twice uneasily, and then made a bolt for the door. But Cole had already pinioned his arms from behind.

' No, my friend,' he said, shaking his head over him, ' you don't leave us just yet, not till I've finished with you at all events ; and if you attempt any violence, I will hand you over at once to the police. I repeat my question, Do you know me ?

' Of course I know you,' replied Macpherson sullenly.

' Of course you know me, and I will tell this company why. Nineteen years ago, ladies and gentlemen, this brute, writhing in my grasp here, who has come to England with a shorn face to profess piety, ran away with my wife, Agnes Summers, whom I had married in St Domingo the year before.'

' My mother ! ' exclaimed Phyllida.

'Yes, child, your unhappy mother, who appears to have expiated her error by a life of suffering. Thank God she is at rest! but you have still to answer to me, Sandie Macpherson, for the wrong you did her. I have tracked you round and round the States for this alone; I have watched and waited for you in vain; and now that you've dropped into my mouth like a ripe plum at the time I least expected it, you needn't think that I will let you go without the punishment I have thirsted to give you.'

'Oh, this must be some dreadful mistake,' said Mrs Freshfield, sinking into a chair, with her handkerchief to her eyes, 'to talk of crime and punishment in connection with a saint like the Laird o' Muckheep, and one whose whole life has been spent in doing good.'

'Ech! but these carles 'ull discover theer mistake before lang, Mrs Fraich-field; an' it's a teerible peenalty they'll ha' to pee foor layin' veeolent hans upon the sacred pair-son o' a Muckheep.'

'Oh no, madam, do not flatter yourself with such a false idea,' said Phyllida. '*Who* should know better than myself what that miserable man is. I who have the misfortune to call him "*father.*" He killed my mother by a long course of cruelty and violence. He sacrificed *me*, his only child, to a man as wicked as himself to conceal his own crime.'

'You're no bairn o' mine,' interrupted Macpherson with a scowl. 'Ay, Mr Cole, but ye needna glare at me after sic a fashion. Ye maun do what ye like wi' me noo; I've had my revenge on ye befoor-hand. Ye didna lose anely your wife by my means, for she brought your bairn along wi' her, and for sixteen years she leeved as my ain dairghter in the Sacramento Valley, and there's many to testify to the truth o' that.'

'*Brute!*' exclaimed Cole, as he nearly shook the life out of him. 'Villain! devil! Was it not sufficient to rob me of one Agnes at a time?'

'*Not* his child!' cried Phyllida, in a transport of delight. 'Oh, there may be some chance of my redeeming the past yet. *Not* belong to that vile, wicked man! Bernard, kiss me. I shall be a better woman than I ever hoped to be.'

'What wood ye be doin' by me?' demanded Macpherson, as Nelson Cole administered a tremendous kick to his person.

'What would I be doing by you?' he repeated scornfully. 'Why, I would like to treat you as you treated her—to take your life from you drop by drop, and see you die by inches in silent, hopeless agony. But you are a brute, and I am a man, and I will not forget that you have restored to me my child.'

'Speer me!' said Macpherson, shivering on his knees.

'Spare you? Did you spare my wife? Have you spared my daughter? For what reason should I spare you?'

'But she wasna' meeried to Cortës—it was no a pair-son that I brought to per-fairm the cereemony. It was joist a tree-ck I played to prevent the gairl fra splee-tin' on us. And noo I ha' tauld ye that, and ane gude tairn desairves anither.'

'Not a parson!' repeated Phyllida; 'not married to Cortës! and I ran away from him the very same day. Oh! Bernard, I am indeed your own. How mercifully I have been preserved for you.'

'I will let you go, then,' said Nelson Cole, addressing Macpherson, 'but not to pollute this country with your presence. Leave England, and never show your ugly face in it again, or I will make the place too hot to hold you.'

'But ye ha' nae proofs—ye canna hand me ower to the police,' said Macpherson anxiously.

'I can make the country ring with your story though, until you are hounded like a leper from the presence of every honest man. And I will do it, excepting on that one condition. Do you understand me ?'

'I do.'

'Go, then, and take your sister with you. We wish no remembrance left behind of the injury you have caused so many here.'

He loosed the creature with a parting shake as he spoke, and Miss Janet, taking her cue from her brother's demeanour, slunk after the Laird o' Muckheep from the room. Then there was a silence, broken only by the weeping of Mrs Freshfield—for every one felt that the next words would be sacred. And so they rung out, like a clarion peal from heaven upon the happy air,—

'Father!'

'My own, own child!'

And Bernard took his wife and placed her in the arms of Nelson Cole.

THE END.

www.ingramcontent.com/pod-product-compliance
Lightning Source LLC
Chambersburg PA
CBHW021715110726
47902CB00005B/1198